*Two bewitching, full-length Christmas
historical romances to sweep you away to
the long-ago worlds of lords and ladies,
of glittering Regency house parties and
intriguing medieval royal courts!*

A

Yuletide
INVITATION

Enjoy the Christmas revels with
talented writers Christine Merrill
and Blythe Gifford

100 Reasons to Celebrate

We invite you to join us in celebrating Mills & Boon's centenary. Gerald Mills and Charles Boon founded Mills & Boon Limited in 1908 and opened offices in London's Covent Garden. Since then, Mills & Boon has become a hallmark for romantic fiction, recognised around the world.

We're proud of our 100 years of publishing excellence, which wouldn't have been achieved without the loyalty and enthusiasm of our authors and readers.

Thank you!

Each month throughout the year there will be something new and exciting to mark the centenary, so watch for your favourite authors, captivating new stories, special limited edition collections...and more!

A *Yuletide* INVITATION

CHRISTINE MERRILL
BLYTHE GIFFORD

M&B

*M&B™ and M&B™ with the Rose Device
are trademarks of the publisher.
Harlequin Mills & Boon Limited, Eton House,
18-24 Paradise Road, Richmond, Surrey TW9 1SR*

A YULETIDE INVITATION © by Harlequin Books S.A. 2008

The Mistletoe Wager © Christine Merrill 2008
The Harlot's Daughter © Wendy B. Gifford 2007

ISBN: 978 0 263 86750 3

009-1208

*Printed and bound in Spain
by Litografia Rosés S.A., Barcelona*

The Mistletoe Wager

CHRISTINE MERRILL

Christine Merrill lives on a farm in Wisconsin, USA, with her husband, two sons, and too many pets – all of whom would like her to get off the computer so they can check their e-mail. She has worked by turns in theatre costuming, where she was paid to play with period ballgowns, and as a librarian, where she spent the day surrounded by books. Writing historical romance combines her love of good stories and fancy dress with her ability to stare out of the window and make stuff up.

Dear Reader,

When I set out to write about Christmas in the Regency, I had to unlearn a lot of our current Christmas traditions. Much of what we do now to celebrate the season did not become popular until Victorian times. No Christmas cards or Santa, of course. And Christmas trees were still quite a novelty in the early nineteenth century.

With no television or radio to entertain them, people passed the time eating and drinking holiday foods, and playing parlour games. As I was doing the research for this story, I came across a game which didn't make it into this book. A player must answer every question asked of him with the word "Sausage." When he laughs, he loses his turn.

A week later, my sons returned from summer camp. They had been surviving without electricity for a week and had learned to play "Sausage" to pass the time.

So although the showier aspects of the Christmas season were years away, people had already found ways to amuse themselves that are still able to tame bored teenagers in the twenty-first century. Very impressive!

Merry Christmas and happy reading,

Christine Merrill

To Jim and the boys. Christmas comes but once
a year. But it lasts twelve months.

CHAPTER ONE

HARRY PENNYNGTON, Earl of Anneslea, passed his hat and gloves to the servant at White's, squared his shoulders, and strode into the main room to face his enemy. Nicholas Tremaine was lounging in a chair by the fire, exuding confidence and unconcerned by his lesser birth. To see him was to believe he was master of his surroundings, whatever they might be. He reminded Harry of a panther dozing on a tree branch, ready to drop without warning into the lives of other creatures and wreak havoc on their nerves.

And he was a handsome panther at that. In comparison, Harry always felt that he was inferior in some way. Shorter, perhaps, although they were much of the same height and build. And rumpled. For, no matter how much time or money Harry spent on his attire, Tremaine would always be more fashionable. And he did it seemingly without effort.

On the long list of things that annoyed him about the man, his appearance was at the bottom. But it was on the list all the same.

The room was nearly empty, but Harry could feel the shift in attention among the few others present as though there had been a change in the wind. Men looked up from their cards and reading, watching his progress towards Tremaine. They were curious to see what would happen when the two notorious rivals met.

Very well, then. He would give them the show they hoped for. 'Tremaine!' He said it too loudly and with much good cheer.

His quarry gave a start and almost spilled his brandy. He had recognised the voice at once, and his eyes darted around the room, seeking escape. But none was to be had, for Harry stood between him and the door. Harry could see the faint light of irritation in the other man's eyes when he realised that he would have no choice but to acknowledge the greeting. 'Hello, Anneslea.' Then he returned his gaze to the paper he had been reading, showing no desire for further conversation.

How unfortunate for him. 'How goes it for you, old man, in this most blessed of holiday seasons?'

The only response was a nod, followed by a vague grunt that could have indicated satisfaction or annoyance.

Harry smiled and took a chair opposite the fire, facing Tremaine. He took a sip from the brandy that a servant had rushed to bring him. He examined the liquid in the glass, holding it out to catch the firelight. 'A good drink warms the blood on a day like this. There is a chill in the air. I've been tramping up and down Bond Street all morning. Shopping for Christmas gifts. Tailors, jewellers, whatnot. And the fixings for the celebration, of course. What's not to be had in the country must be brought back with me from town.' He waved his hand at the foolishness of it. 'I do not

normally take it upon myself. But now that I am alone…'
He could almost feel the ears of the others in the room,
pricking to catch what he would say next.

Tremaine noticed as well, and gave a small flinch. It was
most gratifying.

Harry looked up from his drink into Tremaine's startled
face. 'And, by the by, how is Elise?' It was a bold conver-
sational gambit, and he was rewarded with a slight choke
from his opponent.

The other man turned to him and sat up straight, his in-
dolence disappearing. His eyes glittered with suppressed
rage. 'She is well, I think. If you care, you should go and
ask her yourself. She would be glad of the call.'

She would be no such thing. As he remembered their last
conversation, Elise had made it plain that if she never saw
Harry again it would be too soon. 'Perhaps I will,' he
answered, and smiled as though they were having a
pleasant discussion about an old friend and nothing more.

It must have disappointed their audience to see the two
men behaving as adults on this most delicate of subjects.
But their moderate behaviour had not quelled the under-
current of anticipation. He could see from the corner of his
eye that the room had begun to fill with observers. They
were reading newspapers, engaging in subdued chat, and
gazing out of the bay window while sipping drinks. But
every man present was taking care to be uninterested in a
most focused fashion, waiting for the cross word that would
set the two of them to brawling like schoolboys.

If only it were so easily settled. If Harry could have been
sure of a win, he would have met his opponent on the field

of honour long before now. The temptation existed to hand his jacket to the nearest servant, roll up his sleeves, raise his fists and lay the bastard out on the hearth rug. But physically, they were evenly matched. A fight would impress no one, should he lose it. And Elise would think even less of him than she did now if he was bested in public by Nicholas Tremaine.

He would have to strike where his rival could least defend himself. In the intellect.

Tremaine eased back in his chair, relaxing in the quiet, perhaps thinking that he had silenced Harry with his indifference. Poor fool. Harry set down his empty glass, made a great show of placing his hands on his knees, gave a contented sigh and continued the conversation as though there were nothing strange about it. 'Any plans for the holiday?'

'Has Elise made plans?' There was a faint reproof in the man's voice, as though he had a right to take Harry to task on that subject. Harry ignored it.

'You, I mean. Do you have plans? For Christmas?' He smiled to show all the world Elise's plans were no concern of his.

Tremaine glared. 'I am most pleased to have no plans. I intend to treat the day much as any other.'

'Really. May I offer you a bit of advice, Tremaine?'

He looked positively pained at the idea. 'If you must.'

'Try to drum up some enthusiasm towards Christmas—for her sake, at least.'

In response, Tremaine snorted in disgust. 'I do not see why I should. People make far too big a fuss over the whole season. What is it good for, other than a chance to experience diminished sunlight and foul weather while in close proximity to one's fellow man? I find the experience most unpleasant. If others choose to celebrate, I wish them well. But I do not wish to bother others with my bad mood, and I would prefer that they not bother me.' He stared directly at Harry, so there could be no doubt as to his meaning.

Perfect. Harry's smile turned sympathetic. 'Then I wonder if you will be any better suited to Elise than I was. She adores this season. She cannot help it, I suppose. It's in her blood. She waits all year in anticipation of the special foods, the mulled wine, the singing and games. When we were together she was constantly dragging trees where they were never intended to be, and then lighting candles in them until I was quite sure she meant to burn the house down for Twelfth Night. I doubt she will wish to give that up just to please you. There is no changing her when she has an idea in her head. I know from experience. It is you who must alter—to suit her.'

A variety of emotions were playing across Tremaine's face, fighting for supremacy. Harry watched in secret enjoyment as thoughts formed and were discarded. Should he tell Anneslea what to do with his advice? It had been offered innocently enough. Accuse him of ill treatment in some way? Not possible. Should they argue, Tremaine would gain nothing, for society would find him totally in the wrong. Harry's only offence was his irrational good humour. And Tremaine was at a loss as to how to combat it.

At last he chose to reject the advice, and to ignore the mention of Elise. 'I am adamant on the subject. I have nothing against the holiday itself, but I have no patience for the folderol that accompanies it. Nor am I likely to change my mind on the subject to please another.'

'That is what I thought once.' Harry grinned. 'And now look at me.' He held out his arms, as if to prove his honest intentions. 'I'm positively overflowing with good will towards my fellow men. Of course, once you have experienced Christmas as we celebrate it at Anneslea Manor...' He paused and then snapped his fingers. 'That's it, man. Just the thing. You must come out to the house and see how the feast is properly done. That will put you to rights.'

Tremaine stared at him as though he'd gone mad. 'I will do no such thing.'

The other men in the room were listening with obvious interest now. Harry could hear chuckles and whispers of approval.

'No, I insist. You will see how the season should be shared, and it will melt your heart on the subject. I doubt there is a better gift that I could offer to Elise than to teach you the meaning of Christmas. Come to Lincolnshire, Tremaine. We are practically family, after all.'

There was definitely a laugh from somewhere in the room, although it was quickly stifled. And then the room fell silent, waiting for the response.

If it had been a matter of fashion, or some caustic witticism he was directing at another, Tremaine would have loved being the centre of attention. But today he hated the idea that he was the butt of a joke, rather than Harry. There was a redness creeping from under Tremaine's collar as his anger sought an outlet. At last he burst out, 'Not in a million years.'

'Oh, come now.' Harry pulled a face. 'We can make a bet of it. What shall it be?' He pretended to consider. 'Gentlemen, bring the book. I am willing to bet twenty pounds to Tremaine, and any takers, that he shall wish me a Merry Christmas by Twelfth Night.'

Someone ran for the betting book, and there was a rustling of hands in pockets for banknotes, pens scratching IOUs, and offers to hold the stakes. It was all accompanied by a murmur of agreement that hell would freeze before Tremaine wished anyone a Merry Christmas, so well known was his contempt for the season. And the chance that anything might induce him to say those particular words to Harry Pennyngton were equal to the devil going to Bond Street to buy ice skates.

But while the room was raised in chaos, the object of the wager stared steadfastly into the fire, refusing to acknowledge what was occurring.

Harry said, loud enough for all to hear over the din, 'It does not matter if you do not wish to bet, Tremaine, for the others still wish to see me try. But it will be easier to settle the thing if you will co-operate.' Then he addressed the room, 'Come out to my house in the country, all of you.' He gestured to include everyone. 'Bring your families, if you wish. There is more than enough space. Then, when Tremaine's resolve weakens, you will all be there to witness it.' He stared at the other man. 'And if it does not, if you are so sure of your position, then a wager on it will be the easiest money you could make.'

The mention of finances brought Tremaine to speech— just as Harry had known it would. 'I no longer need to make a quick twenty pounds by entering into foolish wagers. Especially not with you, Anneslea. A visit to your house at Christmas would be two weeks of tedious company to prove something I already know. It would be an attempt to change my character in a way I do not wish. It is utter nonsense.'

Harry grinned. 'You would not find it so if the wager were over something you truly desired. Now that you have received your full inheritance, I suppose twenty quid is nothing to you. I have no real desire to spend a fortnight in your company either, Tremaine. For I swear you are one of the most disagreeable fops in Christendom. But I do care for Elise's happiness. And if she means to have you, then you must become a better man than you are.' He touched a finger to his chin, pretending to think. 'I have but to find the thing you want, and you will take the wager, right enough.' Then he reached into his pocket and pulled the carefully worded letter from his breast pocket. 'Perhaps this will change your mind.'

He offered it to Tremaine and watched the colour drain from the man's face as he read the words. Others in the room leaned forward to catch a glimpse of the paper, but Harry stepped in to block their view.

'For Tremaine's eyes only, please. This is a matter between gentlemen.' For a moment he gave vent to his true feelings and let the words drip with the irony he felt at having to pretend good fellowship for the bastard in the seat in front of him. Then he turned back to the crowd. 'The side bet will in no way affect our fun. And it will be just the thing to convince our victim of the need to take a holiday trip to Anneslea.'

Or so he hoped. Tremaine was still staring at his offer, face frozen in surprise. When he looked up at Harry their eyes locked in challenge. And it was Tremaine who looked away first. But he said nothing, merely folded the paper and tucked it into his own pocket before exiting the room.

Harry smiled to himself, oblivious of the chaos around him.

And now he had but to wait.

CHAPTER TWO

ELISE PENNYNGTON straightened her skirt, smoothed her hair, and arranged herself on the divan in her London sitting room so that she could appear startled when the door to the room opened. Her guest was in the hall, just outside, and it would be careless of her to let him find her in true disarray. With a little effort she could give the impression that she awaited him eagerly, without appearing to be desperate for his company.

As he paused in the open doorway, awaiting her permission to enter, she looked at Nicholas Tremaine and steeled her nerves. Taking a lover was the first item on her list, if she truly wished to be emancipated from her husband. And if she must have male companionship, Nick was the logical choice. In her mind, he had been filed under 'unfinished business' for far too long. He was as elegantly handsome as he had been when he'd first proposed to her.

And she'd turned him away and chosen Harry.

But, since Harry did not want her any more, she was right back to where she had started.

'Nicholas.' She pushed the annoying thoughts of Harry

from her mind, and held out her hands to the dashing gentleman before her.

He stepped forward and took them, raising her fingers to his mouth and giving them a brief touch of his lips. 'Elise.' His eyes were still the same soul-searching blue, and his hair just as dark as the day they'd met, although it had been more than five years.

There was no grey in her hair, either. And she took special care that when they met she looked as fresh and willing as she had at eighteen. Her coiffure was impeccable and her manner welcoming. And her dress was dotted with sprigs of flowers that perfectly matched the blue of her eyes.

Or so Harry had always claimed.

She gave a little shake of her head to clear away that troublesome memory, and gazed soulfully at the man still holding her hands. She was not the naïve young girl he had courted. But surely the passage of time on her face had not been harsh?

If he noticed the change the years had made in her, he gave no reason to think it bothered him. He returned her gaze in the same absently devoted way he always had, and she could see by his smile of approval that he found her attractive.

'Come, sit with me.' In turn, she took his hands in hers, and pulled him down to sit on the divan beside her. He took a place exactly the right distance away from her body—close enough to feel intimate, but far enough away not to incite comment should someone walk in on them together.

She hoped that she had not misunderstood his interest. For it would be very embarrassing if he were resistant to the idea, when she had raised sufficient courage to suggest that they take their relationship to a deeper level. But she had begun to suspect that the event would not happen until she had announced herself ready. It would be so much easier if he were to make the first move. But he had made it clear that he would not rush her into intimacy until she was sure, in her heart, that she would not regret her actions.

For a well-known rake, he was annoyingly protective of her honour.

'Are you not glad to see me?' She gave a hopeful pout.

'Of course, darling.' And after a moment he leaned forward to kiss her on the lips.

There was nothing wrong with the few kisses they had exchanged thus far. Nicholas clearly knew how to give a kiss. There was no awkwardness when their mouths met, no bumping of noses or shuffling of feet. His hands held her body with just the right level of strength, hinting at the ability to command passion without taking unwelcome liberties. His lips were firm on hers, neither too wet nor too dry, his breath was fresh, his cheek was smooth.

When he held her she was soft in his arms, languid but not overly forward, giving no sign that he need proceed faster, but neither did she signal him to desist immediately.

The whole presentation smacked of a game of chess. Each move was well planned. They could both see the action several turns ahead. Checkmate was inevitable.

Of course if it all seemed to lack a certain passion, and felt ever so slightly calculated, who was she to complain of it? She had thought about Nicholas in the darkest hours of her unhappy marriage and wondered how different it might be had she chosen otherwise. Soon she would know.

And if it would ever be possible to gain a true divorce from Harry she must accept the fact that at some point she would need to take a lover, whether she wanted one or not. Her confirmed infidelity was the only thing she was sure the courts might recognise as grounds. But even then, whether she could persuade her husband to make the effort to cast her off was quite another matter.

The matter was simple enough, after all. Harry must have an heir. Since she had been unable to provide one for him, he would be better off free of her while he was still young enough to try with another. But she had grown to see a possible divorce as one more thing in her marriage for which she would need to do the lion's share of the work, if she wished the task accomplished. The last five years had proved that Harry Pennyngton could not be bothered with serious matters, no matter how she might try to gain his attention.

And now Nicholas had pulled away from her, as though he could not manage to continue the charade.

She frowned, and he shook his head in embarrassment. 'I'm sorry if I seem distracted. But the most extraordinary thing happened at White's just now, and we must speak of it. I received an invitation to Christmas.'

She stared at him with a barely raised eyebrow. 'Hardly extraordinary, darling. Christmas is less than two weeks away. It is a bit late, I suppose. You should have made plans by now.'

'Certainly not.' Nicholas, had he had feathers, would

have ruffled them. 'I do not make it a habit of celebrating the holiday. It is much better to use the time productively, in reading or some other quiet pursuit, and to avoid gatherings all together. With so many others running about country drawing rooms like idiots, hiding slippers and bluffing blind men, it makes for an excellent time of peaceful reflection.'

Nicholas Tremaine's aversion to Christmas was well known and marked upon. She had commented on it herself. And then she had placed it on the list of things that she would change about him, should their relationship grow to permanence. 'You are most unreasonable on the subject, Nicholas. If someone has chosen to call you on it, it can hardly be a surprise.'

'But the invitation came from a most unlikely source.' He paused. 'Harry. He's asked me up to the house 'til Twelfth Night, and has bet twenty quid to all takers that he can imbue me with the spirit of the season. He says the celebration at Anneslea Manor is always top drawer, and that I cannot fail to bend. And he invited all within earshot to come as well.' He paused. 'I just thought it rather odd. He's obviously not keeping bachelor's hall if he thinks to hold a house party.' He paused again, as though afraid of her reaction. 'And to induce me to yield he gave me this.' He removed a folded sheet of paper from his pocket and handed it to her.

She read it.

I, Harry Pennyngton, swear upon my honour that if I cannot succeed in making Nicholas Tremaine wish me a Merry Christmas in my home, by January the fifth of next year, I shall make every attempt to give my estranged wife, Elise Pennyngton, the divorce that she craves, and will do nothing to stand in the way of her marriage to Nicholas Tremaine or any other man.

It was signed 'Anneslea', in her husband's finest hand, and dated yesterday.

She threw it to the floor at her feet. Damn Harry and his twisted sense of humour. The whole thing had been prepared before he'd even entered into the bet. He had gone to the club with the intent of trapping Nicholas into one of his stupid little jokes, and he had used her to bait the hook. How dared he make light of something that was so important? Turn the end of their marriage into some drawing room wager and, worse yet, make no mention of it to her? Without thinking, she reverted to her mother tongue and gave vent to her frustrations over marriage, divorce, men in general, and her husband in particular.

Nicholas cleared his throat. 'Really, Elise, if you must go on so, please limit yourself to English. You know I have no understanding of German.'

She narrowed her eyes. 'It is a good thing that you do not. For you would take me to task for my language, and give me another tiresome lecture in what is or is not proper for a British lady. And, Nicholas, I am in no mood for it.'

'Well, foul language is not proper for an English gentleman, either. Nor is that letter. If you understood the process, Elise... He is offering something that he cannot give. Only the courts can decide if you are granted a divorce, and the answer will often be no.'

'We will not know until we have tried,' she insisted.

'But he has done nothing to harm you, has he?' Nick's face darkened for a moment. 'For if he has treated you cruelly then it is an entirely different matter. I will call the man out and we will finish this quickly, once and for all, in a way that need not involve the courts.'

'No. No. There is no reason to resort to violence,' she said hurriedly. 'He has not hurt me.' She sighed. 'Not physically.'

Nicholas expelled an irritated sigh in response. 'Then not at all, in the eyes of the court. Hurt feelings are no reason to end a marriage.'

'The marriage should not have taken place at all,' she argued. 'There were no feelings at all between us when we married. And as far as I can tell it has not changed in all these years.' *On his part, at least.*

'It is a natural thing for ardour to cool with time. But he must have felt something back then,' Nicholas argued. 'Or he would not have made the offer.'

Elise shook her head and tried not to show the pain that the statement brought her. For she had flattered herself into believing much the same thing when she had accepted Harry's offer. 'When he decided to take a wife it was no different for him than buying an estate, or a horse, or any other thing. He did not so much marry me as collect me. And now he has forgotten why he wanted me in the first place. I doubt he even notices that I am gone.'

Nicholas added, in an offhand manner, 'He enquired after you, by the way. I told him you were well.'

'Did you, now?' Elise could feel the temper rising in her. If Harry cared at all for her welfare, he should enquire in person, not make her the subject of talk at his club. 'Thank you so much for relaying the information.'

Nick looked alarmed as he realised that he had misgauged her response to his innocent comment. 'I had to say something, Elise. It does not do to ignore the man if he wishes to be civil about this. If you truly want your freedom, is it not better that he is being co-operative?'

'Co-operative? I am sure that is the last thing on his mind, no matter how this appears. He is up to something.' She narrowed her eyes. 'And how did you respond to his invitation?'

Tremaine laughed. 'I did not dignify it with a response. It is one thing, Elise, for us to pretend that there is nothing unusual between us when we meet by accident in the club. But I hardly think it's proper for me to go to the man's home for the holiday.'

She shook her head. 'You do not seriously think that there was anything accidental in your meeting with my husband, Nicholas? He wished to let me know that he is celebrating in my absence. And to make me wonder who he has for hostess.' She furrowed her brow. 'Not his sister, certainly.' She ran down a list in her head of women who might be eager to step into her place.

'Harry has a sister?' Nicholas asked, surprised.

'A half-sister, in Shropshire. A vicar's daughter. Far too proper to give herself over to merriment and run off to Anneslea Manor for a house party.'

Nicholas frowned. 'You would be surprised what vicar's

daughters can get up to when allowed to roam free. Especially at Christmas.'

Elise shook her head. 'I doubt it is her. More likely my husband is trying to make me jealous by sending the hint that he has replaced me.' And it annoyed her to find that he was succeeding.

'It matters not to me, in any case,' Nicholas replied. 'A tiresome sister is but one more reason for me to avoid Anneslea—the Manor and the man.'

If Nick refused the invitation then she would never know the truth. A lack of response, an unwillingness to play his silly game, would be proper punishment for Harry, and might dissuade him from tormenting her, but it would do nothing to settle her mind about her husband's reason for the jest.

And then a thought occurred to her. 'If we are doing nothing wrong, Nicholas, then there can be no harm in a visit, surely?' Perhaps if she could persuade him to go she would discover what Harry really intended by extending the offer.

Nick was looking at her as though she were no more trustworthy than her husband. 'I see no good in it, either. Harry is all "Hail fellow, well met," when we meet in the club, darling. He is being excessively reasonable about the whole thing. Which is proof that he is not the least bit reasonable on the subject. He wants you to come home, and is trying to throw me out of countenance with his good humour. And he is succeeding. I would rather walk into a lion's den than take myself off to his home for the holiday. God knows what will happen to me once he has me alone.'

'Do not be ridiculous, darling. It is all decided between Harry and me. There was nothing for us to do but face the facts: we do not suit.' She put on her bravest smile. 'We are living separately now, and he is quite content with it. I suspect we will end as better friends apart than we were together. And, while I do not doubt that he has an ulterior motive, I am sure he means you no real harm by this offer.'

'Ha!' Tremaine's laugh was of triumph, and he pointed to her. 'You do it as well. No truly content couple would work so hard to show happiness over their separation. It is a façade, Elise. Nothing more. If I go to Harry's little party in Lincolnshire, I suspect we will be at each other's throats before the week is out. The situation is fraught with danger. One too many cups of wassail, and he will be marching me up a snowy hillside for pistols at dawn.'

'Harry challenge you over me?' She laughed at the idea. 'That is utter nonsense, Nicholas, and you know it.'

'I know no such thing.'

'If Harry were the sort to issue challenges, then it is far more likely that I would be there still, celebrating at his side. But he has given no evidence of caring at all, Nicholas, over what I say or do.' She tried to keep the pain from her voice, for she had promised herself to stop hurting over that subject long ago. 'It is possible that his invitation was nothing more than it sounded. I know the man better than anyone alive, and I can find many defects in him, but I do not fault his generous spirit.'

He had certainly been generous enough to her. After a two-month separation he was still paying all her bills, no matter the size. If he truly cared he would be storming into her apartments, throwing her extravagances back in her face, and demanding that she remove from London and return home immediately. She gritted her teeth.

'But his sense of humour leaves much to be desired. Inviting you for the holiday could be nothing more serious than one of his little pranks. It is a foolish attempt to be diverting at Christmas.'

Tremaine nodded. 'As you will. I will thank him for the generosity of his offer, which has no ulterior motive. And if what you say is true he will be equally polite when I decline it.'

'You will do no such thing. Accept him at once.'

He stared at her without speaking, until she began to fear that she had overstepped the bounds of even such a warm friendship as theirs.

'I only meant,' she added sweetly, 'that you will never know what his true intentions are until you test them. And if we are to continue together, the issue will come up, again and again. If he is mistaking where I mean to make my future, the sooner Harry learns to see you as a part of my life, the better for all concerned. And you need to see that he can do you no harm once he has accepted the truth.'

'But Christmas is not the best time to establish this,' Tremaine warned. 'In my experience, it is the season most likely to make fools of rational men and maniacs of fools. There is a reason I have avoided celebrations such as this before now. Too many situations begin with one party announcing that "we are all civilised adults" and end with two adults rolling on the rug, trading either blows or kisses.'

'I had no idea you were so frightened of my husband.' She hoped her sarcasm would coax him to her side.

'I am not afraid, darling. But neither do I wish to tempt fate.'

She smiled. 'If it helps to calm your nerves, I will accompany you.'

He started at the idea. 'I doubt he meant to invite you, Elise.'

'Nonsense again, Nicholas. It does not matter what he meant to do. I do not need an invitation to visit my own home.' And it would serve Harry right if she chose to put in an appearance without warning him. 'It is not as if we need to go for the duration of the party, after all. A day or two…'

'All three of us? Under the same roof?' Tremaine shuddered. 'Thank you, no. Your idea is even worse than his. But if you wish to visit Harry, you are free to go without me.'

'If I visit Harry alone, then people will have the wrong impression,' she insisted.

'That you have seen the error of your ways and are returning to your husband?'

'Exactly. But if we visit as a couple then it will be understood. And we will not go for the holiday. We need stay only a few hours at most.'

He covered his brow with his hand. 'You would have me traipsing halfway across England for a visit of a few hours? We would spend days on the road, Elise. It simply is not practical.'

'All right, then. We will stay long enough to win Harry's silly bet and gain his promise that he will seek a divorce.' She tapped the letter with her hand. 'Although he probably meant the offer in jest, he has put it in writing. And he would never be so base as to go back on his word if you win.'

If Harry was willing to lose without a fight, then she had been right all along: their marriage was of no value to him, and he wanted release as much as she wished to set him free. But she would never know the truth if she could not persuade Nicholas to play along.

Then a thought struck her, and she gathered her courage along with her momentum. 'And afterwards we will return to London, and I will give you your Christmas present.'

'I have given you my opinion of the holidays, Elise. It will not be necessary to exchange gifts, for I do not mean to get you anything in any case.'

'I was thinking,' she said, 'of a more physical token of gratitude.' She hoped that the breathiness in her tone would be taken for seduction, and not absolute terror at making the final move that would separate her permanently from the man she loved. But if her love was not returned, and there were no children to care for, then there was no reason to turn back. She ignored her rioting feelings and gave Nicholas a slow smile.

Nicholas stared at her, beginning to comprehend. 'If we visit your husband for Christmas? You cannot mean…'

'Oh, yes, darling. I do.' She swallowed and gave an emphatic nod. 'I think it is time to prove that my marriage is every bit as dead as I claim. If you are convinced that Harry carries a torch for me, or that I still long for his attention, then see us together. I will prove to you that your ideas are false. And if it is true that he wants me back, your presence will prove to him that it is hopeless. We will come away from Lincolnshire with everything sorted. And afterwards we will go somewhere we can celebrate in private.

I will be most enthusiastically grateful to have the matter settled.' And she leaned forward and kissed him.

There was none of the careful planning in this kiss that had been in the others, for she had taken him unawares. She took advantage of his lack of preparation to see to it that, when their lips parted from each other, his defences were destroyed and he was quite willing to see her side of the argument.

When he reached for her again, she pulled out of his grasp. 'After,' she said firmly. 'We cannot continue as we are with this hanging over our heads. After we have settled with Harry, we will come back to town and make a fresh start. You may not enjoy Christmas, but I shall make sure that the New Year will hold pleasant memories.'

CHAPTER THREE

HARRY crossed the threshold of Anneslea Manor with his usual bonhomie. It had always been his way to treat everyone, from prince to stablehand, as though he were happy to be in their presence and wished them to be happy as well. If Rosalind Morley had not been in such a temper with him, she could not have helped but greet him warmly. She could feel her anger slipping away, for it was hard not to be cheerful in his presence.

Although his wife had managed it well enough.

'Dear sister!' He held out open arms to her, smiling.

She crossed hers in front of her chest and stood blocking his entrance, in no mood to be charmed. 'Half-sister, Harry.'

'But no less dear for it.' He was not the least bit dissuaded, and hugged her despite her closed arms, leaning down to plant a kiss on the top of her head. 'Did you receive my letter?'

'I most certainly did. And a very brief missive it was. It arrived three days ago, missing all of the important details, and strangely late in the season. I wish to know what you are about, sending such a thing at such a time.'

He tipped his head to the side. 'Sending plans for Christmas? I should think this would be the most logical time to send them. It is nearing the day, after all.'

'Aha!' She poked him in the chest with a finger. 'You know it, then? You have not forgotten the date?'

'December twentieth,' he answered, unperturbed.

'Then you do not deny that in the next forty-eight hours a horde will descend upon us?'

'Hardly a horde, Rosalind. I invited a few people for Christmas, that is all.'

'It will seem like a horde,' she snapped, 'once they are treated to what is in the larder. You said to expect guests. But you cannot tell me who, or when, or even exactly how many.'

'It was a spur-of-the-moment invitation, to the gentlemen at the club,' he said, and his gaze seemed to dart from hers. 'I am not sure how many will respond to it.'

'And what am I to give them when they arrive? Napoleon had more food in Russia than we have here.'

'No food?' He seemed genuinely surprised by the idea that planning might be necessary before throwing a two-week party. If this was his normal behaviour, then Rosalind began to understand why his wife had been cross enough to leave him.

'With Elise gone, Harry, the house has been all but shut up. The servants are airing the guest rooms, and I have set the cook to scrambling for what is left in the village, but you cannot expect me to demand some poor villager to give us his goose from the ovens at the baker. We must manage with whatever is left. It will be thin fare.'

'I am sure the guests will be content with what they have. We have a fine cellar.'

'Good drink and no food is a recipe for disaster,' she warned, trying not to think of how she had learned that particular lesson.

'Do not worry so, little one. I'm sure it will be fine. Once they see the tree they will forget all about dinner.'

'What tree?' She glanced out of the window.

'The Christmas tree, of course.'

'This is some custom of Elise's, is it?'

'Well, of course.' He smiled as though lost in memory. 'She decorates a pine with paper stars, candles and gingerbread. That sort of thing. I have grown quite used to it.'

'Very well for you, Harry. But this is not anything that I am accustomed to. Father allows only the most minimal celebration. I attend church, of course. And he writes a new sermon every Advent. But he does not hold with such wild abandon when celebrating the Lord's birth.'

Harry rolled his eyes at her, obviously amused by her lack of spirit. 'It is rather pagan, I suppose. Not in your father's line at all. But perfectly harmless. And very much fun—as is the Yule Log. You will see.'

'Will I?' She put her hands on her hips. 'I doubt I shall have time to enjoy it if I am responsible for bringing it about. Because, Harry, someone must find this tree and have it brought to the house. And there is still the question of finding a second goose, or perhaps a turkey. If I am to feed a large group, one bird will not be enough.'

'And you must organise games. Do not forget the games.' He held up his fingers, ticking things off an imaginary list. 'And see to the decorations in the rest of the house.'

She raised her hands in supplication. 'What decorations?'

'Pine boughs, mistletoe, holly, ivy. Elise has a little something in each room.' He sighed happily. 'No matter where you went, you could not forget the season.'

'Oh, it is doubtful that I shall be able to forget the season, no matter how much I might try.'

He reached out to her and enveloped her in another brotherly hug. 'It will be all right, darling. You needn't worry so. Whatever you can manage at such short notice will be fine. Before I left London I filled the carriage with more than enough vagaries and sweetmeats. And on the way, I stopped so that the servants might gather greenery. When they unload it all you will find you are not so poorly supplied as you might think.'

Rosalind took a deep breath to calm herself, and tried to explain the situation again, hoping that he would understand. 'A gathering of this size will still be a challenge. The servants obey me sullenly, if at all. They do not wish a new mistress, Harry. They want Elise back.'

His face clouded for a moment, before he smiled again. 'We will see what can be done on that front soon enough. But for now, you must do the best you can. And look on this as an opportunity, not an obstacle. It will give my friends a chance to meet you. They do wonder, you know, that you are never seen in London. I think some of them doubt that I have any family at all. They think that I have imagined the wonderful sister I describe.'

'Really, Harry. You make me sound terribly antisocial.

It is not by choice that I avoid your friends. Father needs me at home.'

He was looking down at her with a frown of concern. 'I worry about you, sequestered in Shropshire alone with your father. He is a fine man, but an elderly vicar cannot be much company for a spirited girl.'

It was perfectly true, but she smiled back in denial. 'It is not as if I have no friends in the country.'

He waved a hand. 'I am sure they are fine people. But the young gentlemen of your acquaintance must be a bit thick in the head if they have not seen you for the beauty you are. I would have thought by now that there would be men lined up to ask your father for your hand.'

'I am no longer, as you put it, "a spirited girl", Harry. I do not need you to act as matchmaker—nor Father's permission should any young men come calling.' And she had seen that they hadn't, for she had turned them all away. The last thing she needed was Harry pointing out the illogicality of her refusals. 'I am of age, and content to remain unmarried.'

He sighed. 'So you keep telling me. But I mean to see you settled. And if I can find someone to throw in your path…'

'Then I shall walk politely around him and continue on my way.'

'With you so far from home, you could at least pretend to need a chaperon,' he said. 'Your father made me promise to take the role, and to prevent you from any misalliances. I was quite looking forward to failing at it.'

Her father would have done so, since he did not trust her in the slightest. But she could hardly fault Harry for his concern, so she curtseyed to him. 'Very well. I will send you any serious contenders for my hand. Although I assure you there will be no such men, nor does it bother me. I am quite content to stay as I am.'

He looked at her critically, and for a change he was serious. 'I do not believe you. I do not know what happened before your father sent you to rusticate, or why it set you so totally off the masculine gender, but I wish it could be otherwise.'

'I have nothing against the masculine gender,' she argued. In fact, she had found one in particular to be most to her liking. 'I could think of little else for the brief time I was in London, before Father showed me the error of my behaviour and sent me home.'

'You are too hard on yourself, darling. To have been obsessed with love and marriage made you no different from other girls of your age.'

'I was still an ill-mannered child, and my rash behaviour gave many a distaste of me.' She had heard the words from his lips so many times that she sounded almost like her father as she said them. 'I am sure that the men of London breathed a hearty sigh of relief when I was removed from their numbers before the season even began.' At least that was true. At least one of them had been more than glad to see the last of her.

'But it has been years, Rosalind. Whatever it was that proved the last straw to your father, it has been forgotten by everyone else. I think you would find, if you gave them a chance, that there are many men worthy of your affection and eager to meet you. There are a dozen in my set alone who would do fine for you. But if you insist on avoiding London, then I must bring London to you.'

'Harry,' she said, with sudden alarm, 'tell me you have not done what I suspect you have.'

'And whatever is that, sister dear?'

'You have not used the Christmas holiday as an opportunity to fill this house with unattached men in an attempt to make a match where none is desired.'

He glanced away and smiled. 'Not fill the house, precisely.'

And suddenly she knew why he had been so cagey with the guest list, giving her rough numbers but no names. 'It is all ruined,' she moaned.

'I fail to see how,' he answered, being wilfully oblivious again.

'There should be a harmonious balance in the genders if a party is to be successful. And it sounds as though you have not invited a single family with a marriageable daughter, nor any young ladies at all. Tell me I will not be the lone partner to a pack of gentleman from your club.'

He laughed. 'You make them sound like a Barbarian invasion, Rosalind. You are being far too dramatic.'

She shook her finger at him. 'You will see the way of things when we stand up for a dance and there is only me on the ladies' side.'

He ignored her distress. 'I do not care—not if you are presented to best advantage, dear one. This party will give you a chance to shine like the jewel you are.'

'I will appear, if anyone notices me at all, to be a desperate spinster.'

'Wrong again. You assure me you are not desperate, and you are hardly old enough to be a spinster.' He held her by the hands and admired her. 'At least you certainly do not look old enough.'

'That has been the problem all along,' she said. 'When I came of age I looked too young to consider.'

'Many women long for your problem, dear. When you are too old, I expect they will hate you for your youth. It is something to look forward to.'

'Small comfort.'

'And you needn't worry. You will not be the only female, and I have not filled the house to the roof with prospective suitors. I believe you will find the company quite well balanced.' He smiled as though he knew a secret. 'But should you find someone present who is to your liking, and if he should like you as well, then I will be the happiest man in England. And to that end, I wish you to play hostess to my friends and to try to take some joy in it for yourself, even though it means a great deal of work.' He was looking at her with such obvious pride and hope for her own welfare that she felt churlish for denying him his party.

'Very well, Harry. Consider my good behaviour to be a Christmas gift to you. Let us hope, by the end of the festivities, that the only cooked geese are in the kitchen.'

For the next two days, Rosalind found herself buffeted along with the increasing speed of events. Harry's carriage was unpacked, and servants were set to preparations. But they seemed to have no idea how to proceed without continual supervision, or would insist that they knew exactly what was to be done and then do the tasks in a manner that was obviously wrong. It was just as it had been since the moment she had stepped over the threshold and into Elise's shoes. At least she'd managed to gain partial co-operation, by begging them to do things as Elise would have wanted them done, as proof of their loyalty to her and in honour of her memory.

It sounded to all the world as if the woman had died, and she'd been left to write her eulogy instead of run her house. But the servants had responded better to her moving speech then they had to anything she could offer in the way of instruction. At some point, she would have to make her brother stir himself sufficiently to retrieve his wife from London. For Rosalind was not welcome in the role of mistress here, nor did she desire it. But it must wait until after the holidays, for she had made Harry a promise to help him for Christmas and she meant to stick to it, until the bitter end.

At last the house was in some semblance of readiness, and the guests began to come—first in a trickle and then a flood. Arrivals were so frequent that the front door was propped open, despite the brisk wind that had arisen. A steady fall of snow had begun in the late afternoon and followed people across the stone floor in eddies and swirls. She busied herself with providing direction to servants, and praying that everyone would manage to find their way to the same room as their baggage.

Couples and families were talking loudly, shaking the snow from their coats and wraps and remarking in laughing tones about the deteriorating condition of the roads and the need for mulled wine, hot tea, and a warm fire. It seemed that Rosalind was continually shouting words of welcome into an ever-changing crowd, promising comfort and seasonal joy once they were properly inside, making themselves at home. Just to the left, the library had been prepared to receive the guests, for the sitting room would be packed solid with bodies should she try to fit all the people together in that room. The great oak reading tables had been pushed to the edges of the room and heaped with plates of sandwiches and sweets, along with steaming pots of tea, carafes of wine and a big bowl of punch.

There were sounds of gratitude and happiness in response, and for a moment she quite forgot the trouble of the last week's preparation. And although at times she silently cursed her brother for causing the mess, she noticed that he was behaving strangely as he moved through the hubbub, making many restless journeys up and down the stairs. It was as if he was anticipating something or someone in particular, and his pleasure at each new face seemed to diminish, rather than increase, when he did not see the person he expected.

And then the last couple stepped through the open doorway.

'Rosalind!' Elise threw her arms wide and encompassed her in an embrace that was tight to the point of discomfort. 'So you are the one Harry's found to take the reins.'

'Elise?' The name came out of her as a phlegm-choked moan. 'I had no idea that Harry had invited you.'

'Neither does Harry,' Elise whispered with a conspiratorial grin. 'But how can he mind? This was my house for so long that I think I should still be welcome in it, for a few days at least. And since he made such a kind point of inviting my special friend, he must have meant to include me. Otherwise he would have left me quite alone in London for the holidays. That cannot have been his intention.'

'Special friend?' Elise could not mean what she was implying. And even if she did, Rosalind prayed she would not have been so bold as to bring him here. If Elise had taken a lover, Rosalind suspected that it was very much Harry's intention to split the two up.

'Have you met? I doubt it. Here, Nicholas—meet little Rosalind, my husband's half-sister. She is to be our hostess.'

When she saw him, Rosalind felt her smile freeze as solid as the ice on the windowpanes. Nicholas Tremaine was as fine as she remembered him, his hair dark, his face a patrician mask, with a detached smile. It held none of the innocent mirth of their first meeting but all of the world-weariness she had seen in him even then. And, as it had five years before, her heart stopped and then gave an unaccustomed leap as she waited for him to notice her. 'How do you do, Mr...?'

But it was too much to hope that he had forgotten her. 'I believe we've met,' he said, and then his jaw clenched so hard that his lips went white. He had paused on the doorstep, one boot on the threshold, snow falling on his broad shoulders, the flakes bouncing off them to melt at his feet. His clothing was still immaculate and in the first stare of fashion. But now it was of a better cut, and from more expensive cloth than it had been. It hardly mattered. For when she had first seen him, Nicholas Tremaine had been the sort of man to make poverty appear elegant.

If his change in tailor was an indication, his fortunes had improved, and wealth suited him even better. In any other man, she would have thought that pause in the doorway a vain attempt to add drama to his entrance, while allowing the audience to admire his coat. But she suspected that now Tremaine had seen her he was trying to decide whether it would be better to enter the house or run back towards London—on foot, if necessary.

The pause continued as he struggled to find the correct mood. Apparently he'd decided on benign courtesy, for he smiled, although a trifle coldly, and said, 'We met in London. It was several years ago, although I cannot remember the exact circumstances.'

Liar. She was sure that he remembered the whole incident in excruciating detail. As did she. She hoped her face did not grow crimson at the recollection.

'But I had no idea,' he continued, 'that you were Harry's mysterious sister.'

Was she the only one who heard the silent words, *Or I would never have agreed to come?* But he was willing to pretend ignorance, possibly because the truth reflected no better on him than it had on her, so she must play the game as well.

'I am his half-sister. Mother married my father when Harry was just a boy. He is a vicar.' She paused. 'My father, that is. Because of course Harry is not…' She was so nervous that she was rambling, and she stopped herself suddenly, which made for an embarrassing gap in the conversation.

'So I've been told.'

'I had no idea that you would be a guest here.' *Please*, she willed, *believe I had no part in this.*

If the others in the room noticed the awkwardness between them, they gave no indication. Elise's welcome was as warm as if there had been nothing wrong. 'How strange that I've never introduced you. Rosalind was in London for a time the year we...the year I married Harry.' She stumbled over her own words for a moment, as though discovering a problem, and Rosalind held her breath, fearing that Elise had noticed the coincidence. But then the moment passed, and Elise took Tremaine's arm possessively. 'I am sure we will all be close friends now. I have not had much chance to know you, Rosalind, since you never leave home. I hope that we can change that. Perhaps now that you are old enough, your father will allow you to come to London and visit?'

'Of course,' she replied, fighting the temptation to remind Elise that Rosalind was her senior by almost two months. Her age did not signify, for her father would never let her travel, and certainly not to visit her brother's wife. If Elise meant to carry on a public affair, no decent lady could associate with her. And the identity of the gentleman involved made an embarrassing situation into a mortifying one.

Elise continued to act as if nothing was wrong. 'I am glad that you have come to stay with Harry. He needs a keeper if he has taken to engaging in daft wagers for Christmas. And this party will be an excellent opportunity for you to widen your social circle.'

'Wagers?' She looked at her sister-in-law with helpless confusion. And then she asked, 'What has Harry done now?'

Elise laughed. 'Has he forgotten to tell you, little one, of the reason for this party? How typical of him. He's bet the men at the club that he can make Mr Tremaine wish him a Merry Christmas. But Nick is most adamant in his plan to avoid merriment. I have had no impact on him, and you know my feelings on the subject of Christmas fun. It will be interesting to see if you can move him, now that you are in charge of the entertainments here.'

'Oh.' This was news, thought Rosalind. For at one time Nicholas Tremaine had been of quite a different opinion about the holiday, much to their mutual regret.

But there was no reason to mention it, for Tremaine seemed overly focused on his Garrick and his hat, as though wishing to look anywhere than at his hostess.

Now Elise was unbuttoning her cloak, and calling for a servant, treating this very much as if it was still her home. It was even more annoying to see the servants responding with such speed, when they would drag their feet for her. It was clear that Elise was mistress here, not her. Rosalind's stomach gave a sick lurch. Let her find her own way to her room, and take her lover as well. She signalled to the servants to help Tremaine, and turned to make an escape.

And then she saw Harry, at the head of the stairs. The couple in the doorway had not noticed him as yet, but Rosalind could see his expression as he observed them. He saw Tremaine first, and there was a narrowing of the eyes, a slight smile, and a set to the chin that hinted of a battle to come. But then he looked past his adversary to the woman behind him.

Resolution dissolved into misery. The look of pain on

his face was plain to see, should any observe him. Then he closed his eyes and took a gathering breath. When he opened them again he was his usual carefree self. He started down the stairs, showing to all the world that there was not a thing out of the ordinary in entertaining one's wife and her lover as Christmas guests.

'Tremaine, you have decided to take up my offer after all.' He reached out to clasp the gentleman's hand, and gave him a hearty pat on the back that belied his look of a moment earlier. 'We shall get you out of the blue funk you inhabit in this jolly time.'

Tremaine looked, by turns, alarmed and suspicious. 'I seriously doubt it.'

'But I consider it my duty,' Harry argued. 'For how could I entrust my wife to the keeping of a man who cannot keep this holiday in his heart? She adores it, sir. Simply adores it.' There was the faintest emphasis on the word 'wife', as though he meant to remind Tremaine of the facts in their relationship.

'Really, Harry. You have not "entrusted" me to anyone. You speak as though I were part of the entail.' Pique only served to make Elise more beautiful, and Rosalind wondered if it was a trick that could be learned, or if it must be bred in.

'And Elise.' Harry turned to her, putting a hand on each shoulder and leaning forward to kiss her.

She turned a cold cheek to him, and he stopped his lips just short of it, kissing the air by her face before releasing her to take her wrap. 'This is most unexpected. I assumed, when you said that you never wished to set foot over my threshold again…' he leaned back to stare into her eyes '…that you would leave me alone.'

Elise's smile was as brilliant as the frost glittering from the trees, and as brittle. 'When I heard that you wished to extend your hospitality to Nicholas, I assumed that you were inviting me as well. We are together now, you know.' There was a barb in the last sentence, but Harry gave no indication that he had been wounded by it.

'Of course. And if it will truly make you happy, then I wish you well in it. Come in, come in. You will take your death, standing in the cold hall like this.' He looked out into the yard. 'The weather is beastly, I must say. All the better to be inside, before a warm fire.'

Tremaine cast a longing glance over his shoulder, at the road away from the house, before Harry shut the door behind him. 'Come, the servants will show you to your rooms.'

'Where have you put us?' Elise asked. 'I was thinking the blue rooms in the east wing would be perfect.'

Rosalind swallowed, unsure of how she was expected to answer such a bold request. Although Harry might say aloud that he wished for his wife to have whatever made her happy, she doubted that it would extend to offering her the best guest rooms in the house, so that she could go to her lover through the connecting door between them.

Before she could answer, Harry cut in. 'I am so sorry, darling. Had I but known you were coming I'd have set them aside for you. But since I thought Tremaine was arriving alone, if at all, I had Rosalind put him in the room at the end of that hall.'

'The smallest one?' Elise said bluntly.

'Of course. He does not need much space—do you, old man?' Harry stared at him, daring him to respond in the negative.

'Of—of course not,' Tremaine stuttered.

Harry turned back to Elise. 'And I am afraid you will have to take the room you have always occupied. The place beside me. Although we are full to the rafters, I told Rosalind to leave it empty. I will never fill the space that is rightly yours.'

The last words had a flicker of meaning that Elise chose to ignore. 'That is utterly impossible, Harry. I have no wish to return to it.'

His voice was soft, but firm. 'I am afraid, darling, that you must make do with what is available. And if that is the best room in the house then so be it.' He turned and walked away from her, up the stairs.

Elise hurried after him, and Rosalind could hear the faint hiss of whispered conversation. Nicholas Tremaine followed after, his retreating back stiff.

CHAPTER FOUR

BY THE time they reached the door to her bedroom, Nicholas had made a discreet exit. And for the first time in two months, Elise was alone with her infuriatingly reasonable husband.

'But, my dear, I cannot give you another room, even if I might wish to. On my honour, they are all full.'

Harry was smiling at her again, and she searched his face for any sign that he had missed her, and had orchestrated the situation just to have her near. But in his eyes she saw not love, nor frustrated passion, nor even smug satisfaction at having duped her to return. He was showing her the same warmth he might show to a stranger. He held a hand out to her again, but made no attempt to touch her.

'I am offering you the best I have, just as I have always done. And you will be more comfortable, you know, sleeping in your own bed and not in a guest room.'

He was being sensible again, damn him. And it was likely to drive her mad. 'It is not my own bed any longer, Harry. For, in case you have forgotten, I have left you.' She said it with emphasis, and smiled in a self-satisfied way that would push any man to anger if he cared at all for his wife or his pride.

Harry responded with another understanding smile. 'I realise that. Although it is good to see you home again, even if it is only for a visit.'

'If you were so eager to see me you could have come to London,' she said in exasperation. 'You were there only last week.'

Harry looked confused. 'I was supposed to visit you? If you desired my company, then you would not have left.' He said it as though it were the most logical thing in the world, instead of an attempt to provoke her to anger.

'You tricked Nicholas into coming here for Christmas with that silly letter.'

'And he brought you as well.' Harry beamed at her. 'I would hardly call my invitation to Tremaine a trick. I promise, I meant no harm by it. Nor by the arrangement of the rooms. Can you not take it in the way it is offered? I wish Tremaine to have a merry Christmas. And I wish you to feel at home. I would want no less for any of my guests.' If he had a motive beyond that she could find no trace of it—in his expression or his tone.

'But you do not expect the other female guests to share a connecting door with your bedroom, do you?' She had hoped to sound annoyed by the inconvenience. But her response sounded more like jealous curiosity than irritation.

He laughed as though he had just remembered the threshold he had been crossing regularly for five years. 'Oh, that.'

'Yes. That, Harry.'

'But it will not matter in the least, for I have no intention of using it. I know where I am not welcome.' As he spoke, his cordial expression never wavered. It was as though being shut from his wife's bedroom made not the slightest difference in his mood or his future.

And with that knowledge frustration got the better of her, and she turned from him and slammed the door in his face.

Nick made it as far as the top of the stairs before his anger got the better of *him*. In front of him Harry and Elise were still carrying on a *sotto voce* argument about the sleeping arrangements. In truth, Elise was arguing while her husband remained even-tempered but implacable. In any case, Nick wanted no part of it. And he suspected it would be the first of many such discussions he would be a party to if he did not find a way back to London in short order.

But not until he gave the girl at the foot of the stairs a piece of his mind. Rosalind Morley was standing alone in the entryway, fussing with the swag of pine bows that decorated the banister of the main stairs. She was much as he remembered her—diminutive in stature, barely five feet tall. Her short dark curls bobbed against her face as she rearranged the branches. Her small, sweet mouth puckered in a look of profound irritation.

It irritated him as well that even after five years he fancied he could remember the taste of those lips when they had met his. It was most unfair. A mistake of that magnitude should have the decency to fade out of memory, not come running back to the fore when one had troubles enough on one's hands. But he doubted she was there by accident any more than he was. And she deserved to know the extent of his displeasure at being tricked by her again, before he departed and left Elise to her husband. He started down the stairs.

She was picking at the boughs now, frowning in disapproval and rearranging the nuts and berries into a semblance of harmony. But her efforts seemed to make things worse and not better. As he started down towards her, the wire that held the thing in place came free and he could see a cascade of needles falling onto the slate floor at her feet, along with a shower of fruit.

'Damn,' she whispered to herself, sneaking a curse where she thought no one could hear her.

'You!' His voice startled her, and she glanced up at him, dropped the apple she had been holding, and stared fixedly at it as it rolled across the floor to land against the bottom step.

'Yes?' She was trying to sound distant and slightly curious, as though she were talking to a stranger. But it was too late to pretend that she had no idea what he meant by the exclamation, for he had seen the panic in her eyes before she looked away.

'Do not try to fool me. I know who you are.'

'I did not intend to hide the fact from you. And I had no idea that you would be among Harry's guests.'

'And I did not know, until this moment, that you were Harry's sister, or I'd never have agreed to this farce.'

'Half-sister,' she corrected.

He waved a hand. 'It hardly matters. You were more than half-loyal to him the day you ruined me.'

'I ruined you?' She laughed, but he could hear the guilt in it.

'As I recollect it, yes. You stood there under the mistletoe, in the refreshment room at the Granvilles' ball. And when you saw me you held your arms out in welcome, even though we'd met just moments before. What was I to think of the offer?'

'That I was a foolish girl who had drunk too much punch?'

He held up a finger. 'Perhaps that is exactly what I thought, and I meant to caution you about your behaviour. But when I stepped close to you, you threw your arms around my neck and kissed me, most ardently.'

Rosalind flinched. 'You did not have to come near to reprimand me, or to reciprocate so enthusiastically when I kissed you.' She stared down at the floor and scuffed at the fallen pine needles with her slipper, looking for all the world like a guilty child.

He shook his head, trying to dislodge the memory. 'Believe me, I regret my reaction, no matter how natural it was. That little incident has taught me well the dangers of too much wine and too much celebration.'

'So you blame me, personally, for ruining Christmas for you?'

'And my chances with my intended, Elise. For when she got wind of what had occurred she left me and married another.'

Nicholas was surprised to see the girl start, as though she was just now realising the extent of her guilt and the chaos her foolish actions had caused. 'You were engaged to Elise? The woman who was in the entry with us just now? My sister-in-law?' Rosalind shook her head, as though she were misunderstanding him in some way.

'The woman who married your brother after you so conveniently dishonoured yourself and me.'

She gave a helpless little shrug. 'But I had no idea, at the time, what I was doing.'

'Because you were inebriated.' He held up a second finger, ticking off another point in his argument. 'And on spirits that I did not give you. So do not try to tell me I lured you to disaster. Although you appeared fine to the casual observer, you must have been drunk as a lord.' He puzzled over it for a moment. 'If that is even a possible state for a girl. I do not think there is a corresponding female term for the condition you were in.'

She winced again. 'I was sorry. I still am. And I paid dearly for it, as you remember.'

'You were sick in the entry hall before your father could get you home.'

If possible, the girl looked even more mortified, as though she had forgotten this portion of the evening in question. 'I meant when I was sent off to rusticate. I never had the come-out that my father had promised, because he said he could not trust me. I am unmarried to this day.'

'You are unmarried,' he said through gritted teeth, 'because your father could not persuade me that it was in my best interests to attach myself for life to a spoiled child.'

'I never expected that you would marry me,' she assured him. 'And I had no wish to marry you. We had known each other for moments when the incident occurred. It would have done no good to pile folly upon folly trying to save my reputation.'

He smiled in triumph. 'Miss Morley, I think I know very well what you expected. For now that I have come to this house the picture is suddenly clear to me. You expected Elise would get word of it and that she would choose your brother over me. And that is just what occurred.'

'Half-brother,' she corrected. 'And I did no such thing. To the best of my knowledge, Harry knows nothing of the happenings of that night. Father kept the whole a secret, and does not speak of it to this day. Harry does not enjoy the company of my father, and seldom visited his mother. We had only just arrived in London, and I did not get a chance to call on him before my behaviour forced the family to leave again. Even now, all my brother knows of that visit is that I did something so despicable that I was sent from London in shame, and that the family is forbidden to speak of it. We could not have the thing fall from memory if it was a continual topic of conversation.'

'You expect me to believe that you were not in collusion with Harry to ruin my engagement to Elise?' He arched an eyebrow at her and glared, waiting for her resolve to break under his displeasure.

She raised her chin in defiance. 'Do you honestly think that my brother would destroy my reputation so casually in an effort to defeat you?'

'Half-brother,' he corrected.

'Even so,' she allowed. 'You may not like him, but do you think Harry is the sort of person who would behave in such an underhanded fashion as to get me foxed and throw me at you? It is not as if he does not care for me at all. He would have no wish to hurt me.'

He paused and considered the situation, trying to imagine Harry Pennyngton as the mastermind of his destruction. While he could imagine Harry viewing an affair of the heart with the same shrewdness he brought to his business dealings, he would never have orchestrated the disaster with Rosalind Morley. More likely, when he had discovered that Elise was free, he had simply capitalised on an opportunity, just as she assumed.

At last, he admitted, 'Harry has always been the most even-handed and honourable of fellows. Elise comments on it frequently.'

'See?' Rosalind poked him smartly in the chest with a holly branch she had pulled from the decorations during her agitated repairs, and a leaf stuck in the fabric of his jacket. 'If he'd had wind of it at the time it is far more likely that he'd have called you out for it, or helped to cover the whole thing up, just as my father wished to do. And he'd have never invited you here while I was hostess, even after all this time. If Elise had learned anything about it she would not have greeted me as warmly as she did just now. I doubt that either of them has a clue as to what happened.' She blinked at him, suddenly worried, and whispered, 'And I would prefer that it stay that way. Which will be difficult, if you insist on arguing about it in a public room.'

Nick took this information in and held it for a while, examining it from all sides before speaking. If it was in any way possible that the girl told the truth, then he must give her the benefit of the doubt. Revelation of the story at this point would turn a delicate situation into a volatile one. He said, 'I have no desire to unbury any secrets during this visit, if it is true that we have managed to keep them hidden. What's done is done. We cannot change the past.'

'This meeting was none of my doing, I swear to you,' she said earnestly, before he could speak, again. 'I would never have agreed to any of it had I known...' He could see the obvious distress in her eyes, and she twisted the holly in her hands until the leaves scratched her fingers and the berries had been crushed. 'I never meant to hurt you or anyone else by my actions. Or to help anyone, for that matter. I simply did not think.' She looked down at the destruction, dropped the twig, and hurriedly wiped her hands on her skirt. She held them out in appeal. 'I am afraid I am prone to not thinking things through. But I have worked hard to improve my character, and the messes I make are not so severe as they once were.'

He nodded, though her unexpected presence still filled him with unease. 'I understand. I am beginning to suspect we are both here for reasons that have little to do with our preference in the matter and everything to do with the wishes of others.'

She said, 'I think Harry hoped that I would have the opportunity to impress eligible male guests with my ability as a hostess. I doubt that will be the case, since my skills are nothing to write home about. In any case, the single gentlemen he promised have failed to materialise. There is you, of course, but if you are with Elise...' She trailed off in embarrassment, as she realised that her babbling had sounded like an invitation to court her.

He watched her for a time, allowing her to suffer a bit, for it would not do for the girl to think he was interested. Whatever Harry had planned for him this weekend, he doubted it would include courting his sister. Rosalind could not tell by looking at him what his real feelings might be for Elise, and he had no wish to inform her of them. But if Elise learned the truth before he could escape, there would be hell to pay.

He said, 'It is very awkward for everyone concerned. Elise wished to come and speak with Harry, and she did not want to come alone. Now that my job as escort has been done, I mean to stay no more than tonight—whatever Harry's plans might be. I suspect I will be gone shortly after breakfast, and I will trouble you no more.'

Rosalind glanced out of the window at the fast-falling snow. 'You do not know how treacherous the local roads can be after a storm such as this. You may find travel to be impossible for quite some time. And you are welcome until Twelfth Night in any case.'

But she looked as though she hoped he would not stay, and he did not blame her. 'Thank you for your hospitality. I trust you will not find it strange if I avoid your company at breakfast?'

She nodded again. 'I will not think it the least bit odd. As a matter of fact, it is probably for the best.' She hesitated. 'Although I do wish to apologise, one last time, for what happened when we first met.'

'It is not necessary.'

'But I cannot seem to stop. For I truly regret it.'

He gave a curt bow. 'I understand that. Do not concern

yourself with it. We will chalk it up to the folly of youth.' And how could he fault her for that? For he had been guilty of folly as well, and was paying for it to this day.

'Thank you for understanding.'

'Then let us hear no more apologies on the matter. Consider yourself absolved.'

But, while he might be able to forgive, he doubted he would ever forget her.

CHAPTER FIVE

ELISE glared through the wood of her bedroom door at the man in the hall. She had not thought when she made this trip that she would end up back in her own room. She would be alone with her memories, and scant feet from her husband, while Nicholas was stowed in the remotest corner of the guest wing like so much discarded baggage. Though he showed no sign of it, she was sure that Harry had anticipated her appearance and sought an opportunity to separate them.

But if he did not want her, then why would he bother? So Harry did not mean to come and take her in the night? Fine. It was just as she'd feared. She meant nothing to him any more. And telling her the truth, with that annoying little smile of his, had removed all hope that he had been harbouring a growing and unfulfilled passion since her precipitate retreat from his house. If he cared for her, an absence of two months would have been sufficient to make him drag her back to his bed the first chance he got, so that he might slake his lust. But to announce that he meant to leave her in peace for a fortnight while she slept only a room away...

She balled her fists in fury. The man had not left her alone for a fortnight in the whole time they had lived together. But apparently his visits had been just as she'd feared: out of convenience rather than an uncontrollable desire for her and her alone. Now that she was not here he must be finding someone else to meet his needs.

The thought raised a lump in her throat. Perhaps he had finally taken a mistress, just as she'd always feared he would. It had been some consolation during the time that they had been together to know that he was either faithful or incredibly discreet in his infidelities. For, while she frequently heard rumours about the husbands of her friends, she had never heard a word about Harry.

And to have taken a lover would have required equally miraculous stamina, for even after five years he had been most enthusiastic and regular in his bedroom visits, right up to the moment she had walked out the door. Then, his interest in her body had evaporated.

If they had not married in haste, things might have been different between them. She should never have accepted Harry Pennyngton's offer when she had still been so angry with Nicholas. She had been almost beyond reason, and had hardly had time to think before she had dispensed with one man and taken another.

But Harry's assurances had been so reasonable, so comforting, that they had been hard to resist. He had said he was of a mind to take a wife. And he had heard that she was in desperate straits. That her parents were returning to Bavaria, and she must marry someone quickly if she wished to remain in England. If so, why could it not be him? He had described the house to her, the grounds and the attached properties, and told her of his income and the title. If she refused him he would understand, of course. For they were little better than strangers. But if she chose to accept everything he had would be hers, and he would do all in his power to assure that she did not regret the decision.

He had laid it all out before her like some sort of business deal. And although he had not stated the fact outright, she had suspected that she would not get a better offer, and would end up settling for less should she refuse.

That should have been her first warning that the marriage would not be what she'd hoped. For where Nicholas had been full of fine words of love and big dreams of the future, Harry had been reason itself about what she could expect should she choose to marry him.

It had been quite soothing, in retrospect, to be free of grand passion for a moment, and to give her broken heart a chance to mend. Harry had been willing to give without question, and had asked for nothing in return but her acceptance.

They had been wed as soon as he'd been able to get a licence. And if she'd had any delusions that he wished a meeting of hearts before a meeting of bodies, he had dispelled them on the first night.

Elise had thought that Harry might give her time to adjust to her new surroundings, and wished that she'd had the nerve to request it. For intimacy had hardly seemed appropriate so soon. They had barely spoken. She hadn't even learned how he liked his tea, or his eggs. And to learn how he liked other things before they had even had breakfast? It had all happened too fast. Surely he would give her a few days to get to know her new husband?

But as she had prepared for bed on her wedding night, she had reached for her nightrail only to have the maid pull it aside. 'Lord Anneslea says you will not be needing it this evening, ma'am.'

'Really?' She felt the first thrill of foreboding.

'Just the dressing gown.' And the maid wrapped her bare body in silk and exited the room.

What was she to do now? For clearly the staff had more instruction than she had over what was to occur. And it was not likely to be a suggestion that they live as brother and sister until familiarity had been gained.

There was a knock at the connecting door between his bedroom and hers. 'Elise? May I come in?'

She gave him a hesitant yes.

He opened the door but did not enter. Instead he stood framed in the doorway, staring at her. 'I thought tonight, perhaps, you would join me in my room.' He stepped to the side and held a hand out to her.

When she reached to take it, his fingers closed over hers, and he led her over the threshold to his room.

It was surprisingly warm for a winter's night, and she could see that the fire was built to blazing in the fireplace. 'I did not want you to take a chill,' he offered, by way of explanation.

'Oh.'

Then he helped her up the short step that led to his bed, and jumped up himself to sit on the edge beside her. He brushed a lock of hair off her face, and asked, 'What have you been told about what will happen tonight?'

'That it will go much faster if I lie still and do not speak.'

His face paled. 'I imagine it will. But expediency is not always the object with these things. If you wish to move at any time, for any reason, then you must certainly do it. And by all means speak, if you have anything to say. If I am causing you discomfort I will only know if you tell me. And if something gives you pleasure?' He smiled hopefully. 'Then I wish to know that as well.'

'Oh.'

'Are you ready to begin?'

'I think so, yes.' She was still unsure what it was that they were beginning. But how else was she to find out?

He kissed her, and it was a pleasant surprise, for other than one brief kiss when he had proposed, and another in the chapel after the wedding, he had offered no displays of affection. But this was different. He rested his lips against hers for a moment, moving back and forth, and then parting them with his tongue.

It was an interesting sensation. Especially since the longer he kissed her the more she was convinced that she could feel the kiss in other parts of her body, where his lips had not touched. When she remarked on it, he offered to kiss her there as well, and his lips slid to her chin, her throat, and then to her breast.

It was wonderful, and strange, for it made the feelings even more intense, and he seemed to understand for his lips followed the sensation lower.

She scrambled away from him, up onto the pillows on

the other side of the bed. Because she understood what it was he meant to do, and it was very shocking. It was then that she realised her robe had come totally undone and he was staring at her naked body. The feeling of his eyes on her felt very much like the intimate kiss she was avoiding, so she wrapped the gown tightly about her and shook her head.

'I have frightened you.' He dragged his gaze back to her face and looked truly contrite. 'Here, let us start again.'

He climbed past her on the bed, and reached for a pot of oil that rested on the night stand. It was scented with a rich perfume, and he took a dab of the stuff, stroking it onto the palm of his hand.

'Let me touch you.'

She tensed in anticipation of his caress. But he sat behind her this time. He slipped his hands beneath the neck of the robe to stroke her shoulders, kissing her neck before rubbing the ointment into the muscles there.

'See? There is nothing to be afraid of. I only mean to give you pleasure.'

And there certainly did not seem to be anything to fear. It was very relaxing to feel his hands sliding over her body, and she found it almost impossible to resist as he pushed the fabric of her robe lower, until he could reach the small of her back.

She was bare to the waist now. And even though he was behind her, and could not see them, she kept her hands folded across her breasts. But soon she relaxed her arms and dropped them to her sides. When he reached around her to touch her ribs, the underside of her breasts and her nipples, she did not fight him. It felt good. And then she leaned back against him and allowed him to play.

When he heard her breathing quicken he put his lips to her ear and kissed her once, before beginning to whisper, in great detail, just what it was he meant to do next.

For a moment her eyes opened wide in alarm, but his hands slipped down, massaging her belly, as his voice assured her that it would be all right. He nuzzled her neck. One hand still toyed with a breast, while the other slid between her legs and teased until her knees parted. The sensation was new, and intense, but he seemed to know just how to touch her until she moaned and twisted against him.

He explained again how wonderful it would feel to be inside her, and demonstrated with his hand, his fingers sliding over her body, inside and out again, over and over, until her head lolled back against him and her back arched in a rush of sensation.

He released her and turned her in his arms, so that he could kiss her again. And then he laid her down on the pillows. And she could see what it was that had been pressing against her so insistently as he had stroked her. She enquired after it.

He explained the differences in their bodies, but assured her that he would enjoy her touch just as she had enjoyed his. Then he kissed her again, and lay down beside her, guiding her hand to touch him.

It gave her a chance to observe him as she had not done before marriage. His own dressing gown had fallen away, and he was naked beside her on the bed. His body was lean and well muscled, although he had never given her the impression of being a sportsman or athlete. His eyes were half closed, and a knowing smile curled at the corners of his lips. He was a handsome man, although she had not thought to notice when he had made his offer to her. His hair was so light a brown as to be almost blond, and he had a smooth brow. His strong chin hinted at power of will, although his ready smile made him appear an amiable companion. There was no cruelty in his green-grey eyes, but a sly twinkle as he reached for her and, with a few simple touches, rendered her helpless with pleasure all over again.

Then he draped his hand over her hip and pulled her close, so her breasts pressed against his chest. His other hand slipped back between her legs, readying her. Her hand was still upon him, stroking gently, and she helped him to find his way to her, then closed her eyes.

He kissed her, and it was almost apologetic as he came into her and she felt the pain of it. But then she felt him moving in her, and against her, and his strength dissolved into need. Finally there was something that she could give to him, an explanation for his generosity. And it all made sense. So she ignored the pain and found the pleasure again, kissed him back as he shuddered in release.

He held her afterwards, and she slept in his arms. The next morning he was cautious and polite, just as he had been before they had married. She remembered the intimacy of the previous night and found it strange that he was still so shy. But she assumed that over time the distance between them would fade.

Instead it was as though the divide between them grew with each rising of the sun. He was friendly and courteous. He made her laugh, and was never cross with her over small things, as her own family had been. He did not raise his voice even when she was sure he must be angry with her.

But he never revealed any more of his innermost thoughts than were absolutely necessary. If he ever had need of a confidante he must have sought elsewhere, for he certainly did not trouble his wife with his doubts or fears.

In truth there was nothing about their relationship that would lead her to believe she was especially close to him in any way but the physical. At first, she thought that he had chosen her because he could find no other willing to have him. He had been too quick to offer, and with such minimal affection. Perhaps his heart was broken, just as hers had been, and he had sought oblivion in the nearest source?

But as time passed he spoke of no previous alliances, and showed no interest in the other women of the ton, either married or single. She had frequent opportunity to see that he could have married elsewhere, had he so chosen. And the compliments of the other girls, when they'd heard that she was to marry him, had held a certain wistful envy. Although he had offered for her, he had treated them all with the utmost courtesy and generosity, and they would have welcomed further interest had any been expressed.

They had done well enough together, Elise supposed. But he had never given her an indication, in the five years they had been together, that he would not have done equally well with any other young woman of the ton, or that his marriage to her had been motivated by anything other than the fortuitous timing of his need for a wife when she had desperately been in need of a husband.

When night came, there had been no question of why he had married her—for his passion had only increased, as had hers. It had been easy to see what he wanted, and to know that she pleased him, and he had taken great pains to see that she was satisfied as well. To lie in his arms each night had been like a taste of paradise, after days that were amiable but strangely empty. Even now she could not help but remember how it had felt to lie with him: cherished. Adored.

Loved.

It was all she could do to keep from throwing open the door between them right now and begging him to hold her again, to ease the ache of loneliness that she had felt since the moment she had left him.

But what good would that do in the long run? She would be happy at night, when he thought only of her. But at all other times she would not be sure what he thought of her, or if he thought of her at all.

He would be pleasant to her, of course. He would be the picture of good manners and casual affection—as he was with everyone, from shopkeepers to strangers. But he did not seem to share many interests with his wife. While he had always accompanied her to social gatherings, she did not think he'd taken much pleasure in them, and he'd seemed faintly relieved to stay at home, even if it had meant that she was accompanied by other gentlemen. He had showed no indication of jealousy, although she was certain that her continued friendship with Nicholas must have given him cause. Her husband had treated Tremaine with a suspicious level of good humour, although they should be bitter rivals after what had gone before.

In time, Nicholas had forgiven her for her hasty parting with him, and his level of flirtation had increased over the years, overlaying a deep and abiding friendship. She'd enjoyed his attention, but it had worried her terribly that she might be a better friend to another man than she was to her husband.

But if Harry had been bothered by it she hadn't been able to tell. He'd either seen no harm in it, or simply had not cared enough about her to stop it.

Most important, if their lack of children had weighed on his mind, as it had hers, she had found no indication of it. In fact, he'd flatly refused to speak of it. The extent to which he'd appeared not to blame her for the problem had left her sure that he secretly thought she was at fault. Her own father had always said that girl children were a burden compared to sons. She dreaded to think what he would have said had his wife provided no children at all.

It had been hard to avoid the truth. She had failed at the one thing she was born to do. She had proved herself to be as useless as her family thought her. Harry must regret marrying her at all.

And on the day that she had been angry enough to leave she had shouted that she would return to her old love, for he at least was able to give her an honest answer if she asked him a direct question about his feelings on things that truly mattered.

Harry had blinked at her. There had been no trace of his usual absent smile, but no anger, either. And he had said,

'As you wish, my dear. If, after all this time, you do not mean to stay, I cannot hold you here against your will.'

Elise had wanted to argue that of course he could. That a real man would have barred the door and forbidden her from talking nonsense. Or called out Nicholas long ago for his excessively close friendship to another man's wife. Then he would have thrown her over his shoulder and marched to the bedroom, to show her in no uncertain terms the advantages of remaining just where she was.

But when one was in a paroxysm of rage it made no sense to pause and give the object of that rage a second chance to answer the question more appropriately. Nor should she have had to explain the correct response he must give to her anger. For if she must tell him how to behave, it hardly mattered that he was willing to act just as she wished.

So she had stormed out of the house and taken the carriage to London, and had informed a slightly alarmed Nicholas that there was nothing to stand between them and a much closer relationship than they had previously enjoyed.

And if she had secretly hoped that her husband would be along at any time to bring her back, even if it meant an argument that would raise the roof on their London townhouse? Then it was positive proof of her foolishness.

CHAPTER SIX

AFTER a fitful night's rest, Nick Tremaine sought out his host to say a hasty farewell. He found Anneslea at the bottom of the stairs, staring out of the window at the yard. Nick turned the cheery tone the blighter had used on him at the club back upon him with full force. 'Harry!'

'Nicholas.' Harry turned towards him with an even broader smile than usual, and a voice oozing suspicion. 'Did you sleep well?'

The bed had been narrow, hard where it needed to be soft, and soft where it ought to be firm. And no amount of wood in the fireplace had been able to take the chill from the room. But he'd be damned before he complained of it. 'It was nothing less than what I expected when I accepted your kind invitation.'

Harry's grin turned malicious. 'And you brought a surprise with you, I see?'

Nick responded with a similar smile, hoping that the last-minute addition to the guest list had got well up the nose of his conniving host. 'Well, you know Elise. There is no denying her when she gets an idea into her head.'

'Yes. I know Elise.'

Anneslea was still smiling, but his tone indicated that there would be hell to pay if Tremaine knew her too well. Just one more reason to bolt for London and leave the two lovebirds to work out their problems in private.

He gave Harry a sympathetic pat on the back. 'And, since you do, you will understand how displeased she shall be with me when she hears that I've had to return to London.'

'Return? But, my dear sir, you've only just arrived.' The other man laid a hand on his shoulder. 'I would not think of seeing you depart so soon.'

Nick tried to shake off his host's friendly gesture, which had attached to him like a barnacle. When it would not budge, he did his best to ignore it. 'All the same, I must away. I've just had word of an urgent matter that needs my attention. But before I go, I wanted to thank you and wish you a M—'

Anneslea cut him off in mid-word. 'Received word from London? I fail to see how. It is too early for the morning post, and, given the condition of the road, I doubt we will see it at all today.'

Damn the country and its lack of civilisation. 'Not received word, precisely. Remembered. I have remembered something I must attend to. Immediately. And so I will start for London and leave Elise in your capable hands. And I wish you both a Mer—'

'But surely there is nothing that cannot wait until after the holiday? Even if you left today you would not arrive in London before Christmas Day. Although you might wish to be a miserable old sinner for this season, you should not make your servants work through Boxing Day to get you home.'

Nick sighed, trying to manage a show of regret. 'It cannot be helped. I have come to tell you I cannot stay. Pressing business calls me back to London. But although I must toil, there is no reason that you cannot have a Merr—'

Before he could complete the phrase sliding from his lips, Harry interrupted again. 'Ridiculous. I will not hear of it. In this weather it is not safe to travel.'

Damn the man. It was almost as if he did not want to win his bet. Which was obviously a lie, for he had seen the look on Anneslea's face at the sight of his wife. The man was as miserable without her as she was without him. Nick stared out of the nearest window at the snow lying thick upon the drive. 'It was safe enough for me to arrive here. And the weather is much improved over yesterday, I am certain. If I depart now I will have no problems. But not before wishing you a M—'

'Not possible.' Harry gestured at the sky. 'Look at the clouds, man. Slate-grey. There is more snow on the way, and God knows what else.' As if on cue a few hesitant flakes began falling, increasing in number as he watched. Anneslea nodded in satisfaction. 'The roads will be ice or mud all the way to London. Better to remain inside, with a cup of punch and good company.'

Nick looked at the mad glint in his host's eye and said, 'I am willing to take my chances with the weather.'

There was a polite clearing of the throat behind them as a footman tried to gain the attention of the Earl. 'My Lord?' The servant bowed, embarrassed at creating an interruption. 'There has been another problem. A wagon from the village has got stuck at the bend of the drive.'

Anneslea smiled at him in triumph. 'See? It is every bit as bad as I predicted. There is nothing to be done about it until the snow stops.' He turned back to the footman. 'Have servants unload the contents of the wagon and carry them to the house. Get the horses into our stable, and give the driver a warm drink.' He turned back to Nick. 'There is no chance of departure until we can clear the drive. And that could take days.'

'I could go around.'

'Trees block the way on both sides.' Harry was making no effort to hide his glee at Nick's predicament. 'You must face the fact, Tremaine. You are quite trapped here until such time as the weather lifts. You might as well relax and enjoy the festivities, just as I mean you to do.'

'Is that what you mean for me?'

'Of course, dear man. Why else would I bring you here?'

The man was all innocence again, damn him, smiling the smile of the concerned host.

'Now, was there anything else you wished to say to me?'

Just the two words that would free him of any further involvement in the lives of Lord and Lady Anneslea. Nick thought of a week or more, trapped in the same house with Elise, trying to explain that he had thrown over the bet and her chance at divorce because he had her own best interests at heart. 'Anything to say to you? No. Definitely not.'

Rosalind stared at the bare pine in the drawing room, wondering just what she was expected to do with it. Harry had requested a tree, and here it was. But he had requested decorations as well, and then walked away as though she should know what he meant by so vague a statement. The servants had brought her a box of small candles and metal holders for the same, sheets of coloured paper, some ribbon, a handful of straw, and a large tray of gingerbread biscuits. When she had asked for further instruction, the footman had shrugged and said that it had always been left to the lady of the house. Then, he had given her the look that she had seen so often on the face of the servants. If she meant to replace their beloved Elise, then she should know how best to proceed—with no help from them.

Rosalind picked up a star-shaped biscuit and examined it. It was a bit early for sweets—hardly past breakfast. And they could have at least brought her a cup of tea. She bit off a point and chewed. Not the best gingerbread she had eaten, but certainly not the worst. This tasted strongly of honey.

She heard a melodious laugh from behind her, and turned to see her brother's wife standing in the doorway. 'Have you come to visit me in my misery, Elise?'

'Why would you be miserable, dear one?' Elise stepped into the room and took the biscuit from her hand. 'Christmas is no time to look so sad. But it will be considerably less merry for the others if you persist in eating the *lebkuchen*. They are ornaments for the tree. You may eat them on Twelfth Night, if you wish.'

Rosalind looked down at the lopsided star. 'So that is what I am to do with them. Everyone assumes that I must know.'

'Here. Let me show you.' Elise cut a length of ribbon from the spool in the basket, threaded it through a hole in the top of a heart-shaped biscuit, then tied it to a branch of the tree. She stood back to admire her work, and rearranged the bow in the ribbon until it was as pretty as the ornament. Then she smiled and reached for another biscuit, as though she was the hostess, demonstrating for a guest.

Rosalind turned upon her, hands on her hips. 'Elise, you have much to explain.'

'If it is about the logs for the fireplace, or the stuffing for the goose, I am sure that whatever you plan is satisfactory. The house is yours now.' She glanced around her old home, giving a critical eye to Rosalind's attempts to recreate the holiday. 'Not how I would have done things, perhaps. But you have done the best you can with little help from Harry.'

'You know that is not what I mean.' Rosalind frowned at her. 'Why are you here?'

She seemed to avoid the question, taking a sheet of coloured paper and shears. With a few folds and snips, and a final twist, she created a paper flower. 'The weather has changed and I was not prepared for it. There are some things left in my rooms that I have need of.'

'Then you could have sent for them and saved yourself the bother of a trip. Why are you really here, Elise? For if it was meant as a cruelty to Harry, you have succeeded.'

Guilt coloured Elise's face. 'If I had known there would be so many guests perhaps I would not have come. I thought the invitation was only to Nicholas and a few others. But I arrived to find the house full of people.' She stared down at the paper in her hands and placed the flower on the tree. 'The snow is still falling. By the time it stops it will be too late in the day to start for London. We will see tomorrow if there is a way to exit with grace.' She looked at Rosalind, and her guilty expression reformed into a mask of cold righteousness. 'And as for Harry feeling my cruelty to him? It must be a miracle of the season. I have lived with the man for years, and I have yet to find a thing I can do that will penetrate his defences.' The hole in the next gingerbread heart had closed in baking, so she stabbed at the thing with the point of the scissors before reaching for the ribbon again.

Rosalind struggled to contain her anger. 'So it is just as I thought. You admit that you are attempting to hurt him, just to see if you can. You have struck him to the core with your frivolous behaviour, Elise. And if you cannot see it then you must not know the man at all.'

'Perhaps I do not.' Elise lost her composure again, and her voice grew unsteady. 'It is my greatest fear, you see. After five years I do not understand him any better than the day we met. Do you think that it gives me no pain to say that? But it is—' she waved her hands, struggling for the words '—like being married to a Bluebeard. I feel I do not know the man at all.'

Rosalind laughed. 'Harry a Bluebeard? Do you think him guilty of some crime? Do you expect that he has evil designs against you in some way? Because I am sorry to say it, Elise, but that is the maddest idea, amongst all your other madness. My brother is utterly harmless.'

'That is not what I mean at all.' Elise sighed in apparent frustration at having to make herself understood in a language that was not her own. Then she calmed herself and began again. 'He means me no harm. But his heart…' Her face fell. 'It is shut tight against me. Are all Englishmen like this? Open to others, but reserved and distant with their wives? If I wished to know what is in his pocket or on his calendar he would show me these things freely. But I cannot tell what is on his mind. I do not know when he is sad or angry.'

Rosalind frowned in puzzlement. 'You cannot tell if your husband is angry?'

'He has not said a cross word to me—that I can remember. Not in the whole time we have been married. But no man can last for years with such an even temper. He must be hiding something. And if I cannot tell when he is angry, then how am I supposed to know that he is really happy? He is always smiling, Rosalind.' And now she sounded truly mad as she whispered, 'It is not natural.'

It was all becoming more confusing, not less. 'So you abandoned your husband because he was not angry with you?'

Elise picked up some bits of straw and began to work them together into a flat braid. 'You would think, would you not, that when a woman says to the man she has sworn herself to, that she would rather be with another, there would be a response?' She looked down at the thing in her hands, gave a quick twist to turn it into a heart, and placed it on the tree.

Rosalind winced. 'Oh, Elise, you did not. Say you did not tell him so.'

Elise blinked up at her in confusion. 'You did not think that I left him without warning?'

'I assumed,' said Rosalind through clenched teeth, 'that you left him in the heat of argument. And that by now you would have come to your senses and returned home.'

'That is the problem. The problem exactly.' Elise seemed to be searching for words again, and then she said, 'After all this time there is no heat.'

'No heat?' Rosalind knew very little about what went on between man and wife when they were alone, and had to admit some curiosity on the subject. But she certainly hoped she was not about to hear the intimate details of her brother's marriage, for she was quite sure she did not want to think of him in that way.

'Not in all ways, of course.' Elise blushed, and her hands busied themselves with another bunch of straws, working them into a star. 'There are some ways in which we are still very well suited. Physically, for example.' She sighed, and gave a small smile. 'He is magnificent. He is everything I could wish for in a man.'

'Magnificent?' Rosalind echoed. Love must truly be blind. For although he was a most generous and amiable man, she would have thought 'ordinary' to be a better description of her brother.

When Elise saw her blank expression, she tried again. 'His charms might not be immediately obvious, but he is truly impressive. Unfortunately he is devoid of emotion. There can be no heat of any other kind if a person refuses to be angry. There is no real passion when one works so hard to avoid feeling.'

Rosalind shook her head. 'Harry is not without feelings, Elise. He is the most easily contented, happy individual I have had the pleasure to meet.'

Elise made a sound that was something between a growl and a moan. 'You have no idea, until you have tried it, how maddening it is to live with the most agreeable man in England. I tried, Rosalind, honestly I did. For years I resisted the temptation to goad him to anger, but I find I am no longer able to fight the urge. I want him to rail at me. To shout. To forbid me my wilfulness and demand his rights as my husband. I want to know when he is displeased with me. I would be only too happy for the chance to correct my behaviour to suit his needs.'

'You wish to be married to a tyrant?'

'Not a tyrant. Simply an honest man.' Elise stared at the straw in her hand. 'I know that I do not make him happy. I only wish him to admit it. If I can, I will improve my character to suit his wishes. And if I cannot?' Elise gave a deep sigh. 'Then at least I will have the truth. But if he will not tell me his true feelings it is impossible. If I ask him he will say that I am talking nonsense, and that there is nothing wrong. But it cannot be. No one is as agreeable as all that. So without even thinking, I took to doing things that I suspected would annoy him.' She looked at Rosalind and shrugged. 'He adjusted to each change in my behaviour without question. If I am cross with him? He buys me a gift.'

'He is most generous,' Rosalind agreed.

'But after years of receiving them I do not want any more presents. Since the day we married, whenever I have had a problem, he has smiled, agreed with me, and bought me a piece of jewellery to prevent an argument. When we were first married, and I missed London, it was emerald earbobs. When he would not go to visit my parents for our anniversary, there were matched pearls. I once scolded him for looking a moment too long at an opera dancer in

Vauxhall. I got a complete set of sapphires, including clips for my shoes.' She shook her head in frustration. 'You can tell just by looking into my jewel box how angry I have been with him. It is full to overflowing.'

'Then tell him you do not wish more presents,' Rosalind suggested.

'I have tried, and he ignores me. Any attempt to express displeasure results in more jewellery, and I am sick to death of it.' She began to crush the ornament she had made, then thought better of it, placing it on the tree and starting another. 'Do you wish to know of the final argument that made our marriage unbearable?'

'Very much so. For I am still not sure that I understand what bothers you.' Rosalind glanced at the tree. Without thinking, Elise had decorated a good portion of the front, and was moving around to the back. Since the Christmas tree situation was well in hand, Rosalind sat down on the couch and took another bite from of the biscuit in her hand.

'Harry had been in London for several days on business, and I was reading the morning papers. And there, plain as day on the front page, was the news that the investments he had gone to look after were in a bad way. He stood to lose a large sum of money. Apparently the situation had been brewing for some time. But he had told me nothing of the problems, which were quite severe.'

'Perhaps you were mistaken, Elise. For if he did not speak of them, they could not have been too bad.'

The tall blonde became so agitated that she crumpled the straw in her hand and threw it to the floor. 'I was in no way confused about the facts of the matter. They

referred to him by name, Rosalind, on the front page of
The Times.'

That did look bad. 'Surely you do not hold Harry responsible for a bad decision?'

'I would never do such. I am his wife, or wish that I could
be. Mine is the breast on which he should lay his head when
in need of comfort. But when he returned home, do you
know what he said to me when I asked him about his trip?'

'I have not a clue.'

'He said it was fine, Rosalind. *Fine!*' Elise repeated the last
word as though it were some unspeakable curse. 'And then
he smiled at me as though nothing unusual had happened.'

She paced the room, as though reliving the moment.

'So I went to get the paper, and showed him his name.
And he said, "Oh, that." He looked guilty, but still he said,
"It is nothing that you need to worry about. It will not
affect your comfort in any way." As if he thought that was
the only thing I cared about. And then he patted me on the
hand, as though I were a child, and said that to prove all
was well he would buy me another necklace.'

She sagged onto the settee beside Rosalind and stared
at the straws littering the floor. 'How difficult would it have
been for him to at least admit that there was a problem in
his life, so that I did not have to read of it in the papers?'

'He probably thought that you were not interested,'
Rosalind offered reasonably. 'Or perhaps there was nothing
you could do to help him.'

'If I thought it would help I would give him the contents
of my jewel case. He could sell them to make back his in-
vestment. They mean nothing to me if all is not well. And

if that did no good, then I would help him by providing my love and support,' Elise said sadly. 'But apparently he does not need it. And if he thinks to keep secret from me something so large that half of London knows it, then what else is he hiding from me?'

'It is quite possible that there is nothing at all,' Rosalind assured her, knowing that she might be wrong. For she had often found Harry closed-mouthed about things that pained him greatly. It was quite possible that Elise's suspicions were well grounded. She wished she could slap her foolish brother for causing his wife to worry, when he could have solved so many problems by telling her the whole truth.

'And when I told him, in pique, that I quite preferred Nicholas to him, for he at least had the sense to know that I was capable of reading a newspaper, Harry smiled and told me that I was probably right. For Nick had finally come into his inheritance. And at that moment, he had the deeper pockets. But Harry said he could still afford to buy me earrings to go with the new necklace if I wished them. So I left him and went to London. And he bought me a whole new wardrobe.' The last words came out in a sob, and she stared at Rosalind, her eyes red and watery. 'Is that the behaviour of a sane man?'

Rosalind had to admit it was not. It made no sense to open his purse when a few simple words of apology would have brought his wife running home. 'He was trying to get on your good side, Elise. He has always been slow to speak of his troubles, and even slower to admit fault. It is just his way.'

'Then *his way* has succeeded in driving me away from him. Perhaps that was what he was trying to do all along.

He certainly made no effort to keep me. I said to him that perhaps I was more suited to Nicholas, and that our marriage had been a mistake from the start.'

'And what did he say to that?'

'That he had found our marriage most satisfactory, but that there was little he could do to control how I felt in the matter.'

'There. See? He was happy enough,' said Rosalind. She picked up the ornament from the floor and offered it back to Elise, thinking that the metaphor of grasping straws was an apt one if this was all the ammunition she could find to defend her idiot brother.

Elise sniffed and tossed the straw into the fire, then took a sheet of paper and absently snipped and folded until it became a star. 'He said it was *satisfactory*. That is hardly praise, Rosalind. And the way he smiled as he said it. It was almost as if he was daring me to disagree.'

'Or he could have been smiling because he was happy.'

'Or not. He always smiles, Rosalind. It means nothing to me any more.'

'He does not smile nearly so much as he used to, Elise. Not when you are not here to see. Harry feels your absence, and he is putting on a brave front for you. I am sure of it.' There was truth in that, at least.

'Then he has but to ask me to return to him and I shall,' she said. 'Or I shall consider it,' she amended, trying to appear stubborn as she busied herself with the basket of ornaments, putting the little candles into their holders.

But it was obvious that, despite initial appearances, Elise would come running back to Harry in an instant, if given any hope at all. And Harry was longing for a way to get her back.

Rosalind considered. While neither wished to be the first to make an overture, it might take only the slightest push from a third party to make the reconciliation happen.

And so she began to plan.

CHAPTER SEVEN

HARRY watched Tremaine retreating to the library. Merry Christmas, indeed. Apparently the miserable pest had seen through the trap and was trying to wriggle out of it, like the worm he was. But his hasty departure would solve nothing, and his forestalling of the bet would anger Elise to the point that there was no telling what she might do. If she got it into her head that she was being rejected by both the men in her life, she might never recover from the hurt of it.

Thank the Lord for fortuitous weather and stuck wagons. It would buy him enough time to sort things again, before they got too far out of hand. And if it gave him an opportunity to deal out some of the misery that Tremaine deserved? All the better.

'Harry.' Rosalind came bustling out of the drawing room and stopped her brother before he could escape. 'What is really going on here?'

'Going on?' He made sure his face showed nothing but innocence, along with a sense of injury that she should accuse him of anything. 'Nothing at all, Rosalind. I only wished to entertain some members of my set for the holiday, and I thought...'

His little sister set her hands upon her hips and stared at him in disgust. 'Your wife is here with another man. And you do not seem the least bit surprised. As a matter of fact you welcomed her new lover as though he were an honoured guest.'

'In a sense he is. He is the object of a bet I have made with the other gentlemen. I guaranteed them that I could make Tremaine wish me a Merry Christmas.'

'Why on earth would you do that?'

He grinned. 'Perhaps my common sense was temporarily overcome with seasonal spirit.'

Rosalind frowned at him. 'Or perhaps not. Perhaps you have some plan afoot that involves ending the separation with your wife. Or did you bet on her as well? And what prevailed upon the odious Mr Tremaine to accept your challenge? I do not understand it at all.'

'Then let me explain it to you. I told Tremaine that I would facilitate the divorce Elise is so eager for, if he would come down to the country and play my little game. I knew he would take the information straight to Elise, and that she would insist they attend—if only for the opportunity to come back here and tell me to my face what she thought of the idea. I expect she is furious.'

'And you think by angering her that you will bring her closer to you? Harry, you do not understand women at all, if that is your grand plan.'

'But I know Elise.' He smiled. 'And so far it is going just as I expected it to.'

'If you know her so well, then you should have been able to prevent her from leaving in the first place. Do you understand what you have done to her to make her so angry with you?'

He was honestly puzzled as he answered, 'Absolutely nothing. As you can see from the house, her wardrobe, her jewels, she can live in luxury. And if this was not enough I would go to any lengths necessary to give her more. I treat her with the utmost respect. I do not strike her. I do not berate her in public or in private. I am faithful. Although I have never denied her her admirers, I have no mistress, nor have ever considered a lover. I want no one but her, and I am willing to give her her own way in all things.' He gestured in the direction of the library. 'I even tolerate Tremaine. What more can she ask of me? There is little more that I can think to give her.'

Rosalind paused in thought for a moment. 'You spoil her, then. But you must cut her off if she means to belittle you so. If she has a taste for luxury, deny her. Tell her that you are very angry with her over this foolishness and that there will be no more gifts. Tell her that you wish for her to come home immediately. That will bring her to heel.'

'Do not speak that way of her.' He said it simply for he did not mean to reprove his sister, since she got enough of that at home. 'Elise is not some animal that can be punished into obedience and will still lick the hand of its master. She is a proud woman. And she is my wife.'

'It seems she does not wish to be.'

'Perhaps not. But it is something that must be settled

between the two of us, and not by others. And perhaps if you had lived her life…'

Rosalind laughed. 'I would gladly trade her life for mine. You will not convince me that it is such a tragedy to be married to an earl. Even in separation, she lives better than most ladies of the ton.'

He shook his head. 'You should understand well enough what her life was like before, Rosalind, and show some sympathy. For her parents were every bit as strict to her as your father has been to you. I met her father, of course, when I offered for her. Her mother as well. It would not have been easy for her if she had been forced to return home after the disaster with Tremaine. The man betrayed her, and so she broke it off with him. It was the only reason she was willing to consider my offer.'

Rosalind bit her lip, as though the situation was unusually distressing to her. 'A broken engagement is not the end of the world. And you saved her from any repercussions. It could not have been so horrible to have you instead of Mr Tremaine.'

He shrugged. 'Perhaps not. I have endeavoured to make her happy, of course. But in losing Tremaine she lost any dreams she might have harboured that her marriage would be based in true love. Her parents did not care what happened to her as long as her brother was provided for. It was for him that they came to England. They wished to see him properly outfitted and to give him a taste for travel. Her presence on the trip was little more than an afterthought.' He remembered her brother Carl, who was as sullen and disagreeable as Elise was charming, and gave a small shudder.

'Before I came into the room to speak to her father I heard him remonstrating with her before the whole family for her refusal of Tremaine. He called her all kinds of a fool for not wishing an unfaithful husband. Told her if her mother had seen fit to provide a second son, instead of a useless daughter, then the trip would not have been spoiled with tears and nonsense. Her father swore it mattered not to him who she might choose, and that if she wouldn't have me then he would drag her back home by her hair and give her to the first man willing to take her off his hands.

'When I entered, and she introduced me, I assumed he would show some restraint in his words. But he announced to me that if the silly girl did not take her first offer she must take mine, whether she wanted it or no. He complained that they had spent a small fortune in launching her at what parties were available to them in the winter. They had no wish to do it again in spring, when she might be shown to her best advantage and have a variety of suitors. She stood mutely at his side, accepting the abuse as though it were a normal part of her life.'

Harry clenched his fists at the memory, even after several years. 'If I was not convinced beforehand that she needed me I knew it then. How did they expect her to find a husband with the season still months away? My offer was most fortuitous.' He remembered the resignation with which she had accepted him, and the way she had struggled to look happy as he took her hand. 'And she has been most grateful.'

'Then why is she not living here with you, instead of at Tremaine's side in London?'

'While it was easy enough for her to break the engagement, it has been much harder to tell her heart that the
decision was a wise one. And at such times as there is
trouble between us, she cannot help but turn to him and
wonder if she made a mistake.' He sighed. But he made
sure that when he spoke again it was with optimism. 'But,
since I can count on Tremaine to be Tremaine, if she thinks
to stray, she always returns to me, sadder but wiser.'

'Is he really so bad, then?'

He made note of the curious look in Rosalind's eyes as
she asked the question, as though she was both longing for
the answer and dreading it.

'He is a man. No better or worse than any other. I
imagine he is capable of love if the right woman demands
it of him.'

A trick of the morning light seemed to change his sister's
expression from despair to hope and back again. So he said,
'But Elise is not that woman and never has been. He was
unfaithful to her, you know.'

'Perhaps the thing that parted them was an aberration.
Things might be different should they try again.'
Rosalind's voice was small, and the prospect seemed to
give her no happiness.

He gave her a stern look. 'I'm sure they would be happy
to know that their rekindled love has your support. But I
find it less than encouraging.'

'Oh.' She seemed to remember that her behaviour was
of no comfort to him, and said, 'But I am sure she could
be equally happy with you, Harry.'

'Equally?' That was the assessment he had been afraid of.

Rosalind hurried to correct herself. 'I meant to say much happier.'

'I am sure you did. But I wonder what Elise would say, given the chance to compare? Until recently I could not enquire. For at the first sign of trouble, she rushed off to London to be with Nicholas Tremaine.'

Rosalind eyed him critically. 'And you sat at home, waiting for her to come to her senses?'

For a moment he felt older than his years. Then he pulled himself together and said, 'Yes. And it was foolish of me. For I knew how stubborn she could be. It is now far too late to say the things I should have said on that first day that might have brought her home. She has ceased arguing with me and begun to talk of a permanent legal parting. But despite what I should have done, or what she may think she wants, I cannot find it in my heart to let her go. There will be no offer of divorce from me, even if Tremaine can remain stalwart in his hatred of Christmas.' He frowned. 'Which he shows no sign of doing.'

He cast her a sidelong glance. 'This morning he seemed to think he could lose easily and escape back to London. But it does not suit my plans to let him go so soon. If there is any way that you can be of help in the matter...'

Rosalind straightened her back and looked for all the word like a small bird ruffling its feathers in offended dignity. 'Is that why you invited him here while I am hostess? Because if you are implying that I should romance the man in some way, flirt, preen...'

He found it interesting that she should leap to that conclusion, and filed it away for further reference. 'On the contrary. I mean to make Christmas as miserable an experience for him as possible, and keep him in poor humour until Elise is quite out of patience with him. I was thinking something much more along the lines of an extra measure of brandy slipped into his glass of mulled wine. Enough so that by the end of the evening his mind is clouded. While good humour may come easy at first, foul temper will follow close on its heels in the morning. But the thought of you forced into the man's company as some sort of decoy?' He shook his head and smiled. 'No, that would never do. To see my only sister attached to such a wastrel would not do at all.' He watched for her reaction.

'Half-sister,' she answered absently.

He pretended to ignore her response. 'No, I think he should have more brandy than the average. I doubt laudanum would achieve the desired effect.'

'Laudanum?' She stared at him in surprise. 'Are you seriously suggesting that I drug one of your guests?'

'Only Tremaine, dear. It hardly counts. And it needn't be drugs. If you can think of a better way to keep him off balance…'

'But, Harry, that is—' she struggled for words '—surprisingly dishonourable of you.'

'Then, little one, you are easily surprised. You did not think I had invited the man down here to help him in stealing my wife? I am afraid you will find that I have very little honour on that particular subject. So I did not follow Elise to town to compete for her affections? What point would there have been? Look at the man. More town bronze than the statues at Westminster. He has so much polish I swear I could shave in the reflection. I did not wish to go to London and challenge the man, for I doubt I could compare with him there.'

Harry rubbed his hands together. 'But now we are on my home turf. He knows nothing about country living, or the true likes and dislikes of my wife. And he has no taste at all for the sort of simple Christmas diversions that bring her the most joy. It will take no time at all for him to wrongfoot himself in her eyes, and his disgrace will require very little help from me. When that happens I will be here to pick up the pieces and offer myself as an alternative, just as I did before. If you wish to help me in the matter of persuading Elise to return home, then I wish to hear no more talk of bringing her to heel. Help me by helping Tremaine to make an ass of himself. I will see to Elise, and things will be quite back to normal by Twelfth Night.'

CHAPTER EIGHT

ROSALIND left her brother and his mad plans alone in the entry hall. If what he was saying was true, then their marriage must have been as frustrating as Elise had claimed. The man had no clue what was wrong or how to fix things. And, worse yet, he refused to stand up to his wife, no matter how much she might wish for it.

This would be more difficult than she'd thought.

As she walked past the door to the library she paused, noticing the mistletoe ball from the doorway had fallen to the floor. She stared down at it in dismay. That was the problem with bringing live things into the house in such cold weather. There was always something wilting, dying or shedding leaves. And even with the help of the servants, she was hard pressed to keep pace with the decay. She shook the tiny clump of leaves and berries, patting it back into shape and re-tying the ribbon that held it together. Then she looked up at the hook at the top of the doorframe. It was hardly worth calling a servant, for to fix the thing back in place would be the work of a moment.

She reached up, her fingers just brushing the lintel, and

glanced across the room at a chair. She considered dragging it into place as a step, and then rejected the idea as too much work. The hook was nearly in reach, and if she held the thing by its bottom leaves and stretched a bit she could manage to get it back into place, where it belonged.

She extended her arm and gave a little hop. Almost. She jumped again. Closer still. She crouched low and leaped for the hook, arm extended—and heard the stitching in the sleeve of her dress give way.

The mistletoe hung in place for a moment, before dropping back on her upturned face.

'Do you require assistance?' She caught the falling decoration before it hit the floor and turned to see the head of Nicholas Tremaine peering over the back of the sofa. His hair was tousled, as though he'd just woken from a nap. And he was grinning at her, obviously amused. Even in disarray, he was as impossibly handsome as he had been the day she'd met him, and still smiling the smile that made her insides turn to jelly and her common sense evaporate.

She turned away from him and focused her attention on the offending plant, and the hook that should hold it. 'Have you been watching me the whole time?'

Tremaine's voice held no trace of apology. 'Once you had begun, I saw no reason to alert you to my presence. If you had succeeded, you need never have known I was here.'

'Or you could have offered your help and saved me some bother.'

He paused, and then said, 'If you wished assistance, you would have called for a servant. I thought perhaps you drew some pleasure from it.' He paused again. 'I certainly did.'

She reached experimentally for the hook again. 'You could at least have done me the courtesy to mention that you were in the room. Or in the house, for that matter. You said that you wished to be gone.'

He sighed. 'I assumed you had looked out of the window this morning and guessed the truth on your own. You were right and I was wrong. I am told by your brother that the roads are quite impossible, the drive is blocked, and I am trapped. So I have gone to ground here by the library fire, and I was doing my best to keep true to my word and stay out of your path.' She heard the rattle of china and glanced over her shoulder to see his breakfast things, sitting on the table beside the couch.

'When you realised that your plan was not working, you could have given me warning that I was being observed. It would have spared me some embarrassment.'

He gave a slight chuckle. 'It is not as if I am likely to tell the rest of the company how you behave when we are alone together.'

She cringed. 'I did not say that you would. I have reason to trust your discretion, after all.'

'Then are you implying that my presence here embarrasses you?' He let the words hang with significance.

It did. Not that it mattered. She turned back to look at him. 'Perhaps it is my own behaviour that embarrasses me. And the fact that you have been witness to more than one example of the worst of it.'

He laughed. 'If I have seen the worst of your behaviour, then you are not so very bad as you think.'

She gave him her most intimidating glare, which had absolutely no effect. 'Tell me, now: are you accustomed to finding Elise leaping at doorframes, like a cat chasing a moth?'

'No, I am not. But then, she would not have need to.' His eyes scanned over her in appraisal. 'She is much taller than you are.'

'She is tall, and poised as well, and very beautiful.' Rosalind recited the list by rote. 'She will never know how vexing it is to find everything you want just slightly out of reach. It all comes easily to her.' And Elise, who had two men fighting over her, would never have to cope with the knowledge that the most perfect man in London still thought of her as a silly girl. Rosalind glared at the hook above her. 'I must always try harder, and by doing so I over-reach and end up looking foolish.'

'Perhaps you do.' His voice was soft, which surprised her. And then it returned to its normal tone. 'Still, it is not such a bad thing to appear thus. And I am sure most people would take a less harsh view of you than you do of yourself.'

She picked at the mistletoe in her hands, removing another wilted leaf. Behind her, there was a sigh, and the creak of boot leather. And then he was standing beside her and plucking the thing from between her fingers.

She looked up to find Tremaine far too near, and grinning down at her. 'I understand your irritation with *me*, for we agreed to keep our distance,' he said. 'I have been unsuccessful. But what has that poor plant ever done to you, that you treat it so?'

She avoided his eyes, focusing on the leaves in his hand, and frowned. 'That "poor plant" will not stay where I put it.'

He reached up without effort and stuck it back in its place above their heads. Then he tipped her chin up, so she could see the mistletoe—and him as well—and said innocently, 'There appears to be no problem with it now.'

As a matter of fact it looked fine as it was, with him beneath it and standing so very close to her. For a moment she thought of how nice it might be to close her eyes and take advantage of the opportunity. And how disastrous. Some lessons should not have to be learned twice, and if he meant to see her succumb again he would be disappointed. 'Do not try to tempt me into repeating mistakes of the past. I am not so moved.'

He smiled, to tell her that it was exactly what he was doing. 'Are you sure? My response is likely to be most different from when last we kissed.'

Her pulse gave an unfortunate gallop, but she said, in a frigid tone, 'Whatever for? What has changed?'

'You are no longer an inexperienced girl.'

'Nor am I as foolish as I was, to jump into the arms of a rake.'

He smiled again. 'But I was not a rake when you assaulted me.'

'I assaulted you?' She feigned shock. 'That is doing it much too brown, sir.'

'No, really. I cannot claim that I was an innocent babe, but no one would have called me a rake.' He held a hand over his heart. 'Not until word got round that I had seduced some sweet young thing and then refused to do right by her, in any case.'

'Seduced?' The sinking feeling in her stomach that had begun as she talked to Harry was back in force.

'The rumours grew quite out of proportion to the truth when Elise cast me off. Everyone was convinced that something truly terrible must have happened for her to abandon me so quickly.'

Her stomach sank a little further.

He went on as though noticing nothing unusual. 'And it must have been my fault in some way, mustn't it? Although I was not exactly a pillar of moderation, I had no reputation for such actions before that time. But it is always the fault of the man, is it not? Especially one so crass and cruel as to refuse to offer for the poor, wounded girl because I was already promised to another. And then to deny her father satisfaction, for fear that I might do the man injury.' He leaned over her. 'For I am a crack shot, and a fair hand with a blade. And your father, God protect him, is long past the day when he could have hurt me.' He put on a face of mock horror. 'And when I refused to make a full explanation to my betrothed, or give any of the details of the incident? Well, it must have been because it was so very shameful, and not because it would have made the situation even more difficult for the young lady concerned.'

'You needn't have used my name. But I would not have blamed you for giving the truth to Elise. It was not your fault, after all.' She wished she could sink through the floor, along with the contents of her heart.

'When she came to me with the accusation, I told her that the majority of what she had heard was true. I *had* been caught in an intimate position with a young lady, by the girl's father. But I had not meant to be unfaithful to her, it would not happen again, and she must trust me for the rest.' He frowned. 'That was the sticking point, I am afraid. Her inability to trust. The woman has always been quick to temper. She broke the engagement and went to Harry. I happily gave myself over to sin. And thereby hangs a tale.'

'So you are telling me not only did I ruin your engagement, and spoil Christmas for ever, I negatively affected your character?'

'It is not so bad, having a ruined character. I have found much more pleasure in vice than I ever did in virtue.' He frowned. 'And after all this time the woman I once sought has come back to me.'

Her anger at him warred with guilt. Elise and Harry were in a terrible mess, and she might have been the cause of it all. But how could Tremaine stand there, flirting so casually, as though it did not matter? 'She might have come back, but she is foolish to trust you. What would she think of you, I wonder, if she found you and I here, alone together?'

'I think she would go running right back into Harry's arms, as she did once before.' He seemed to be considering something for a moment, before reaching out to brush his knuckles against her cheek. 'But enough of Elise. I know what she has done these past years, for we have been close, although not as close as I once wished. At no time did she ever mention that Harry had a sister.'

Rosalind cleared her throat, to clear her head, and stepped a little away from him, until he was no longer touching her. 'Half-sister.'

'Mmm.' His acknowledgement of her words was a low

hum, and she thought she could feel it vibrating inside her, like the purr of a cat. 'If it was not a trick, as I first suspected, is there some reason that they kept you so well hidden?'

She swallowed hard, and when she answered her voice was clear of emotion. 'Harry and my father do not get on well. He was sent away to school when we were still young, and took the opportunity to spend all subsequent holidays with his own father's family, until he was of age. Then he came to London.' She hung her head. 'I remained at home, where I could not be an embarrassment to the family.'

He was still close enough that if she looked up she could admire his fine lips, see the cleft in his chin. And she remembered the feel of his cheek against hers, the taste of his tongue. She had lost her freedom over a few kisses from that perfect mouth. And somehow she did not mind.

She could feel him watching her so intently that she feared he could read her thoughts, and he said, 'What did you do in the country, my little black sheep? Did you continue in the way you set out with me? Were there other incidents of that kind, I wonder, or was I an aberration?'

Rosalind pulled herself together, pushed against his chest and stepped out of the doorway further into the room. 'How rude of you to assume that there were. And to think that I would tell you if I had transgressed is beyond familiar.'

He turned to follow her and closed the distance between them again. 'But that does not answer my question. Tell me, my dear Rosalind, have there been other men in your life?'

'You were hardly in my life. And I most certainly am not your dear...'

'Ah, ah, ah.' He laid a finger on her lips to stop her

words. 'Whether I was willing or no, I was your first kiss. But who was the second?'

'There has not been a second,' she answered, trying to sound prim. But his finger did not move from her lips, and when she spoke it felt rather as though she were trying to nibble on his fingertip. His mouth curled, and she shook her head to escape from the contact. 'I learned my lesson, I swear to you. There is nothing about my conduct of the last years that is in any way objectionable.'

'What a pity.' He leaned away from her and blinked his eyes. 'For a moment I thought Christmas had arrived, in the form of a beautiful hostess every bit as wicked as I could have wished. But if you should have a change of heart and decide to throw yourself upon my person, as you did back then, I would make sure that you would have nothing to regret and much more pleasant memories.'

She turned away and looked out of the window, so that he could not see the indecision in her face. The offer had an obvious appeal. 'How dare you, sir? I have no intention of, as you so rudely put it, *throwing* myself upon your person.'

'Did you have that intention the last time, I wonder?'

'I have no idea what I thought to accomplish. It was the first time I had drunk anything stronger than watered wine, and I did not know my limitations. One cup of particularly strong Christmas punch and I lost all sense.'

He raised his eyebrows. 'And how is the punch at this house?'

'Nothing I cannot handle.'

'If you have returned to the straight and narrow, then you are no use to me at all.' He turned and walked away from her, throwing himself down on the couch as though he had forgotten her presence. 'Whatever shall I do now, to give Elise a distaste of me? For if that fool brother of yours does not come up to snuff soon and reclaim his wife, I am likely to end up married to her after all.'

She looked at him in surprise, and then she blurted, 'Do you not mean to marry Elise?' It was none of her business, but it turned the discussion to something other than herself, which suited her well.

'Elise is already married.' He said it flatly, as though stating the obvious, and stared up at the ceiling.

It was her turn to follow him. She stood before him, hands on hips, close enough so that he could not pretend to ignore her. 'Elise is separated from Harry. If she can persuade him, she will be divorced and free. What are your intentions then?'

'Divorce is by no means a sure thing,' he hedged. 'I would have to declare myself in court as her lover. And even then it might amount to nothing. But it would drag the whole affair into the public eye.'

'Do you have issues with the scandal of it?'

He shrugged. 'If I did, then I would be a fool to escort her now. It is no less scandalous to partner with her while she is still married.'

'Would you think less of her should she be free? Would she be beneath you? Because that would put things back to the way they were before I spoiled them.' She sighed, and dropped her hands to her sides, remembering the look in her brother's eyes when he had seen his wife in the doorway. 'Although it would hurt Harry most awfully.'

Nicholas gave her a tired look, and stretched out on the couch with his feet up and a hand over his eyes. 'There is nothing wrong with Elise, and no reason that I would find her unfit to marry if she were free. Save one.' He looked as though the words were being wrenched out of him. 'I do not love her.'

'You do not…' Rosalind looked confused. 'But she has come back to you again, after all these years. And when I spoke to her, she seemed to think…'

'What she understands to be true is in some ways different from what I have come to believe.' He turned his head to her, and there was a look of obvious puzzlement on his face. 'At one time I would have liked nothing better than to meet her in church and unite our futures. But in the years since she turned me down in favour of Harry?' He shrugged. 'Much time has passed. I still find her beautiful, and very desirable—for, while I am circumspect, I am not blind to her charms. I enjoy her company, and I value her friendship above all things. But I seriously doubt, should we marry, that I will be a more satisfactory husband than the one she already has. Once the novelty began to pale she would find many aspects of my character are wanting. And for my part? She broke my heart most thoroughly the first time she chose another. But I doubt when she leaves me this time that it will cause similar damage.'

'How utterly perfect!' Rosalind reached out and pulled his boots onto the floor, forcing him to sit up.

'Oh, really?' He was eyeing her suspiciously. 'And just why would you say that?'

She sat down on the couch beside him, in the space his

legs had occupied, trying to disguise her obvious relief. 'I will explain shortly, if you can but answer a few more questions to my satisfaction. If you do not want her, then why did you take her back?'

He scratched his head. 'I am not sure. But I suspect that force of habit brought her to me, and force of habit keeps me at her side.'

'That does not sound very romantic.'

'I thought at first that it was lust. A desire to taste the pleasures that I was once denied.' He gave her a significant look. 'But our relationship has not yet progressed to such a stage, and I find myself most content with things as they are.'

'You two are not…? You do not…?' Rosalind took her most worldly tone with him, and hoped he could not tell that she lacked the understanding to ask the rest of the question. For she was unsure just what *should* be happening if the relationship had 'progressed'. But she had wondered, all the same.

'We are not, and we do not.' He was staring at her in surprise now. 'Are you seeking vicarious pleasure in the details of Elise's infidelity? For you are most curious on the subject.'

'Not really.' She gave him a critical appraisal in return. 'I think it is quite horrid that she left Harry, and even worse that you took her in. But if it was all for an ember of true love that smouldered for years, though untended, it would give me some measure of understanding. And I would find it in my heart to forgive her.'

'But not me?' he asked.

'I would suspect you of being an unrepentant rogue,

Tremaine, as I do in any case. For you seem ready to ruin my brother's marriage not because you love deeply, but because you are too lazy to send Elise home.'

He flinched at her gibe. 'It will probably spoil your low opinion of me, but here is the real reason I encouraged her to remain in London. I recognise a friend in dire need, and I want to help her. She is lost, Miss Morley. She will find her way right again, I am sure. But until that time better that she be lost with me than with some other man who does not understand the situation and chooses to take advantage of her weakness.'

'You are carrying on a public affair with my sister-in-law for her own good?'

Tremaine smiled. 'And now please explain it to your brother for me. I am sure he will be relieved to hear it.'

'I think Harry doubts your good intentions.'

His smile widened to a grin. 'I know he does. I think he invited me down here for the express purpose of keeping me away from Elise during the holiday. To the susceptible, Christmas can be a rather romantic season. I believe we both know what can happen in the proximity of wine and mistletoe.'

He looked at the ceiling and whistled, while she glared steadfastly towards the floor.

'Do you know how he attempted to trick me into this visit? By offering to divorce his wife if I won his silly bet. He probably thought I could not resist the challenge of besting him. Little did he suspect that I would tell Elise all, and she would insist on coming as well. It must gall him no end to see the two of us here.'

Rosalind cleared her throat. 'I think you would be surprised at how much he might know on that matter. But pray continue.'

Tremaine laughed. 'For my part, were I a jealous man, I would be enraged at the amount of energy my supposed intended spends in trying to attract her husband's attention by courting mine. She means to go back to him, and he is dying to have her back. There is nothing more to be said on the matter.'

'I will agree with that,' said Rosalind. 'For I have never met a couple better suited, no matter what they might think.'

He nodded. 'We agree that they belong together. And she does want to come home to him, since he did not come to London and get her. So be damned to Harry's machinations for the holidays. I have devised a plan of my own.'

'Really?' Someone else with a plan? She could not decide if she should meet the news with eagerness or dread.

'Harry's scheme, whatever it might be, requires my eagerness to win his wife away from him. In this he does not have my co-operation. I have kept her safe from interlopers for two months now, but it is time she returned home. I was hoping to find my host, lose the bet, and make a hasty escape before Elise realised what had happened. In no time, I would have been back in London. And she would have been back here with Harry, where she belongs.'

She shook her head. 'Until such time as Harry loaned her a coach so that she could leave him again. Which he will do, the moment she asks. It will do no good at all if you leave only to have Elise following in your wake.'

Tremaine grimaced in disgust. 'Why on earth would

Harry lend her a coach? I have brought her as far as Lincolnshire. If he lacks the sense to hold on to her once he has her again then you can hardly expect me to do more.'

Rosalind replied, 'Elise's main argument with the man seems to be that he is too agreeable. And he has admitted to me that he would deny her nothing. If she wished to leave, he would not stop her.'

'Damn Harry and his agreeable nature,' he said. 'In any case, the snow is keeping me from the execution of my plan, since it required a rapid getaway and that appears to be impossible.' He stared at her for a moment. 'But finding you here adds an interesting ripple to the proceedings. Considering our history together, and the results that came of it, I thought perhaps…'

'That I would allow you to dishonour me again to pre-cipitate another falling-out with Elise?' She gave him a sceptical glare. 'While I cannot fault you for the devious-ness of it, I do not see what good it would do. You might have escaped marriage to me once, but I expect Harry would call you out if you refused me now.'

He glared at her. 'Very well, Miss Morley. You have proved my plans to be non-starters. I shall fall back on my last resort, of taking all my meals in this room and avoiding both the lord and the lady of the house until I can leave. Unless you have a better idea?' The challenge hung in the air.

She smiled back. 'I was hoping you would ask. For I have a far superior plan.' Or rather Harry had, if she could get Tremaine to agree with it. It would be quite hopeless if he meant to hide in the library the whole visit.

He favoured her with a dry expression, and reached for his teacup to take a fortifying sip. 'Do you, now?'

'Of course. You admit you are concerned with Elise's welfare. And, while I wish her well, I am more worried about Harry. If we are in agreement that what they need for mutual happiness is each other, then it makes sense that we pool our resources and work together to solve their difficulties.'

'Because we have had such good luck together in the past?'

She sniffed in disapproval. 'I would not be expecting you to do anything more than you have done already. Pay courteous attention to Elise. Be her confidant, her escort, her friend. But to do that you must come out of this room, participate in the activities I have planned, and see that she does as well. Your mere presence may be enough to goad Harry to action on the matter, if he is the one who must apologise.'

'That is exactly what I fear.' Tremaine shuddered theatrically. 'Although Harry seems to be a mild-mannered chap, I've found in the past that this type of fellow can be the most dangerous, when finally "goaded to action". If your plan involves me meeting with violence at the hands of an irate husband...'

'I doubt it will come to that.'

'You doubt? Miss Morley, that is hardly encouraging.' He spread his hands in front of him, as though admiring a portrait. 'I can see it all now. You and the other guests look on in approval as Harry beats me to a bloody pulp. And then, Elise falls into his arms. While I wish them all the best, I fail to see the advantages to me in this scenario.'

'Do not be ridiculous, sir. I doubt Harry is capable of

such a level of violence.' She considered. 'Although, if you could see your way clear to letting him plant you a facer…'

'No, I could not,' He stared at her in curiosity. 'Tell me, Miss Morley, are all your ideas this daft, or only those plans that concern me?'

'There is nothing the least bit daft about it. It is no more foolish than taking a lover in an effort to get her to return to her husband.' She stared back at him. 'You will pardon me for saying it, but if that is the projected result of an affair with you, it does not speak well of your romantic abilities.'

'I have the utmost confidence in my "romantic abilities". But if you doubt them, I would be only too happy to demonstrate.'

She cleared her throat. 'Not necessary, Tremaine. But, since you are concerned for your safety, we will find a way to make Harry jealous that involves no personal harm to you. Is that satisfactory?'

'Why must we make him jealous at all? If I stay clear of him, and we allow time to pass and nature to take its course…'

'Spoken as a true city-dweller, Tremaine. If you had ever taken the time to observe nature, you would have found that it moves with incredible slowness. The majestic glaciers are called to mind. So deliberate as to show no movement at all. And as cold as that idea.'

He shook his head. 'Spoken by someone who has never seen the ruins of Pompeii. They are a far better example of what happens when natural passions are allowed their sway. Death and destruction for all who stand in the way. Which is why I prefer to keep my distance.'

'You have seen them?' she asked eagerly.

'Harry and Elise? Of course. And I suspect that, although they do not show it outright—'

'No. The ruins of Pompeii.'

He stopped, confused by the sudden turn in the conversation. 'Of course. I took the Grand Tour. It is not so unusual.'

She leaned forward on the couch. 'Were they as amazing as some have said?'

'Well, yes. I suppose. I did not give it much thought at the time.'

She groaned in frustration. 'I have spent my whole life sequestered in the country, drawing the same watercolours of the same spring flowers, year after year. And you have seen the world. But you did not think on it.'

'You are sequestered in the country because you cannot be trusted out of sight of home,' he snapped.

'Because of one mistake. With you.' She pointed a finger. 'But I notice you are to be trusted to go wherever you like.'

'That is because I am a man. You are a girl. It is an entirely different thing.'

'Please cease referring to me as a girl. I am fully grown, and have been for some time.' She glared up at him. 'My diminutive stature has nothing to do with youth, and should not render me less than worthy—despite what Elise might have to say on the subject of what constitutes a good match.'

He was staring at her with a dazed expression. 'Indeed. You are quite tall enough, I am sure. And what does Elise have to do with it?'

'She was speaking on the subject of her marriage to Harry,' Rosalind admitted. 'I still find it very hard to understand, but she seemed to think it important that Harry was tall.'

Tremaine furrowed his brow, and took another sip from his cup. 'That makes no sense. He is no taller than I, certainly. Perhaps even a little shorter.'

'But just right in the eyes of Elise, I assure you. She made a point of assuring me that physically he is a magnificent specimen, and that they are very well suited.'

Tremaine choked on his tea.

'Is something the matter?'

'Not at all. It is just I think you have misunderstood her.'

'Whatever else could she mean?'

He was looking at her in a most unusual way. 'Perhaps at another time we can discuss that matter in more detail. But for now, do not concern yourself with it. I suspect it means that there are parts of married life that she is eager to resume. And that I have brought her home not a moment too soon. We need not concern ourselves with Harry's good qualities. If we wish success, we would be better served to improve on his deficiencies. And, much as I dislike the risks involved, we must do what is necessary to make him reclaim his wife's affection.'

Rosalind smiled at his use of the word 'we'. Perhaps they were working towards the same end, after all. 'My thoughts exactly.'

He returned her smile. 'Well, then. What does she want from him that we can help her achieve?'

'I know from experience that Harry can be the most frustrating of men.' She frowned. 'If he does not wish you to know, it is very hard to divine what it is that he is thinking. Hence our current predicament. I have no doubt that he adores Elise. But she cannot see it, even after all these years.'

Tremaine frowned in return. 'Can she not see what is obvious to the rest of us?'

'I think she wishes him to be more demonstrative.'

'Which will be damned difficult, you will pardon the expression, with her hanging upon my arm. If he has never made any attempt to dislodge her from it, I fail to see what I could do to change things.'

She patted him on the arm in question. 'You have hit on the problem exactly. She wishes him to *do* something about you.'

Tremaine ran a hand over his brow. 'And I would rather he did not. Is there anything else?'

'She wishes he would talk to her so that she could better understand him.'

He furrowed his brow. 'They have passed the last five years in silence? That cannot be. I would swear that I have heard him utter words in her presence. Is it a difficulty of language? For I have found Elise's comprehension of English to be almost flawless.'

Rosalind closed her eyes for a moment, attempting to gather strength. 'She wishes him to speak about important matters.'

'Matters of state, perhaps? How odd. She has shown no interest in them when speaking to me.'

Rosalind burst forth in impatience. 'This has nothing to do with English lessons or a sudden interest in politics, Tremaine. Elise wishes Harry to speak openly about matters that are important to *her*.'

'Oh.' He slumped in defeat. 'Then it is quite hopeless. For he would have no idea what that would be. The minds of women are a depth that we gentlemen have not been able to plumb, I'm afraid.'

'Don't be an idiot,' she snapped. 'There is nothing so terribly difficult to understand about women, if you make an effort. We two are conversing well enough, aren't we? You do not require the assistance of a guide to understand me?'

He paused for a moment and answered politely, 'Of course not. But you are more direct in your communication than Elise.'

She smiled graciously, preparing to blush and accept the compliment.

Then he said, 'Almost masculine.' He paused again. 'And why do you persist in calling me just Tremaine, and not Mister? If you prefer, you may call me Nicholas.'

'I do not.' She stood up and moved away from him. 'Nor do I think your behaviour proves you worthy of an honorific. Tremaine will do. And you may continue to call me Miss Morley. And now that we have got that out of the way, are we in agreement about the matter of Elise and Harry? Will you help me?'

'Since it is likely to be the only way you will allow me any peace? Yes, I will help you, Miss Morley. Now, go about your business and let me return to my nap.'

CHAPTER NINE

HARRY sighed in satisfaction as he climbed the stairs towards his bed. The day had gone well enough, he supposed. The house had buzzed with activity. Wherever he went he had found people playing at cards or games, eating, drinking and merrymaking, with Rosalind presiding over all with an air of hospitable exasperation. The only faces that had seemed to be absent from the mix were those of Tremaine and his wife.

The thought troubled him, for he suspected that they might be together, wherever they were, enjoying each other's company. And it would be too obvious of him to pound upon his wife's door and admit that he wished to know if she was alone.

He almost sighed in relief as he saw her in the window seat at the top of the stairs. She was just where she might have been if there had been no trouble between them, sitting in her favourite place and looking out onto the snow falling into the moonlit park below.

He stepped up beside her, speaking quietly so as not to disturb her mood. 'Beautiful, is it not?'

'Yes.' She sighed. But it was a happy, contented sigh, and it made him smile.

'I expect it will make tomorrow's trip into the trees a difficult one.'

'You still mean to go?' She looked at him in obvious surprise.

'Of course. It will be the morning of Christmas Eve. We went out into the woods together often enough that I have come to think of it as a family tradition. Would you like to accompany me?'

She looked excited at the prospect, and then dropped her gaze and shook her head. 'I doubt that would be a good idea.'

He laughed. 'It is not as if we are planning an assignation. Only a sign of friendship. If we cannot be lovers we can at least be friends, can't we?'

'Friends?' The word sounded hollow and empty coming from her. She was making no attempt to show the world that she was happy with their situation.

It gave him hope, and he continued. 'Yes. We can have a truce. If you wish Tremaine to be your lover, then why can I not occupy the position he has vacated and be your trusted friend?'

'You wish to be my friend?' Now she looked truly puzzled.

'If I can be nothing else. Let us go out tomorrow, as we have done in the past. We will take Tremaine with us, so that he can share in the fun. If he is what you want, then I wish to see him well settled in my place before I let you go. Tomorrow I will pass the torch.'

'You will?' If she wanted her freedom, his offer should

give her a sense of relief. But there was nothing in her tone to indicate it.

'Yes. I had not planned on your visit, but now that you are here it is a good thing. We cannot settle what is between us with you in London and me in the country. If you wish an end to things, then it is better if we deal with them face to face, without acrimony. Only then will you truly be free.' He let the words sink in. 'You do wish to be free of me, do you not?'

'Yes...'

There was definitely doubt in her voice. He clung to that split second of hesitation as the happiest sound he had heard in months.

'Very well, then. If there is nothing I can do that will make Tremaine lose the bet, on Twelfth Night I will honour my word and begin divorce proceedings. For above all I wish you to be happy. Merry Christmas, Elise.'

'Thank you.'

She whispered it, and sounded so very sad that it was all he could do to keep from putting his arms around her and drawing her close, whispering back that he would never let her go.

'Let us go to bed, then, for it will be an early morning.'

She stood and walked with him, towards their rooms.

Would it be so wrong to take her hand and pull her along after him to his door? Although her manner said that she might not be totally opposed to the idea, neither was there proof that she would be totally in favour of it. It would be best if he waited until he had a better idea of what she truly wanted.

He put his hands behind his back and cleared his throat.

'About our disagreement of yesterday, over the arrangement of the rooms. After we had gone to bed, I realised how
it must look to you. And I apologise if you took it as an
effort to control your behaviour. You have made it clear
enough to me that it is no longer any business of mine
what occurs in your bedroom. If there is a reason that you
might wish to lock the connecting door, I will allow you
your privacy.'

'For what reason would I wish privacy?' She sounded
confused by the idea. Perhaps even after two months
Tremaine was an idle threat to their marriage. She shrugged
as though nothing could occur to her, and gave a tired
laugh. 'In any case, what good would it do to lock the door
against you? You have the key.'

He held his hands open in front of him. 'I have all the
keys, Elise. I could open the door of any room in which you
slept. You must have realised that when you came home.
But do you really think me such a villain that I mean to
storm into your room without your permission and force
myself upon you?'

She caught her breath and her eyes darkened. For a
moment his threat held definite appeal.

Then he cleared his throat and continued, 'Am I really
the sort who would take you until you admitted that there
was no place in the world that you belonged but in my arms
and in my bed?'

She froze for a moment, and then glared at him. 'No,
Harry, you are not. On more careful consideration, I think
that I have nothing to worry about. Goodnight.'

And, perhaps it was his imagination, but the way she

carried herself could best be described as stomping off to her room. When the door shut, he suspected that the slam could be heard all over the house.

The next morning Harry was up well before dawn, had taken breakfast and dressed in clothes suitable for the weather before going to roust Tremaine. He could not help but smile as he pounded smartly on the door to the poor man's bedroom. He could hear rustling, stumbling noises, and a low curse before the door in front of him creaked open.

Tremaine stood before him, bleary-eyed and still in his nightshirt. 'Eh?'

'Time to get up, old man.'

Tremaine squinted into the hall and croaked, 'Is there a problem?'

'No problem at all. Did I forget to tell you last night? So sorry. But you *must* be a part of today's proceedings. Elise is expecting you.'

'Then come for me in daylight.'

'No, no. What we are about must be done at dawn. And on the morn of Christmas Eve. There is no better time. Pull on some clothes, man. Warm ones. Your true love is awaiting you in the hall.'

At the mention of Elise Tremaine's eyes seemed to widen a bit. Then he stared back at Harry, as though trying to gauge his intentions. At last he sighed with resignation, and muttered something that sounded rather like, 'Damn Rosalind.' Then he said, 'A moment.' And then he shut the door.

'A moment' proved to be the better part of a half an hour. Tremaine appeared at the door again, no happier, but reasonably well dressed for Harry's purposes, in a fine coat of light wool and soft, low shoes. He stepped into the hall and shut the door behind him. It was only then that he noticed the axe in Harry's hands. 'What the devil—?'

Harry nudged him with the handle and gave him a mad grin. 'You'll see. You'll see soon enough.'

Tremaine swallowed. 'That is what I fear.'

'Downstairs.' He gestured Tremaine ahead of him, and watched the cautious way the man passed him. There was a tenseness in his shoulders, as though his back was attempting to climb out of his coat while his head was crawling into it. His neck seemed to have disappeared entirely. He did not relax until he saw Elise, pacing on the slate at the foot of the stairs, probably assuming that Harry would not cut him down dead in front of a lady.

'There you are.' Elise was trying to display a mixture of irritation and trepidation at what was about to occur, but she could not manage to disguise the same childlike excitement that she had shown whenever they had done this in the past. It made Harry happy to look at her. 'I was not sure if you would still hold to the practice.'

Harry smiled. 'Perhaps if you had not come home I might have forgone it. But if you are under this roof then Christmas will be every bit as full as you would wish it to be. And if we are to do it at all, then we must bring Tremaine, so he will know what is to be expected of him next year.'

If she meant to rescue the poor man, she gave no indication of it. Instead, she nodded with approval. 'Let us go, then.'

'Go where?' Tremaine had found his voice at last.

'Outside, of course. To cut the Yule Log.'

'Oh, I say. You can't mean…'

'A massive oak. I have just the thing picked out.' He turned back to his wife, ignoring the stricken look on Tremaine's face. 'You will approve, I'm sure, Elise. The thing is huge. Sure to burn for days, and with enough wood for two fireplaces.'

'Really?' She was smiling at Harry as though he had offered to wrap her in diamonds. Any annoyance at the chill he would take tramping about the grounds in a foot of fresh snow was replaced by the warm glow of her presence.

But the Christmas spirit did not seem to be reaching Tremaine. He grumbled, 'Surely you have servants to do this?'

Harry shook his head. 'I could never expect them to do such. It is tradition that we choose one ourselves. Elise is very particular about the choice, and she enjoys the walk. I could not begrudge her the experience.'

Elise looked at Tremaine in disapproval. 'You are not dressed for the weather.'

'Here—we can fix that.' Harry removed his own scarf and wrapped it twice around Tremaine's neck, pulling until it constricted. 'There. All better. Let us proceed.' He opened the front door wide and shepherded them through.

Elise took to it as he had known she would. Though she might claim to adore the city, she needed space and fresh air to keep her happy. She strode out into the morning, with the first glints of sunlight hitting the fresh snow, twirled and looked back at them, her face shining brighter than any star. 'Isn't it magnificent?'

Harry nodded in agreement. As he looked at her, he felt his own throat close in a way that had nothing to do with the tightness of a scarf. She was so beautiful standing there, with the dawn touching her blonde hair. And he thought, *You used to be mine.* He chased the thought away. He would make her come home again. For if he had lost her for ever he might just as well march out into the snow, lie down and wait for the end.

He looked around him—anywhere but at Elise. For until he had mastered his emotions he could not bear to look in her face. And he saw she was right: with a fresh coating of snow over everything, and frost and icicles clinging to the trees, it was a most beautiful morning indeed.

Tremaine merely grunted.

'This way.' Harry pointed to the left, up a low hill at the side of the house. 'In the copse of trees where we used to picnic.' He set off at a brisk pace.

Elise followed him easily in her stout boots and heavy wool skirt. 'You do not mean to take the tree where we…' She was remembering their last picnic in the oak grove, and her cheeks were going pink in a way that had nothing to do with the cold.

He cleared his throat. 'Not that one, precisely. But very nearby. This tree is dying, and we will have to take it soon in any case. Why should it not serve a noble purpose?'

Behind them he could hear Tremaine, stumbling and sliding and cursing his way up the hill. He was falling further behind as Elise drew abreast of Harry.

She said softly, 'I am still amazed that you are willing to do this after what has gone on between us. Although you always complied with my wishes, you complained about the bother of it in years past.'

He appeared pleased, and looked at the ground. 'Perhaps I did. But I found, though I meant to leave it off, that the habit was ingrained. Although I complained to you, perhaps I enjoyed it more than I knew.' He glanced back over his shoulder. 'In future you will have Tremaine to complain over it, when he takes my place. But for myself I mean to spend a quiet hour on a winter morning, watching the sun come up.'

She smiled at him in approval, and then blushed and looked away. He glanced back again, so that she could not see his answering smile, and called, 'Keep up, Tremaine, or you shall miss the best part.'

The tree he had chosen had been carefully notched by a servant, so that most of the work was done and it would fall correctly. In truth, there was so little left to do that it was fortunate the thing had not fallen on its own in the storm. A few blows of the axe would give the impression to his lady love of manly competence without undue exertion.

He stepped around to the far side and swung the axe into the wood. It struck with a satisfying clunk that made Tremaine flinch. 'See? We strike thusly.' Harry swung again, and felt the unaccustomed labour jar the bones of his arms. After several Christmases just like this, at least he was prepared for the shock. It was much better than it had been the first time his wife had suggested the activity. 'It takes only a few strokes to do the job.' He smiled at his adversary again. 'Step away from that side, sir. For the tree is likely to come down when I least expect it.' He took a short pause, turned so that Elise could not see the expression on his face, and stared at Tremaine, not bothering to smile. 'I would hate for an accident to befall you.'

Tremaine fairly leapt out of the way, standing safely behind him. The man was terrified of him.

Harry grinned to himself and swung again. 'It is a dangerous business, using an axe.' *Clunk.* 'No end of things can go wrong. Should the handle slip in my hands, for example.' *Clunk.*

He glanced up at his wife's friend, who had gone bone-white with cold and fear. Harry offered him the axe. 'Here. You must try. For I expect Elise will wish you to learn the ways of this.'

Tremaine muttered low, under his breath, 'If you think next year will find me chopping wood for the holiday, you are both quite mad. I have no property in the country, nor do I plan to acquire one. And I seriously doubt that I will be motivated to march through Hyde Park with a weapon in my hands, doing damage to the landscaping.'

'Oh, Nicholas,' Elise laughed. 'What a droll idea.'

But Tremaine took the axe from Harry's hands, and looked relieved to have disarmed him. Harry stepped back as the other man took a mighty swing at the oak, overbalanced, and fell on his seat in the snow.

'Hmm. It does not seem that you have the hang of it yet. Best let me finish it after all.' He retrieved the axe, and a few more chops and a stout push was all it took. There was a loud cracking noise, and he put out an arm to shield Elise. Tremaine scrambled to safety, away from the falling tree.

It crashed to the ground and they stared at the thing for

a moment—Tremaine in disgust, and Elise with obvious satisfaction. Then Tremaine said, 'I suppose now you will tell me that we must drag it back to the house?'

Elise giggled, and Harry said, 'Oh, no. Of course not. This is still much too green to burn. This is the log for next year's festivity. Some people save the cutting for Candlemas, but we have always done it on Christmas Eve morn. And this year it is my gift to you, Tremaine. You will need it next year, when you celebrate Christmas with Elise.' He gestured to the enormous tree on the ground before them. 'You can take the whole thing back with you when you return to London. The servants will take care of it in good time. They are just now bringing in last year's log. We shall see it when we go back to the house.'

'Mad.' Tremaine stared at them in amazement. 'You are both quite mad.' Then he turned from them and stalked back to the house, sliding ahead of them on the downward slope.

Harry looked after him. 'I do not think Tremaine appreciates my gift.'

Elise looked after him as well, trying to look stern, although a smile was playing around her lips. 'That was horrible of you, you know. To drag the poor man out in weather like this. And so early in the morning. He abhors mornings.'

Harry tried to focus on the snow-covered back of the retreating man. Not on the beautiful woman at his side and what her smile might tell him about her intimate knowledge of Nicholas Tremaine's morning routine. 'A pity. For it is the most beautiful time of day. You still enjoy mornings, do you not? Or have your ways changed now that you are not with me?'

'I still enjoy them,' she admitted. 'Although they are not so nice in the city as they are here. It is the best time to ride, though. For many are still sleeping from the night's revelry, and the park is nearly empty.'

'Oh.' He tried not to imagine what a handsome couple his wife and Tremaine would make on horseback in Rotten Row.

'But the city is quite empty at Christmas. And I will admit it would have been lonely to remain there.' She hesitated. 'I must thank you for inviting…Tremaine.'

She had remembered, too late, that she had not been included in the invitation. There was an awkward pause.

'I am glad that you chose to accompany him,' Harry said firmly. 'For I would not wish you to be alone. And I hope Christmas will be very much as you remember it.' He glanced down the hill towards the house. 'You have brought many changes to Anneslea since we married.'

'Really?' She looked surprised, as though she did not realise the merriment she'd brought with her when she'd come into his life. 'Was not Christmas a joyous time when you were a boy?'

He shrugged. 'Much like any other day. When I was small my father was often ill, and there was little cause for celebration. My stepfather, Morley, did not hold with foolishness on a holy day. And once I came here, to stay with Grandfather?' He shrugged again. 'It was a very quiet festival. There was dinner, of course. And gifts.' They had arrived back at the house. A footman grinned as he opened the front door, and they entered the front hall to the smells of pine and spices and an air of suppressed excitement. He looked around him. 'But it was nothing like this. Thank you.' His voice very nearly cracked on the words.

'You're welcome, Harry.' Her eyes were very round, and misty blue in the morning light. Then she looked away from him quickly, letting a servant take her outer clothes and enquiring about tea, which was already poured in the library, just as it had been in years past. It was still early, but any guests who had risen would be in the dining room taking breakfast. For a time it would be just the two of them, alone together.

In the library, she glanced around the room with a critical eye. And Harry noted with some satisfaction that she seemed unconcerned by the presence of only two cups on the tea tray. Apparently, after his disgrace in the woods, she did not care that Tremaine would be left to fend for himself.

'Do you mean to have Rosalind here for Christmas from now on?' she said softly.

'It depends, I suppose, on whether Morley allows it. But I do not know what I would have done without her help this year.'

Elise looked up from her cup, her eyes still wide with sympathy. 'Does she know that the family recipes as they are written are not accurate?'

'Eh?'

'Rosalind. There are changes in the Christmas recipes, and she should remember to remind Cook.'

Harry waved a dismissive hand. 'I expect she will manage as best she can. It will be all right.'

'Perhaps I should help her.'

'No,' Harry said, worried that her sudden interest in the menu was likely to take her away from him again. 'There is no need, I'm sure. No one will notice if things are not quite up to standard.'

She stared at him. 'Really, Harry. You have no idea how difficult a house party can be.'

He looked warmly at her. 'Only because you made it look so easy, my sweet. But you need not bother.' He gave a slight sigh. 'I will want you here tonight, of course. When it is time to light the Yule Log. For it is still very much a part of you, since you helped me to choose it. And I've still got a piece of last year's log, so that we may light the new one properly.'

Her agitation seemed to fade, and she smiled a little, remembering.

'If we have any regrets from the old year we can throw them on the fire,' he announced. 'Next year we shall start anew.'

She set her teacup down with a click. 'And behave as if none of this has happened?'

He sighed. 'Is it really necessary to retread the same ground? If you are ready to come home, then I see no reason to refer to any of this again.'

'If I am ready to come home?'

He had spoken too soon, and ruined all that had gone before. For the coldness had returned to her voice, and she was straightening up the tea things and preparing to leave him.

'Perhaps I should go to my room and dress for the day. If you will excuse me?'

He followed her to the door and in a last act of desperation held up a hand to stop her as she crossed the threshold, touching her arm and pointing above them. 'Mistletoe.'

She frowned. 'You can't be serious.'

'Not even for old times' sake?'

'Certainly not.' She reached up and caught the thing by a twig. She pulled it down, then threw it to the floor at his feet.

He stared at it, unsure whether to be angry or sad. 'Pity. I would have quite enjoyed it. I think it is your kiss I miss the most. But there are so many things about you that I miss it is hard to tell.'

'Miss me?' She laughed. 'This is the first I have heard of it. It seems to me that you are managing quite well without me, Harry.'

'It bothers you, then, that I have put Rosalind in charge?'

'Not particularly.'

'But something has made you unhappy again. Are you ready to discuss why you are here?' he asked.

'Whatever do you mean?'

'You have come back to me, Elise, just as I knew you would. It was no real surprise, seeing you. I had a devil of a time persuading Tremaine to take the invitation, but I knew if he came you would not be able to stay away. And I was right.' He looked at her, searching her expression for some evidence that she was weakening again.

'It should not be so terribly strange that I would wish to return with him. I lived here for several years, and associate many happy memories with the place.'

Harry sighed. 'Do you really? When you left I thought you never wished to see the place again. Or was it just the owner you wished to avoid? Because you must have known I'd be here as well.'

'I hold you no ill will,' she insisted, staring at him through narrowed eyes and proving her words a lie. 'And, since you have not said otherwise, I assume you agree that our separation is for the best.'

'You wished to part, not I. Do not mistake my unwillingness to beg for you to return as agreement.' And then his desire to hold her got the better of him, and he stepped even closer. 'There is very little separation between us at this moment.' He grabbed her wrist and pulled her to him, so her body rested tight against him.

'That is none of my doing and all of yours.' But she did not push him away.

He calmed himself so as not to alarm her. Then he put his mouth to her ear and whispered, so softly that only she could hear, 'Kiss me, Elise. Just one more time. I will enjoy it, and you will as well. I would make sure of the fact.' He felt her tremble and knew that he was right. When his lips met hers he would make her forget all about her argument with him. She would think of nothing but how he made her feel, and that would be the end of their troubles.

'I did not come here because I missed your kisses.' She pulled away from him, and the small rejection stung worse than all the others combined.

'And yet you were the one to come home.'

'For a brief visit. There are things in my room…'

'Things?' He laughed, for he had been sure that she would come up with a better lie than that when they finally had a chance to speak. 'If that is all you wanted, then you could have saved me a small amount of personal pride had you come alone, in January, rather than trailing after Tremaine when the house is full of guests.'

'I am not trailing after him,' she snapped.

Harry took a deep breath, for it would not do to lose his temper with her. 'It is all right,' he responded. 'I've grown quite used to it, really.'

But clearly it was not all right to her. He had misspoken again, and she was working herself into a rage. 'You did not expect me to live for ever alone, once we parted?'

'That is not what I mean, and you know it. I knew when you finally left me that you would go straight to Tremaine for comfort. I have expected it for many years.'

Anger and indignation flashed hot in her eyes, as though she could pretend the truth was not an obvious thing and her leaving had been all *his* fault. 'When I *finally* left you? What cause did I ever give you to doubt me?'

'It was never a question of doubt, Elise.' He tried to keep his tone matter-of-fact, for there was no point in fuelling her anger with his. 'I have always known that I was your second choice.'

'How utterly ridiculous,' she snapped. 'I married you, didn't I? Are you saying you doubted my innocence?'

'I am saying nothing of the kind. I am saying that I was not your first choice when you wed. You might have accepted my offer, but Tremaine offered for you first. You might have chosen me, but you always regretted that it could not have been Nicholas. I have had to live with the fact for five years, Elise.' He struggled to hide the hurt in his tone, and instead his voice sounded bitter. 'I had hoped that you would put him behind you once you were married. I would not have offered for you otherwise. But I realised almost from the beginning that it was not to be the case.'

'You realised?'

There was something in the sound of her voice that was almost like an accusation, and he could feel his carefully managed control slipping away. 'It did not take you long to make up with the man. Less than a year. The quarrel that parted you would have mended easily had you been willing to wait. It was really most annoying to listen to you complain, at the end, about *my* lack of devotion. For you have been so clearly devoted to another. Did you expect me to remain for ever the benighted fool who had married you? In the face of your continued indifference? In time one learns to harden one's heart, Elise.'

He was almost shouting by the time he'd finished. And then he laughed again, at the shocked expression on her face. 'Although what you expect by accompanying your lover to our home for Christmas I cannot imagine. Did you hope to create a dramatic scene for the diversion of my guests? Is it not bad enough that you have finally worked up the courage to be unfaithful to me? Must you parade it in front of me as well?' He shook his head, and his voice returned to normal. 'I never in all these years felt you to be so cruel. Perhaps I did not know you as well as I thought.'

Which was foolish, for he had known all along that that was what she would do. He had wanted her to come with Tremaine, had planned for the eventuality. And now he was angry to the point of shouting because his plans had come to fruition. It made no sense at all.

But it was too late to call back the words, or to explain that he wished to discuss things with her in a rational manner. Elise's cheeks had grown hot with anger and shame, but no words were issuing from her lips, and she was staring at him as though she no longer knew him.

As he waited for her response, a part of him wanted to beg her forgiveness, forestall her reaction. But why should he take all the blame when she was the one who had left? It was long past time for her turn to be hurt and frustrated and embarrassed.

It did him no good to feel sure that he was in the right on this. Instead of vindication, he was suddenly sick with the taste of truth. He had spoken too much of it, all in one go, and it sat in his stomach like an excess of Christmas dinner.

Did she expect him to swallow his pride as well, before she was willing to come home? If the silence went on much longer she would see him on his knees, begging her to return.

Then she spoke, and her voice was cool and even. 'So I finally know, after all this time, what you really think of me. It is most gratifying that our separation has given you the ability to speak your mind. And I find I have nothing to add to it.'

Then she turned and walked from the room, leaving him all over again. He stared down at the mistletoe at his feet, and then kicked it savagely aside, before gathering enough composure to meet his guests for breakfast.

Elise walked back towards her room, numb with shock. She could hear Harry turn and walk in the opposite direction, towards the dining room. She was glad of it, for if he spoke one more word to her she would burst into tears and not care who saw her. After all her complaints over not knowing her husband's true feelings, he had finally given them to her. And she found that she liked him better as he had been.

What had happened to the man she'd married? The amiable fellow who had tolerated her behaviour without question? In two months he'd been replaced by an angry stranger who looked at her with hard eyes and a mouth set in bitter disapproval. It was as though he was meeting her for the first time, and was thoroughly disappointed with what he saw.

Why had she come here? It had seemed like a sensible decision at the time. Either she would prove to herself and everyone else that she had put her marriage behind her, or she would make it up with Harry and go back to her old life. She had hoped that she would come back to the house and understand why he had married her in the first place. He would prove that he needed her, even if there were no children, and she would see that her fears were foolishness, and learn to accept his natural reserve as an aspect of his character, not a reflection upon her person.

For a moment she had been sure it was true. He had spoken so fondly of the changes she'd made in his life. And then had proved that he did not need her to preserve them. The last thing she had expected was to find him getting on with things without her help.

And, even worse, that he would come out and admit that there had been a problem from the first, just as she had suspected. Worse yet, it did not sound as if she could easily gain his forgiveness, and the love she wanted. He had spoken as though he had no hope for a closer relationship with her. He had offered for her never expecting to receive her love, or to give his in return. But they could have drifted along in peace and pleasantry had she not chosen to rile him in an effort to fix things.

Rosalind was approaching from the other end of the hall, and Elise reached out to her in desperation. 'I need to talk to you. There is a problem.'

Rosalind replied, 'If it is about the eggs I must argue that they are not at all my fault. I hardly think if one makes a simple suggestion to Cook that a touch more seasoning would be appreciated, that it should result in so much pepper as to make the whole tray inedible. Lord Gilroy took a large portion and grew so red in the face that I feared apoplexy. I—'

Elise grabbed her sister-in-law by the wrist and pulled her into the drawing room. 'It is not about the eggs.'

'What else has gone wrong, then? It is so early in the day that there cannot be more.'

'It is your brother. He is angry with me.'

Rosalind smiled with satisfaction. 'And you have no trouble recognising the fact? That is wonderful news. For it means you are beginning to solve your difficulties.'

'It is not wonderful. It is really quite horrible. He thinks I am faithless.'

Rosalind stared at her and made a face. 'Did you think that taking a lover would assure him of your fidelity? I know things are different in Bavaria, Elise. But they can't be as different as all that.'

'Nicholas is only a friend, nothing more.' She squeezed

Rosalind's arm. 'You must believe me. I would never be untrue to Harry.'

Rosalind disengaged her arm and said, 'While I have no trouble believing you, it is what Harry thinks that matters.'

'If Harry were really bothered he should have said something before now.' She realised too late how defensive she sounded—and how guilty.

Rosalind was looking at her in annoyance. 'You have said yourself that Harry does not speak about anything that bothers him. Did you think that this would be different?'

'Perhaps I was trying to make him jealous.' It was difficult to say the words, for they proved that she had known what she was doing was wrong.

Rosalind nodded. 'You were lonely. And by his silence Harry made it easy for you to stray. He is lucky the situation is not worse than it is.'

Elise let out a small sigh of relief. At least Rosalind did not hold her weakness too much against her. 'I wanted Harry to notice me. But now that he has, what am I to do? I would send Nicholas away, but with the weather he cannot get to the end of the drive, much less back to London.' And then she remembered the offer she had made to get him to bring her home. 'And I will have to apologise to Nicholas as well, for I fear I have given him the wrong idea of my feelings.'

Rosalind stared at her, offering no help.

Elise continued. 'We are all stuck here together, the house is full of strangers, and if we argue everyone in London will hear of it. What am I to do?'

Rosalind replied with a helpless shrug. 'I assumed you

would not have come here if you did not have some idea how to proceed once you had talked to Harry. Did you not have a plan? Everyone seems to be full of them nowadays. It is quite the thing.'

'I was so angry with him I did not think.'

'And he was not angry enough. And now you are less angry, and he is more so.' Rosalind nodded. 'In no time at all balance shall be achieved and you shall both be equally annoyed.' She said it as though this were supposed to be good news, and wiped her hands on her skirts.

Elise shook her head. 'But I do not wish to be annoyed with Harry. I wish us to be happy together. If I return to find that we are both still cross, leaving will have been an exercise in futility.'

Rosalind stepped past her towards the hall, gaining speed as she went. 'There is nothing more I can do for you at the moment. I must run to the entry hall and decorate the Yule Log, so that tonight we can throw the whole thing into the fire and burn those same decorations to ashes. I am sure I will be in a much better mood to discuss futile behaviour, after that is done.'

CHAPTER TEN

ROSALIND hurried down the hallway, taking sips from the cup of tea in her hand. It was tepid. But since she had not managed lunch, it was all she was likely to have until supper, and it would have to do. Since the moment she had arisen there had been something that needed doing, or fixing, or seeing to. Harry's friends seemed to think that the food was either overcooked or raw, they found their rooms too hot or too cold, and the servants could not manage to please any of them without constant supervision.

After watching her decorate the Christmas tree, she had nurtured hopes that Elise would see the chaos, take control of the house, and set things to right again. But after one conversation with Harry the woman could not manage to do anything more useful than wring her hands.

It was most distressing.

As Rosalind passed the open door of the library she noticed that the mistletoe was no longer in its place. Was there something wrong with the thing that it could not seem to stay fixed to the door? Was the nail loose? Tremaine had placed it quite securely yesterday. What had happened now?

She searched the floor and found it had not fallen, as she'd expected, onto the doorstep, but had pitched up against the wall, several feet away. Someone must have kicked it by mistake, for it did appear somewhat the worse for wear. She glared at it, as though blaming it as a trouble-maker, then shook it roughly and gave it a half-hearted toss in the direction of the hook above her.

It hung for a moment, and then dropped back into her teacup, splashing the contents onto her bodice. Unlike yesterday, there was no sound of muffled laughter. But she took a chance before acting further.

'Tremaine, I need you. Get up from that couch and be of use.'

There was a sigh from the other side of the room. 'How did you know I was here?'

'I have been everywhere else in the house, for one reason or another, and I have not seen you all day. So, by process of elimination, you must be hiding in the library—just as you promised you would *not*.'

'And what in God's name do you mean to involve me in now? I have had quite enough of the festivities, and the fun, as you call it, has barely begun. Do you know what your brother attempted this morning?'

'Whatever it was, he has managed to annoy Elise no end.'

'Annoy her?' Tremaine's angry face peered from behind the couch. 'When I left them they were as happy as love-birds. It seems she was not bothered by the sight of her husband threatening me with an axe, or attempting to freeze me to death. And I have ruined my best pair of shoes by walking through the snow. My valet is beyond consolation.'

'As I have told you before, Tremaine, Harry means you no real harm. He is only teasing you because seeing you in a foul temper amuses him. My brother thinks that you have a lack of Christmas spirit, and I'm afraid I must agree with him.'

Nicholas punched the couch cushions in disgust. 'I do not deny the fact. And, since Harry has sufficient spirit for two men, he pretends that he wishes to share it with me.'

She looked down at the dripping mistletoe in her hand, gave it another shake to remove the tea, and reached for the doorframe again. 'If you would be so kind as to take it, then you could save some of us a world of effort. I can be every bit as persistent as my brother, if you give me reason. And if you try to avoid my scheduled activities, I will find a way to force your participation in them. It would be easier for both of us if you could at least pretend to enjoy them.'

He stood and walked slowly towards her. 'I will participate, Miss Morley. But you far overstep the bounds of our limited acquaintance if you think you can make me enjoy the fact. I am a proper gentleman of the ton. And as such I live by certain rules. Conversation should flow freely, but truth should be kept to an absolute minimum. In the Christmas season truth runs as freely as wine.' He made a sour face. 'But the wine is endlessly seasoned with cloves. And therefore undrinkable.'

'So you have an aversion to truth? And cloves? I can do little about the cloves, for they are all-pervasive, but I suppose spontaneous honesty is reason enough to avoid the holiday. Harry and Elise are proving that even if the truth is spoken it is oft misinterpreted. And then there is the very devil to pay. He has finally admitted that he is angry with her.' Rosalind looked heavenward for understanding. 'And yet, she is surprised.'

Tremaine shook his head in pity. 'He'd have been better to hold his tongue. When it comes to women, if you admit to nothing you will have less to apologise for later.'

'I find the fault is with her. One should never ask a man to reveal the contents of his mind if one does not already know what they are.' Rosalind smiled. 'But until they have fought they cannot make up. Some progress has been made. And the game I have chosen for tonight will be perfect to rejoin the two of them. They will be back in each other's arms and laughing together in a matter of minutes. I suspect, once that has happened, the temptation will be great to stay where they are. But you must help fill out the room so that it doesn't look too suspicious.' She looked him up and down. 'You need do nothing more strenuous than take up space. In less than an hour you will be back on that couch, and none the worse for it.' She tapped the mistletoe against her teacup, awaiting his response.

He yawned, as though to prove that taking up space was near the limit of his endurance. And then he said, 'How can I resist you when you put it so appealingly? Here, now. Will you stop fooling with that accursed thing.' Her tapping had turned into a nervous rattling of china, and with surprising alacrity he snatched the kissing ball out of her hand and put it in place on the hook, above her head. And then he stood perfectly still, totally alert, looking down at her. His mouth turned into a curious smile.

She felt the bump as her back met the doorframe, for she'd scrambled out of reach of his arm without even realising it.

And then he laughed. 'You are much more cautious than you once were.'

'And you are no less prone to flirt. But, since I know you wish to return to London alone, I see no point in indulging you.' She took another step, which brought her back into the hall and well out of harm's way. 'I will expect to see you in the drawing room this evening, Tremaine. And we will see if you are still so interested in fun and games when my brother is present to chaperone me.'

After a hearty Christmas Eve dinner, Harry gathered the guests in the drawing room for the lighting of the Yule Log. Elise was pleased to see that the trunk of the ash they had chosen the previous year was large enough to fill the fireplace from end to end.

Rosalind had spent a good portion of the afternoon draping it with garlands of holly and ivy, tied on with red bows, until it was almost too pretty to burn. And she had sighed dramatically as she directed the servants to put it on the grate.

Harry produced a charred piece of last year's log and doused it liberally with brandy before thrusting it into the embers and watching it flare to life.

The crowd gave an appreciative 'Ahh' and several people stepped closer to offer toasts.

When Harry felt ceremony had been properly served, he touched the old log to the new and held it until the decorations upon the new log caught. Then he threw his torch into the fireplace.

'There you are, my friends. The Yule Log. May it burn long and joyfully. If you have any regrets of the previous year, now is your chance to throw them upon the fire and start anew.' He looked significantly at Elise as he reached into a basket of kindling and tossed a handful of pine needles upon the fire, watching them flare.

Elise stared at the basket of needles, and at the crowd around them. Did he mean her to do penance, in front of all these people? But what good would it do to stand in front of the guests and wordlessly declare herself a failure as a wife? Even if she could prove herself sorry for her indiscretion with Nicholas, there was so much she could not change. Without a miracle, next year was likely to be as barren as this had been.

When she did nothing, he gave a moment's thought and added a second handful of needles to the fire. Then he smiled, changing easily back into the jovial host. 'Come, everybody—wassail and mince pies!' He made a few steps in the direction of the refreshment table, until he was sure that the guests were well on their way, then turned back to face Elise on the opposite side of the fire.

'Elise. A word, please, in the study.' Harry beckoned to her to follow him and left the drawing room, walking down the corridor and away from the crowd. His smile was as pleasant as it had always been, with none of the rancour it had held that morning. But his tone was that of a husband who took it for granted that a command would be obeyed.

It rankled her to see him falling right back into the pattern of the last five years. Even though she no longer lived with him, he was acting as though there was nothing strange between them, and ordering her from room to room while pretending that she was free as a bird and could do as she liked.

She hesitated. If she wished to come home, then she must learn not to fight him over little things. But if he did not want her back, then what was the point of obeying? At last she sighed, and nodded, and followed him to the study, letting him shut the door behind her.

He turned and faced her, and he must have seen the anger growing in her—and the shame. For a moment he seemed at a loss for words. He held his hands out in front of him and opened his mouth. Then closed it again, and put his hands behind his back, pensive. At last he said, 'I notice that you did not throw anything onto the fire tonight. Am I to take it that you have no regrets?'

'Of course I have regrets,' she said. 'But do you think a handful of burned pine needles and dead silence is a sufficient apology?'

He shrugged. 'Sometimes, when one does not know what to say, it is better to keep silent.'

'But not always.' She looked earnestly at him. 'It is possible, when one cares deeply about another person, to forgive harsh words said in the heat of the moment.'

He frowned and stared at the ground. 'But not always.' He dipped a hand in to his pocket, removing a jewellery box. 'I have your Christmas gift.' He offered it to her.

'Harry…' And now she was at a loss for words, but her mind was crying, *Tell me you didn't.* Their marriage was in a shambles, and he meant to gloss it all over with another necklace. At last she said, 'This is not necessary.'

He gave her another empty smile. 'Gifts rarely are. It defeats the point, when one has ample means but denies necessities to someone all year, to mete them out at Christmas, pretending that they are gifts. That is miserliness in the guise of generosity.'

She pushed the box back to him. 'I mean that it was not necessary for you to buy me a present. I do not wish it.'

'How do you know? You do not know what is inside.' He held it out to her again.

'It is not the contents of the box that concern me. I do not wish another gift from you, Harry.'

For a moment she thought she saw pain in his eyes, before he hid it in sarcasm. 'And yet you have no trouble with my paying for your apartment or settling your bills? You take things from me every day, Elise.'

He was deliberately misunderstanding her, so she struck back at him. 'If it bothers you so, then set me free. Then I would not take another thing from you, Harry.'

He nodded. 'Because you prefer Tremaine, now that he can afford to buy you the things you need?'

'His inheritance has nothing to do with my leaving you.'

'It was merely a fortunate coincidence that six months after his uncle died you went to London to be with him? You barely allowed him enough time to mourn before you returned to his side.'

She started in surprise. It had not occurred to her when she had left how that might look to the casual observer. Or, worse yet, to her husband. 'If you think I left you because of Tremaine, then you do not understand the problem at all.'

'I understand the problem well enough. I have a wife who prefers the company of another.'

'If you wish to see it that way then there is little I can do to change your mind,' she snapped. 'But in truth you have a wife who left because she was tired of being held at a distance. I can understand, Harry, if you are not happy with me. Or if you do not wish to take me into your confidence. But if you do not want me, must you blame me for seeking companionship elsewhere?'

'I do not want you?' He laughed. 'You do not want *me*, more like. Has Tremaine shown you the letter? I assume that is why you are both here? So that he can win his bet and you can gloat over it.'

'That letter was foolishness itself. Do you think our marriage is some kind of joke? And it was most cruel of you to make me a part of it. I did not think you capable of such base behaviour.'

His eyes held the hooded look they had sometimes, and he looked away from her briefly before saying, 'You would be surprised what I am capable of when it comes to you, Elise. But my cruel trick succeeded in making you angry enough to return home for Christmas.'

She moaned in exasperation. 'Really, Harry. If all you wanted was a visit at Christmas, then you had but to come to London and ask me.'

He thrust the jewel box back into his pocket and glared into the fire. 'And the answer would have been no. Or you would have insisted that we discuss a divorce.'

It surprised her to see him looking so sullen. And without intending it, her tone became softer. 'At least we would have been talking again, and the matter of our future could have been decided one way or another. But you felt the need to trick me into doing what you wished instead of asking me outright, and taking the risk that my answer might not be to your liking.' She stared at him, willing him to understand. 'If you do not see the wrong in that, then perhaps you will never understand why I am unhappy with you.'

He grabbed a poker and jabbed at the logs in the grate. 'I understand you well enough to know that you were eager to come back to me for an argument. But I do not think you returned home to climb the hill with me at dawn and watch the sun rise, as you did this morning.'

She swallowed for a moment as the memory of that simple pleasure returned to her. 'You are right. And thank you for that. There is much we need to talk about, Harry. But it has been a long time since we have done something just for pleasure's sake. It felt good to put our differences aside for a few moments.' She hesitated. 'I enjoyed it very much.'

He set the poker aside, wiped his hands on a handkerchief, and then patted the box in his pocket, smiling. 'Then you will enjoy this as well.'

A lump of bitterness formed in her throat at the thought of the jewel box again. 'I brought nothing for you in exchange, you know.'

His voice dropped low. 'There is only one thing I want from you.' He stepped towards her and reached out, taking her hand in his. 'That is for you to return home to me, and for things to go back to the way they were.'

'I would not want to return to what we had, Harry,' she said, surprised that he had not seemed to notice the emptiness they'd shared. 'You cannot continue to pretend that nothing was wrong any more than you can buy my co-operation with jewellery.'

He shook his head in amazement, as though he really did not see a problem. 'I am not attempting to buy you, Elise. I should not need to. We are married, after all. You have been mine for five years.'

His words shocked her back to anger. 'So I am already bought and paid for? Is that the way you see me?'

'What a daft idea. I never said so,' he answered.

'Perhaps because you speak so rarely.'

'Then I will speak now, if you are willing to listen,' he said, and smiled. But for a moment, before the affability returned to his face, she saw frustration underneath. 'I did not mean that I had bought you. I meant that I should not have to buy you now. Do you expect me to outdo Tremaine in some way, to win you back? I had hoped that when we married your choice was fixed. But now I am not so sure.'

She threw her hands into the air. 'I have been gone from your house for two months, Harry. And your best response, after all this time, is that you are "not so sure" I am gone.'

He scoffed. 'You did not expect me to take this division between us seriously, did you? It would serve you right if I went ahead with the divorce you seek and left you to marry Tremaine. But I have forgiven you for it. Now, let us put aside this silly quarrel. I will give you your Christmas present, and we can return to the main room and explain to Tremaine that his presence is no longer required.'

He offered the box to her again, and she knocked it from his hand onto the floor. 'It does not matter to me, Harry, if you have "forgiven" me for leaving. For if you think so little of me, and take our marriage for granted in such a way, how can I ever forgive you?' And with that she stormed from the room.

In the drawing room, Rosalind grabbed Nick by the arm, almost jostling the cup of wassail from his hand.

'Dear God, woman,' he drawled. 'Can I not enjoy a moment's peace?'

'The guests are getting restless. We must start the games soon. Harry has gone off somewhere.' Her eyes darted to the open doorway. 'And Elise appears to be in a state and is headed for her room. Stop her!' She gave him a shove towards the open door that spilled even more of his punch. 'I will find my brother.'

Nick stumbled out into the hall and hurried to catch up with Elise. 'Darling, where are you headed at such an alarming pace? The night is young, and I long for your company.'

She turned on him with a glare, and responded in a torrent of unintelligible German.

He grinned. 'I gather you have been talking to your husband?'

'That man. If I spend one more moment in his company I swear I shall go mad.'

He gestured to the drawing room. 'Then spend a moment with me. I have brought you a cup of wassail.' He held his cup out to her.

She took it, and stared down at it. 'This cup is empty, Nicholas.'

He slipped an arm around her waist, guiding her back to the party. 'Perhaps it is only waiting to be filled.

Optimism, Elise. We need optimism at times like this. Twelfth Night will be here soon enough, and then we shall go back to London and I will help you to forget all about this.' He gave her waist a little squeeze.

She blinked, as though just remembering what she had promised him. 'That will be wonderful, Nicholas. I can hardly wait.' But she said it with a sickly smile that proved she had not been living for the moment they would become one. 'I believe I might need a cup of punch after all.'

'I thought you might.' He shepherded her to the refreshments and she downed a cup of wassail, hardly stopping for breath. It was not flattering to see that the thought of intimacy with him required so much fortification. Alcohol could not help but make Harry more appealing to her, so he reached for the ladle and helped her to a second cup.

'I have found another who is willing to play,' Rosalind announced from the doorway. She was ignoring Harry's lack of enthusiasm as she hauled him back into the room by his elbow. 'The more people we have, the more fun it shall be.'

As they passed, Harry stared at Nick's hand, which was still resting on his wife's waist while he plied her with liquor. Harry shot him a look of undisguised loathing before turning to his sister. 'Yes, Rosalind. I think we should all like a diversion.'

'And what exactly is this game we are all so eager to play?' Nick asked dryly.

'Blind Man's Bluff,' Rosalind said. 'And, Harry, as host you must go first.'

Nick thought to remind her that it was rarely polite to

put guests last, but he could see the stubborn glint in Rosalind's eye and elected not to challenge her.

'I will blindfold you, and you must identify your guests.' She was tying a handkerchief around Harry's face, and spinning him so that he lost all direction.

Guests who were not interested in playing moved to the corners of the room. Elise looked to the exit with longing, and then to Harry, as though trying to decide between the two.

But Rosalind hurried to close the door, and put her back to it, making the decision for her. 'Quiet, everyone, let Harry try to find you.'

Nick swore silently, and nudged Elise towards the centre of the room and into the game. With Rosalind blocking the door, his escape was thwarted as well. If Harry's eyes were covered, there was little he could do to affect the man. It would have been an excellent opportunity to get away. He shot Rosalind a murderous look.

She shrugged and cocked her head towards the other players, as though telling him to pay attention to the game.

While Nick was distracted by her, Harry lumbered past him, on his blind side, and stamped mercilessly on his toe. 'Eh—what was that?' He stumbled, turned back as though to find Tremaine, and then veered left at the last minute, catching another guest by the shoulders. 'Let me see.' He patted at the man, placing his hands on an ample stomach. 'Cammerville. I do not need eyes to tell it is you.'

The gentleman laughed and sat down.

'That's one down.' Harry swung his arm out wide through the open air and laid hands on a young lady, reaching carefully to touch her hair. 'And the younger of the Misses

Gilroy, I believe. For there are your pretty curls.' Then he marched purposefully towards Elise, who took a deep breath and froze like a rabbit, waiting to be caught.

Nick hoped that the game they were really playing would be over once Harry had caught his wife. Elise looked more resigned than happy to be playing, but at least she was no longer as angry as she had been in the hall. But Harry stopped at the last moment and turned, moving across the room again, away from his wife.

Elise put her hands on her hips and glared at his back in disgust.

On his way to wherever he thought he was going, Harry managed to catch himself on a small table and tip it, sending a carafe of wine cascading down the leg of Nick's best buff trousers.

He stifled an oath and mopped at the stain with his handkerchief.

Rosalind glared at him, making frantic gestures that he should hold his tongue and keep to the spirit of the game.

'I have upset something,' announced Harry, grinning without remorse.

Rosalind reached him from behind and spun him, giving him a forceful shove to send him back towards Elise.

Harry lurched again in the direction of his wife, only to catch another woman by the shoulders. 'And this is the elder Miss Gilroy. For I have danced with you before, and recall you as being most slim and just this tall.' The girl dissolved into a shower of giggles.

Elise's countenance darkened with the clouds of a returning storm. As Harry made another pass through the room, instead of avoiding him she stepped in front of him, so that he could not help but run into her.

He swung his arms wide again, turned suddenly, and reached high instead of low, catching Tremaine by the throat. 'What's this, then? Have I caught the turkey for tomorrow's dinner?'

He gave a warning squeeze, and Nick gagged slightly.

'Oh, no. Not a turkey at all. It is Tremaine. I recognise that artfully tied cravat. You're out of the running, old man. Sit down.' He released his throat, spun him around and gave a sharp push to his shoulders that sent him stumbling towards the sofa. 'And stay out of my way.'

The other people in the room laughed knowingly.

He turned again, 'How many is that, then? Almost everyone? But there must be someone left.' He walked deliberately past his own wife again.

Elise was getting angrier by the minute, and was now actively trying to be found—repeatedly stepping into his path, only to be avoided as he seized and identified someone else.

Nick was near enough to Rosalind to hear her fervent whispering. 'Don't toy with her, Harry. Do not toy with her. She does not appreciate it.'

But either Harry did not hear or did not care. He was still pretending that he did not know the location of his wife. He groped in the empty air to the right of her, and when she moved into his path he turned again. It was plain to all there that he was deliberately avoiding her.

'Where is she?'

Several guests laughed, and a young girl called out, 'Behind you. Look behind you.'

At last, Elise could control her temper no longer. 'If you seriously wish to find her, she will be in her bedroom. With the door locked.' Elise gave her husband an angry shove, then marched past him and through the drawing room door.

The room went silent, waiting to see what would happen next. When Harry yanked off the blindfold he looked, for a moment, as though he were torn between staying and following her. And then he smoothed his hair and let out a hearty laugh, to prove that there was nothing seriously wrong.

The guests relaxed and laughed with him.

Rosalind caught Nick before he could leave the room to find Elise. He frowned at her. 'You need some practice, I think, in your tying of the blindfold. Your brother could see us all, clear as day.'

She let out an exasperated puff of air. 'Of course he could. It would make little sense for him to have wandered around blind.'

'That is the point of the game, is it not?'

'When you are in a room with your wife and her lover it is never a good idea to be blind.'

'He has pretended blindness on the subject long enough,' said Nick, with a growing understanding of Harry's predicament.

'But now it is long past time for him to stop pretending.' She glared in the direction of her brother. 'I am so angry with Harry that I can hardly speak. He must have known what I was about by tying the handkerchief the way I did. I gave him an excellent opportunity and he wasted it. But if I question him on it, he will claim that he knows his wife better than I. And she will return to him in her own good time and there is little else to be done about it.'

'You gave him no choice but to act as he did, Rosalind. I had my doubts, when he welcomed me into his home, but the man does have his pride. He wants his wife back, but he does not want to be forced to admit the fact in front of an audience.'

'And why ever not? Admitting that you love your wife is nothing to be ashamed of.'

Nick shook his head. 'Perhaps not. But to solve this problem someone must be willing to sacrifice their pride. And each one is still hoping that it can be the other.'

'It might be easier for us to reconcile them were they not so perfectly suited in their bullheadedness.'

He glared at her. 'It might also be easier if you would include me in the plans that you are making. At least a small warning would have been welcome just now. The man positively mauled me, and I had to stand there and take it in good humour.'

'It serves you right,' she said with vehemence. 'You are quite horrible, you know.'

'I am no worse than I have ever been.'

'And no better than you should be. Harry is right in one thing, Tremaine. You need to change your ways. And, while it pains me to see Harry and Elise struggling with pride, I have no compunction in sacrificing yours. If this season gives you a chance to do penance, then so be it. You may start afresh in the New Year.'

'What if one suspects that no matter what one does the next year will be no different from the last?' He shook his head. 'I find it no cause for celebration.'

'Only if you are unhappy with your life,' she said. 'I thought you claimed to be content. If so, another year of the same will not bother you.'

Damn her for making him think on it. For as he did he realised that he was far too bored to claim contentment. 'And you are so content in yours, then?' He gave her a sour smile.

She lifted her chin. 'My view of the future is somewhat more optimistic than yours. I do not worry myself over the things I cannot change, and apply myself diligently to those things that I can. I view the New Year as a promise that things do not always have to be the same.' She held out a hand. 'While the book is closing on 1813, there is no telling what 1814 will bring us. You might be a better man.'

Nick stood too close to her, and was satisfied to see the flash in her eyes that proved she was not so immune to his charms as she pretended. 'Are you still convinced there is something wrong with me as I am now?'

Instead of responding playfully to his comment, she looked at him in all seriousness and said, 'Yes, there is. You wonder how it is that you manage to be in such trouble with Harry, and why your life does not change from year to year. But you have only your own behaviour to blame for it.' She glanced towards the hall, in the direction of the absent Elise. 'I saw the two of you together when I brought Harry into the room. And I saw the look you gave her as she left. Do not tell me that you were not about to follow her. It is more than difficult, trying to get the two of them to co-operate and reconcile. If you can muster enough sense to set her free, then it will be much easier for all of us.'

CHAPTER ELEVEN

THE next day, Nick was lying on his back on the library sofa, struggling to enjoy the peace and quiet of Christmas afternoon. The roads to the village were better, but still suspect. So the party had forgone church and let Harry lead them in morning prayer in the dining room. After luncheon, the servants had hitched up sleighs, and Harry had taken the majority of his guests to go ice skating on a nearby stream. Others had retired to their rooms. There had been no sign at all of Elise since she had taken to her room the previous evening.

He felt a touch of guilt over that point. But jollying her back into good spirits would mean he must forfeit the afternoon, which was going just as he preferred it: dozing with a full stomach, in air scented faintly with pine and punch, and none of the frenetic eagerness to make fun where none was needed. Nor did he wish to give Rosalind Morley fuel for her spurious argument that he did not know how to let well enough alone when it came to his ex-intended. If Elise needed cheering, then perhaps it was time for her husband to do the job.

It had occurred to him that if he wished any real peace, it would be a far better idea to stay in his own bedroom than to stretch out in a common area, where he was likely to be interrupted at any moment. But he had rejected the idea for the illogical reason that it would give him too *much* privacy. Rosalind would not think to look for him if he rested in his room. And he had to admit that he was growing to expect a disruptive visit from the sweet Miss Morley as part of his daily routine. He had promised to stay out of her way, and he had meant to be true to his word. It was no fault of his that she insisted upon searching him out.

His mind ran over and over their conversation of the previous evening. She seemed to think that he was still to blame for the troubles between Harry and Elise, even though he was doing everything in his power to rejoin them. Had he not brought her home? Was he not doing his best to stay clear of them while they sorted out their difficulties?

And had he not immediately fallen back into his role of devoted admirer the minute he'd seen Elise's unhappiness? Damn it all, he did not want to lie with her any more than she wanted his attentions. But the suggestion of it had been enough of a distraction to coax her back to the punch bowl.

Now, despite nagging doubts about the wisdom of it, he would leave Elise to have her sulk. He would be sure to point the fact out when Miss Morley put in an appearance with whatever scheme she was currently hatching. There was no telling what chaos she was likely to bring with her when she came today. He smiled. Although she was a most annoying young lady, at least she did not bore him.

Nick glanced at his watch, and was surprised to see it was almost three. Several hours had passed in relative silence, and he should have been able to settle his mind and get the sleep he'd been craving. Although the library sofa was much more comfortable than the miserable mattress his host had allotted him, he could not seem to find peace.

He looked over the back of the couch at the mistletoe, still hanging in its proper place above the door. On impulse he rose and removed it from the hook, dropping it on the floor under a table. Then he went back to his place by the fire and pretended to sleep.

Rosalind came into the room a short time later, but took no notice of the missing decoration. Instead, she strode directly to his hiding place, coming round to the front of the couch to slap at the sole of his boot. 'Wake up, Tremaine. I have plans for you.'

He pretended to splutter to consciousness, looked up at her, and hurriedly closed his eyes again. 'Then I am most assuredly still asleep. Please leave me in peace.'

'There is much work to be done if you wish to go home alone.'

'Far more than that, I wish to go home alive. And the best way to assure my safety is to stay right here, far away from Harry. The man laid hands on me yesterday. He cannot be trusted.'

'You are being silly again. It was an innocent game.'

When she scolded him, her curls bounced in a most amusing fashion, and he had to force himself not to smile at her. 'The game was innocent enough. But I do not trust some of the players any further than I can throw them.' No more than he trusted Rosalind. He suspected that she had other reasons for wishing him to play.

'You have nothing to fear from Harry. I have known the man almost a quarter of a century. Although he might threaten, he would never do you bodily harm.'

He laughed. 'When you reach that advanced age, little one, and make such claims, then I shall take your word.'

She glared down at him. 'Twenty-five is not an advanced age, and it is most unflattering of you to call it so. The fact that I am near to it does not put me so far beyond the pale.'

Four-and-twenty? But she could barely be eighteen now. He was convinced of it. He looked at her more closely. But hadn't he thought the same thing when he had met her the first time? And that had been years ago. If she was twenty-four, then… He counted upon his fingers.

His silence must have unnerved her, for she said, 'Do not fall asleep again, Tremaine. The festivities have not been so strenuous as to require rest in midday. And if you mean to imply that my conversation bores you to unconsciousness, I swear I shall box your ears.'

He gave a little cough. 'Twenty-four?'

'Twenty-five next month.'

'But you are…'

She gritted her teeth. 'Older than Elise. Just barely. And still single. But I look much younger and always have. Or were you about to say *tiny*? For if you mean to comment on my lack of height as well as my advanced age then you will have nothing more to fear from Harry. I will do more damage to you than he ever shall.'

For a moment, he could swear that he was looking at the

same gamine he had found in the hallway at the Grenvilles' ball, five Christmases ago. The only change in her was the cynical glint in her eyes and the determined set to her mouth. 'You look no different than you did when I first met you.'

She put her hands on her hips. 'Considering how well our first meeting went, I hardly know what you mean by that. But I shall assume you mean to compliment me. I hope you are not so cruel as to torment me with my appearance? There is little I can do to change it.'

'I thought you much younger when we first met. You were standing in the doorway of the ballroom, behind a potted palm, watching everyone else dance.'

She smirked. 'You remember that now, do you?'

'I never forgot it.'

'But when my father caught us kissing you announced, "I have never seen this girl before in my life." I assumed that we were keeping to the established lie and pretending that our dance had never occurred.'

'It was only an hour before we kissed. So technically I had not met you before. Not before that night, at any rate.'

'Technically?' She nodded sceptically. 'My father assumed that I had kissed a man without even taking the time to learn his name. It was very awkward for me.'

'But when we danced,' he said haltingly, 'you told me that you were not yet out.'

'I'd have made my come-out in spring, if Father had allowed me to remain in London. Twenty would have been a bit later than the other girls, of course. But not too late.' There was a wistful note in her voice, and she took a moment to crush it before continuing in a normal, business-like tone, 'But a come-out is not necessary for a happy life. Only so much foolishness.'

'You were nineteen?'

'As were you, once.' There was another long pause as she came to understand him. 'You mean when we first met? Well, yes. Of course I was. You did not think I had escaped from the schoolroom to accost you? It was only my father's stubbornness, not my age that left me lurking outside the ballroom instead of dancing with the others.'

'But you were nineteen,' he repeated numbly.

'The night we met?' She shrugged. 'It did not matter. My father has very strict ideas on what is proper and improper for young ladies. Girls who are not out should not dance, no matter their age.'

As he remembered that night, he knew there had been girls much younger at the party, giggling in corners, begging for gentlemen to stand up with them and being no end of a nuisance—just as there were in the house today. He had assumed Rosalind to be one of them. But she had been of marriageable age, and yet still denied the pleasure of adult company. Her actions made more sense.

'That was rather strict of him.'

'Perhaps. But there was little to be done about it.'

'And you say you had not tasted wine unwatered?'

She stared at him, as if daring him to doubt her. 'I had not. If you were to speak to my father on the subject, I still have not.' She made a face. 'He does not approve of strong spirits. He drinks his wine with water as well, and forgoes brandy entirely. He says that consumption of alcohol by gentlewomen is most improper.' She smiled. 'It is fortunate for me that I am the one who does the pouring in our household. For, while he trusts me to follow his wishes, he really has no idea about the contents of my glass.'

He tried to imagine what it would be like to have to forgo wine with a meal and could not comprehend it. It was as if she had been trapped in childhood, with no escape on the horizon. 'And he still does not allow you to travel to the city, even after years of good behaviour?'

'I am not encouraged to leave the house at all. He sent me to Harry, of course, because my brother was in need. But I suspect that says more about his disapproval of Elise than anything else.' Rosalind made another stern face. 'He has much to say on the subject of foreigners and their strange ways, and he is none too secret about the satisfaction he feels at Harry's marital difficulties. He will expect a full report of them when I return home. Which will be very soon, should he get wind of the festivities I have organised. I do not care to hear what he will say when he finds out that I have been stringing holly on a Yule Log.'

'How utterly absurd,' Nick replied. 'It is an innocent enough diversion, and most enjoyable.' If one could manage to ignore the nuisance of going into the woods and focus on the blazing fire in the evening. He gave a nod to her. 'And I must say, the thing was most attractively decorated, before Harry set it to light.'

Rosalind looked amused. 'Are you a defender of Christmas now, Saint Nicholas?'

'I do not defend Christmas so much as believe that small pleasures are not a threat to character or a black mark upon the soul.'

'On that point you and Harry agree. It is one of the reasons I see so little of Harry, for he cannot abide my father's treatment of his mother, nor of me. And Father has very little good to say about him.' She sighed. 'But my father means well by it, although he may seem harsh to others. It has done me no real harm. And I must admit, I bring much of his censure on myself. For I have a tendency to small rebellions, and can be just as stubborn as Harry when I've a mind.'

It made Nick unaccountably angry to see her resigned to her future, caring for a man who was obviously impossible to please. And the idea that she had to moderate a temperament which he found quite refreshing, irritated him even more. He said, 'If a wild bird is caged long enough, even for its own protection, it will beat its wings against the bars. If it does itself an injury, whose fault is it? The bird's or the one who caged it?'

'If you are attempting to draw some parallel between me and the bird, then I wish you would refrain from it. The fault would lie with the bird. For, while such creatures are lovely to look at, they are seldom held up as an example of wisdom and good sense.'

She was standing close enough to him that the smell of her perfume blended with the pine boughs on the mantel and the other inescapable smells of Christmas, turning the simple floral scent she wore into something much more complex and sensual. It was just as tempting as he remembered it, and just as hard to ignore. He wondered if it had been the same for her. For all along she had been old enough to understand temptation, but lacking the experience to avoid it. He smiled in sympathy. 'It seems I have done you an injustice, Miss Morley. For this explanation of your behaviour on the night we met puts the event in a whole new light.'

'I thought we had agreed not to speak of that again,' she muttered, and tried to turn away.

He put a finger under her chin and urged her to look up at his face. 'After you were forced to apologise repeatedly for something which was no real fault of yours? What you were doing was not so unusual, compared with other girls of your age. If you lacked seasoning or sense, it was because your family did not train you to know what was expected of you. They thought that they could confine you until the last possible moment and then thrust you into the light, where you would exhibit flawless behaviour with no practice. When you failed, it was more their fault than yours.' He hung his head. 'And mine as well. I might have behaved quite differently had I known the circumstances involved. And I do not remember at any time giving you the apology that you deserve in response.'

She swallowed. 'It is not necessary.'

'I beg to differ.' He moved so that he was standing before her, and said, 'Give me your hand.'

She was obviously trying to come up with a response that would make things easier between them, but none was forthcoming.

So he reached, and took her hand in both of his. 'I am sorry for what occurred that night,' he said. 'The fact that you were behaving without caution did not require me to respond in kind. If anything, I should have been more circumspect, not less. You have been punished inordinately for it, although I have always deserved the majority of the guilt. Please forgive me.'

He was staring into her eyes, and it made things difficult. For it reminded him of the way she'd looked at him that night, and how it had made him feel, and why it had been so easy to throw caution to the winds and kiss her when he had known he had no right to.

But this time she managed to look away from him, instead of drawing nearer. 'Of course,' she said, and then she closed her eyes and dropped her head, as though praying that humility would be sufficient to bring this awkward scene to a close.

He brought her hand to his lips and held it there. Her skin was soft against his, and he lingered over it for longer than a simple apology would warrant, imagining what it might be like to kiss her palm, her wrist, and all the rest of the white skin leading to her lips. And then he smiled, remembering that this was what had caused the problem five years ago. The suspicion that all parts of Rosalind Morley were eminently kissable, and his sudden, irresistible compulsion to test the theory.

And now she was looking up at him again, over her outstretched hand, as though the kiss were causing her pain when he suspected that it was an excess of pleasure that was the problem. Should he take another liberty with her, she would yield—just as she had the last time. And he would probably run away from her—just as he had been running his whole life, from any situation that smacked of responsibility.

And so he released her, smiling. 'There. I hope it is settled at last. There is nothing wrong with you, Rosalind Morley. Nothing at all. Never mind what your father says, or what others might think of you. You are perfect just as you are.'

It occurred to him, in an idle, confusing way, that it would take a lifetime to catalogue the things about her that were perfectly suited to his temperament.

'Thank you.' Her voice sounded hoarse, as though it were difficult for her to speak. He wished that she would call him Tremaine, and return some sharp rebuke that would put things back to normal between them. But instead she murmured, 'I must go. To see about…something. And you must come as well. I…' She touched her hand to her forehead, trying to remember, and then looked into his eyes again and went very still.

Her vision cleared and she muttered, 'Apples. That is it. We are bobbing for apples. Harry is there. I have managed to get Elise to come out of her room, but she is looking very cross with him, and threatening to go back to bed with a megrim.'

'So I must let your brother drown me to put her into good humour again?'

'If you would be so kind.'

She held out her hand to him, and he was more than ready to follow wherever she might lead. But when he smiled at her, she looked so worried that he put on his most perturbed expression and yawned. 'The least you could do is deny it, you know. If you wish me to behave, you will do much better with flattery than you do with the truth.'

'If I flatter you, it might cause your head to swell more

than it already has.' She gave him her usually cynical smile. 'I dare not risk it, Tremaine. Come on, then. We can finish this business by New Year if we apply ourselves to it.'

CHAPTER TWELVE

ROSALIND pushed him into the hallway ahead of her, announcing, 'I have found him.'

Harry beamed in triumph. 'And about time. Do not think that you can avoid the party, Tremaine. It is hardly keeping in the spirit of the bet if you do not try.'

Nick sighed, and prepared for a dunking. 'Very well, then. What have I to do to get you to leave me alone?'

'Play our little game.' Harry led him into the hall and gestured expansively towards the centre of the room. 'We have all had a turn, and the other guests are eager to see how you fare.'

True to his word, there was a large crowd gathered around a basin of water, and the air smelled of apples. The daughter of a lord was holding a fruit in her hand and shaking the water from her pretty blonde locks, and everyone was laughing heartily and congratulating her on her success.

There were calls of encouragement from the crowd, accompanied by drunken laughter.

Tremaine approached the pan of water with caution, and

looked down at the abused fruit floating there. He stalled. 'And I am to…?' He looked down into the water again.

'Put your face in, grab an apple and bite.' Harry was grinning.

He knew that Harry would never be so foolish as to kill him in front of witnesses. The worst that would happen would be a wet head. Embarrassing, of course. But not so terrible, really. It would be over in a minute. Nick stepped up to the basin, bent awkwardly at the waist, and placed his face near the water.

He dutifully chased one of the remaining apples around the edge of the pan, while Harry stood behind him, pretending to offer encouragement.

'You have nothing to be afraid of.'

Harry was laughing at him, the miserable bastard. But he could hear Elise laughing too, so he soldiered on.

'The water is not so very deep. You will not drown,' Harry said. And then he whispered, directly into Nick's ear, 'I'm right behind you.'

Nick leaned too close to the water, trying to escape him, and took a quantity of it up his nose. He gasped and shot upright again, coughing, to the laughter of the crowd around him.

Harry clapped him smartly on the back to clear his lungs. 'There, there. You have it all wrong. You are not to drink the water. You are to eat the apple. Try again.'

He glared at Harry and stared at Rosalind. 'This is part of your brilliant plan, is it?'

She gave him a frustrated smile, and said, 'Take your

turn and let others have a chance.' She rolled her eyes and cast a significant glance at Elise.

'Very well. But if anything untoward occurs I will hold you responsible, even in the afterlife.'

'Tremaine, do not be an ass.' She pushed past her brother, took him by the back of the neck, and pushed his face down into the water.

This time he had the good sense to hold his breath, and came up dripping, with an apple in his mouth. To complete the humiliation of it, Elise was leading the crowd who laughed at his discomposure.

'That was not so bad, was it?' Rosalind grabbed him by the collar and pulled him out of the way of the next player. Then she took the apple from his mouth and offered him linen to dry his face.

'Did I perform to your satisfaction?' he asked, tipping his head to drain the water from his ear.

'You were most amusing. Elise is laughing again—at you, and in front of Harry. That cannot but help put him in a good mood.' She took a bite from the apple that he had caught.

He watched her slender fingers caressing the fruit, her red lips, so memorably kissable, touching the place where he had bitten, the delicate workings of her pale throat as she chewed and swallowed. And suddenly he knew how Adam must have felt when Eve came to him with a wild scheme that he knew would end in disaster. He had agreed, because how could he have refused her, even if it meant the ruin of all?

'It will not be long, I think, before Harry decides his pride is not so very important.' She looked speculatively at

Elise. 'Then perhaps I shall be able to turn the rest of the party over to his wife.'

'And when she is back as mistress of this house what shall you do?' he whispered. 'Do you mean to see Pompeii, then? Once you have your freedom?'

The apple froze, halfway to her mouth, and she gave him a blank stare. 'What do I mean to do? Harry is right, Tremaine. You are an idiot. Harry will send me home after the holidays. I will return to Shropshire and my needle-work, my jelly-making and my good works.'

He snorted at the idea. 'Do you miss home so much?'

'I do not miss home in the slightest. But where else am I to go?' She took another bite of the apple.

He watched her lick a drop of apple juice from her lip, and fought down the desire to suggest some good works she might try that had nothing to do with making jelly. 'Now that you have left your father's house, you might enjoy travelling. For you seem to have a taste for adventure.'

She laughed. 'Tell me, sir, when you are in the city, what do you drive?'

He thought for a moment. 'At this time I have several carriages. A curricle, of course, and a high-perch phaeton as well. Pulled by the finest pair of matched blacks in London.'

She gave a little moan of pleasure, and then looked him square in the eye. 'We have a pony cart, which Father allows me to drive to the market in Clun. But only when the weather is fine and no one else is free to take me. The rest of the time I must walk.' She pulled a stern face, probably mimicking her father. 'But never alone. My father warns against the dangers present for young ladies travelling alone. But what they are I have no idea.' She gave a dry sigh. 'A trip to Pompeii might have seemed a lark to you, but it would be no more likely for me than a trip to the moon.'

Rosalind was making her future sound quite grim, so he rushed to reassure her—and himself—that it needn't be so. 'Do not fear, little one. Some day you will find a man who will take you to Italy.' Although he found that thought to be strangely annoying.

She spun the apple core on its stem, looking for a place to set it. 'I do not understand why everyone is so convinced that I cannot find a husband. As it so happens, I find them frequently enough. And then I find them wanting. I have had three proposals, just this year. All fine, upstanding men, who were willing to offer me a life no different from the one I have: full of restrictions and cautions and common sense. It appears being a wife is little different from being a daughter, and so I will have none of it. In this, at least, I am in full agreement with Elise. If a husband does not offer the love and respect I truly desire, and means to treat me no better than an overgrown child or an inanimate object, then it is better to do without.'

This took him aback. 'You have refused suitors?'

'Yes, I have. The rest of the world does not find me so repellent as you must, Tremaine.'

Here he was supposed to offer a compliment. But his glib tongue failed him, and the best he could manage was, 'I would hardly say you were repellent.'

She gave him a tired look and batted her lashes. 'I shall cherish your sweet words on my journey back to Shropshire.'

'But there must be some other alternative. Another place you could go…' He racked his brain for a better answer.

She set the apple core on the tray of a passing servant, and took back the linen she had given him to wipe her hands on it. 'There is not. The fact of the matter is this: I have no other female relatives, and a father who wishes help with his parish. When I am finished here I will go where everyone expects me to go. Where I am needed.' She tipped her head to the side. 'Although I must say the parish would be better off if my father was encouraged to marry the widow who comes to see to the cleaning of the church. She is a very organised woman, and a skilled housekeeper. He is very fond of her. They would make an excellent match.'

'If this woman is so well suited to your father, then why does he not offer for her?'

'Because then what would become of me? While the widow is suited to my father, I do not like her at all. And two women under the same roof would be one too many, when those women are not in harmony. Any progress my father has made in finding a new wife will be thwarted by my return home.'

He could not be sure, but he thought for a moment she glanced at him in a most strange way, and the pause before her next words was a touch longer than normal.

'Unless there is any reason that I should not go back to Shropshire.'

'When your brother is finished with you he means to send you back to your father, with no care for your future?' The thought rankled, for it was most sweet to see this girl doing everything in her power to help the brother who cared so little for her.

'When he presented the idea of a house party, he offered me my pick of the bachelor guests to prevent my flight.' She glanced around the room and frowned. 'Of course since he neglected to invite any single gentlemen, it has done me no good to entertain them. I have never seen so many happily married men, so many wives and children.' She gave another sidelong glance at Tremaine. 'You are the only unattached man in the house.'

'That was most unfair of him,' Tremaine agreed. 'But do not worry. I am sure when you least expect it you will find someone to suit your tastes.'

'The men who seek me out are hoping for a moderation in my character.' She glanced in the direction of Elise. 'Someone more like my sister-in-law, who has grown in the last few years from a naïve and somewhat awkward girl into a polished lady. I, on the other hand, am very much as you found me when we first met: wilful, short-tempered, and prone to acting in haste and following with regret.'

He suppressed a smile. 'I will admit your personality is more volatile than Elise's.'

She shrugged. 'When the men of England come to value volatility over grace and candour over artifice, then I shall have my pick of them. Now, if you will excuse me, I should see to the other guests.' She walked across the room to Elise, and said something that made the other woman laugh.

He took a moment to admire the two women together, and had to admit they had little in common. Elise's cool beauty was paired with an equally cool wit. The sort that made a man long to melt the icy exterior and find the warm heart beneath. And Rosalind? Her kisses were as tart as Elise's were sweet. And her skin and hair tasted of cinnamon and pepper.

He stopped and blinked. It had been years, and yet he could remember everything about that single kiss as though he had stolen it moments ago. With each new sight of her, the past had come flooding back, sharper than ever. She smelled the same, her skin was just as soft, and her face held the same mix of devilment and innocence.

He glanced across the room at Elise, and tried to remember the kisses that he had shared with her the year they'd met. There had been months of dancing, laughter, and a few passionate stolen moments alone. But it was all a vaguely pleasant blur, and not nearly so clear as their time spent in friendship since. Try as he might, he could not sort the incidents of his engagement, supposedly the happiest time of his life, from his time spent with the dozens of other pretty girls he had known before and since.

But he could still remember every moment of the hour he had spent with Rosalind Morley. The way he had felt when he'd looked at her. The way she'd felt in his arms. And how he had known it would be wrong to kiss her and done it anyway. She had positively glowed with an unsuppressed fire, and he had been helpless to resist.

A sensible man would have pulled her out from under the mistletoe that night and sent her home to her father before anything untoward happened. It would have been far better to douse the fiery spirit, even if it had turned her tart wits to bitterness. Only a fool would have leapt into the flames and laughed as he burned.

A fool, or a man in love.

He turned away quickly and took a sip of his drink, hoping for a soothing distraction. But the spices in the mulled wine heated his blood rather than cooled it. Love at first sight. What an utterly prosaic notion. It lacked the sophistication of lust or the banal thrill of debauchery. It was gauche. Naïve. A simplistic explanation for a natural physical response to finding a beautiful young girl alone and willing, and taking advantage of the opportunity to kiss her senseless.

And running away had been a natural response as well. He had given little thought to what the girl might have felt over it. She would have given the incident too much significance, since she had nothing to compare it with. He knew better. That brief intimacy, and his resulting obsession with it, was a result of too much whimsy in a season given over to such behaviour. To avoid such revelry in the future was the best way to keep one's head and prevent further mistakes.

He had ignored the vague feeling that his perfectly acceptable engagement to Elise was a misalliance of the worst sort. And the faint sense of relief he'd felt when Elise had rejected him. The feeling that he was very lucky to be free of it. His subsequent inability to find anyone to suit him better was merely selectiveness on his part. It did not mean that he'd given his heart away on a whim, several Christmases ago, and lacked the courage to find the girl and retrieve it.

He shook his head. This was not an epiphany. This was temporary insanity—brought on by too many parlour games, too much punch, and a severe lack of oxygen from too many nights packed in tight at the fireside next to people who were happier in their lives than he. One did not make life-altering decisions based on a brief acquaintance with a girl, no matter how delectable she might be. And, even worse, one should not make them in the presence of mistletoe.

Should he manage to get clear of his attachment to Elise, if he wished for the change to be permanent he should run and keep running. It would be even wiser to give a wide berth to Harry Pennyngton and all of his extended family.

He took another sip of wine.

But where would be the fun in that?

His sip became a gulp, and he choked and spluttered on it, gasping to catch his breath.

A hand hit him sharply between the shoulderblades, to help him clear his lungs. And then hit him again out of sheer spite.

'Anneslea,' he gasped.

'None other.' Harry was grinning at him again, revelling in Nick's distress. 'First I see you nearly drown in the apple bucket, and now in a single glass of wine? It is a good thing I am here to take care of you. Heaven knows what might happen if you were left on your own.'

There was probably a double meaning in his words, just as there always was. But suddenly Nick found it impossible to care. He took in a great gulp of air, reached out and took Harry by the shoulders to steady himself, and announced, 'I am a faithless cad.'

Harry clapped him on the back again. But this time it

was in camaraderie. 'You have realised it at last, have you? Good for you, sir. And a Merry Christmas to you.' Then he disengaged himself and headed back to the apple barrel.

Nick stared after Harry, wondering if the man had interpreted that as an apology, or just a random statement of fact. Apparently, he had come to some level of self-awareness. But what was to be done about it? If he ran to Rosalind with the news, he was not positive that his discovery would be welcome. And even if it was, he did not dare risk breaking her heart again until he was sure how things would come out.

But if all went as planned, Elise would be home for good in a few short days, and Rosalind would be faced with a return trip to Shropshire. If he could bide his time until then, Rosalind might be open to possibilities that might prevent her homecoming.

He grinned to himself. Even if she had doubts about a future with him, it would take only a closed door, some mistletoe, and a few moments' persuasion to convince her of the advantage in total surrender.

Elise stared down at the apples floating in the basin and forced a bright smile. Her head still ached, and her eyes felt swollen and sandy from crying. But she had promised herself there would be no more sulking in her room. After last night's outburst it would not do to let the guests see that she was upset.

Of course her husband's continual rejection of her during the game had hurt her. He had known all the girls in the room by touch, and had joked and laughed with them. In his study, he had claimed to want her back. But he had shown no sign of it a moment later. And now she must smile and chat with the women he had hugged as though nothing was wrong.

She focused her attention on the apples and dipped her face into the water, deep enough so that it lapped at her cheeks, cooling the fire in them. And if, while submerged, she imagined either of the Misses Gilroy, plunged headfirst into the same water until their hair dripped and their gowns were ruined? Then at least no one could see it in her face.

She caught an apple easily in her teeth, and rose to laughter and applause. She set the fruit on the small table beside the basin, and turned to find Harry right behind her, holding out a towel.

He grinned at her. 'Very good, my dear. Very good indeed.' And she noticed his eyes shift away from her face, lower, to the neckline of her gown.

She could feel a drop of water sliding slowly down her skin, ready to disappear into the hollow between her breasts. Was it this that was drawing his attention? She took the towel from him. And then, as though she were flirting with a stranger, she offered him a languid hand. He took it, and led her away from the apples.

She dabbed carefully at her face with the towel, taking care to leave the single drop of water quavering on the swell of her breast. When they reached a quiet corner of the room she paused and looked up, to catch him staring again. For a moment, she expected him to give her a guilty smile to acknowledge that he was behaving improperly, and fix his gaze upon her face. For this was her husband, not Nicholas or some other gentleman of the ton.

But, although he must know that she had caught him, he continued to stare at her body as though the passage of the water were of the utmost importance to him. He wet his lips like a man parched from too long without a drink, and gave a small sigh of longing as it disappeared from sight. When he met her gaze again, his eyes were a dark, smoky green. And for a moment she was sure that honour, pride and propriety meant nothing to him. Even though they were in a crowded hall, if she gave the slightest of nods he would bury his face between her breasts, find that drop and kiss it away.

She felt a thrill of desire, just as she always did when Harry looked at her with that strange intensity. But this time it was heightened by abstinence, and the fact that he was admiring her so obviously, in so public a place. If he had been brazen before she'd left she would have scolded him. Told him to wait for evening, until they were upstairs. And he would have laughed and complied with her wishes, banking his desire until they were safely behind bedroom doors.

But he had been behaving quite unpredictably of late. It was possible she might never again see that look in his eyes. And suddenly dread mixed with desire, and she knew that it was of the utmost importance to hold his interest.

So she played the coquette, just as she would with a gentleman whose affections were not guaranteed. She touched the skin of her throat with one hand, spreading the fingers until they gave the briefest caress to the track the water had followed, and then traced the neckline of her gown. 'It is surprisingly warm in the house today, is it not?'

'Indeed.' His reply was innocent enough, but his eyes followed the progress of her hand.

'The water was most refreshing.' She smiled at him, gazing through her lashes. 'I am surprised that you have not taken a turn.'

'Alas, I have no skill in apple-bobbing. But there are other games I prefer.' His voice was a purr, and the invitation it held was clear.

Would it be success or failure to give in to desire, just for a night? It would not solve their problems, but at least she would be sure that he still wanted her. 'But so many games require a partner. It is most frustrating to find oneself unmatched when one wishes to play.'

'Very,' he agreed.

She bit her lip and pretended to hesitate. 'You seemed quite taken with the young ladies of the Gilroy family during yesterday's game. Perhaps either of them would suit?' She waited for the assurance that he would much prefer someone else.

Instead, he said, 'It is an interesting idea. They are both lovely girls—well-formed, fair of face. And on the whole I find them both to be good company. Too young, of course. Although their mother remarked, after you had left the room, that Lord Gilroy always retires early. I suspect she is also in search of a partner.' And he glanced away from her, to Lady Gilroy, who was wearing a dress cut far too low for daytime, and bending over the apple barrel to call attention to the fact.

He looked back to Elise, and she could feel the jealous colour rising in her face, spoiling her efforts to appear coy and detached. 'It is no business of mine,' she snapped. 'I am sure it does not matter who you choose to partner you.'

He sighed. 'You are wrong, of course. I'm sure it would hurt some people very much.'

Me. It would hurt me. Even the thought that Lady Gilroy was interested caused an ache in her heart. It was even worse than seeing Harry's innocent flirting with her daughters. But she must remember where she was, and the number of prying eyes around her. For she had a shameless urge to grab him by the arm and plead with him to assure her she had nothing to fear.

He continued. 'Think of Lord Gilroy, knowing that his wife is eager to give her attentions to another. It is most difficult to suffer in silence.'

Suffering. He was right to call it that. For now, with each minute they were apart, she would know that he was free, and she would worry that he might choose to exercise that freedom. It did not matter that he did not care for her, nor that there were other women who would be a better wife than she had been. She was overcome with a desperate, selfish desire to have her old life back.

Harry was staring across the room in the general direction of Lord Gilroy. 'I suppose it is easier to let people think he does not care than to appear a tired old fool who cannot keep his wife satisfied.'

Oh, God. Perhaps it meant nothing. Perhaps he was only speaking of Gilroy, and not of himself. If it mattered to him, why had he not spoken? If he truly cared for her, then every smile that she'd given to Nicholas, every dance, every shared laugh, would have been like a knife in her husband's heart.

'Harry?' Her voice was shaking, as were her knees. In fact it felt as if her whole body were trembling, afraid of the answers to the questions she must ask him.

'Darling?' He reached out and took her hand again, gave it a squeeze of encouragement.

'Anneslea!' Lord Cammerville was tottering over to them, smiling broadly and gesturing with his glass. 'So good to see you with your lovely wife at your side again.'

Harry gave a slight bow of pride.

Elise smiled as well, letting the curses flow in her mind. Why had the fat old toad chosen *now* to interrupt them?

'And how have you managed to keep that delightful sister so well hidden from society? You are truly fortunate to be surrounded by such beauty.'

'Hardly surrounded, Cammerville. This is the first time I've been able to enjoy the company of both of them for an extended period. Rosalind's father, the Reverend Morley, has very little faith in my ability to watch out for the girl, even though it is long past time for him to let her fly the coop.'

Elise turned her wrath upon the absent Morley. 'He is very foolish. There can be no better place for her than with you if she wishes an introduction to polite society.'

Harry gave a surprised smile in response to her small compliment. 'If you asked her father's opinion, I doubt it would be the same. I was eight when he married my mother, and he still looks on me as a wilful schoolboy with a decadent upbringing that has permanently flawed my character. Didn't think much of my late father or his family, I'm afraid. Couldn't abide Grandfather, who was Anneslea before me.'

Cammerville laughed knowingly. 'Tried to cane the title out of you, did he?'

Harry winced, and laughed in response.

'He beat you?' Elise stared at him in surprise. For he had never mentioned any such thing.

'Spare the rod and spoil the child,' Cammerville answered.

Harry nodded. 'And Morley was a firm believer in biblical retribution—especially when it concerned the sin of pride.'

'Why did you not tell me?' It was the wrong time to ask him, in a room full of people. But suddenly it was urgent that she know.

He considered for a moment. 'Have I not? Hmm. I thought I had.' He shrugged in apology. 'I find I am happier if I do not think on him much. As I am sure he is content not to think of me.'

'Is that why you left home so early? Rosalind said that you found it easier to stay at Anneslea with the old Earl. And that she hardly saw you at all until after she was grown-up.' She reached out and touched his sleeve.

He smiled at her in reassurance. 'That is the way we like to remember the facts, yes. I came to live with my Grandfather Pennyngton because Lincolnshire was closer to my school than our home in Shropshire. It was much easier to come here for holidays.' He shrugged again. 'But I suspect that if we measured the distance it would have been a much shorter trip to the rectory, and on roads that were better and less affected by weather. The truth of the matter was Morley would not have me at home, and I had no desire to return. Nothing my mother could say would sway him.'

'That was most unfair of him.'

'I cannot say I blame him overly. By the time I was thirteen I was nearly as tall as he was.' He gave Cammerville a knowing wink. 'The day came when I disagreed with his parental advice. So I snatched the stick from his hand and broke it over his back.'

Cammerville laughed so hard that tears ran from his eyes, and Harry laughed as well.

'You struck him?' Elise looked at him in continued amazement.

He must fear that she was angry with him for keeping secrets, for he hurried to say, 'I doubt that Rosalind has heard that story either. It is one of the many things that we do not discuss in my family. Nor do we dwell on the fact that Morley threw me, bag and baggage, from his house. But that is the real reason I ended up with my father's family.'

'That is horrible.' She looked back and forth between his smile and Cammerville's obvious amusement, and her lip trembled in sympathy for the little boy he had been.

Harry reached out and laid a comforting hand on her shoulder, as though surprised by her strong reaction to something that had been over and done with for almost twenty years. 'It was not so terrible. It was quite possible that I earned the punishment he gave me. After Father died I was well on the way to having an uncontrollable temper. Grandfather took me in and put me right. He taught me that one does not need to rage to accomplish what one desires. One can do as much by patience as one ever can with temper.'

'Perhaps you learned too well,' she murmured. 'But it was better, if Morley beat you, that you remained away.'

'And in time I demonstrated my improved character to him, and he allowed me home to visit Rosalind.' He frowned. 'Of course it was too late to heal some wounds. I only saw my mother once before she died.'

'He separated you from your mother?' Her voice was an anguished bleat, and Cammerville laughed at her tender heart.

Harry blinked, and absently brushed a lock of hair out of his eyes. 'It had to happen eventually, once I went away to school. The miserable old goat brought the whole family up here for Christmas, after I was of age. Of course, he turned around in only a day and rushed them all home again. But I had a very nice dinner with mother and Morley that evening.' He put his arm around her shoulders and gave her a cautious hug. 'It was fine, really. And over very long ago. Nothing to be so distressed about.'

'Oh, Harry.' Now she was both tearful and slightly disgusted with him. And he was giving her such a puzzled look, as though he knew he had done something wrong but had no idea what it might be. Like a lost little boy.

She stamped her foot, trying to drive the sob back down her throat, and whimpered, 'Excuse me, Lord Cammervile.' Then she seized the towel from Harry's hand and hurried towards the door.

Behind her, she could hear Cammerville's explosive, 'Women, eh? They are an eternal mystery. Is it too early for a brandy, do you think?'

And Harry's response. 'Let us find Rosalind and see where she is hiding it. I feel strangely in need of cheer.'

Elise hurried into the hall before the tears could overtake her. Of all the times for her husband to open up and reveal his soul it would have to be when they were chatting with one of his more ridiculous friends, in a room full of people. Lord Cammerville must have thought her quite foolish to be near to crying over a story that they thought was nothing more than a common fact of boyhood.

But not to her. Never had she seen her father raise a hand to Carl. Nor had her brother reason to respond in anger to punishment. And the sight of Harry running a hand through his hair like a lost child, telling her how one mistake had cost him his mother...

She gulped back another sob.

'Here, now, what is the matter?' Nicholas reached out and seized her by the arms, arresting her flight. 'Crying in a common hallway? What is the cause?' He looked happier than she had seen him in months, but his expression changed quickly to concern.

'I have done something terrible.'

He looked doubtful. 'Surely not?'

'I have left my husband.'

'Not again.' He drew away from her in alarm.

'No. Before. When I left him to come to you, Nicholas.' And she took him by the arms, trying to get him to listen. 'I teased him, and it hurt. And then I left him when he needed me.'

'And you have noticed this now?' Nicholas shook his head in amazement. 'Very well. And what do you mean to do about it?'

'I do not know. You are a man. Tell me. What can I say to him that will make it all better?'

'Say to him?' Nick responded with his most rakish

smile. He put his hands on her shoulders and looked deep into her eyes. 'Oh, darling, I doubt you need say anything at all to have a man at your feet. You have but to wait until the guests are safely asleep, and open your bedroom door. You will not need words after that.'

There was the sound of masculine throat-clearing, and an inarticulate noise of female distress. And then her husband and his sister walked past them, down the hall.

Harry looked his usual calm, collected self. But Rosalind was nearly overcome with emotion, her eyes darting from Elise, to Nicholas and back, trying to choose whom she should scold first.

When she slowed, Harry took her by the arm and pulled her along, refusing to let her stop. But as they passed he gave Nicholas an arch look that made the man carefully release Elise's arms, as though he were taking his finger off the trigger of a primed pistol. Then Harry smiled to his sister, and said, 'The brandy, Rosalind. Remember the brandy. We shall find a glass for you as well. Your father will not approve, but so be it.'

CHAPTER THIRTEEN

ROSALIND'S foul mood continued unabated through dinner, despite the small glass of brandy Harry had given her to calm her nerves. While he'd said it was flattering to have a sister so devoted to one's happiness as to be reduced to spluttering rage by the scene of one's wife and her lover in a position that could be considered by some as compromising, he'd assured her it was hardly a reason to ruin Christmas dinner.

His assurances that it did not require action had been met with frustrated cries of, 'Oh, Harry,' and elaborate threats on her part to chase down Tremaine and make him pay bitterly for his lack of manners.

A rumour from the cook that the evening's goose was past its prime and too tough to eat had driven the scene temporarily from her mind, and Harry had made a mental note to reward the kitchen staff generously on Boxing Day for the timely distraction. He had smiled to himself in satisfaction and poured another brandy. For, after seeing the tears in his wife's eyes over his tragic childhood, he doubted that Tremaine, annoying though he might be, was making as much progress as it appeared.

After a dinner of goose that had been more than tender enough for his taste, Rosalind stood and announced, 'Tonight, for those who are interested, we shall have dancing in the ballroom. Come and join us once you have finished your port.'

Harry followed her out of the dining room and down the hall to the ballroom. 'If you can still manage a ball, darling, you are a magician.'

'And how so?' Her gaze was defiant, her smile frozen and resolute.

'There are no musicians,' he said reasonably. 'They did not arrive today—probably because of the bad weather. I am certain we can forgo the dancing and no one will mind.'

'It is not the first problem I have had with this party of yours,' she said through gritted teeth. 'And I doubt it will be the last. But if we cancel the dancing then I will have to find a better activity to pass the evening, and I can think of none. Besides, the room has already been decorated and the refreshments prepared. The servants have moved the pianoforte to the ballroom, and I am more than capable of playing something that the guests can dance to.'

'But if you are playing then you cannot dance yourself,' he pointed out.

'It is only polite that I sit out in any case.' Her voice was cold reason. 'It is slightly different than I feared, but I was marginally correct. Your numbers are unbalanced, and in favour of the women. Several families have brought daughters, and there are no partners for them. Better that I allow the others to dance in my place.'

'But no one expects you to forgo the pleasure all evening,' he said. 'You do not have to play for the whole time.'

'Really it is no problem. I enjoy playing. And I will have the opportunity to sit down while doing it.' The look in her eye said if the party knew what was good for it, they would dance and be glad of it, because she did not wish to be crossed.

Harry put on his most fraternal smile. 'But you also enjoy dancing, do you not? I can remember the way you stood on my boots and let me waltz you around the drawing room.'

She gave him a pained look. 'Twenty years ago, perhaps. Then, it was not so important to have a partner.'

He clutched at his heart. 'I am no partner? You wound me, Rosalind.'

'You are my brother,' she said firmly. 'And if you are the only unpartnered man in the room I suppose it is not improper that we dance. But it would be far more pleasant for me if you stand up as a courtesy to the daughters of your guests than with me out of pity.' For a moment she did sound a bit pitiable. But then she snapped, 'If you cannot manage that, then perhaps you should dance with your wife. It is what you want to do, after all. It does no good to pretend otherwise. But for myself? I prefer to remain at the keyboard. Thank you very much.'

Guests had begun to filter into the room behind them, and she sat down and began to play a tune so brisk that they could not resist standing up to dance.

Harry did as she'd bade him and offered his hand to a blushing girl of sixteen. He was gratified to see the look on her face, as though the room could hardly contain her joy at being asked. When they stood out, he had an oppor- tunity to view the others in the room.

His wife was standing up with Tremaine, of course. They made a most handsome couple, as they always had. Their steps were flawless, their smiles knowing. It was painful to see them together, so he smiled even wider and raised a glass of champagne in toast to them.

Rosalind sat at the piano, playing a seemingly endless progression of happy melodies. To look at her was to suspect that the instrument in front of her had done her an injury, and that she wished to punish it with enthusiastic play. Her eyes never wavered from the empty music stand in front of her, even though she was playing it all from memory, and her hands hammered away at the keys with an almost mechanical perfection. She seemed to focus inward, and there was no sign that the sights she saw were happy ones.

And suddenly Harry felt the fear that if something was not done he would see her in the same place next year, and the year after, ageing at the piano stool, the lines in her face growing deeper and her expression more distant as the world laughed and went on without her.

So he smiled his best host's smile, remarked to all within earshot that it was a capital entertainment, and encouraged them to help themselves to refreshment when the music paused. If they thought him a naïve cuckold, so be it. Perhaps after this holiday they would have no reason to. But, no matter what became of him, he would not allow Rosalind to become the sad old maid who kept his house.

He turned to the girl beside him, pointed to Rosalind, and enquired if she played as well.

'Not so well, sir. But I have lessons. And my piano master says I am his most proficient pupil.'

'I would see my sister stand up for a set. But first I must find someone to replace her at the instrument. Can you help me?'

The girl was radiant at the thought.

Very good, then. He was only being a good host by making the offer.

He went to Rosalind. 'Dear sister, I have a favour to ask of you.'

She sighed, but did not pause in her playing. 'Another favour? Am I not busy enough for you, Harry?'

He laughed. 'Too busy, I think. Templeton's daughter was remarking at what a fine instrument this appears to be, and it seems she is a musician. But obviously not much of a dancer, for she trod upon my toes on several occasions. If she is thus with the other guests it might benefit all to have her play for a time and rest from dancing. If you could give up your seat to her, I would be most grateful.'

Rosalind considered for but a moment. 'It would be for the best—if she does not seem to mind.'

'Very good. Have a glass of champagne, and I will see her settled here.

He installed the Templeton girl at the piano, then watched as his sister visited the refreshment table and became occupied with haranguing the servants about the dwindling supply of wine. When he was sure she would take no notice of him, he swallowed his distaste, refreshed his smile with another sip of wine, and strode into the room to find a partner for Rosalind.

'Tremaine—a word, if you please?'

It was always a pleasure to see the way the man cringed when Harry addressed him directly, as though snivelling and subservience were sufficient apology for all he had done.

'Harry?' He took a deep sip from his glass.

'I need a favour from you.'

'From me?' Now the man was totally flummoxed. And then suspicious. His eyes narrowed. 'What can I do for you?'

Jump off the nearest cliff. Harry pushed the idea to the back of his mind, readjusted his smile, and said, 'I need a dancing partner. Not for me, of course.' He gave a self-deprecating laugh. 'For m' sister. She will not stand up from the damn piano if she must stand with me. And you are the only man in the room who could pass, in dim light, for eligible.'

Tremaine looked past his usual partner towards Rosalind, who had seated herself next to a potted palm, almost out of sight of the crowd. His face took on a curious cast in the flickering light of the candles. 'And she does love dancing,' he said. His voice was distant, as though lost in memory.

Harry wondered if he needed to repeat his request, and then the man next to him seemed to regain focus.

'Of course,' he said. 'You are right. She should not be forced to sit out the whole evening because of some misplaced sense of duty to her guests.'

'Make her think it is your idea, for I doubt she will do it for me. She was most cross that I even suggested she dance before.'

'Yes. Yes, of course.' And Tremaine strode across the room and passed by Elise as though she did not even exist.

Elise raised her eyes to follow him, and nodded with approval when she saw him go to Rosalind.

Tremaine smiled his cynical London smile and bowed to Rosalind, offering his hand.

Rosalind shook her head, gave him an outraged glare, and replied with something tart and equally cynical, which must have amused him. He laughed, and then repeated his offer, with a deeper bow and hands held open in front of him.

She tossed her head, and made a great show of getting up, against her better judgement, to take his hand and let him lead her into the room. But Harry could see the faint flush of guilty pleasure on her face, and the exasperated curve to the lips that had replaced her stoic lack of expression.

Harry went to stand next to the girl at the piano, who was looking nervous now that the attention was to be on her. 'Something simple to start, I think. You can manage a waltz, can you not? They are slow, and the beat is steady.'

The girl nodded and began.

When Rosalind realised what was about to occur, alarm flashed across her face, and the pink in her cheeks was replaced by white. She hissed something to her partner, stepped away from him, and made to sit down.

But Harry watched as Tremaine caught her hand easily in his and pulled her back into the dance, giving another slight bow before putting his arms about her.

She still hesitated for a moment, and then looked down at the floor and coloured again, as though she would be anywhere in the world but where she was. But as the dancing began she relaxed. Her small body settled into the circle of his arms like a sparrow seeking warmth in the winter.

For his part, Tremaine stood close enough to her that she could not see his face. He gazed over her head and past her, into the room. And wherever he was it was not in the present. His eyes were looking somewhere very far away, some place that gave him both great happiness and great pain, for there was more sincere emotion in his eyes than Harry had ever seen. The man was in torment, and yet there was a faint smile on his lips.

For a moment Harry sympathised.

As the couple danced it was not with the easy, perfectly matched grace of Tremaine and Elise, but as one person. Their steps were not flawless, but their mistakes matched their successes, and the false notes in the music did nothing to hinder them.

And then the dancing was over, and Rosalind pulled away from him and rushed from the room.

After a moment's hesitation Tremaine went after her, his urbane lope failing to disguise the speed of his response.

Harry sighed. That answered that. It would be even more complicated than he had hoped. But it was just as he had always feared, and he could not pretend surprise.

CHAPTER FOURTEEN

ELISE watched the couple on the dance floor too, trying to disguise her ill ease. They were an unusual pair, for Nicholas was a head too tall to dance easily with Rosalind. But they were attractively matched in colouring. And of a similar temperament. If circumstance had been different, and Elise had been hostess at Harry's side, she would have seated the two together at meals just to see what became of it. It was disturbing that the idea held such appeal. For it showed her how easy it would be to forget the man who had stood by her side for so long, and had so graciously escorted her back to this house, although he must have known what it might mean.

She watched the dancers take another turn, and saw the expression upon Nick's face. The most incorrigible rogue in London looked the picture of restraint—and none too happy about it. For a moment Elise flattered herself that it was for her benefit, to show his loyalty. But only for a moment. She knew the man too well for that. He must want the girl in his arms most desperately to make such a great effort not to want her.

And as he turned again she could see Rosalind. It was as though the girl were dancing to her favourite tune on the edge of a cliff—for she was clearly struggling not to enjoy the waltz, nor her contact with the man who danced with her.

So that was the way it was to be. It pained Elise to think that she had not matched the two long ago, for Rosalind needed a way to escape from her father, and Nick needed a steady hand to hold his. She shook her head at her own folly. Rather than help him she had stood in his way, making it more difficult for him to leave her. How great a fool she was, to realise it now that things had grown so complicated.

But perhaps it would be easier if Tremaine wished a parting as much as she did. At least she would not be obliged to break his heart before returning to Harry. For, after their conversation of the afternoon, she was sure she meant to return—if he would still have her.

She frowned. Had she gained anything by her two months away? She suspected that once she was back in his house, Harry would cease his complaints about her loyalty and drop easily back into the role of affectionate but distant husband. She must learn to tolerate his silences without complaint now he had shown her the reason for them. And she would not trouble him any more with Nicholas, or any other foolish flirtations.

Although Harry had not run to fetch her from London, he had at least admitted, aloud, that he wanted her back. And she knew she wanted to be with him, perhaps even more than she had before. If he was willing to overlook their barren union, then she should count her blessings.

Most men would not have bothered to disguise their dissatisfaction with her, or to mask their disappointment in false smiles and silence. Perhaps she should learn to view Harry's self-restraint as a gift.

She saw Nicholas whisper something to his partner, and the girl started like a frightened fawn. Then she broke from him and left the room.

For a moment Elise thought to go after her, but she saw Nick glance once around the room to see if the other guests had noticed. Then he followed in the girl's wake.

'I wonder what has got into Rosalind?' Harry had come to stand by her side.

'She is probably overcome with the burden you have forced on her with this party. It was most unfair of you to saddle her with it at so little notice.' Elise gave him a mildly disapproving look, and then smiled to prove it a joke.

He smiled and answered back, 'Perhaps it is unfair to my sister to say so, but you would not have had the trouble she has. I have seen you rise to greater challenges than this without faltering. Should we go and see to her, do you think?' He paused dramatically. 'But wait. I saw Tremaine go after her. So I needn't worry. He is very good at taking care of women in distress, is he not?' His expression was supremely innocent, but he was obviously trying to make her jealous.

'I have always found him so,' she answered with an equally blasé look, ignoring the bait. If he did not wish to question her directly about what he had witnessed in the hall, then did she really need to explain it? And then she remembered how he had been in the afternoon. And she responded in kind, 'Sometimes things are not as they appear.'

He glanced at her, as though surprised at her acknowledgement. And then he gave a small sigh, of fatigue or relief, and said, 'So I assumed.'

The girl at the piano began another waltz, and he bowed to her, holding out a hand. 'Will you favour me with a dance?'

When she hesitated, he added, 'You need not read too much into it. It is only a waltz. I trust Tremaine will not mind if I borrow you for a few moments?'

He was working very hard to appear neutral, but she could see the challenge in his eyes.

So she answered it. 'It does not matter to me what Nicholas thinks.' And she took his hand and let him lead her onto the floor.

It felt so good to be back in his arms again that she had to struggle for a moment to keep herself from saying it aloud. Would it be too much, too soon, to admit tonight that she wished to come home? Though a truce had been declared for Christmas Day, she was not sure it would last. And it would serve her right if he wished to toy with her a bit, as punishment for leaving, before accepting her apology.

Her hopes rose when he said, in a carefully polite tone, 'It is good to dance with you again. Yet another of the many things I've missed since you have gone.'

He was willing to make the first move, to make things easier for her. She leaned back to get a better look into his face, surprised at his choice of words. 'Oh, Harry. You loathed dancing.'

He laughed and shook his head. 'Not true. I made a great show of loathing it. Because I so liked the things you were willing to do to coax me into it.'

She blushed at the memory of long nights spent in his arms after various balls, and he laughed again.

'But now I must take what pleasures you will allow, with no more foolish dissembling to gain ground.' He squeezed her hand, and tightened his fingers on her waist as he spun her around the floor.

She relaxed and let him lead her, enjoying the feel of his strength. Tonight she would do as Nicholas had suggested and open the connecting door between their rooms. And everything would return to the way it was.

'I shall know better,' he said, 'when next I seek a wife.'

She stumbled against him. He was teasing her again. Or did he mean it? She tried to match his tone as she responded, 'Do you have plans of that nature?'

'It all depends on what the future holds for us. I shall know if Tremaine is serious about keeping you by his actions this holiday. If he is true to his word, then we shall see about the divorce.' He paused for a moment. 'If you still wish for it, that is.'

Here was her chance to admit that her feelings on the subject had changed. She approached the subject elliptically, as he had. 'I understand,' she said, 'that the courts of England are not likely to be co-operative in the matter of a divorce. Once the bonds between two people are set they are not to be easily broken.'

'That is probably for the best,' he answered. 'But there should be some regard to the happiness of the individuals involved. It would not be good to force someone to remain if they were truly unhappy.'

And she had been miserable.

That was why she had left. She had loved him dearly, and still did, but it had not been enough to make a happy marriage. If she came back to him, perhaps for a while she could pretend that his silence didn't matter to her. She would forgo the companionship of other men so as not to arouse his jealousy, and she would learn to speak around the things that were most important to her, so as not to upset the delicate balance between them. But if it was to be just the two of them, alone until death?

'We are not likely to have any children,' she blurted, unable to avoid the truth a moment longer.

He tensed. 'Are they necessary for a happy union?'

'I assumed, when you offered for me, that they must be a primary concern to you. There is the title to consider, after all.'

'Well, yes, of course.' He glanced around them. 'I just choose not to discuss it in the middle of a crowded ballroom.'

She all but forgot the promise she had made to herself to be patient with his reticence. Once she came home she might never get a second chance to say what she needed to. 'No, Harry. You choose not to speak of it at all. You have left me to guess your opinions on the matter.'

'We are speaking of it now, aren't we?' He lowered his voice, hoping that she would follow suit.

She looked from her husband to the people around them. 'I know. It is the wrong venue, if we do not want our problems known to all of London. But at least I know that you cannot walk away in the middle, before you have heard what I mean to say.' She took a deep breath. 'In daylight, you treat me like a child if I wish to discuss matters of importance. But at night it is clear that you know I'm a grown woman, for you do not wish to talk at all. You visit me regularly enough. But I assume that you are hoping for a result from those visits. It must be gravely disappointing to you.'

She felt his spine stiffen. And suddenly it was as though she were dancing with a block of wood. 'I was under the impression that you enjoyed sharing a bed with me.'

'I never said I did not.'

He began to relax again, and his fingers tightened on her waist in a way that offered a return to intimacy should she be inclined.

She continued. 'But, pleasurable or not, I am beginning to think that nothing will come of it.'

'Nothing?' He grew stiff and cold again. 'And I suppose you think you will do better with someone else? Is this one more way that you believe Tremaine to be my superior?'

'I did not say that.' For she was not the one that needed an heir.

'But neither are you denying it.' He stopped dancing and released her. 'Go to him, then, and see if it is better. It is obvious that I have nothing that you want. And I certainly cannot buy you children.' Then he turned and left her alone on the floor.

Rosalind leaned against the closed door of the library and felt the breath come out of her in a great, choking sob. She had done an excellent job controlling her emotions, in regard to Tremaine. And now it was all collapsing. It had taken years to convince herself that her first response to him had been the result of alcohol and inexperience. She had been sure that if she met him again she would find him no different from a hundred other town bucks. He would be no more handsome, no quicker to take advantage of a foolish girl, than if he were a man of better character.

But in comparison to the other men of her experience he was still perfection: sharp-witted, urbane and funny. And at such moments as he chose to turn his attention upon her he was no easier to resist than he had been that first day. And when they danced…

It was not fair. It simply was not. To be in the arms of a man one barely knew and feel convinced that one was home at last, finally in the place where one belonged. To feel all the wrongness and confusion of the rest of her life vanish like a bad dream. And to know that when the music ended she would find that she had confused dreams and reality again. Nicholas Tremaine was the fantasy. Not all the rest.

If she could have a moment alone to gather her wits she would return to the ballroom as though nothing strange had happened. She would claim any redness of the eyes as brought about by cinders from the Yule Log.

'Rosalind? Open the door, please. We need to talk.'

She glared at the wood, as though she could see through it to the man on the other side. 'I think we have talked more than enough, Tremaine. I have nothing to say to you at the moment.'

'I need to know that you are all right before I return to the dancing.'

'I am fine. Thank you. You may go.'

'Rosalind! Open this door.' He was speaking more

loudly than necessary, perhaps so that he could be heard clearly through the oak.

She rubbed at the tears on her cheeks. 'Don't be an ass. I am perfectly all right. Go back to the dancing, and to your…your…usual partner.' The words came in little gasps. Even without opening the door it would be obvious to him that she was crying. She winced at having revealed herself so clearly.

'Now, Rosalind.' His tone had changed to coaxing. 'What you think you saw in the hall today—it was nothing.'

'Nothing?' she parroted back. 'Tell that to Harry, for he says much the same thing. But I am not blind, nor foolish, nor too young to know better. I can recognise "nothing" when I see it. "Nothing" is what we share. But you and Elise have "something".'

'Barely anything, really. We are old friends, just as I have told you. Exceptionally close, of course.'

'Everyone knows about your "close" friendship, Tremaine. As apparently they always have. Nothing has changed in all these years. Everyone here can talk of nothing else.' She tried not to think of that first foolish Christmas, when she had had no idea of the truth. And how much easier it had been to know only half the facts.

He cleared his throat. 'It is not quite as it once was. When I first met you, Elise and I had an understanding, and I was not free. Now? Now we have a different sort of understanding. And until I can sort it out I cannot call my future my own.'

'Your future is no concern of mine, Tremaine. Nor do I wish to speak of how it once was. Frankly, I would rather forget the whole thing. I wish it had never happened.'

There was a long pause. 'And is that why you ran from the room after we danced? Because it reminded you of the first time we waltzed? I remember it well.' His voice had gone soft again, quiet and full of seduction. 'You were spying on the other dancers. I put a finger to your lips, to let you know that what we were doing was to be secret, and I pulled you out of the doorway and waltzed you around the corridor.'

She remembered the finger on her lips, and the feel of his arms. And how, when she had been confused by the steps, he had held her so close that he could lift her feet from the ground and do the dancing for both of them, until she had dissolved into giggles. And then the giggles had changed to something much warmer, almost frightening. He had set her back down on her feet rather suddenly, and put a safe space between them to continue the dance. She wrapped her arms tightly around her own shoulders, trying to focus on the disaster that had ended the evening and not on how wonderful the dancing had been. But she would always remember her first waltz as a special thing, no matter what had come later.

His voice was quieter, more urgent. 'And I distinctly remember thinking, Ah, my dear, if only you were older…'

She dropped her arms to her sides. 'Really? Well, I am quite old enough now. And it makes no difference. Elise still leads you about like a puppy, and you still dawdle behind, sniffing after any available female. And if any of them get too close, you have Elise and your poor broken heart as an excuse to remain unmarried. Do not think you can play that game with me, Tremaine, for I know how badly it will end.'

'Rosalind.' He said it softly, and she waited for what might come next.

When nothing did, she said, 'Go back to the ballroom, Tremaine. And leave me in peace. Just as I wish you had done five years ago.'

There was another pause, before she heard the sound of his footsteps retreating down the corridor to the ballroom. She crept further into the room and went to sit on the sofa, where she had so often found Tremaine. She laid her hand upon the cushion, imagining that there was still some warmth there. Why did everything have to be so complicated, so unfair? She was quite sure that of the four of them she was the least to blame for the mess they were in. Why was *she* the one who was being punished? For she suspected that, despite what he might feel for her, in the end she would be no closer to Nicholas Tremaine than she had ever been. He was everything that she longed for and always had been. But for the fact that he did not want her, he would be perfect.

The door of the library opened and Elise stalked into the room, showing no respect for her privacy. She dropped down on the couch beside Rosalind and stared into the fire. 'I do not understand your brother in the slightest.'

Rosalind glared at her, wishing with all her heart that she would go away and take her close friend with her. 'Then you are truly suited. For neither does he understand you.'

'Harry claims to want me back. But now that I am here we do nothing but argue.'

'You were doing that before, were you not?'

'I was arguing. But he did not respond. And now?' She

shrugged. 'It seems I can do nothing to please him. He misunderstands me at every turn, and I cannot convince him that I do not prefer the company of Nicholas.'

'Perhaps because he finds you in Tremaine's arms in a public hallway begging you to give in to his desires?'

Elise stared at her in confusion, and then said, 'Today? That is not at all what was going on.'

Rosalind cast a jaundiced eye upon her. 'And did you tell Harry that?'

'I told him that things were not as they appeared.'

'Small comfort. You will not unbend sufficiently to put his mind at rest, but you still think all your problems are caused by what he does or does not say?'

'You do not understand,' Elise argued. 'He becomes even angrier when I speak the truth.'

'Well, let me be forthcoming, since you set such a high price on honesty,' Rosalind snapped. 'You were unhappy before you left because you did not know his mind, but now that you know it you are still not satisfied. Perhaps you are the one who cannot be pleased, Elise.'

Elise shook her head. 'That is because he is not being logical. One moment he wants me, the next he tells me he would marry again. He tortures Nicholas, but tells me to go back to him. He wants our life to be just the way it was before I left. But if I must lie to him, and tell him all is well, then what good will it be to either of us?'

'Before he was trying to hide the truth, to keep the peace. But now that he must face facts, he is as angry and stubborn as you are.'

'Me?'

'Yes. You. You refuse to admit that you were happy, just as much as he refuses to admit his unhappiness. And if neither of you can manage a happy medium?' Rosalind sighed. 'Then I expect you will continue to make those around you even more miserable than you make yourselves.'

'We are making other people miserable?' Elise gave her a blank look. 'I fail to see how. Everyone here seems to be having a delightful time.'

Rosalind stood up and threw her hands in the air. 'I stand corrected. All is well, and everyone who matters is perfectly happy. And, since that is the case, I need not concern myself with the situation. I am going to my room.' She stalked to the door of the library. 'And it will serve you all right if I do not come out until Easter.' With that she stamped out of the room, allowing herself the luxury of both a muttered curse and a slam of the door.

Elise waited until she was sure that her sister-in-law had gone well away, and then followed slowly up the stairs to her own room. Was it only a few hours ago that she had been convinced her problems were almost over? And now Harry was angry with her and Rosalind even angrier. Only Nicholas was still her friend. But it was most unwise to rely on him any longer if he wished to be free. Rosalind was right: she was making everyone around her miserable.

Elise sighed in defeat. The sooner she learned to hold her temper and her tongue, the better it would be for all concerned. She would go to her husband, take all the blame onto herself, and beg him to take her back. Perhaps she would never have the sort of marriage she wanted, but anything would be better than the chaos around her now, and the aching loneliness she had felt when Harry had left her on the dance floor.

She sent her maid away and undressed hurriedly, leaving the clothes in a pile on the floor. She rummaged in the wardrobe for the dressing gown she had worn on her first night with Harry. Would he remember it after all this time? Perhaps not. But if Nicholas was right it would not matter overmuch. Once she had come back to his bed Harry would cease to be angry with her. And if she could lie in his arms each night, the days would not be so bad.

She wrapped her bare body in the silk and went to the connecting door. For a moment she was afraid to touch the knob. What would she do if he had locked it against her? But it turned as easily as it always had, and she opened the door and entered her husband's room.

To find it dark and empty. The candles had not been lit. The fire was banked low in the grate. And the bed was cold and still neatly made.

She hesitated again, and then went to it, climbing in and crawling beneath the covers to wait for Harry. The night wore on, and the linen was cold against her skin. So she pulled her wrapper tight around her, curled into a ball and slept, shivering through fitful dreams.

She awoke at dawn, still alone.

CHAPTER FIFTEEN

THE next day, Rosalind felt even worse than she had after storming off to her room. She'd spent the night staring up at the ceiling, thinking of all the things that had gone wrong and all the ways the people in her life had failed her. And after a few fitful hours of sleep she had woken to find that her problems were not just a bad dream. The house was just as she'd remembered it: full of people she did not want to see ever again, and manned by servants who were just as slow and disobedient as ever. But, since it was Boxing Day, she was obliged to thank them for the fact, and respond to the lack of service with light duties and generosity.

After a cold breakfast she went down to the library, to take it all out on Tremaine. He was lounging in his usual place by the fire, eyes closed and feet up, as though the struggle of tying his own cravat had caused him to collapse in exhaustion.

She pushed his boots from their place of elevated comfort. When they hit the carpet she glared down and kicked them for good measure. 'Get up this instant. You are required in the drawing room.'

He sighed. 'For what possible reason could you need me? Are there not enough drunken fools available to bend to your will? I swear, I still have the blue devils from last night.'

So the tenderness while they had danced was to be explained by an excess of champagne? She said, in a voice that she hoped was painfully loud, 'Then it is about time you learned moderation. A headache is no more than you deserve. Now, get up.'

He draped an elegant hand over his brow. 'Do you show such cruelty to all your guests, Miss Morley? Or do you reserve it especially for me? If I were in my right mind I'd return to London immediately.'

'Do not think you can fool me with idle threats. The roads have been clear for several days, but you are still lying about on this couch, insisting that you will leave at any moment. If you mean to go, then stand up and do it.'

'Very well, then. I admit it. I intend to stay for the duration of this farce, until I can see Elise safely back into the arms of her loving husband.'

She glared down at him. 'As always, I cannot fault you for your devotion to Elise. Let us hope, once she is settled and you are long gone from this place, that you can find some other woman who is worthy of such unwavering affection. But for now you will have to content yourself with my company, and I need your help.'

He gave an elaborate sigh, to prove that her words had little effect upon him. 'Very well. I am your humble servant, Miss Morley. What do you require of me now?'

'Elise is out of temper with Harry again. She looks as if

she has not slept a wink. Harry is little better. He appeared at breakfast still in his evening clothes, smelling of brandy.'

'And what am I to do with that? Make possets and sing lullabies?'

Rosalind smothered the desire to kick him again, and to keep kicking him until she had made her feelings known. She took a deep breath and said, 'We are having charades. Elise adores the game, and I'm sure she will play to show the world that nothing is wrong. Harry means to remain in whatever room has the punch bowl, so he is easily controlled. I have prepared clues to remind them of the happiness that is married bliss. The game will either leave them in the mood for reconciliation or murder. At this point I do not really care which. Either would solve my problem.'

'And what do *I* have to do with all of this?'

She narrowed her eyes. 'You need merely be as you are—incorrigible, irritable and unbearable. Harry cannot help but shine by comparison.'

He sat up and glared back at her. 'You have no idea what it means to know of your confidence in me. You have decided I'm unbearable, have you?'

She lifted her chin and said, with all honesty, 'Yes. I have.'

'I was dragged here against my better judgement. For reasons that have nothing to do with the sincere celebration of the holiday and everything to do with schemes concocted by you and your brother. I am forced to be the bad example so that everyone else may shine. And yet you find fault with my behaviour?' He had gone white around the lips, and was looking at her with a curious, hard expression, almost as though she had hurt his non-existent feelings.

She shifted uncomfortably from foot to foot, and for a moment she was tempted to retreat. But then her anger at him got the better of her, and she retorted, 'You talk as though you are the injured party in all this. I am sorry, Nicholas, but you are not. In my experience, you are just as I have described you. You are wilful, self-serving, and have no thought to the comfort of anyone but yourself. Because of this, you are finally getting what you deserve.'

He stood up and came near to her. When he spoke, his voice was so soft that only she could hear it. 'You have a very limited experience where it concerns me.'

She shook her head. 'I have more than enough.'

He stared at her for a long moment, as though there was something he wished to say. Or perhaps he was awaiting a sign from her.

She glared all the harder, and deepened her frown.

At last, he said, 'In your eyes I will always be a monster who ruined you and then abandoned you. Very well, then. Let us play-act. And I shall be the villain, since you have cast the parts.'

He stepped past her and stalked to the door. On his way he stopped, looked down at the floor, and scooped up the tattered ball of mistletoe, which was out of place again. Then he turned back, glared at her, and threw the thing into the library fire.

Nick preceded Rosalind into the drawing room and took a place at the back of the room, arms folded. The little chit had all but told him that he was repellent to her, and now expected him to do her bidding like a common lackey.

Rosalind Morley had never been anything but trouble to him from the first moment he had laid eyes on her—cutting up his peace, altering his plans, and disappearing in body but remaining stuck in his mind like a burr, a constant irritant to his comfort. He had wondered on occasion what had become of her after they had first parted. In moments of weakness he had even thought about enquiring after her, before common sense had regained the upper hand. If a single dance with her had turned into his life's most fateful kiss, there was no telling what a casual meeting or a friendly letter might become.

And his fears had proved true. For after only a few days in her company his life had been turned upside down. There she stood at the front of the room, with a false smile on her face, acting for all the world as if she did not even notice him. Which was a total falsehood. He could feel when they were together that she was attracted to him, and he had a good mind to go up there and drag her back to the library, to give her a demonstration of the flaws in his character. No matter what she might claim, once the door was closed it would take only a few moments to prove that her character was no better than his. And afterwards he would have her out of his system and could go back to London in peace.

At the front of the room, Rosalind continued to explain the rules in an excessively cheerful voice that gave the lie to everything he had just seen. 'First we must choose who is to guess and who is to help with the clues.' She scanned the crowd. 'I must stay here, since I already know the answer, but I will need two helpers.'

Elise came to her side immediately, and looked hopefully across the room to Harry.

Harry began to rise unsteadily from his chair. Very well, the two would play nicely together, just as Rosalind wished. But that did not mean that Nick had to waste his time watching over them. He began a subtle retreat towards the door, hoping that Rosalind had forgotten her original plan after his outburst in the library.

But she was ignoring Harry, and had turned her attention to the doorway. 'Mr Tremaine. You as well, I think.'

So she still meant to involve him in this? He turned back into the room and saw the dark look on Harry's face before the man collapsed back into his seat with an easy and devious smile. Whatever Rosalind had planned, the results were not likely to be as she expected. Nick strode to the front of the room, conscious of all eyes upon him.

'The rules are simple,' Rosalind announced to the group gathered before her. 'I have a riddle, and the answer is a three-syllable word. If you cannot guess the word from the riddle, we will act out the parts to help you. Here is the riddle:

Vows are spoken, True love's token, Can't be broken.'

She passed a folded piece of paper to Elise, and then to Tremaine.

Elise frowned.

Nick read it, then stared at Rosalind. 'This is a four-syllable word. Not three.'

She gritted her teeth. 'It does not matter.'

'I think it does if you mean people to guess the answer.'

She glared at him. 'And if I do not care for them to guess

too quickly,' she whispered, so that Elise could not hear, 'it does not matter at all.'

She had that wild look in her eye again, that she normally used on mistletoe. And she was turning it on him. He glared back at her. 'You are right, it does not matter.'

'Here, Elise,' Rosalind said, smiling too brightly. 'You must take the first clue.'

Elise read the clue again and stepped forward. She stooped to lift an imaginary object and then remove from the ground another, which appeared to be a key. She made a great show of placing it in a non-existent lock and opening an invisible door to step through. There were the expected calls of, 'Doorknob,' 'Enter,' and Harry's muttered, 'Leave.'

'Don't be an idiot, Harry,' Rosalind whispered, loud enough so that everyone could hear. 'It is clear that she is coming back.'

'Clear to you, perhaps,' he responded, looking more sullen than Nick had seen him all week.

Elise frowned in his general direction, and then went back to her play-acting. She pretended to look back over the threshold and notice something on the ground, to go back to it and stare down and carefully wipe her shoes.

Whereupon Harry announced, in a clear voice, 'Husband.'

Elise's glare was incandescent, and to stop the outburst that she knew was coming Rosalind announced, 'I should think it is obvious. The answer is—'

Nick put his hand over her mouth, stopping the word. 'You cannot make the riddle and give us the answer,' he announced, giving everyone a false grin. 'Where would be the fun in that?'

'Door,' announced someone in the crowd.

Elise pointed to her feet.

'Feet.'

'Shoes.'

'Dirt.'

'Mmmmmmm,' said Rosalind, around the edges of his fingers.

At last someone shouted, 'Mat.' And he could feel Rosalind, sagging in relief against his hand. He released her.

She looked out at the other guests and announced, 'And now the next word. Tremaine, you must do this one.'

He gave a deep sigh and turned to face the crowd, making a great dumb show of pouring wine from a bottle into a glass. He drank from his imaginary glass, then held it up to the light to admire it, held it out to the crowd and deliberately ran his finger along the rim.

'Wine.'

'Drink.'

'Drunkard,' shouted Harry. 'Inebriate. Wastrel.'

Rosalind put her hands on her hips. 'It is not the person you are supposed to look at, Harry. It is the thing in his hand.'

'Philanderer,' Harry supplied, ignoring her guidance.

Nick took an involuntary step towards him, before regaining his temper and pointing to the imaginary glass in his hand.

'It starts with an R,' Rosalind supplied, and gave an encouraging look to the audience.

'Rascal. Reprobate,' Harry answered. 'Rake.'

'Now, see here…' Nick threw down his imaginary glass and balled his fists.

Rosalind muttered, 'Rim,' under her hand, until a member of the audience took the hint and shouted it.

Nick stalked back to where she was sitting. 'I have had quite enough of this. I wish a resolution to these issues as much as you do. But if it means that I must stand before the entire room while your brother attacks my character for the amusement of the other guests—'

She answered, making no attempt to whisper, 'Oh, really, Tremaine. Stop protesting and play the game. After all, you did steal the man's wife.'

'He did not steal me,' Elise announced. 'I went willingly.'

Tremaine and Rosalind turned to her and whispered in unison, 'This is none of your affair.'

She held up her hands and said, 'Very well, then.' And took a step back.

'Elise is right,' Tremaine muttered back. 'The current problems are none of my doing and all of theirs. I am an innocent bystander.'

'Innocent? Oh, that is rich, sir. The picture of you as an innocent!'

'And now I suppose we are talking of what occurred the night we met? As I remember there were two involved, and not just one. And if that event had not transpired, then today it would be Harry attempting to steal Elise away from *me*.' He stopped. Perhaps that was exactly what would have occurred. For he could much more easily imagine Harry stealing Elise than he could imagine himself exerting the effort to take her away.

'As if Harry would ever do such a thing. Look at him.' Rosalind held out a hand. 'He is the picture of innocence.'

They paused in their whispered argument to look out at Harry, who smiled and offered a wave.

'And there you go again with your twisted notions of guilt and innocence.' Nick looked at Harry again. The man appeared to be harmless, just as he always had. But, from the first, there had been a resolute glint in his eye that did not match the mild exterior.

'He is wondering what we are arguing about.' Rosalind flashed a bright, false smile in the direction of Harry, and nudged Nick until he did the same. 'So, let us go back to the game for now. We will continue this discussion when there are not so many people present.' There was something in her tone that said they would be doing just that, as soon as the guests were out of earshot.

He nodded in agreement and thrust the last clue to Elise. 'Here, take this.'

'I think it is Rosalind's turn,' Elise responded meekly.

'Take it,' Rosalind said with finality, transferring her anger to Elise. 'The last clue.' Rosalind gestured to Elise as she walked to the front of the room.

'I certainly hope so,' Nick replied, then looked at the other guests. 'But it is a two-syllable word.'

Rosalind slapped his arm. 'I said it does not matter.'

'And I beg to differ.'

'Shh.' Elise stared at them, hands on hips, as though she were viewing a pair of unruly children, and they fell to silence.

Elise mimed reaching into her pocket and removing something.

'Handkerchief?' someone supplied.

Tremaine glared into the crowd. 'And how many syllables might that be?'

Elise held the object up between her fingers, then made a great show of opening it and reaching inside.

'Bag?'

'Reticule?'

'Purse.'

She gave an approving nod, and then removed something from it and counted objects out into her hand.

'Coins.'

'Pounds.'

'Notes.'

'Money!' shouted Harry, rising from his chair. 'No surprise that this clue should come from you, Elise. For it is the only thing you care about, is it not?'

Elise's hands dropped to her sides and her eyes narrowed. 'Harry, you know that is not true.'

His chin lifted. 'And I say it is. When I offered for you, your eyes fairly lit as I told you my income. And what were we arguing about the day you left? Now that Tremaine has come into his inheritance you are no longer at my side but at his.'

There was a fascinated murmur from the crowd around them, as though they were finally getting the Christmas entertainment they had hoped for when accepting the invitation.

'You still think this is all about money, then?' Elise laughed. 'And so you *would* like to think. For it removes any blame in this from you, Harry. You, who spent all these years trying to buy my affection. If you had been less quick to give of your pocket and more willing to share of yourself, then we would not be having this argument.'

He stood up. 'I have given you everything I can, Elise.'

'And I say you have not. For Nicholas is the one who has given me love.'

'Because it cost him nothing.'

Nick took another step towards Harry. 'First I was a drunkard, then a rake. And now I'm cheap, am I?'

Rosalind pulled on his arm to draw him out of the line of fire.

Elise stepped towards her husband. 'Even though I chose another, he has given me love and faithfulness and honesty.'

'Ha!' cried Rosalind, unable to contain herself. 'If you knew—'

'Not now.' Nick pulled her back. 'It will not help, Rosalind, I swear to you.'

Elise ignored the interruption. 'But for one misstep. And that was years ago.' She turned back to him and said, as an afterthought, 'It was a mistake ever doubting you, Nicholas.'

'No, it wasn't,' whispered Rosalind.

But Elise had returned her attention to Harry. 'And an even bigger mistake to marry *you*.' She swept from the room.

Harry dropped back into his seat, shocked into silence.

Nick turned to Rosalind, gesturing wide to encompass the mess she had made of things. 'There. See what you have done with your little game? She wants nothing to do with him now he has insulted her. I must go and see if I can mend the damage you have caused.'

She reached for his arm. 'That is the last thing you should do, Tremaine. Let them work this out for themselves. For it is your meddling that is the cause of half their problems.'

He laughed and pulled away from her. 'You dare to

accuse me of meddling in the affairs of others, after the games you have had us playing? You have done more than I to tinker with something you do not understand. And a fine pass it has brought us all to.'

He was following Elise out through the door, even if his mind was telling him Rosalind was right. He would be better off to wash his hands of the whole affair.

'Go, then,' Rosalind shouted. 'Follow her, if her happiness means so much. Follow her, just as you always do. I hope it brings you what you deserve.'

The words struck him in the back like blows, but his feet did not slow their pace. She was right. The last thing he should be doing was following another man's wife down the hall to offer her comfort. If she was so in need of it then it was her husband who should provide it, not some other man.

And it was not as if Harry would deny her. He had been quick enough to sense her distress when he offered for her, and it had been plain to see from the man's enraptured expression after the wedding that his offer had had nothing to do with seizing an advantageous opportunity, and everything to do with his hopeless love for Elise.

If Nick had had the sense to keep himself out of their way couple would have been able to solve their problem on their own. But here he was, still insinuating himself into a situation he had no real desire to join.

He stopped at the open door to the library and turned to make his retreat. But it was too late. Elise had caught sight of him. She gave a watery moan of, 'Nicholas,' and held a limp hand out to him.

And, as he had always done, he sighed and went to her.

'I swear what he said is not true,' she sobbed. 'It was never about your money. Or even about his. Perhaps at first it made a difference. It was nice that an earl had offered for me. And I thought, Oh, Nicholas shall be so jealous, when I accepted. For he could give me much more than you could back then. But mostly I was afraid that no one would want me at all.'

Nick nodded and sat beside her, putting an arm around her shaking shoulders.

'But once we were married it changed. He was so good to me, and so kind. I could not help having tender feelings for him. I felt very guilty about it at first. For it seemed like a final betrayal of what we had together. And that is why I have worked so hard to see that we remained friends.'

'And I have always been your friend in return.' He gave her a small hug. 'For I did not wish you to think you had been abandoned, just because your future did not lie with me.'

'But now?' She shook her head. 'I wonder if it has all been a mistake. Does he really care about me at all?'

'I am sure he does.' But why was the ninny tarrying? If he wished to keep his wife he must come and tell her so. 'Perhaps he is not good with words.'

'He was good enough with them back in the drawing room.' He could feel her tense. 'I think he has finally given me the truth of it, just as I wanted him to. But why did it have to happen in front of all those people? He thought me a fortune-hunter, and in secret he regrets marrying me. He is wrong. But I love him enough to want him to be happy, and to have a wife he respects. And a family. And that is why I cannot go back.'

Nick held her as she composed herself, and silently damned her husband to seven types of hell. If he could not come and force some sense into his wife, then at least he might have given Nick more powerful ammunition to defend him. For after the debacle in the drawing room, her assessment of her marriage appeared to be accurate.

'He cannot mind your spending too much. Even while you are away he supports you, does he not?'

'He is obligated. And I have accepted it because I could not think of another way. But I certainly cannot take his money after what he has said.' She paused, and then drew closer. 'Whatever might happen in the future, I cannot live as a burden on Harry any longer.' She paused again. 'Nicholas, do you remember our discussion before we came to this house, and my promise to you?'

'Vaguely.' He felt a wave of disquiet.

'When I said that if you did this for me there would be no more barriers between us?'

'Yes.' *No.* At least he did not wish to remember what he was sure she must be talking about.

'I may never be free by the laws of the land, but my heart has no home.' She paused again. 'It is yours if you still want it.'

After all these years, how could he tell her that he did not? She had expectations of him, just as surely as if he had offered for her. If her husband would not have her, then it was his responsibility to take on her care. Even if they did not marry, he could offer some sort of formal arrangement that would give her security. It would make her little better than a mistress in the eyes of society, but that could not be helped. Perhaps if they left London they could leave the scandal behind as well. But wherever he lived, it would mean that he could have nothing to do with Harry Pennyngton's sister, for the sake of all concerned.

'Of course, darling,' he said, closing his eyes and accepting the inevitable.

And he felt the relief in her, for she must have suspected by now that he did not want her either. He did not have the heart to tell her she was right.

She looked up at him, obviously expecting something. 'Is this not worthy of a kiss?'

'Of course,' he said absently, and kissed her.

She was still looking at him in the same strange way. 'A real kiss, Nicholas.'

'That was not?' He tried to remember what he had done.

She was smiling sadly. 'It appeared to be. But it was an attempt to save my feelings wrapped up in a pretty package. Can you not kiss me as though you mean it?'

'Now?' There was an embarrassing squeak in his voice that undid all his efforts at urbane sophistication. Kiss her as if he meant it? Now was as good a time as any. It was long past time. For how could one tell the person that the world had decided was one's own true love that one longed for freedom to marry another?

'Yes, Nicholas.' Her lashes were trembling, and there was a hitch in her voice. 'I can never go back to Harry. It is quite impossible. But that does not mean that I must be alone for the rest of my life. On my darkest days, I feared that there was some deficiency in me that rendered me unworthy of true love. Perhaps there was some flaw in my character that had left me without heart. At such times it has been a great comfort knowing that your love remained true after all these years. I would tell myself, If my husband does not want me, then at least there will always be Nicholas.'

He closed his eyes, trying to look as if he was gratefully accepting the compliment that all but sealed his doom. Did she not recognise the difference between love and flattery when it was right before her? It was not possible that Harry was devoid of the emotion that she was so convinced *he* held for her in abundance.

She held out her arms to him and closed her eyes, looking no happier than he felt.

What had that imbecile Harry hoped to prove by behaving as he had in the drawing room just now? And why would he not swallow his pride and come and get his wife this instant? Tremaine had a good mind to find the fellow and punch him in the nose.

He stared at the woman in front of him, stalling for time. 'Perhaps it would be better to wait until we are back in London.'

She searched his expression, trying to read the meaning in it. Then she leaned forward and touched the lapel of his coat, and dropped her gaze so that he could not see her expression. 'If we are to do it at all, there is no reason to delay. I cannot wait for ever in expectation that things will change between my husband and myself. It will soon be a new year, Nicholas, time to put the past behind me. And I think things will be easier between us once we have jumped this particular hurdle.'

'Oh.' His hand shifted on her shoulder, and he could not help giving it a brotherly pat. It wasn't terribly flattering to have the act of physical love viewed as a hurdle. If she would admit the truth to herself, she would see that she wanted this even less than he did.

'Yes. I am certain of it.' But her voice didn't sound the least bit certain, and he feared there were tears at the edge of it.

'If you are sure, then,' he said, and waited for her to come to her senses.

And then she stopped talking and came into his arms, all trembling beauty. That was the way it had always been with Elise. Almost too beautiful to resist, even though she had never been right for him. Her body pressed tight to his, soft and yielding, and her face tipped up to give him easy access for his kiss. Perhaps she was correct, and giving in to lust was all it would take to clear his head of romantic nonsense. So he tried to kiss her in the way she wished to be kissed, as though it mattered, and made every effort to drum up the old passion he had felt for her so long ago.

Her response to him was just as devoid of true desire as his was to her. After a time she pulled away from him and looked up, disappointment and awareness written plainly on her face. When she spoke, her voice was annoyingly clear of emotion. 'This is not working at all as I expected.'

'No,' he answered in relief. 'It is not.'

'I suppose it is too much to hope that you are feeling more than I am on this matter?'

'I am sorry, but I am not. If there were anything, Elise, I would tell you. But do not think that I am disguising my true feelings for you to save your marriage. I will be your friend for ever, but I do not love you in the way you desire.'

She pulled away from him, stood up. And as she walked towards the door she looked sad, but strangely relieved. 'All this time I have been so afraid that I was supposed to be with you. And now? Things are not as I expected at all.'

He nodded, following her. 'I will admit to being somewhat surprised on that point as well. When you came back, I thought perhaps… But, no. I have suspected for some time now that it was not meant to be.'

She sighed in annoyance. 'And when did you mean to share this knowledge with me? For if you meant to take advantage of the situation, Nicholas Tremaine, I swear…'

He held up his hands in surrender. 'I do not know why everyone expects the worst from me, for I am utterly blameless in this. It is not as if I sought you out.'

'You have flirted with me all these years, Nicholas.'

'You and everyone else, darling. I am incorrigible. You have told me so on many occasions. And you never for a moment took me seriously. It is only since the trouble between you and Harry that you have given me real consideration. Frankly, I found it to be rather alarming, and most out of character for you. But I thought, as your oldest and dearest friend, that if you meant to do something foolish you might as well do it with me.'

'You thought you would spare me pain by entering into a dalliance with me?'

He smiled. 'Better me than another. I never claimed to be a noble man, Elise. I am a rake, pure and simple. But I sought to be the lesser of two evils, and I think, after a fashion, that

I have succeeded. Never mind what the world thinks has occurred. We have done nothing that your husband will not forgive.'

Her face darkened. 'And what makes you think that my husband cares to forgive me?'

Damn his tongue for speaking of Harry too soon. He did not wish, at this delicate juncture, to spoil progress towards reconciliation. 'I am merely saying that should you ever wish to return to him, my conscience is still clear. I have not broken your heart. I have not even truly engaged your affections.'

'Neither has he.'

Tremaine resisted the urge to inform her that a woman whose affections were not fully engaged would not be going to such trouble to exact revenge. 'Even so, if you do not wish to settle for less than a full commitment from your husband, you need hardly settle for less than you deserve from me.'

She considered the situation. 'You think that I should choose another lover, then?'

Once again he felt himself losing control of the situation. 'That is not what I said at a—'

'Tremaine!' Harry's hand fell on his shoulder, heavy as death, and yanked him away from Elise. Then Harry pushed him back to the wall, and stared into his eyes, too close. 'I have had quite enough of your interference in the matter of our marriage. It has been difficult enough to have you sniffing about the edges, waiting for my wife to stray. I have tolerated it for Elise's sake. But if you mean to cast her off and pass her on to some other man? You are a heartless cad, sir. You are filling my wife's head with nonsense, and you are to stop it this instant.' His face had the same amiable smile it always had, but this time the tone of his voice was menacing. 'Or I will be forced to take action.'

'Ha!' Elise's response was a shrill laugh. 'You will take action, now, will you? After all this time?'

Nick could feel the fists of the man holding him begin to tense on the lapels of his jacket. 'Elise,' he said in warning. 'Do not goad the man.'

Elise ignored him, as it had always been her nature to do. 'I have been gone for months, Harry. And I have been with Nicholas all that time.'

'But not any more,' Nick announced, hoping that it would end the matter.

She smiled with pure malice at her husband. 'I suppose you can imagine what has occurred?'

Judging by the look on Harry's face as he stared at Nick, he was doing just that.

Nick gave him an ineffectual pat on the arm. 'It does no good to let one's imagination run free and create scenarios where none has existed. She's all yours, old man, and always has been.'

'I am not,' Elise insisted. 'I am not some possession of yours, Harry. And if I wish to take one lover, or a dozen, there is no way you can stop me.'

'Oh, really?' Harry was angry enough to strike someone, and since he would never raise his hand to a lady, no matter how vexing she might be, Nick closed his eyes and waited for the punch. Then, just as suddenly as Harry had grabbed him, he pulled him off balance and pushed him out into the hall, slamming the door after him.

Nick hit the wall opposite the door and bounced off it, landing on the floor with a thump. He leaned his back against the wall in relief, and waited for his head to clear. The situation was solved at last. Judging by the look on Harry's face as the door had closed, Elise would be given no more opportunities to roam. And even if she did, Nick would be risking life and limb should *he* involve himself in the situation. In any case, she had admitted that he was not the true object of her affections. If she could not manage to solve the problems in her marriage she would not come back to him again, hoping to regain the past.

Which meant he was free.

What a strange thought. For he had been free all these years, hadn't he? There was no wife to tie him down. Since his break from Elise he had sampled all the pleasures available to an unattached man in the city. He had indulged whims to the point of boredom, and was more than ready to give them up and settle down. But there had been something holding him back from seeking an end to his solitude.

In the background there had always been Elise—unattainable and yet his constant companion. For even when she had married he had grown used to the idea that he was in some way still responsible for her happiness. He had feared that while she might tolerate his mistresses and small infatuations, and laugh at his penchant for opera dancers and actresses, any serious attachment of his to another would break her heart.

But if she was returning to her husband, this time it would be in soul as well as body. He stared at the closed door in front of him, then rose to his feet, surprised at the lightness of his heart. He would always be her friend. But it was as if some bond had snapped, a tie that had held him so long it had felt more like security than restriction. As though he had been staring at a brick wall so intently he no longer knew if he was outside or inside of it.

And now there was nothing to prevent him from doing what he suspected he had wished to do from the very first.

CHAPTER SIXTEEN

ROSALIND stopped to retie a bow on the Christmas tree, only to be rewarded by a shower of needles on the rug beneath. After Harry's embarrassing outburst, and the disappearance, one by one, of the key players in the domestic drama, the audience had escaped to the dining room for luncheon and gossip.

She was in no mood to hear the scene reworked by curious strangers, so had remained behind with the pretence of refreshing the decorations. She kicked the needles into a small pile at the base of the tree, only to see more fall onto the cleared spot of carpeting. The silly pine had no right to die on her so quickly. How was she to keep the candles lit even for one more night with the tree in this condition? Well, they could carve 'Happy New Year' on her tombstone if they were burned in their beds because of the decorations.

Not that she was likely to remain here much longer. If things had progressed as she thought, Harry had finally come to his senses and she would be back in her own bed in Shropshire long before Candlemas. And Tremaine was still full of excuses, and no closer to offering for her than he had been all those long years ago.

She walked to the drawing room door and stretched and strained until she had pulled down the mistletoe ball. Without thinking, she began to shred the leaves in her hands. What had possessed her to hang the things all through the house, so she could not get a moment's reprieve from them? Damn all mistletoe, anyway. She was likely to see everyone else in the house put it to good use, but gain nothing by it herself.

She could hear steps in the hall, clicking on the marble at the far end. Tremaine, she thought, for there was the distinctive tap of his fine leather boots. But he was coming indecorously fast. What had started out at a measured pace on the marble was growing faster with each step. She ducked her head out into the hallway to see if she had guessed correctly.

At the sight of her, he sped up. And when he reached the rug that began at the entry hall, it was at a dead run.

She looked both ways, searching for the cause of the disturbance. 'What is it? Is something amiss? Do I need—?'

In a moment he was upon her, pushing her back into the room, closing the door and yanking the destroyed plant from her hand. Then he pinned her against the doorframe, his hand twisted in her hair, the mistletoe crushing beneath it, and his lips came down to hers with surprising force.

It was just as wonderful as she remembered it from the first time they'd kissed: the smell of him, the feel of his hands, the warmth of his body near to hers. She opened her mouth, as he had taught her then, to find the taste of his tongue against hers was deliciously the same.

If she was not careful, the end result would be the same as well. He would kiss her, and then he would leave. So, no matter how much she was enjoying it, she gathered her will and pulled away from him, trying to appear shocked. 'Tremaine, what the devil are you doing?' she managed, before he overpowered her weak resistance and stopped her speech with another kiss.

Actually, there was no question of what he was doing. He was driving her mad, just as he had when she was young and foolish. She could feel her pulse racing to keep up with her heart, and felt the kiss from her mouth to the tips of her toes, and every place in between. It did not matter any more than it had the first time that this was wrong. She wanted it anyway.

He pulled away far enough to speak. 'What I am doing, darling, is settling once and for all the location of the mistletoe. You have been standing under it for days, a continual source of temptation. I feel I have done an admirable job of ignoring the fact. But no longer.'

She struggled in his grasp, shocked to find that his other hand had settled tight around her waist, holding her to him in a way that was much more intimate than the brief meeting in their past. The situation was getting quickly out of hand. 'I did not think it mattered to you.'

'And I find I can think of nothing else.' When he realised that he was frightening her, he relaxed for a moment, smoothed her hair with his hand and looked into her eyes. There was a softness in his expression, a tenderness that she had not seen since the day they had first met. Then he smiled, and was just as wicked as he ever was. He kissed her again, into her open mouth, before she could remember to stop him, thrusting with his tongue, harder and harder, until she gave up all pretence of resistance and ran her hands through his hair and over his body, shocking herself with the need to touch and be touched.

'I suppose,' she said breathlessly when he paused again, 'that when someone catches us here you will insist that this is all my doing, just as you did before.' She regained some small measure of composure and pushed at his hands, trying to free herself from his grip. But as she struggled against him she suspected that, despite the trouble it would cause, total surrender was utterly superior to freedom.

'On the contrary. This time, if you wish, you may claim yourself the innocent victim of my animal lust.' And he kissed her again, dominating her easily, to prove that any attempt to escape him was quite futile.

'Really?' She smiled, delighted, and stopped fighting. His head dipped to nuzzle her neck. 'I have never been an innocent victim of anything before.'

He laughed against her skin. 'I thought not. I expect once we are married you shall prove even more difficult to handle than Elise would have been.'

Married? She did her best to frown at him, for it would not do to appear too eager after all the time she had waited for this. 'I expect you are right. If, that is, I decide to marry you. You have not offered as yet, nor have I accepted.'

'I have owed you a proposal for over five years. I assumed your answer would be yes.'

'Never assume,' she said, a little breathlessly. 'I would rather die an old maid than spend another Christmas as I've spent this one—as someone's dutiful wife, cooking geese and tending to the ivy.'

He reached out and took her fingers, bringing them to his lips, drawing them into his mouth to suck upon the tips until she gasped. 'If you marry me, your hands will never touch another Yule Log.' He held them out, admiring the fingers and kissing each one in turn. 'But they would look very attractive wrapped around the reins of a curricle in Hyde Park.'

Her eyes sparkled. 'You would let me drive?'

He smiled back. 'We must see if you have the nerve for it. And you would have to be very good to me, of course. But if you indulge my every whim, how can I deny you yours? We will discuss that later.' He tucked a sprig of mistletoe into his pocket and kissed her again, until she was quite breathless.

'Later?' She caught at his hand as it reached to touch her breast. 'You are being quite wicked enough now, Tremaine.'

'Not hardly,' he answered back, then kissed her once more until she let him caress her. 'You have led a most sheltered life, Miss Morley. And you are utterly unprepared to deal with a reprobate such as myself. But I will be only too happy to educate you in the ways of the world. For instance, I'm sure you will agree that this is much more shocking than a few kisses under the mistletoe.' And his hand slipped beneath the neckline of her gown.

His fingers found her nipple and began to draw slow circles about it. He was right. Judging by the way it was making her feel, it was much worse than kissing. 'You mustn't,' she whispered, and then arched her back to give him better access. 'If someone finds us…'

He pinched her. 'Then I shall be forced to marry you immediately.' He sighed. 'Which is just what I mean to do in any case. I cannot wait another moment. I must have you, darling. And I cannot very well remain under this roof and do what I wish to do with you. I have just left off trying to seduce Harry's wife, and now I mean to ruin his sister? I must show some respect for the poor man. It is Christmas, after all. He deserves to be rid of me. And absconding with his hostess in the middle of a house party is a fitting gift, considering what kind of host he has been to me.' Then he smiled. 'But I have not given you a gift either, have I?' And his other hand slipped beneath her skirts.

'Tremaine, whatever are you doing?'

'You will know soon enough, love.' And she felt his hand caress the bare skin of her leg above her stocking. 'Now, speak. Will you have me?'

She had wanted nothing more for as long as she could remember. But she was afraid he would stop trying to persuade her if she gave in too easily. Was it the knowledge that he was touching her so intimately, or the touch itself that was so compelling? She smoothed down her skirt, to hide what his hand was doing, and tried to appear uninterested. 'I doubt my father will approve of you.'

'Then we shall not tell him until it is too late to matter.'

His fingers travelled up, until they could go no further, and then gave a gentle caress that caused her to gasp in shock. She decided it was definitely the touch that was affecting her, for he had increased the speed of his stroking and was driving her mad with it. His fingers played in a gentle rhythm against her body, reaching places that she had never thought to touch, and creating a jumble of new sensations that made it much easier to feel than to think.

She could barely hear him as he said, 'Now that the roads are clear, it's Gretna for us, my love. And then to bed.'

'I have never...never...never been to Scotland,' she gasped, and grabbed his shoulders for support, trying and failing to hold on to common sense as the feelings built in her.

'Then it will be a day of firsts for you.'

He held her in place against the wall, one hand tightening upon her breast and the other teasing between her legs. She was not sure what was happening, but she knew at any moment that she would have no choice but to say yes, most emphatically, to anything he might ask.

So she closed her eyes and leaned her head back against the wall. With her last strength she whispered, 'Show me Pompeii, Tremaine, and I am yours for ever.' And then she gave herself over to him, and dissolved in pleasure at his touch, accepting his proposal repeatedly and with surprising enthusiasm.

He laughed and kissed her throat. 'Tomorrow, if you ask for it, I will give you the world. But tonight, Vesuvius is nothing compared to what you shall have.'

CHAPTER SEVENTEEN

ELISE had heard Nicholas's body strike the wall with some considerable force. It had surprised her, for although she knew Harry was strong enough, he was not usually given to displays of brute strength. But now, as he turned back to face her, she began to wonder if she had ever known him at all.

It was not yet noon, his clothing was a mess, and he smelled of brandy. His face had not seen a razor that morning, and a slight stubble emphasised the squared set of his jaw. Everything about him seemed larger, more intimidating than she remembered, and he was advancing on her in a way that might have seemed threatening if she hadn't known that it was only Harry Pennyngton. But then he reached her, and before she quite knew what was happening he had taken her in his arms and crushed her body to his in a kiss she could almost describe as ruthless.

'Harry, whatever are you doing?'

'What I should have done months ago,' he said through gritted teeth. 'We are going to settle what is between us once and for all.'

'I thought it was settled,' she said.

'For you, perhaps. Since dear old Harry has allowed you to do whatever you want, in the vain hope that you will grow tired of wandering and come home. But I am done with patience.'

'If you think that I am so easy to control as all that, you had best think again, Harry.' She squirmed in his arms, expecting him to release her, but instead he held her tighter, until she gasped with pleasure.

'Easy to control?' He released her then, and she swayed against him. 'You are more trouble than any two wives. I am sure that the sultans of Arabia do not have the challenges in dealing with an entire harem that I have with you.'

'If I am so much trouble, you had best divorce me and save yourself the bother.' She started towards the door.

But he was past her in a flash, and pushed her back into the library ahead of him. Then he stepped in after her and slammed the door. 'On the contrary, my dear. I have no intention of letting you go. Especially if you mean to throw Tremaine aside and take another lover.'

She stopped and stared at him. 'Whatever difference should it make to you, who I choose to be unfaithful with?'

'I have always known, should you choose to leave me, that it would be for Tremaine. For you have wondered from the first if your decision in marrying me was a wise one. But now that you have had a chance to compare us, I hope that I appear more favourably in your mind.'

'Harry,' she groaned, 'that is the most cold-blooded thing I have ever heard. If you are willing to stand aside and allow me a lover for purposes of comparison, then it proves you don't love me in the slightest.'

'Not a lover, Elise. Only Tremaine. He has been as regular a feature in our marriage as a dog, lying beside the fireplace. Lord knows, I have often had to kick the blighter out of the way to regain your attentions. But it is my good fortune that he has as much initiative as an old dog as well.'

'I beg your pardon?' she said indignantly. 'Nicholas Tremaine is a notorious rake, with a very passionate nature.'

Harry scoffed. 'And no threat at all to our marriage. If he were half the man you claimed he'd never have let me take you away. Failing that, he'd have hounded you day and night, until you could no longer resist the temptation and allowed him into your bed. Instead, I have borne his half-hearted flirtation with you in good humour, knowing that it would lead to nothing. That in the end you went to him, and not the other way round, should tell you everything you need to know about his grand passion for you.'

The words hit close to home, and she felt like a fool for not noticing earlier. But at least Harry did not seem jealous any more. And then, as though unable to resist, she taunted him again. 'If what you say is true, and he does not have a burning desire for me, then I am sure there is someone who does.'

Harry's eyes narrowed. 'Oh, Elise, I have no doubt of it. But if you think you will be allowed to seek any further than this room for such a man you are sorely mistaken.'

He was finally angry enough to show her the truth that she wanted to see, and his words sent desire pulsing to the centre of her being. She pushed him again. 'Seek in this room a man with sufficient passion to hold my attention? If you had sufficient passion, Harry, I would not be looking elsewhere.'

If she had hoped for a reaction there was none apparent. His smile was the same vaguely placid one that he often wore. But there was a strange light in his eyes that had not been there when last she'd looked.

'Very well, then. If you wish a demonstration of the depth of my feelings…'

Before she realised what he had done, he'd locked the door behind her, torn the key from the hole and pitched it into the fireplace.

She stared into the embers, and she thought she could see the metal as it heated to glowing. 'Harry, what the devil are you doing?'

'Making it impossible for you to leave the room before we have finished our discussion. I imagine the fire shall be almost out by the time I am finished with you, and then you will be able to retrieve the key and open the door.' He said it in a way that made her think discussion was the last thing on his mind, and she felt another thrill go through her—one that she had been missing for over two months.

'Now, let me describe to you how I am feeling.'

And then she felt the desire start to fade, for it seemed they were only going to have another silly argument. 'You are going to tell me *now* how you feel? After five years of nothing, you have told me more than enough of your feelings in the last few days. Must I hear more of them? For I have had quite enough.' But when she looked at him, staring into his eyes, she wondered if that was true.

'Really?'

'You have made it quite clear that I have lost your trust. And I am sorry, Harry. I know I've given you cause to doubt me. But until recently I did not think it mattered to you how I behaved. I am sorry. There—I have said it. Though we did comfortably well together, proximity has not made us into lovers. You deserve more. As do I.'

'More comfort than I have given you?' he sneered. 'My pockets are deep, Elise, but they are not bottomless.'

She slapped at his shoulder. 'I cannot make you understand, and I am tired of trying. I do not wish you to buy me a new dress, or a diamond, or even a larger residence, so that I can live in luxury without you. If you want, you can take it all back. Sell every last jewel and turn me out on the streets in my shift. I do not care a jot for any of it if I cannot have a marriage that is more than remuneration for services rendered.'

'Am I to understand that you wish a meeting of hearts, and not just an equitable living arrangement?' He smiled.

'Exactly.' She was relieved that at last he understood her. But she found it strangely disappointing that it might mean he'd let her go.

'What utter nonsense.'

'Harry, it is not nonsense at all. It is what I have longed for all my life.' She reached out a hand to push his shoulder, to move him out of her way. But he caught it easily, sliding his palm over hers, wrapping his fingers around it and squeezing tightly, rubbing the ball of his thumb slowly over the pulse-point beating on her wrist.

'But, Elise, what kind of a fool would I be to give my

heart to you now, knowing that you have ignored it for so many years?'

'Me?'

'When I sought to court you, as smitten as any young buck in London, you all but ignored me. You struggled to hide your disappointment when you married me. Since that time, you have been everything a man could desire in a wife. I have had all I could want save one thing.'

She thought of the children that should be gracing their home, and felt a moment's pain.

'You have not loved me.'

She started.

'And so I have kept my distance as well. For there is nothing more pathetic than a man so lost in love that his wife leads him like an ape on a string for the amusement of the ton. But now, after you have left me, you expect me to show you the depths of my feelings and risk ridicule or indifference?'

It was as if he was throwing her own thoughts back at her, and she found she had no way to answer for them. There must be something she could say that would make it all right between them, but for the life of her she could not think of the words.

When he realised that a response would not be forthcoming, he sighed. 'Very well, then.'

She feared that she had lost him with her hesitation.

And then he kissed her.

The strength of her reaction came as a shock, and she wondered how she had ever become convinced that he was taking her for granted with the casual affection he displayed. He seemed to put no effort into arousing her. But he had managed it all the same. Where Nicholas Tremaine's kisses had been skilled enough, but not particularly passionate, Harry's lacked grace in their eagerness to bring her pleasure. In the months they had spent apart he had forgotten none of what she enjoyed, and now he was using all of his accumulated knowledge against her, until she caught fire in his arms.

He was kissing her with every last ounce of desire, his tongue sliding past her teeth and his lips devouring hers. And it no longer mattered what he had said, or not said, whether he loved her, hated her, or cared neither way. She could not help it that a small moan of pleasure escaped her lips, and then a somewhat louder moan of disappointment when he pulled away from her.

His voice was low and husky when he spoke. 'Do you still doubt the state of my heart after all we have been to each other?'

He had brought her close to climax with the force of his kiss. So she gathered her breath and whispered, 'The fact that you are a skilled lover does little to tell me your true feelings.'

He allowed himself a satisfied grin. 'So I am a skilled lover, am I?'

She was near to panting with eagerness as she said, 'I am sure there are many as talented as you, who care only for the pleasure to be gained from the act of love and not the woman they share it with.'

'Really?'

'Nicholas, for instance—'

And his lips came down upon hers again, stopping her

in mid-sentence. This kiss was rougher, and more demanding, and his hands held her tight to his body as he rubbed his hips against hers. He was hard and ready for her. When he felt her growing soft and weak in response, near ready to give in, he pulled away from her again.

'There will be no more talk of Tremaine, Elise. For I do not care what he thinks when alone with a woman. I can speak only for myself when I say that it is much more pleasurable when one has the love of one's partner. And if, after tonight, I have not gained yours, then there will be no point in our continuing. If you do not love me with your whole heart, then I do not want you back.'

He would not take her back? She was struck by the shock of the idea. For she had believed for so long that he did not love her, it was a surprise to think he had feared the same.

'You want my love?' she asked softly.

He buried his face in her neck, inhaling the scent of her. 'As I have wanted it from the first day we met. I still remember the first time I saw you, standing in a doorway at some party or other. I cannot remember anything else about that night but you. You wore blue satin, and it matched the colour of your eyes. I had to force my way through a crowd of suitors to gain your hand for a dance.'

'That was a long time ago,' she murmured, trying to ignore the feeling of his lips on her throat so that she could hear his words over the singing in her blood.

'Barely an instant. You are no less beautiful. You were so bright—glowing like a diamond.'

She tried to remember the last time he had spoken to her

thus, with anything more than polite approval. 'I did not know you had noticed my appearance.'

He raised his head to look into her eyes. 'Every hour of every day. Just to look at you was a pleasure, and still is. But you belonged to someone else, and I thought there was no hope. Can you blame me, then, for using Tremaine's downfall to my advantage?'

She pulled away and looked at him in surprise. 'And how did you do so? For we were parted before you offered.'

For a moment the old Harry was back, hesitant, guarded, evasive. 'The anonymous note you received? Telling of his perfidy? It was from me.'

The shock of it shook her to her very core. 'You lied to me?'

'It was the truth. The girl involved was Rosalind. As much her fault as his. But he was not blameless, for it was his flirting that led her to disaster.'

'Rosalind?' And suddenly the pieces of Elise's life began to fall together. The strange behaviour of her sister-in-law, and the even stranger behaviour of Tremaine.

'I should have called the bastard out instead of keeping what he did a secret. But Morley wished the thing covered up, and rushed her back out of town. And then I saw my opportunity to hurt him, and to have you as well. I sent the note, and I would do it again in a heartbeat.' He squared his jaw in defiance. 'If you believe I won you through unfair means, then so be it. I would have done anything to part the two of you. That the man was too decent to dishonour my sister further and tell you the truth came as a great relief to me. For I realised too late that I had jeopardised her reputation further by hinting at the facts. But he was not honourable enough to marry her, and he deserved some punishment for it—not the reward of your love as well.'

'You deliberately ruined my engagement?' He had changed her life to suit his own desires, tricked her into his bed and pleasured her until she was helpless to resist. The thought should have enraged her. But the rush of emotion she felt was closer to lust than anger.

'I was mad with wanting you.' And then he added, as if it should mitigate what he had done, 'You would not have suited. Tremaine is too shallow, and would not give you the safety and security of home that you desire. You would have discovered it yourself eventually, to your own regret, if I had not intervened.' He frowned. 'But if I had known that I would never be free of the man, and that you would still be pining for him five years later, perhaps I would not have bothered.'

'I have not been pining for him,' she snapped. 'I have made every effort to be a good wife to you, just as you deserved.'

He snorted. 'I got what I deserved, all right. A woman beautiful, passionate, and in mourning for the man she had given up. But willing to do her duty to the husband she never wanted. I am not sorry for what I did to get you. I would do it again to have even a day with you in my arms, though your heart was divided. But, believe me, I paid the price.' He looked at her again, his eyes strange and sad. 'For I will always wonder what it would have been like had you loved me first.'

As he spoke, it sounded as though something was over. Which was strange, because perhaps nothing had ended at all.

'I cannot tell you what might have been,' she said. 'I only know that my future does not lie with Tremaine, no matter the past.'

Harry looked at her with a slow, hot smile that made her insides melt.

'And what do you mean to do tomorrow?' He pulled her a little closer, and her body shocked her with remembrance.

'Tomorrow?'

'Yes, tomorrow. If you mean to leave both me and Tremaine, and find another lover, it will have to wait for morning. I have plans for you tonight.'

'Harry, it is barely noon.' Her breath came out in a little squeak. It surprised her, for it sounded almost as if she was frightened by her mild milquetoast of a husband.

'I am well aware of the fact. For now, it is you and me and the library fire, my love. And, by God, if you go out through that door tomorrow morning, I will see to it that you remember what you have left.' Then he pushed her back to the door and kissed her so hard that she thought her lips must bruise.

'Harry,' she gasped, when he allowed her a moment to breathe.

'Indeed.' He was after the hooks on her gown, pulling until she felt them give.

'Stop it this instant. This is my best dress.'

'I will buy you another.' She heard the faint pop of seams and the rip of lace and silk as he pushed the dress down to her waist and ran his tongue along the tops of her breasts, where they peeked over her stays, before setting to work on the laces at her back.

She slapped at his hands, trying to slow his progress, for desire was rising in her again. 'At least let us go upstairs to my room.'

His hands froze, and he looked up from his work. 'If you like your bedroom so well, then I will allow you to return to it. Tomorrow. But today I mean to have you, here and now, in whatever way I care to.'

She swallowed, and felt her knees go weak as another wave hit her. She let out a shaky sigh before saying, 'Suppose someone discovers us?'

'The door is locked.' He plunged a hand beneath her skirts and stroked between her legs, and then laughed in triumph because there was no way for her to hide the evidence of her desire.

'But they might hear.'

He stroked again, and slipped a finger into her, making her moan. 'I expect they will.' And he settled his mouth over a nipple and thrust again with his hand, harder and faster, until she shuddered and groaned his name.

He raised his head to look at her, critically, but with a small smile playing about his lips. 'There. That is how I prefer you. Unable to argue with me.'

It was difficult to argue when her body was crying for more. But, since he was growing more passionate with each objection she raised, she found the strength to disagree. 'Do not think you can persuade me so easily, Harry Pennyngton. I have no intention of giving you your way in this. Unlock the door and let me go.'

'She has found her tongue again,' he murmured. 'A sharp tongue, but a pretty mouth.' And he kissed her again, biting at her lips and taking what little sense she had left. Then he scooped her legs out from under her and carried her into the room.

She kicked. 'Put me down this instant.'

He dropped her onto the chaise longue and stood over her, undoing his cravat. 'You are down. Stay where you are while I get out of these blasted clothes. And know this: if you run, I will catch you.'

As she watched him undress, her heart was pounding so that she feared she would dissolve into ecstasy before he had even touched her. 'If you do not stop this instant I shall scream.'

He was grinning now. 'I certainly hope so—eventually.' He threw his jacket down beside her and pulled his shirt over his head. 'Our guests will find it the most diverting entertainment of the year, but it will not dissuade me from what I mean to do.'

She propped herself up on her elbows and made to swing her legs onto the floor. But he blocked her, and she kicked at his knee with her slipper. 'Harry, be reasonable.'

He glanced down at her as he stripped off the last of his clothing. 'I have tried for five long years to be reasonable, Elise. And today reason fails me.' Then he knelt on the chair, with his legs straddling her, caught her hands in his and pinned them to the cushion beside her head.

She had to admit that it was difficult, under the circumstances, to maintain a level head. He was poised at the entrance of her body, and she lifted her hips to greet him as he plunged into her.

He gave a long, slow stroke that was so good it made

her gasp, then leaned away to look at her, trapped beneath him. 'There—that is more like it.'

'This changes nothing,' she said, but the words came out in short pants as he thrust again.

'You are the one who wishes change, not I.' His breathing was barely laboured, but she could see a sheen of sweat glowing on his body. 'For my part, you are perfect just as you are.'

She groaned. 'You say that now. But when we are clothed you will say nothing at all.'

'How would you know what I say, since you show no desire to be at my side?' His thrusts increased their tempo, bordering on violence, and she could feel the pressure building inside her, ready to break. 'At least when I bed you I know that you are not thinking of another.'

And in truth she could think of nothing at all but him, and what he could do to her. Her body was liquid, hot and wet. Release was moments away. A few more thrusts would send her spinning over the edge. And he knew what he was doing to her, for he had five years' practice in making her respond. He slowed again and began to withdraw. She bucked her hips under him, trying to deepen the penetration.

And then he gritted his teeth in a pained smile, and said, 'Speak my name. Tell me that you want me.'

'Harry,' she whispered.

He gave a single thrust. 'Louder.'

'Harry, please.' She pushed against him, wriggling her hips.

'That's better. Now, tell me there will be no other but me. Tell me, or I swear I will withdraw and leave you unfinished.'

'You can't,' she gasped.

'I can.' And he thrust gently, just enough to keep her on edge.

It was so good that she didn't care what came tomorrow if she could have this moment. 'Not fair,' she panted.

'All's fair in love and war,' he muttered against her throat, and thrust into her again.

'Love?' He was filling her senses, and she struggled to remember if he had ever used the word to her, even in jest.

He paused again, and then rocked gently against her until she was trembling under him, dying for release. 'You are the one that wants war, not I. Now, tell me you love me. That you will be mine for always.'

He was moving slowly inside her, awaking every nerve. She struggled to reach for him, but he held her fast. She whipped her head from side to side, until she found his wrist and rubbed her cheek against it, groaning. 'I am yours, heart and mind and body. Always. Please...' And she felt her body clench at the words, and then go to pieces in spasms of rapture.

He felt it too, and laughed, then fixed his mouth on hers and smothered her screams of pleasure as he pounded into her body. He fell shaking against her, helpless with the strength of his own release.

When she could catch her breath, she whispered, 'I do love you, Harry. Truly.'

In response, he released a surprisingly shaky sigh and whispered back, 'At last. I despaired of ever hearing you admit it. I have loved you to distraction since the first moment I saw you.'

'You have?' She could not keep the wonder from her voice.

'Indeed.'

'You never said so.'

He laughed. 'I thought I had made it abundantly clear when we came together.'

'I knew you were happy with me in that way,' she whispered.

He groaned. 'Delighted. Ecstatic. Delirious.'

'But I thought perhaps a good marriage should be more.'

'A good marriage is whatever we choose it to be, my darling,' he whispered back, and kissed her again. 'And while ours happens to be a very satisfying physical relationship, I feel it *is* more than that. Do you know how I have missed you since you have been in London? The sound of your voice, the sight of you each morning at breakfast, the little things you did to bring joy to my life every single day. My only regret has been that I gained you through trickery. I was afraid that some day you might discover the truth and I would lose you. It seemed as though I was for ever on guard, lest in some impulsive moment I revealed too much. But you left me anyway. The secrecy was for naught.'

He looked worried now that he had told her. Could that have been the great mystery all along? That he had loved her past all honour, since the very first? She felt the thrill of it go through her. And then she relaxed against him for what seemed like the first time. For why did she need to be wary of losing a man who wanted her with such uncontrollable passion? She noticed the way his arm drew her tight, as it always did after they made love, as though he would never let her go. Perhaps it had always been thus and she had never noticed.

She turned her face to him and kissed his chest. 'It was very wicked of you,' she said. 'But I think I can forgive it after all this time.'

He broke into a grin, then, and hugged her again.

She blinked. 'If you can forgive me for Tremaine. I did not understand how you felt.'

He stroked her hair. 'If you have come back to me, then what does the past matter?' He looked away from her then, and said, as though it did not matter, 'Of course it made me very jealous.'

She poked him in the ribs. 'You worked very hard at hiding it until just recently. I did not think you cared a jot for how I behaved.'

'I told myself that he would take no greater liberties than he had already, even when you were free. But if I was wrong…' He paused again, and said with difficulty, 'I understand how much you long for children. But I have not been able to give them to you.' He paused and touched her belly. 'If there is any reason why you might need to return to him, or any likelihood of an occurrence that we might need to explain, then it would be best if you told me sooner and not later.'

She could feel the tenseness between his shoulderblades as he waited for her answer. But his grip on her did not loosen. It stayed as protective and gentle as ever, even as he discussed the possibility of raising another man's bastard. She looked up at him, and for the first time she was sure, beyond a doubt, that he loved her.

'Harry,' she whispered, and hugged him back. 'You have nothing to fear. There has never been anyone but you. Nor will there be.' She frowned, and then pushed forward with her own greatest fear. 'There will be no surprises of that kind because of my time away. But what if there are to be no surprises at all? Even after I come home? We have been together for years, Harry, and nothing has happened. It has been so long.' And she waited, afraid that he would turn from her again.

He smiled, and it was sad, and then he gathered her close to him again. 'It has. But we are not too old yet, I think. And if we are not blessed then we will have to content ourselves with the future God has sent us. In any case, there is not another woman in the world I would wish at my side.'

He reached for his jacket and pulled it over them, to try to keep back the chill. It was hopeless, for the narrow tails did little to cover their bare legs, and they struggled with it, tangling together until she was laughing again. Then he reached into a pocket and withdrew the box he had offered her before.

'Look what I still have for you. Will you accept your gift from me now? You have given me what I want.' He kissed down the side of her neck. 'Let me give this to you.'

Her laughter disappeared at the sight of the box. He had made her laugh. Made her believe in him again. But here he was with another jewellery box, likely to stop talking and spoil it all. 'Must you?'

He shook his head and smiled softly. 'You do not want more jewels? I fear I do not understand women at all. I certainly do not understand you, darling, although if you open this box you will see that I am trying to do better.' He hesitated. 'But, before you do, let me assure you that the thing you read in the paper was nothing. I swear. There is no problem with money that will not fix itself, given time. Do not think that the value of this gift implies a lack of funds.'

She leaned back to examine his face, and was surprised to see the trepidation there. It did seem that he was unusually worried about her response.

'Do not be silly, Harry. It is not the value of the gift that matters to me. It never has been. As I have told you, time and time again, I do not wish any more jewellery from you. But if you mean to give me the thing, and I can no longer avoid it, then let us get it over with.' She steeled herself and reached for the box.

He was obviously rethinking the wisdom of his gift, for he pulled it away from her at the last minute. 'We will see how serious you are when you say that. For the contents of this box are really nothing at all. Nothing more than foolishness. But when I made it for you I did not think how it might appear…'

'You *made* it for me?' Surely she had not heard him correctly.

But he nodded, and coloured like an embarrassed schoolboy. 'We will go to London and get you a real gift once the guests have gone…'

'We most certainly will not,' she said, and snatched the box from his hands, popping open the lid.

Inside, lying on a bed of velvet, as though it came from the finest jeweller in London, was a tiny straw heart,

threaded through with the same ribbon she had used for the
Christmas ornaments.

He poked it with a finger. 'I fear I am not much good at
braiding, although I have seen you do it often enough. I
worked for the better part of an afternoon, and the results are
still quite sad. But I wanted to give you my heart on a string
for Christmas. You have always had it, you know. But I did
not truly miss it until you were gone. I am empty without you.'

She kissed him then, with an enthusiasm that took him
quite by surprise. She was crushing the box between them,
and further mangling his gift, not caring in the least
whether it was crooked, or crude, as long as it came from
her darling Harry.

He pulled away, catching his breath. 'It is all right, then?'

'It is the most perfect thing I have ever seen.' She picked
up the ribbon and held it out to him. 'Put it on me—for I
mean to wear it until Twelfth Night.'

He was embarrassed again. 'Not in front of the guests,
surely?'

'Until you wish to take it off me again.' She gave him
an inviting smile and rubbed her bare leg against his. He
sighed happily in response, and took the necklace from her.

There was a knock at the door.

Which they ignored.

His hands were at the back of her neck, fumbling with
the ribbon, but his lips were on her throat, warming the
place where the straw was lying. She snuggled back into
the wool of his jacket, squirming against him to distract
him, until he had to start all over again and give her even
more kisses while he re-tied the bow.

The knock came again—this time more insistent. And a polite clearing of the throat which, if it was to be heard through the heavy oak door, must have been as loud as a normal man's shout. It was followed by the butler's soft, 'Your lordship? I would not normally trouble you, sir. Under the circumstances... But this is urgent.'

Elise wondered what it could possibly be that should be deemed that important, and hoped it was nothing Rosalind had done. For one more evening the house must run itself, without her help.

Harry rolled his eyes and gave an exasperated groan. He answered, 'A moment, please.' Then he slipped out from under the jacket and covered her up again, struggling into trousers and shirt, going barefoot to the door. He tried the knob, and then remembered the key, still hot in the coals. 'Do you have your keys, Benton?' he muttered. 'You must open the door from your side. I will explain later. Or perhaps not.'

A moment later, there was a rattling of the lock, and the door opened far enough for the butler to proffer a piece of paper.

Harry took it, unfolded the thing, and read in silence for a moment before exploding with an oath. 'Damn the man. Damn him to hell. For that is where I will send him once I catch him. I cannot believe the audacity.'

'What is it, dear? Who do you mean to send to hell?' She could not help but smile when she looked at him.

'Your lover.' He glared down at her. 'I dare say you will be none too happy with him either. Tremaine has run off to Scotland. And he has taken my sister. I swear, Elise, this is outside of enough.' He slapped the note in his hand. '"Dear Harry—" And whenever have I been the least bit *dear* to the blighter? "—I wish you well in this happiest of seasons." Ha! "May it bring you a happy reunion with our beloved Elise." Our beloved? The nerve of the man… "Since my services are no longer needed, I must away. And since you no longer need Rosalind as hostess she means to join me. We travel north to Gretna Green, and then to warmer climes. Do not expect to hear from us until spring, for Rosalind craves more adventure than Shropshire can offer, and I do not wish to deny her. Merry Christmas. Your new brother, Tremaine."'

Harry shook the paper again, and then crumpled it in his fist. 'The bastard has stolen my sister.'

'Your half-sister,' Elise reminded him. 'Who, lest you have forgotten, is well of age, and should have married long before now.'

'But to Tremaine?' Harry made a face as though he was tasting something foul. 'Tremaine.' He shook his head and mouthed the name to himself again. 'Why must it be him?'

'I think that should be plain enough. They love each other.'

'Well, of course,' he spluttered. 'I have known that for years. But I thought he would at least have the decency to court her as he should, make an offer and wait for the banns to be read. Instead he has rushed my little sister over the border like some lust-crazed animal. And he has done it while she was in my care. What am I going to tell Morley? I suspect when he hears of this he will burst from apoplexy.' Harry considered for a moment. 'Which means that some good has come of it, I suppose.' He stared down at Elise.

'You are taking this surprisingly well.' And he smiled at her, in joy and relief, and forgot all about Rosalind.

Elise supposed she was. After all they had been through perhaps she *should* feel something other than joy at the prospect of Tremaine happily married to someone else. But she could not.

'It was time for Nicholas to marry as well. He is a dear man, but he can be a bit of a nuisance. Now that there is someone to watch out for him, his character will be much improved.' She leaned on her elbow and stared at her husband, the love of her life, and fingered the heart at her throat. She gave a theatrical sigh. 'While I cannot begrudge your sister her happiness, I confess that it makes me feel somewhat undesirable.'

'Never,' he breathed. 'Not while I live.'

She held out her arms to him as he walked back to her. 'Show me.'

* * * * *

The Harlot's Daughter

BLYTHE GIFFORD

After a career in public relations, advertising and marketing, **Blythe Gifford** returned to her first love – writing historical romance. Now her characters grapple with questions about love, work and the meaning of life, and always find the right answers. She strives to deliver intensely emotional, compelling stories set in a vivid, authentic world. She was a finalist in the Romance Writers of America's Golden Heart™ Award competition for her debut novel, *The Knave and the Maiden*. She feeds her muse with music, art, history, walks and good friends. You can reach her via her website, www.BlytheGifford.com

For my mother, a trailblazer.
And with great thanks to Pat White,
who kept me going

Author Note

My fascination with the English royal bastards
began in school when I read a novel about the
mistress of one of the sons of Edward III. Her
romance had a happy ending. She married her
prince, her children were legitimised and their
descendants sat on the throne of England.

The story was a testament to the role that love
has played in shaping history.

The story of Edward III's notorious mistress,
Alice Perrers, did not end so happily.
Universally hated, she was stripped of her
position and her wealth when the king died. Her
children rate barely a footnote in history.

Yet her daughter intrigued me. What was it
like to grow up nearly a princess and then be
banished from the court? How would she view
love, and the world, as a result? This story is my
answer to the questions.

And it reflects my view of the role love plays in
shaping the history of our lives.

I hope you enjoy it.

CHAPTER ONE

Windsor Castle,
Yuletide, 1386

THE *shameless doxy dragged the rings right off his fingers before the King's body was cold.*

They used to whisper that and then look sideways at her, thinking that a ten-year-old was too young to understand they slandered her mother.

Joan had understood even then. It was all too clear the night the old King died and her mother, his mistress of thirteen years, gathered their two daughters and fled into the darkness.

Now, ten years after her father's death, Joan stood poised to be announced at the court of a new King. Her mother hoped Joan might find a place there, even a husband.

Foolish dreams of an ageing woman.

Waiting to be announced, she peeked into the Great Hall, surprised she did not look more outdated wearing her mother's made-over dress. It was the men's garb, colourful and garish, that looked unfamiliar. Decked in blues and reds, gold chains and furs, they looked gaudy as flapping tournament flags.

Except for one.

Standing to the left of the throne turned away from her, he wore a simple, deep blue tunic. She could not see his face fully, but the set of his jaw and the hollow edge of his cheek said one thing: unyielding.

For a moment, she envied that strength. This was a man whose daily bread did not depend on pleasing people.

Hers did. And so did her mother's and sister's.

She pulled her gaze away and smoothed her velvet skirt. Please the King she must, or there would be no food in the larder by Eastertide.

As the herald entered the Hall to announce her, she heard the rustling skirts of the ladies lining the room. They whispered still.

Here she comes. The harlot's daughter. No more shame than her mother had.

She lifted her head. It was time.

Amid the whispers, Lady Joan, twenty summers, illegitimate daughter of the late King and his notorious mistress and the most unmarriageable woman in England, stepped forward to be presented to King Richard II.

Lord Justin Lamont avoided Richard's court whenever possible. He had braved the crowded throne room only because he had urgent news for the Duke of Gloucester.

Last month, Parliament had compelled the reckless young King to accept the oversight of a Council headed by his uncle, Gloucester. Since then, Justin had been enmeshed in the business of government. He was only beginning to uncover the mess young Richard and his intimates had made of the Treasury.

Thrust upon the throne as a boy when his grandfather died, Richard had inherited the old King's good looks without his strength, judgement or sense. Instead of spending taxes to fight the French, he'd drained the royal purse with grants for his favourites.

When he demanded more tax money, Parliament had finally baulked, installing the Council to gainsay the King's outrageous spending.

Now, the King had put forth another of his endless lists of favours for his friends, expecting the new Council's un-questioning approval.

He would not get it.

'Your Grace,' Justin said to Gloucester, 'the King has a new list of gifts he wants to announce on Christmas Day. The Council cannot possibly approve this.'

Distracted, the Duke motioned to the door. 'Here she comes. The doxy's daughter.'

Justin gritted his teeth, refusing to turn. The mother's meddling had near ruined the realm before Parliament had stepped in to save a senile King from his own foolishness. This new King needed no more misguidance. He was getting that aplenty from his current favourites. 'What do they call her?'

'Lady Joan of Weston,' Gloucester answered. 'Joan the Elder.'

Calling her a Weston was a pleasant fiction, though the old King's mistress had passed herself off as Sir William's wife while she bore the King's children. 'The Elder?'

Gloucester smirked. 'There were two daughters. Like bitch pups. Call "Joan" and one will come running.'

Wincing at the cruelty, Justin reluctantly turned, with the rest of the court, to see whether the daughter carried the stain of her mother's sin.

He looked, and then could not look away.

Her mother's carnality stamped a body that swayed as if it had no bones and her raven hair carried no hint of the old King's sun-tinged glory. 'She looks nothing like him,' he murmured.

Gloucester whispered back, 'Maybe the whore simply whelped the children and called them the King's.'

Justin shook his head. 'She moves like royalty.'

Head high, she stared at a point above the King's crown, walking as if the crowd adored instead of loathed her.

But then, just for a moment, she glanced around the room. Her eyes, violet, brimming with pain, met his.

They stopped his breath.

Wide-eyed, still looking at him, she did not complete her step. Tangled in her gaze, he forgot to breathe.

Then she gathered herself, lifted her skirt and approached the throne.

He shook off her spell and looked around. No one had noticed that her eyes had held his for an eternity.

She dipped before the King, head held high. Justin thought of the lad on the throne as a boy, though, at twenty, he had been King for half his life. Yet he still played at kingly ceremony, instead of grappling with the hard work of governing.

'Lower your gaze,' the King said to the woman before him.

A flash of fury stiffened her spine. Then, she bent her neck ever so slightly.

'Kneel.'

She dropped gracefully to her knees as if she had practised.

Justin took a breath. Then another. Still the King did not say 'rise'. A smothered cough in the crowd breached the silence.

Her hands hung quietly at her sides, but her fingers twitched against the folds of her deep red skirt.

He squashed a spark of sympathy. The woman's glance had been enough to warn him. Her mother had bewitched a King. He would be on guard.

He had been deceived by a woman's eyes once—long ago.

Ioan had known the King would test her. *Kneel.* So she did. Her mother had taught her well. *Read his needs and satisfy them. That is our only salvation.* This one needed deference, that was obvious. She would give him that and whatever else he asked if he would grant them a living from the royal purse.

At least there was one thing he would not ask. The blood of the old King flowed through both their veins. She would not have to please a King as her mother had.

She heard no whispers now. Silent, the court watched as the King left her on aching knees long enough that she could have said an extra Paternoster for her mother's sins.

Eyes lowered, she looked toward the edge of the wide-planked floor. The men's long-toed shoes curled like a finger crooked in invitation. She stifled a smile. Men and their vanities. Apparently, they thought the longer the toes, the longer the tool.

Yet when her eyes had met those of the hard-edged man at the fringes of the crowd, she had nearly stumbled. His severe dress and implacable gaze sliced through the peacocks around the throne sharply as a blade. For that instant, she forgot everything else. Even the King.

A thoughtless mistake. She had no time for emotion. Only for necessity.

Finally, the King's high-pitched voice called a reprieve. 'Lady Joan, daughter of Sir William of Weston, rise and bow.'

With no one's hand to lean on, she wobbled as she stood. Forcing her shaking knees to support her, she curtsied, then dared lift her eyes.

Tall, thin, and delicately blond, King Richard perched on the throne overlooking the hall. A golden crown graced his curls. An ermine-trimmed cloak shielded him from the draughts. She wondered whether his cheeks were clean shaven from choice or because the beard had not yet taken hold.

His slope-shouldered wife sat beside him. Her plaited brown hair hung down her back, a strange affectation for a married queen. Of course, Joan's mother had whispered, after six years of childless marriage, she wondered how much of a wife the Queen was.

'We hope you enjoy this festive time with us, Lady Joan,' she said. Her eyes held a gentleness that was missing from the King's.

Joan, silent, looked to the King for permission.

He waved his hand. 'You may speak.'

'Thank you, your Grace.'

He sat straighter and lifted his head. 'Address us as Your Majesty.'

'Forgive me, Your Majesty.' She bowed again. A new title, then. 'Your Grace' had served the old King, but that was no longer adequate. This King needed more than deference. He needed exaltation.

The Queen's soft voice soothed like that of a calm mother after a child's tantrum. 'I hope you will not miss Christmas at Weston Castle too much, Lady Joan.'

She suppressed a laugh. A Weston in name only, she had never even visited the family estate. It was her mother and sister she would be thinking of during the Cristes-mæsse, but no word of them would be spoken aloud. 'Your invitation honours me, Your Majesty.'

Queen Anne said, 'Perhaps you might pen a short poem for our entertainment.'

'Poem, Your Majesty?'

'Not in French, only in English. If you feel capable.'

She swallowed the subtle insult. The Queen's words denigrated not only her mother, but Joan's ten years spent away from Windsor's glories. Still, as a daughter of the King, she had been taught both English and French. 'Your Majesty, if my humble verse might amuse, I would be honoured.'

The King spoke, 'Of course you would, Lady... What was your name?'

'Joan, Your Majesty.'

He frowned. 'I do not like that name. Have you another?'

'Another name, Your Majesty?' Odd, she thought, then she remembered. The King's mother had been called Joan. And his mother had been a bitter enemy of hers. Of course she

could not be called by the name of his beloved mother. 'Yes,
Your Majesty, I do.' It would not be the Mary or Elizabeth
or Catherine he expected. 'My mother also calls me Solay.'

'*Soleil?*' he said, with the French inflection. 'The sun?'

'Yes.'

'Why would she give you such a name?'

She hesitated, fearing to speak the truth and unable to
think of a way to dissemble. 'She said I was the daughter
of the sun.'

Whispers ricocheted around the floor. *I was the Lady
of the Sun once,* her mother had said. The Sun who was
King Edward.

The King dismissed her with a wave. 'Your name
matters little. You will not be here long.'

Fear twisted her stomach. She must cajole him out of
anger and gain time to win his favour.

'Your use of the name honours me,' she said quickly, 'as
much as the honour of knowing I share the exalted day of
your birth under the sign of Capricorn.' She knew no such
thing, but no one cared when she had come into the world.
Even her mother was not sure of the day.

He sat straighter and peered at her. 'You study the stars,
Lady Solay?'

She knew little more of the stars than a candle maker, if
the truth be told, but if the stars intrigued him, flattery and
a few choice phrases should suffice. 'Although I am but a
student, I hear they say great things of Your Majesty.'

He looked at her sharply. 'What do they say?' he said,
leaning forward.

What did he want to hear? She must tread carefully. Too

much knowledge would be dangerous. 'I have never read yours, of course, Your Majesty.' To do so without his consent could have meant death. She thought quickly. The King's birthday was on the twelfth day of Christmas. That should give her enough time. 'However, with your permission, I could present a reading in honour of your birthday.'

'It would take so long?'

She smiled and nodded. 'To prepare a reading worthy of a King, oh, yes, Your Majesty.'

The King smiled, settling back into the throne. 'A reading for my birthday, then.' He turned to the tall, dark-haired man on his right. 'Hibernia, see that she has what she needs.'

She released a breath. Now if she could only concoct a reading that would direct him to grant her mother an income for life. 'I will do my humble best and be honoured to serve Your Majesty in any way.'

A small smile touched his lips. 'I imprisoned the last astrologer for predicting ill omens. I shall be interested in what you say.'

She swallowed. This King was not as naïve as he looked.

Done with her, he rose, took the Queen's hand and spoke to the Hall. 'Come. Let there be carolling before vespers.'

Solay curtsied, muttering, 'Thanks to Your Majesty', like a Hail Mary and backed away.

A hand, warm, touched her shoulder.

She turned to see the same brown eyes that had made her stumble. Up close, they seemed to probe all she needed to hide.

The man was all hardness and power. A perpetual frown furrowed his brow. 'Lady Joan, or shall I say Lady Solay?'

She slapped on a smile to hide the trembling of her lips. 'A turn in the carolling ring? Of course.'

He did not return her smile. 'No. A private word.'

His eyes, large, heavy lidded, turned down at the corners, as if weighed with sorrow.

Or distrust.

'If you wish,' she said, uneasy. As he guided her into the passageway outside the Great Hall, she turned her attention to him, ready to discover who he was, what he wanted and how she might please him.

God had blessed her with a pleasing visage. Most men were content to bask in the glow of her interest, never asking what she might think or feel.

And if they had asked, she would not have known what to say. She had forgotten.

Yet this man, silent, stared down at her as though he knew her thoughts and despised them. Behind him, the caroller's call echoed off the rafters of the Great Hall and the singers responded in kind. She smiled, trying to lift his scowl. 'It's a merry group.'

No gentle curve sculpted the lips that formed an angry slash in his face. 'They sound as if they had forgotten we might have been singing beside the French today.'

She shivered. Only God's grace had kept the French fleet off their shores this summer. 'Perhaps people want to forget the war for a while.'

'They shouldn't.' His tone brooked no dissent. 'Now tell me, Lady Solay, why have you come to court?'

She touched a finger to her lips, taking time to think. She must not speak without knowing whose ear listened. 'Sir, you know who I am, but I do not even know your name. Pray, tell me.'

'Lord Justin Lamont.'

His simple answer told her nothing she needed to know. Was he the King's man or not? 'Are you also a visitor at Court?'

'I serve the Duke of Gloucester.'

She clasped her fingers in front of her so they would not shake. Gloucester had near the power of a king these days. Richard could make few moves without his uncle's approval, a galling situation for a proud and profligate Plantagenet.

She widened her eyes, tilted her head and smiled. 'How do you serve the Duke?'

'I was trained at the Inns of Court.'

She struggled to keep her smile from crumbling. 'A man of the law?' A craven vulture who never kept his word, who would speak for you one day and against you the next, who could take away your possessions, your freedom, your very life.

'You dislike the law, Lady Solay?' A twist of a smile relaxed the harsh edges of his face. For the first time, she noticed a cleft in his chin, the only softness she'd seen in him.

'Wouldn't you, if it had done to you what it did to my mother?' Shame, shame. Do not let the anger show. It was over and done. She must move on. She must survive.

'It was your mother who did damage to the law.'

His bluntness shocked her. True, her mother had shared the judges' bench on occasion, but only to insure that the King's will was done. Most judges could not be trusted to render a verdict without an eye on their pockets.

Solay kept her brow smooth, her eyes wide and her voice low. 'My mother served the Queen and then the King faithfully. She was ill served in the end for her faithful care.'

'She used the law to steal untold wealth. It was the realm that was ill served.'

Most only whispered their hatred. This man spoke it aloud. She gritted her teeth. 'You must have been ill informed. All her possessions were freely given by the King or purchased with her own funds.'

'Ah! So you are here to get them back.'

She cleared her throat, unsettled that he suspected her plan so soon. 'The King honoured me with an invitation. I was pleased to accept.'

'Why would he invite you?'

Because my mother begged everyone who would still listen to ask him. 'Who can know the mind of a King?'

'Your mother did.'

'A King does as he wills.'

A spark of understanding lit his eyes. 'Parliament turned down her last petition for redress so she has sent you to beg money directly from the King.'

'We do not beg for what is rightfully ours.' She lowered her eyes to hide her anger. Parliament had impeached one of the King's key advisers last autumn, then given the five Lords of the Council unwelcome oversight of the King. It was an uneasy time to appear at court. She had no friends and could afford no enemies. 'Please, do not let me detain you. My affairs need not be your concern. You must have many friends to see.'

'I'm not sure that anyone has many friends these days,

Lady Solay. You asked about my work. Among my duties is to see that the King wastes no more money on flatterers. If you try to entice him into raiding the Exchequer on your behalf, your affairs will become my concern.'

The import of his words sank in. She risked angering a man who had power over the very purse strings she needed to loosen.

'I only ask that you deal fairly.' A vain hope. She had given up on justice years ago.

She stepped back, wanting to leave, but he touched her sleeve and moved closer, until she had to tip her head back to see his eyes. He was tall and lean and in the flickering torch fire, his brown hair, carelessly falling from a centre parting, glimmered with a hint of gold.

And above his head hung a kissing bough.

He looked up and then back at her, his eyes dark. She couldn't, didn't want to look away. His scent, cedar and ink, tantalised her.

Let them look. Make them want, her mother had warned her, *but never, never want yourself.* Yet this breathless ache— surely this was want.

He leaned closer, his lips hovering over hers. All she could think of was his burning eyes and the harsh rise and fall of his chest. She closed her eyes and her lips parted.

'Do you think to sway me as your mother swayed a King, Lady Solay?'

She pushed him away, relieved the corridor was still empty, and forced her lips into a coy smile. 'You make me forget myself.'

'Or perhaps I help you remember who you really are.'

Her smile pinched. 'Or who *you* think I am.'

'I know who you are. You are an awkward remnant of a great King's waning years and glory lost because of a deceitful woman.'

Gall choked her. 'You blame my mother for the King's decline, not caring how hard she worked to keep order when he could not tell sun from moon.'

When he did not know, or care to know, the daughter he had spawned.

'I, Lady Solay, *can* tell day from night. Your mother's tricks will not work on me.'

Then I must try some others, she thought, frantic.

What others did she know?

He *had* made her forget herself. She had been too blunt. Next time, she must use only honeyed words. 'I would never try to trick you, Lord Justin. You are too wise to be fooled.'

Muttering a farewell, she turned her back and walked away from this man who lured her into anger she could ill afford.

Shaken, Justin watched her hips sway as she walked, nay, floated away. He had nearly kissed her. He had barely been able to keep his arms at his side.

He had been taken in once by a woman's lies. Never again.

Still, it had taken every ounce of stubborn strength he could muster not to pull her into his arms and plunder her mouth.

Well, nothing magical in responding to eyes the colour of purple clouds at sunset and breasts round and soft. He would not be a man if he did not feel something.

'There you are.' Gloucester was at his elbow. 'What possessed you, Lamont, to whisper secrets to the harlot's daughter?'

Gloucester's harsh words grated, although Justin had thought near the same. 'Such a little difference, between one side of the blanket and the other,' he said, turning to look at the Duke. 'You share a father. You might call her sister.'

Gloucester scowled. 'You are ever too outspoken.'

'I'm just not afraid to tell the truth.' But about this, he was. The truth was that he had no idea what possessed him to nearly take her in his arms and he did not want to dwell on the question. 'The woman sought to tempt me as her mother did the old King.'

'You looked as if you were about to succumb.'

'I simply warned her that she would not be permitted to play with King Richard's purse.'

Gloucester snorted with disgust. 'My nephew is a sorry excuse for a ruler. The French steal my father's land and all the boy does is read poetry and wave a little white flag to wipe his nose. As if a sleeve were not good enough.' Gloucester sighed. 'Now, what was it you wanted to tell me?'

Justin brought his mind back to the King's list. 'He wants to give the Duke of Hibernia more property.'

'And what of my request?'

Justin shook his head.

Gloucester exploded. 'First he gives the man a Duke's title that none but a King's son has ever held. Then he gives him a coat of arms adorned with crowns. Now he gives him land and leaves me at the mercy of the Exchequer? Never!'

'I'll tell him, your Grace. Right after vespers.' To Justin

had fallen the task of delivering bad news. He was not a man to hide the truth. Even from the King.

But he suspected that Lady Solay was. Nothing about her rang true, including her convenient birthday. As he and Gloucester returned to the hall, Justin wondered whether one of the old King's servants might remember something of her.

If she believed she was going to tap the King's dwindling purse with honeyed kisses, she would be sorely disappointed.

He would make sure of that.

CHAPTER TWO

IN THE hour after sunset, Justin strode towards the King's chamber, dreading this meeting. The King expected an answer on his list of grants. He wasn't going to like the one he would hear.

But Justin would deliver it, and quickly. He had another mission to accomplish before the lighting of the Yule Log.

Entering the solar, Justin saw Richard on his knees, hands clasped. He paused, thinking the King at prayer, but when Richard dropped his pose and waved him in, Justin saw an artist, squinting over his parchment, sketching.

As Justin forced a shallow bow, the artist left the room, handing his drawings to the King.

'Aren't these magnificent, Lamont?' The man had drawn Richard kneeling before a group of angels. 'The gold of heaven will surround me here and my sainted great-grandfather will stand behind me.'

Only young Richard would call the man a saint. 'Your great-grandfather died impaled on a poker for incompetence in government.' And sixty years ago, most had cheered at his death.

The King narrowed his eyes. 'He was deposed by ruffians who had no respect for their King. Do you?'

Justin clenched his fingers, his sergeant-at-law ring digging into his fist. 'I respect the King who respects his realm and the advice of his barons.'

Years ago, Justin had respected this King. Then, the young boy bravely faced rebellious peasants and promised them justice. That promise, like so many others, had been broken many times over.

Frowning, the King put down the sketches. 'It's abominable, having to go to the Council every time I need the Great Seal. Give me the list.'

'The Council has said no.'

The King, stunned, merely stared at him. Only the crackle of the fire broke the silence.

'Even to Hibernia?' he asked, finally.

'Especially to Hibernia. The man tarries at court with his mistress while his wife waits at home in embarrassment.'

'You go too far!' The King shook his fist. His voice rose to a squeak. 'That's not the Council's concern. These are my personal gifts, not governmental ones.'

Obviously, the King did not understand the new order. 'They affect the Treasury, so they come under the Council's purview.' There might be a legitimate grant or two on the list, but in the end, he suspected, he would be serving summons to the lot of them. 'Until we complete a full review of the household expenses, there will be no new grants.'

'Is this the legal advice you gave the Council?' The King spat 'Council' as if he hated the very word.

'Parliament made the law, Your Majesty.'

'And by that law a Council can rule a King?'

'For the next year, yes.'

The King narrowed his eyes. 'You tell your Council that by Twelfth Night I want the seal affixed to this list. The entire list.' A wicked smile touched his lips. 'And add a grant of five pounds for the Weston woman.'

Justin clenched his jaw. The amount would barely keep a squire for a year, but the woman had done nothing to earn it. The King was simply trying to flaunt his power. 'I will convey your message,' he said. 'I do not expect them to change their minds, particularly for the woman.'

Barely suppressed fury contorted the King's face. 'Remember, Lamont, according to your precious law, by this time next year, I will be King again.'

The King's very softness of speech caused him to shiver. This was a man who never forgot wrongs.

Well, that was something they had in common.

As Justin left the room, laughter laced the halls as the court gathered for the lighting of the Yule Log. He did not slow his steps. The Lady Solay had to be stopped. Quickly.

Scolding herself for speaking harshly to Lamont, Solay took her small bag of belongings to the room she was assigned to share with one of the Queen's ladies-in-waiting, wondering whether the choice was an omen of the King's favour or a sign that he wanted her watched.

She unpacked quickly as Lady Agnes, small, round, and fair, hovered in the doorway. 'Lady Solay, hurry. We mustn't miss the celebration.'

Shivering in her outgrown, threadbare cloak, Solay

crossed the ward with Lady Agnes, who had not stopped talking since they left the room.

'The Christmas tableaux for his Majesty tomorrow will be so beautiful. I am to play a white deer, his Majesty's favourite creature.' Agnes had come to England from Bohemia with Queen Anne and still trilled her *r*s. 'And for the dinner, the cook is fixing noodles smothered in cheese and cinnamon and saffron. It's my very favourite.'

Solay's mouth watered at the thought. Her tongue had not touched such extravagant sweetness in years. As they entered the hall, Solay looked around the room, relieved when she did not see Lord Justin.

All her life, she had ignored the prejudice of strangers, yet, unlike all the others, his condemnation had unearthed her long-banked anger, exposed it to the air where it threatened to burst into flame, stirring her to fight battles long lost.

Worse, he had touched something even more dangerous. Close to this man, she felt *want*. The unruly emotion threatened the control she needed if she were to control those around her. And her ability to influence others was her family's only hope.

Lady Agnes left to attend the Queen, who was touching the brand to the kindling beneath the Yule Log. Solay looked for another woman companion, but each one she approached drifted out of reach.

The men were not so reticent. One by one they came to study her face and let their eyes wander her body. Feeling not a speck of desire, she turned the glow of her smile on each one, circling each as the sun did the earth.

She learned, as she smiled, that the King had bestowed a new title, Duke of Hibernia, on his favourite courtier.

The men did not smile as they told her.

'Congratulations, Lady Solay.' Justin's words came from behind her. 'The King has put your name on his list already.'

Only when she heard his voice did she realise she'd been listening for it. Yet surely the excitement she felt was for the news he brought and not for him. 'His Majesty is gracious.' She wondered how gracious an amount he'd given.

'The Council is not. It will not be allowed. The Council cares not that you pick a birth date to please the King.'

Her cheeks went cold. 'What do you know of my birth?' Few had known or cared when she came on to this earth. The deception had been harmless. Or would be unless the King found out.

'One of the laundresses served your mother twenty years ago. She remembers the night of your birth very clearly. It was the summer solstice and all the castle was awake to hear your mother's moans.'

She bit her lower lip to hold back a smile of delight. Her birthday. She finally knew her birthday.

But she must cling to the tale she'd told. 'She must have mis-remembered. It was many years ago.'

'She was quite sure she was right. And so am I.'

Fear swallowed her reason. If the King were to believe her reading, he must have no doubts about her veracity. 'Would you take the word of a laundress over that of a King's daughter?'

'The laundress has no reason to lie. The King's daughter apparently does.'

She raised her eyes to Justin's, forgetting to shield her desperation. 'You haven't told the King?'

'No.'

Relief left her hands shaking. 'He need not know.' Surely a few light words and a kiss would cajole this man to silence. She touched his arm and leaned into him, pleading with her eyes. Her lips parted of their own accord. 'It was harmless, really. I thought only to flatter him.'

The angry set of his lips did not change as he stepped away. 'When next you think to flatter the King, remember that, for the next year, the power belongs to the Council.'

Fear smothered her joy. Now that he knew the truth, he held a weapon and could strike whenever he pleased. This man, so able to resist a woman's persuasion, must want something else.

She had a moment's regret. She had thought he might be different. 'I see. What is it you want for your silence?'

He raised his brows. 'Don't confuse my character with yours, Lady Solay. I do not play favourites.'

'So you will hold your tongue and then call the favour I owe you when it's needed.'

Seemingly surprised, he studied her face. 'Do you trust no one?'

'Myself, Lord Justin. I trust myself.'

'Surely someone has given you something without expecting anything in return?'

Her thoughts drifted to memory. All those courtiers who had fawned over her mother while the King lived disappeared the night he died. All their kindnesses, even to a little girl, had only one purpose—access to his power. 'Not that I remember.'

'Then I am sorry for you.'

She saw a trace of sadness in his eyes, and steeled herself against it. 'I don't want your pity. You'll want something some day, Lord Justin. They all do.'

'You are the one who wants something, Lady Solay. Not I.' He turned his back and left her standing alone in a crowded room.

She shrugged as the next man approached. What Lord Justin said did not matter. His actions would tell the tale.

Justin strode down the stairs and out into the upper ward, glad to be free of her. The dark, her nearness, went to his head like mulled wine.

He should go to the King immediately with her deception, he thought, rubbing his thumb across the engraved words on his ring. *Omnia vincit veritas.* Truth conquers all. Just tell the king she had lied and she would be gone.

But all around him, the court was surging across the ward towards the chapel for midnight Mass. It was hardly the time to interrupt one's monarch to say…what? That the Lady Solay had lied about her birthday? What lady had not? The King, never too careful of his own word, might either take it as a compliment or as an affront.

Justin's footsteps slowed. He could imagine the look on Richard's face. After the King digested the fact, the cunning would creep into his eyes. Then, just as she predicted, he would hold the knowledge as a weapon, waiting to use it until she was most vulnerable. And despite everything, Justin knew that the Lady Solay was vulnerable. When her violet eyes pleaded with him, they reminded him of another woman's. A woman so desperate she—

He blocked the painful memory as he walked by the Round Tower, looming in the centre of the castle's inner ward. There was no need to reveal Solay's secret tonight. The threat alone would give her pause. Besides, the Council would never approve her grant, so what did it matter?

But as he entered the chapel and bowed before the altar, the knowledge of her lie, and the desperation that caused it, lay in his gut like an undigested meal.

Right next to the admission that, for once in his life, he was holding back the truth.

Beside Lady Agnes, Solay walked out of the midnight Mass with a stiff neck from craning to watch the King. She knelt when the King knelt, rose when the King rose, following his movements as closely as his shadow.

At least she did until Lord Justin blocked her view. He moved to his own rhythm, never glancing at the King, or at anyone else, except once, when he caught her eyes with an expression that seemed to say, 'Can't you even be yourself before God?'

Who was he to judge her? she thought, shivering beneath her thin cloak. He did not know her life.

But he already knew a secret that threatened her. And her clumsy attempt to kiss him had made matters worse.

Everyone wanted something. If she could learn what he wanted, perhaps she could help him get it in exchange for his silence.

Agnes must know something. 'Lady Agnes,' she began, 'what do you—?'

'I need the room to myself tonight,' Lady Agnes whispered back, not looking at her.

Craving the few hours of rest between the Christmas Eve and Christmas dawn Masses, Solay opened her mouth to protest, then stopped. This was why Agnes had offered to share a room with her. Agnes needed someone to cover for her when she had a rendezvous.

Lady Agnes had chosen wisely. Solay murmured her assent.

As the crowd fanned out across the inner ward toward the residential apartments, she wondered where she might pass the night. Lagging behind the others, she slipped around the Round Tower and over to the twin-towered gate her father had built before she was born. Perhaps it would shelter her tonight.

She slipped inside and started up the stairs, but, halfway up, she heard a noise in the darkness below. She climbed faster. Another set of footsteps echoed hers.

Who could it be? Even the guards had been given a Christmas respite.

The man was gaining on her.

Holding her skirts out of the way, she tried to run, but he was faster. As the scent of cedar touched her, her heart beat faster, the fear replaced with something even more dangerous.

'Lady Solay, you must be lost.'

She turned, holding back a laugh at the very idea. 'I cannot be lost, Lord Justin. I was born here.' The castle had been her playground when she was near a princess. At the memory, her chest ached with loss long suppressed.

'Born here, yet you can't seem to remember the day and you don't know the difference between the gate tower and the residential wing.' He took her arm. 'I'll take you to your room.'

'No!' She pulled her arm free, and turned gingerly on the narrow stair. He was still too close. 'Sleep is difficult for me,' she said. That, strangely, was true. She wondered why she had shared it with him.

'So you wander the castle like a spectre?'

She grabbed an excuse. 'I was going to study the stars to prepare for the King's reading.' He would not know that a horoscope came from charts and not from the sky.

He moved closer. 'Then I will accompany you.'

She released a breath, not caring whether he believed her. At least Agnes was safe.

Their steps found the same rhythm as they climbed to the top of the Tower. Cold air rushed into her lungs as they emerged from the dark stairway on to the battlements. After the darkness of the Tower, the night, lit by stars, seemed almost bright, although the half-moon shed only enough light to polish the strong curve of his jaw.

He waved his hand towards the sky, a gesture as much of dismissal as of presentation. 'So, milady, look out on the stars and make what sense of them you will.'

She looked up and her heart soared, as it always did. How many sleepless nights had she spent trying to discern their secrets? Now, like familiar friends, their patterns kept her company when sleep would not come.

She hugged herself, trying to warm her upper arms. He moved behind her, his broad back cutting the wind, suddenly making her feel sheltered, though his voice turned cold. 'Strange method of study. In the dark. Without notes or instruments.'

'I only need to watch them to learn their meaning.'

He snorted. 'Then all soldiers should be experts on the stars.' Behind her, he took her by the shoulders, his breath intimate as he whispered in her ear, 'Do you know any more of the stars than you do of your birth date?'

She swallowed. Was it his question or his nearness that caused her to tremble? 'I know more than most.'

Yet of the stars, like many things, she knew only the surface. By memorising the list of ascendants in her mother's Book of Hours, she had gleaned enough to impress most people, but only enough to tantalise herself.

Thankfully, he let her go and leaned against the wall next to her. 'You could not know what takes the University men years to learn.'

His dismissal rankled. 'I *had* years.' Years after they left court and her mother was busy with suits and counter-suits.

His dark eyes, lost in shadow, gave her no clue to his thoughts. 'And did the stars give you the answers you sought?'

His question surprised her. She had studied the heavens because she had nothing else to do. She had studied hoping they might explain her life and give her hope for the future. 'I am still searching for my answers, Lord Justin. Did you find yours in the law?'

He turned away from her question, so silent she could hear the lap of the river out of sight below the walls.

'I was looking for justice,' he said, finally.

'On earth?' She felt a moment's sympathy for him. How disappointing his life must be. 'You'd do better to look to the stars.' The stars surely had given her this time alone with him. She should be speaking of light, charming things that might turn him into an ally. 'Let me read yours. When were you born, Lord Justin?'

He frowned. 'Do you think your feeble learning can discover the truth about me?'

She touched his unyielding arm with a playful hand. 'My learning is good enough for the King.'

Her fingers burned on his sleeve. She swayed towards him.

He picked up her hand. All the heat between them flowed from his fingers and into her core. He held her a moment too long, then dropped her hand away from his arm.

'The King cares more for flattery than truth.' His voice was rough. 'I would not believe a word you say.'

She waved her hand in the air, as if she had not wanted to touch him at all. As if his dismissal had not hurt her. 'Yet you believe in justice on earth.'

'Of course. That's what the law is for.'

Was anyone so naïve? 'And when the judges are wrong? What then?'

'The condemned always claim they've been unjustly convicted.'

Fury warmed her blood. Parliament had given her mother no justice. 'Even if the judgement is right, is there never forgiveness? Is there never mercy?'

'Those are for God to dispense.'

'Oh, so justice lives on earth, mercy in Heaven, and you

happily sit in judgement confident that you are never wrong.' She laughed without mirth.

'You believe your mother should be exonerated.'

Surprised he recognised a meaning she had missed, she was silent. Better not to even acknowledge such a hope. Better not to picture her mother back at court and revered for the good she had done. 'She was brought back to court before the year was out.' Restored to her position beside the King for his last, painful year.

'Not by Parliament.'

'No, by the King himself. The Commons never had the right to judge her. And neither do you.'

'It is you I judge. You've lied about your birth date. I suspect you are lying about why you are not abed. It seems truth means nothing to you.'

'Truth?' He talked of truth as if it were more valuable than bread. She held her tongue. She had already been too candid. If she angered him further, he would never keep her secret. 'Perhaps each of us knows a different truth.'

'There is only one truth, Lady Solay, but should you ever choose to speak it, I would scarce recognise it.' His voice brimmed with disgust.

'You do not recognise it now. My mother was a great helpmate to the King.'

He shook his head. 'Even you can't believe that.' A yawn overtook him. 'I'm going to bed. I leave you to your stars and your lies.'

'Some day when I tell you the truth, you will believe it,' she whispered to his fading footsteps.

Shivering and alone under a sky that seemed darker than before, she crossed her arms to keep from reaching for him as he descended the stairs.

CHAPTER THREE

SOLAY snatched only an hour of sleep after Mass, then spent the feast day watching Justin and wondering whether he planned to expose her lie. Finally, exhausted, she escaped for a nap as soon as the King left the Christmas feast.

Her respite was brief. Before dark, Lady Agnes bustled into the room, carrying a white robe and two bare branches. 'Here's my costume for the disguising.' She held up the simple off-white shift and waved the branches over her head. 'Will I not look like a hart?'

A knock relieved Solay of responding. Agnes would resemble a horned angel more than a white stag.

At the door, a page, garbed in a vaguely familiar livery of three gold crowns on a blue background, handed Agnes a note and ran. She read it, then, smiling, closed the door.

'I need you to take my part in the disguising,' she whispered.

'I would be honoured,' Solay told her, trying to place the page's livery. How bold to ignore the King's entertainment for a private tryst. Did lusting make one so mad?

'Quick. We haven't much time.' Agnes helped Solay

into the undyed gown, slipped a linen hood over her face, and tied the branches around her head.

'Tell me what I must do.' Beneath the hood, she squinted, trying to see out of the eye holes.

'Just watch the others in white. Do as they do and at the end, curl up at the feet of the one who plays the King.' Agnes stopped tugging on the robe and peered through the slits in the hood to meet Solay's gaze. 'They must think you are me.'

Behind the hood, Solay laughed. 'I'm disguised and I've just come to court. Who will recognise me?'

'Everyone saw you yesterday.'

Everyone watched in glee as the King humiliated her, Agnes meant. And then, of course, the men had come for a closer look.

But only Justin had really seen her.

Agnes squeezed Solay's fingers. 'Please. Do not remove your hood, no matter what. Too many know what part I was to take.' Agnes opened the door a crack, looked both ways, then pushed Solay into the hall. 'And thank you,' she whispered, her round blue eyes full of gratitude.

Solay crept down the stairs to the Great Hall, fingers touching the cool stone wall for balance. The branches wobbled uncertainly at the back of her head. Anonymous beneath her white hood, she felt strangely free as she entered the Hall.

Until she saw Justin.

Head down, he huddled with three other men. He was not costumed, of course. This man refused to disguise himself or his feelings.

As she walked towards the masked group gathering at

the end of the Hall, his gaze drifted from the conversation to follow her. Knowing he was watching, she realised that Agnes's costume exposed her ankles and hung slack around her hips. She turned her back on him and touched her hood to make sure her hair was covered. A stray dark lock would betray her.

The King's herald called for silence and she pulled her attention back to the tableau. Like a mirror, the scene reflected the King who observed it. A pretend King sat on a mock throne. Heavenly beings in blue surrounded him. Beasts of the field came to lie at his feet.

As she moved to her place, the court seemed as much of a façade as the play, beautiful on the surface, but concealing each player's true nature. When she lay at the foot of the false throne and heard the applause, she wondered which player had donned Agnes's lover's garb.

'Up. Now,' someone behind her whispered.

Around her, players moved into the audience, pulling them into the scene. As she rose to follow, she glimpsed a deep blue robe through the slits in her hood. All around them, laughing men and women joined the pretty scene, posing like statues. Afraid to look up, she saw a hand, grasped it and pulled.

At his touch, her fingers seemed to dissolve. For that moment, there was no separation between them.

He ripped his hand away, refusing not with the good-natured, temporary reluctance of the rest, but with stubborn belligerence.

She made the mistake of looking up.

Beneath the heavy brows, she saw no doubt in his eyes. It was Justin. And he knew her.

She turned, reaching with both hands to draw in two courtiers next to him, trying to escape. As the real and the pretend court merged, the King applauded and some of the disguisers lifted their masks.

Ducking behind the pretend throne, Solay fled into the hall. The man in the King's garb left, too, mask still in place, turning in the opposite direction.

She had almost reached the stairs when Justin's voice licked her back.

'You do not raise your hood with the rest, Lady Solay.'

'You mistake me.' She climbed the first two stairs, back to him. Perhaps a carefully rolled *r* would fool him. 'I am a white hart, pious and pure.'

'You are neither pious nor pure and your accent sounds nothing like the Lady Agnes.'

She lowered her eyes, her lashes scraping the linen hood, still hoping to deny who she was.

Too late. He pulled off the hood, letting the fake antlers skitter down the stairs, and took her chin in his hand, forcing her to look into his eyes, dark with anger, and something more.

His breath touched her cheek. 'And her eyes are not the colour of royalty.'

Her lips parted and she struggled to catch a breath that did not smell of him.

He swayed nearer, his lips dangerously close to hers. One more breath, and they would touch.

He let her go and held out the hood. 'No, I see you are nothing like a hart.'

She snatched it back, her breath still coming fast. What

good would she be to Lady Agnes now? 'Did you not think I played the part well?'

He dusted his palms, to brush off her touch. 'It seems all of life is a disguising to you, a deception for amusement.'

''Tis not true,' she said, though the idea gave her pause. She had mirrored the others in the play, just as she did every day, playing a part to please the watcher.

'Where is Lady Agnes this evening?' he asked, ignoring her answer.

'She was taken ill. She did not want to disappoint their Majesties.'

'So you lie for others as well as for yourself.'

'Why do you assume I lie?' Not only did the man demand truth, he had an uncanny knack of discerning it.

'Because I saw Lady Agnes just after the feast. She was laughing and excited about her part in the disguising. Where is she?'

'She was taken to her bed suddenly,' she said, hoping still to hide Agnes's sin.

'I'm certain she was, but not by illness and not alone.' His strong brows furrowed with disapproval.

'I told you, she didn't feel well.' Her tongue ran away with her, trying to make him believe. 'She must have eaten too much of the noodles and saffron.'

'You are the only one who thinks that Hibernia's trysts with Lady Agnes are a secret.'

Her cheeks went cold. 'I am newly come to court.' Where ignorance of such secrets was dangerous. No wonder the page's livery looked familiar. The Duke was the

King's dearest companion. Poor, foolish Agnes. 'And if that is so, there's nothing to be gained by speaking of tonight.'

'You seem to have nothing but secrets, Lady Solay. Don't expect me to keep them for ever.'

'I denied you a kiss last night.' She had been told a woman's body could enslave a man, though she knew little of how. She leaned close to him, feeling her breasts soft against his hard chest, fighting her traitorous body as it weakened next to his. 'Perhaps you want it now?'

He raised his arms. She waited, wanting him to take her.

Instead, his hands curved into fists. Nothing else moved except the truth of his response, pounding below his waist.

Then, he pushed her away. 'You are just like your mother.' He spat the words like a curse.

She gripped his sleeve, fighting her anger. She had tried to tell him about her mother, but this implacable man had no compassion. And now, her foolish move had only strengthened his mistrust.

She swallowed her emotions and tried to think clearly. 'What do you want? What can I give you?'

The harsh planes of his face held no more feeling than a stone. 'Nothing. The Council will not be swayed by kisses, Lady Solay.' He uncurled her fingers from their grip on his sleeve. 'And neither will I.'

Shaking, Solay watched him leave, fear drowning both her want and her anger. She knew how to charm men. She had even cajoled the King, but this man, this man could resist everything she offered. This man could ruin it all.

She slipped the hood over her head and hurried back to her room, knocking cautiously before entering.

She opened the door to the scent of lovemaking. The smell tugged at her. What would that be like, to share such closeness?

She shut the door behind her. Dangerous. It would be dangerous.

Agnes sprawled under the covers, tears streaking her rounded cheeks.

Had Agnes's sad lesson come so soon? 'What's the matter?'

'His wife comes tomorrow.'

She had wondered where the Duchess was while all the King's favourites were gathered at Windsor. Perhaps she had stayed home to avoid humiliation. 'She travels on Christmas day?' The rumours must have driven her to protect herself. No wonder the urgency to bed him one more time. Surely, Agnes would see him no more after his wife arrived.

Agnes shrugged her answer, speechless in the face of disaster. She folded a little white piece of cloth and blew her nose.

Solay sat on the side of the bed and patted her arm. 'It's all right. Everything will work out,' she said, without sincerity. Such naïveté could only lead to pain. What had the silly goose expected? That he would leave his wife for his mistress?

Agnes sat up in bed, sniffing back the tears. 'I know. You're right. I must be patient.' She squeezed Solay's hands. 'Thank you. You're a true friend.'

She blinked. She had known few women and never one who had called her friend. Women did not like her, as a rule.

Agnes blew her nose again and tried to smile. 'Now, tell me—how was the disguising? It was beautiful, no?'

'Oh, yes. The King clapped loudly.'

'No one recognised you?'

She turned away as she folded the wrinkled linen hood and slipped out of the shift. 'Nothing has changed.' Based on what Justin had said, the Duke and Agnes had no secrets left. 'Tell me, Agnes. What do you know of Lord Justin Lamont?'

Agnes's smile slipped into a frown. 'He's a terrible man. He's the one who led Parliament to impeach the King's Chancellor.'

Solay shuddered. Worse than a man of law, worse than a Council member. He was a man who would manoeuvre Parliament to destroy those closest to the King, just as her mother's enemies had done. 'So he truly is the King's foe.'

Agnes leaned forward. 'They want to attack my dear Duke as well,' she whispered, as if afraid someone might hear, 'but they do not dare. He is the King's right arm.'

Agnes had let slip her lover's identity. The poor girl truly believed he was safe, but in times such as these, no one was safe. Still, if Agnes trusted her, perhaps Solay could glean something useful. 'Lord Justin does the Council's legal work?'

Agnes snuggled back under the covers with a pout. 'I suppose. Who knows how any man spends his time when not with a woman? Documents, diplomacy, bookkeeping.' She shrugged, as if it were unimportant.

Solay stared, stunned. Her mother had taught her that the work of the King was the work of the world. While feminine arts gave them diversion, money and power, law and war ruled the earth. How could Agnes not care about those things?

'But that's not what you really want to know,' Agnes continued, with a catlike smile. 'I saw him watch you with hunger during the Christmas feast. You want to know what kind of man he is.'

'He is the King's enemy.' *And mine.* 'That is all I need to know.'

'But not all you want to know. He's handsome, isn't he? Many women think so, but he has refused them all.' Agnes tilted her head. 'I heard he was to be wed, many years ago, and the girl died.'

'So he mourns still?' Somehow, he did not seem like a man who pined for a dead love.

'He has no interest in marriage.'

'His family allows it?' He was certainly nine and twenty. The family must want an heir.

'He is a second son. His brother has many children. But beware, Solay. He and the Lords Appellant would destroy the King.'

Should Justin demand more than kisses for his silence, how could she refuse? 'He does not tempt me. I am only trying to learn who's who.'

'Good. I saw you with the Earl of Redmon. He might make a good husband. His wife died on Michaelmas and he has three children who need tending. He might not be too particular. I mean…' A blush spread over her cheek-bones. 'I'm sorry.'

'It's all right.' There would be no marriage for Solay. She had nothing to offer a husband but her body, unless the mere taste of royalty might titillate a man. 'I am not thinking of a husband.' Her hopes lay with a grant from the

King, not with a group of lords with temporary power, and if she were to please the King, she must produce a horoscope and a poem.

'Tell me, Agnes, who is the King's favourite poet?'

CHAPTER FOUR

As the Lord of Misrule pranced around the table two days after Christmas, Justin felt no Yuletide spirit.

Across the room, Solay laughed gaily at something John Gower the poet said.

Justin was not laughing.

He sank his teeth into the roast boar. At least the King had bowed to convention and put a whole pig on the spit for the Yule feasts. Usually, the meat at table was spiced, sugared, and so shredded you could eat it with a spoon.

Robert, Duke of Hibernia, had left the King's side to wander the room and now stood laughing with Solay. That man alone was enough to make him scowl. He was so close to the King that he seemed to fancy that he, too, was royal.

And judging by her wide-eyed attention to him, Solay knew it as well.

He heard her husky laugh again.

Just like her mother, she would lie and cheat and use anyone to get what she wanted. He had avoided her for the past two days, but, mistrustful of her motives, had watched her from afar.

Be honest with yourself, Lamont. This has nothing to do with your distrust of her. You just can't keep your eyes off the woman.

How had he let himself be guiled into holding her lies? Now her falsehoods tainted him, too, and, instead of thanks, she accused him of some subversive purpose. He should expose her and have her expelled from court.

But then he would remember the pain in her eyes.

He was ever the fool for a woman in pain.

More than a fool, for the pain he thought he saw was probably as false as her offered kisses.

Gloucester joined him, swilling wine from his goblet. 'Your eyes are ever upon the Lady Solay.'

'Her eyes have turned on every man in the room.' Most had leered at her as long as she'd let them. 'I even saw her talking to you.'

Gloucester smiled. 'She has her mother's talent for pleasing powerful men, but if she seeks a husband, she'll be hard pressed to find one who will have her.' He lifted his goblet in a parting toast and laughed, moving on down the hall.

Husband. Startled, Justin looked for her in the crowd. She was smiling at the Earl of Redmon, a recent widower as a result of his third wife's fall down the stairs. Why had he never thought of marriage for her? A husband would do her more good than a grant, if he came with enough property and a willingness to take on Alys of Weston as a mother-in-law.

And the right husband would not require the Council's approval. Only the King's.

He looked to the dais. Despite the joy of the season, the King's scowl matched Justin's own. Since he had told the King that the Council refused his appointments, Richard had been in a foul mood.

Tonight, he sulked while the poor fool, the Lord of Misrule, tried to create merriment by ordering the most unlikely couples to embrace.

The Fool forced Hibernia into an embrace with Lady Agnes. Hibernia and Agnes seemed to be enjoying it mightily. The man's wife did not.

Solay had assumed a bland smile. He wondered what it hid.

The thought deepened his frown, so when the Fool waved his crown before Justin's eyes, blocking his vision of Solay, Justin only grunted.

The Fool would not be dissuaded. 'Now here's another man who needs to show more Yuletide cheer. Who would you like to kiss this evening?'

'No one. Leave me be.'

'Ah, but your eyes have been on the Lady Solay. Would you like to put your lips on her as well?'

Hearing her name, Solay turned to look.

His entire body surged to answer. He had refused her kisses before, but those she fawned over tonight might not. The wine had loosened his resistance. Surely, he, too, deserved a taste. 'Yes,' he answered. 'I would kiss the daughter of the sun.'

Her eyes widened and her lips parted, as if she inhaled to speak, but no words came.

The diners next to him went silent. Was it because he

dared kiss the daughter of a King? Or because no one wanted to be reminded of who she was?

The jester's babbling broke the awkward silence. 'The Lord of Misrule makes all things possible.' He grabbed Justin's hand and pulled him around the table, to face Solay.

Trapped in the jester's grip, Justin watched her eyes darken with desire, and regretted his honesty. What would happen when he took her lips? He steeled himself against her. Nothing. She was a woman, nothing more.

The Lord of Misrule laughed merrily. 'Your wish is my command. Kiss the lady!'

She was too close now, close enough that her scent engulfed him. She smelled of rose petals hidden in a golden box, sweet, yet protected by metal that only fire would melt.

He wanted to take her in his arms, crush her to him and ravish her lips with his. He wanted to possess her, yet something warned him that she would possess him instead.

Her lips parted, but her eyes did not droop with desire. They were open, wide with fear.

He put his hands on her arms, deliberately holding himself away from her body, leaned over and put his lips on hers.

Her lips were soft as he'd expected, but they lay cool and unyielding beneath his. When she did not respond, something burst within him. She had teased him for days. For all those other men, she supplicated and simpered.

He would have what she offered.

He pulled her close, feeling her breasts, soft, pressing against him. Suddenly, he did not care who she was or where they were. He wanted her kiss, yes, but whatever else she hid, he wanted that, too.

The kiss she had dangled before him for days blossomed and the impossible scent of roses made him dizzier than the wine. When she opened to him, he took her lips and thrust his tongue into her mouth, wanting to taste all of her. Her stiffness became softness and he tightened his arms, fearing she would fall if he let go.

And only the beat of the jester's wand on his shoulder brought him to himself.

'The man's eaten nothing but oysters all night,' the jester said.

Drunken laughter around them brought heat to his cheeks.

He pulled away, torn between desire and scorn, and glimpsed on her face the truth he'd sought.

She wanted him.

Her eyes were dark with desire, her mouth ripe with lust. Then she touched her lips and blinked the softness from her eyes, and for once he was grateful—her disguise protected them both.

The jester turned to Solay. 'Since you have suffered this dullard's embrace, you deserve a wish of your own. What boon can I grant the lady?'

She grabbed her goblet and lifted it toward the King's table. 'I desire to toast our gracious Majesties, King Richard and Queen Anne. Long life, health and defeat of all their enemies.'

Tapered fingers hugging the chalice, she lifted it to drink, but instead of looking at the King, her eyes met Justin's.

He touched his goblet to his lips, wishing the wine could wash away her kiss.

Now that he had tasted her, he could no longer deny that

her body tugged at his loins. Her eyes put him in mind of bedchambers and the pale skin of her inner wrist made him want to see the pale skin of her thighs.

All the better, then, if she took a husband, although none of the popinjays at court seemed right. As long as she kept out of the King's Treasury, she was no concern of his.

Gloucester returned to his side. 'How does she taste?'

Like no one else in the world. ''Twas but a Yuletide jest.'

'You obviously enjoyed it,' Gloucester said. 'And you put her in her place.'

The words kindled his shame. She had succumbed, yes, but he had forced her. No matter that she had tried to tempt him earlier. He had let his desire overrun his sense, spoken his want aloud, then forced it upon her.

And he had promised himself never to force a woman. He knew too well the bitter results.

For that, she deserved an apology.

Unable to sleep, Solay looked out of the window at the last star fading in the blue dawn light. An insistent rooster heralded the coming day, yet beside her in the bed, Agnes slept undisturbed, her gentle, drunken snore ruffling the air.

Solay, too, felt drunk, perhaps from the wine or the sweetness of the almond cake.

Or perhaps from his kiss. It still burned her mouth and seared her mind, speaking of promises not to be hoped for, particularly from a man who hated her.

Wide awake, she rolled over. What boon does the lady want? the Fool had asked. She wanted such simple things. To be safe. To be looked at without scorn. To sleep through the night without worrying whether they would have food to meet the morrow. To see her mother smile and hear her sister laugh.

And tonight, God help her, she wanted him.

She crept from bed and grabbed her cape as Agnes snored on. Crossing the ward, she climbed again to the roof of the tower. As a child, she had loved to watch the sun rise. Each time, she could begin life anew. For those few moments when first light touched the world, she had had no one to please, no one to *be* but herself.

Here, as the winter wind quieted in anticipation of the life-giving ball of light, she could believe that the stars ruled people's lives and that she was truly a daughter of the sun.

She recognised his steps, surprised that, after only a few days, she knew his gait. As he reached the ramparts, she composed her smile and turned, dizzy at the sight of him.

Impossible hopes danced in her heart. 'Did the Lord of Misrule send you after me again?'

He held himself stiffly, his hands clenched as if to keep from reaching for her. 'We must talk.' The words seemed forced. 'About the kiss.'

Kiss. The word lingered on lips that had moved soft and urgent over hers. The memory brought heat to her cheeks and to places deeper inside. 'What is there to say?'

'I should not have forced you.'

So. He regretted his passion now. Well, she would not reveal her weakness for him. He would only use it against her in the end. She shrugged. 'It is Yuletide. It meant nothing.'

'Really?'

His question trapped her. To admit he moved her would

leave her with no defence. *Oh, Mother, how do I protect myself against the wanting?*

'Of course not.' She crafted a light and airy tone so he would not know she had dissolved at his kiss and no longer recognised the new form she found herself in. 'You took no more than I had offered.'

'Well, then…' He nodded, finishing the sentence and the incident. His rigid muscles relaxed, but he did not move closer. 'What brings you to the roof, Lady Solay? It is too late to see the stars.'

'I come to watch the sun.'

She was grateful that the breeze quickened and blew his scent away from her. One more step and she might reach for his shelter.

'The sun is near its lowest point, Lady Solay. It has withdrawn its light from the world.'

His words brought back her childhood fears. Sometimes, as her life had changed, she had watched for the sun to rise, uncertain that it really would. 'Yet it was at this, the darkest hour upon earth, that the brightest son was born.'

'Are you speaking of the Saviour or the King?'

She smiled. The analogy had not occurred to her, but it might make a flattering conceit for the King's reading. 'Both.'

'The sun comes up every morning.' He leaned on the battlements, facing her. 'Why do you find it worthy of watching?'

'Why? Just look.'

He turned.

In anticipation of sunrise, the sky erupted in colour— bruised purple at the horizon, then striped blue, and finally brilliant pink. 'The heavens are more reliable than your justice. The sun comes up every morning.' Her words came out in a whisper. 'Even in our darkest hours.'

'Have you had many of those?'

'Enough.' More than dark hours. Dark years after the death of the old King snuffed the life-giving sun from their sky.

'But you survived.' No compassion softened his words.

She blocked the memories. She had spoken too much of herself and her needs. 'Has the world never been harsh to you?'

'No more than to most.' Pain gilded his answer, but whatever weakness had sent him to the roof in near-apology was gone when he looked at her. 'Do not try to play on my sympathies. You will not change my mind about your grant.'

The memory of the kiss pulsed between them. Could an appeal to his sense of justice change his mind? 'King Richard has given his clerks more than we would need.'

'And the clerks didn't deserve it either.'

'Don't deserve?' Despite her resolution, harsh words leapt to her tongue. 'The King is the judge of that, not you.'

'Not according to Parliament.'

'Parliament!' She spat the word. 'Those greedy buzzards stripped us of everything, not only what the King had freely given, but lands my mother acquired with her own means.'

'Lands she took from others and did not need.'

'She needed them to support us after his death.'

'She had a husband to take care of her, more fool he. Better to ask for a husband to support you.'

'Now you mock me.' Husbands were for women with dowries and respected families. 'No one would have me.'

'If the King decreed, someone would.'

'Then perhaps I shall ask him.' The very idea left her giddy.

He grabbed her arms and forced her to look at him. Some special urgency burned behind his eyes. 'Don't let him force you. Only wed if it is someone you want.'

Her heart beat in her throat as she looked at him. That was why her mother had warned her against this feeling. If the King decreed, it would not matter whom she wanted.

She stepped back and he let his hands drop. 'If someone weds me, be assured that I will want him.'

Disgust, or sadness, tinged his look. 'And if you don't, you'll tell him you do.' The brilliant colours of daybreak faded as the sun emerged. The sky had no colour; the sun, no warmth. 'Here's your sun, Lady Solay,' he said, turning towards the stairs. 'May it bring you a husband in the New Year.'

As his footsteps faded, the image he had suggested tantalised her like the dawn at the edge of the day. Marriage. Someone to take care of her.

She pulled her cloak tighter and let the wind blow the fantasy away. Better to focus on pleasing the King with a pleasant poem and a pretty future.

But Justin's suggestion tugged at her. Perhaps he had deliberately shown her the path to circumvent the Council.

If the King had no power to grant her family a living, he might find an alliance for her with a family that would not allow hers to starve.

And if the King were gracious enough to find her a husband, she would take whomever he gave, even if the man's kisses did not make her burn.

CHAPTER FIVE

As the sun rose to its pale peak on the last day of the year, Solay set aside the astrology tables in despair. She read no Latin, so she could understand none of the text. In a week, the Yuletide guests would be gone, and she with them unless she could create a story from the stars to please a King.

Before she wove a fiction, she had tried to decipher the truth, but the symbols in the chart the old astrologer had drawn blurred before her eyes.

She trusted no one for help except Agnes. When she had asked what ill omens the old astrologer had seen, Agnes's already pale face turned white.

'He said the King must give up his friendship with the Duke of Hibernia or the realm would be in danger.'

No wonder the man had been jailed.

Idly, she flipped through the tables of planets, wondering when Lord Justin Lamont had been born. He had the stubbornness of the Bull, but his blunt speech reminded her of the Archer. Perhaps one of them was the ascendant and the other…

Foolishness. She put the tables aside and turned to her real work. Her future lay in the hands of the King, not in the kisses of Justin Lamont.

She studied the King's birth chart again. Some aspects didn't match the temperament of the King she knew. Aggressive Aries was shown as his ascendant, yet he seemed the least warlike of kings.

The eleventh house was that of friends; the twelfth of enemies. Surely just a slight shift could move the Duke from one to the other.

A different time of birth would do it.

She turned pages with new energy. She would populate the chart as she wished and suggest it had changed because she used a different time of birth.

Smiling, she began to draw.

By late afternoon, she derived a chart that suited her purpose, and, it seemed, the King much better. A square formed the centre of the chart, Capricorn, his sun sign. Four triangles surrounded it, forming the four cardinal points as triangles from each side. Then, the additional eight houses formed another square around the first.

The shift clustered more planets in the house of friends, but it also described his character more accurately. From this one, she could spin a happy future for the King and, she hoped, for her family.

She hesitated. If it were dangerous to change her own time of birth, what would she risk to change the King's?

Yet it was the only answer she had. At least she was sensible enough to tell him no bad news. No one was likely to know enough to dispute her conclusions and, if anyone did, she would laugh and say she was only a woman and not a real astrologer.

Justin's mind wandered as the Court wasted the afternoon listening to bad verse penned by courtiers playing poet. The words flowed around him unheard. He had spent the last week telling himself that he was relieved that the kiss had meant nothing to Solay, though it galled him that she could swoon in his arms like a lover and then laugh. He should have expected nothing less. Even the woman's body lied.

Across the room, she was fawning over Redmon again. Since he had told her to seek a husband, Justin judged every man she spoke to for the role. She would have few choices. The man must have money, not need it, for she would bring no dowry. He must be acceptable to the King, but not too important, for if he were, he would get a better bride.

She gave the Earl a dazzling smile as it came her turn to present. Then, she licked her full, lower lip, cleared her throat, glanced at Justin and started to read.

They call them men of law, an empty boast
They claim that law means justice
But justice comes quickest to him that pays the most.

His cheeks burned. Though no one looked his way as they laughed, he knew her words were directed towards him. Her poem told an amusing tale of a dishonest lawyer, brought to justice by a benevolent and pure King. The verse lacked polish, but it showed promise. The words were clever.

More than clever. Something about them seemed very familiar.

After the King applauded heartily and the afternoon's entertainment ended, Justin sought her out. Her small triumph had touched her lips with an easy smile.

'A pretty poem, Lady Solay,' he said. 'Did you suggest the subject to John Gower?'

Solay's smile stiffened. 'What makes you ask that?'

He did not dignify her lack of denial with an answer. 'I did not think him a man to be swayed by kisses.'

She did not blush, which made him think she had not tried physical persuasion of the King's favourite poet. Odd, he felt relieved.

'The idea was his, not mine. He told me he was trying something new and if the King did not like the poem, Gower would put it aside. Since the King liked it very much, I dare say he will finish it and then tell the King and they will both think it a good joke.'

'So now I must keep secrets for John Gower's sake, not yours?'

Behind the pleading look in her eyes he saw the shadow of resentment. It must gall her to beg his co-operation. 'You wouldn't spoil the surprise, would you, just because the verse doesn't flatter you?'

Shocked, he realised he had never even considered it. 'It is Gower you wronged, not me. You sling borrowed barbs about lawyers, but you know nothing about me at all.'

'I know you helped Parliament impeach the King's Chancellor on imaginary charges.'

'The charges were real.'

'Not real enough, I see.' She nodded towards the Earl of Suffolk, laughing with the King. 'The man is with us today.'

He gritted his teeth. 'The King released him. Not Parliament.' Richard had imprisoned the man for a few weeks, then, as soon as Parliament had gone home, set him free as if Parliament had never ruled. As if the law meant nothing.

She lowered her voice to whisper. 'You say you care about truth, but others say you care more about destroying those closest to the King.'

'And you let others decide what you think.'

She didn't answer, but turned to smile at Redmon across the room. The man smiled back, broadly, and she started to leave.

'I hope you are not thinking of him as a husband.'

She kept searching the room, not meeting his eyes to answer. 'When you suggested marriage you did not request approval of the choice. In fact, you told me only the King could decide.'

One of the young pups across the room winked at her, elbowing his companion, and she gave him a slow smile.

The boy's grin grated on him. 'That one is not looking on you as a wife,' he growled.

'How do you know?'

'Because I am a man.'

'Well, the Earl of Redmon is.' Behind the lilt in her voice he heard the edge of anger.

'Did the stars tell you so?'

'He was born under the sign of the goat. We should get along well enough.'

'Did the stars also tell you that he is old and rich with wealth and sons and three dead wives? All he needs is someone to grace his bed. That should not be difficult for you.'

She gasped, but instead of satisfaction, he felt remorse. 'You fault me for failing some standard of your own devising. What do you expect of me, Lord Justin?'

'Only what I expect of anyone. To be what you are.'

She dropped the smile and let him see her anger. 'No, you expect me to be what you think my mother is.' She turned to leave.

'So each of us judges the other wrongly, is that what you think?' He grabbed her hand, stopping her as if he had the right.

The shock was almost as great as touching her lips.

Both of them stared down at their clasped hands, her hand, cool in his, his large, blunt fingers, covering her pale skin.

And something alive moved through him, the feeling of kissing her all over again. Then, he had been in his cups. Easy to explain being set afire by a beautiful woman. But this… He had simply touched her hand and now stood transfixed, unable to—

'Lord Justin, please.'

He looked up. This time, her slow, sultry smile was for him.

He dropped her hand. As she walked across the room to Redmon, he could swear she put an extra sway in her hips.

He smothered his body's quick response. He was

finished with this dangerous woman. Whether she married
or not was none of his affair as long as she did not dip her
hand into the King's purse.

Justin and Gloucester approached the King's solar shortly
before noon on the last day of the Yuletide festivities. Their
visit would be short and unpleasant, but at least Solay
should be gone at the end of it.

'Lamont? Did you hear me?' Gloucester's voice interrupted his thoughts.

'Sorry,' he answered. 'What did you say?'

'I'm going to throw this list in his face.'

Justin gathered his thoughts. It would fall to him to keep
things civil when the royal tempers slipped loose.

As they entered, King Richard extended his hand, im-
perially as if it held a sceptre. 'The list. Give it to me.'

Justin held out the list of grants to be enrolled on the
Patent Rolls 'with the assent of the Council'. 'The Council
has approved these four.'

The King glanced at the list. 'Where are the rest? Where
is Hibernia? Where is the woman?'

'They have not been allowed,' Justin said.

'Not been allowed? It is the King who allows!'

'Allowed?' Now it was Gloucester who yelled. 'You've
allowed France to seize our lands instead of defending them!'
he snapped, sounding more like an uncle than a subject.

Richard reached for his dagger. 'You impugn the power
of the throne? I'll have you hanged.'

They lunged towards each other, tempers flaring, while

the guards hung back, uncertain whether to protect the King or Gloucester.

Justin stepped between them. 'Please, Your Majesty, Gloucester.' Each stepped away, glowering.

Richard gritted his teeth. 'I will see *all* these grants allowed, including...' he looked at Gloucester, hate glowing in his eyes '...the one for the harlot's daughter.'

'You'll see none of them,' Gloucester said. 'Least of all that one!' He stomped out of the room without asking for leave.

Richard stood rigid with shock. Or anger.

Justin repressed his resentment. The King cared nothing for Solay except as a pawn to infuriate his uncle and the Council. 'Your Majesty, the Council has finished its review. There will be no more grants.'

Richard turned to Justin, his entire face pinched with rage. 'Be careful, Lord Justin.' His voice quavered with anger. 'Your Council may have power now, but I was born a King. Nothing can change that, especially not you and your puny law.'

A shiver slithered down Justin's back. When this man returned to power, he would grab what he wanted without a care for justice or the law. And Justin had been very, very much in the way of what he wanted.

On the afternoon of the twelfth day of Christmas, Solay was ushered into the King's private solar to present her reading. The King dismissed everyone but the Queen and Hibernia, an indication that he was taking her reading very seriously.

Solay's fingers shook as she smoothed the parchment with her new drawing. Her family's fate lay on its surface.

'Your Majesty,' she began, 'was born under the sign of the goat on the day three kings were in attendance on the babe in the manger. Surely this is auspicious. In addition—'

'This is all well known,' Hibernia scoffed. 'Can you tell us nothing new?'

She put aside the chart. Hibernia had tolerated her for Agnes's sake, but after what the last astrologer had said about him, he had no love of the art.

'Well, I believe there may be.' Her breath was shallow. Now. Now she must risk it. 'Is Your Majesty sure you were born near the third hour after sunrise?'

Silence shimmered. How could one doubt the King?

'Of course I'm sure. My mother told me.'

Next to him, Anne put a gentle hand on his arm and gave Solay a look that was hard to decipher. 'Why do you ask?'

Solay swallowed. 'My calculations suggest the hour was closer to *nones*.' That would have meant the middle of the afternoon.

'Impossible,' said the King.

Queen Anne stared at Solay, then turned to her husband and whispered. The King's eyes widened and they both stared at her.

She swallowed in the lengthening silence.

'Who told you this?' the King said.

'No one. I was simply trying to read the planets. Of course, I am no expert and could easily be wrong.'

'But you could not easily be right.'

She looked from one to another. 'Am I right?'

The Queen spoke with her customary calm. 'Richard's mother once told me she had put out a false time of birth so as not to give the astrologers too much power.'

Her body burned with a heat that did not come from the hearth. Power. The unfamiliar fire of power. The truth of her startling prediction had given her something she had never before possessed.

Power enough for him to fear.

The King leaned forward, pinning Solay with eyes that held an uneasy mixture of apprehension and curiosity. 'What new knowledge does that give you?'

She looked down at her chart, trying to think. Too much knowledge would be dangerous. 'There are differences in the two ascendants. Yours is now Gemini and your moon is in Aries.'

'But what does that mean?'

Flattery first. Then the request.

'Your people revere you, Your Majesty. You are a singular man among men, whose wisdom surpasses ordinary understanding.' She swallowed and continued. 'And you are exceedingly generous to faithful friends and those of your blood.'

'Such as you?' His smile was hard to decipher.

She should have known that a King had heard all the ways to say 'please'. 'And so many others.'

His mouth twisted in derision, but fear still haunted his eyes. 'What does it tell you,' he whispered, 'of my death?'

She took a deep breath. If she predicted long life incorrectly, they would only think her a poor astrologer. If she predicted death correctly, she could be accused of causing it.

'I see a long and happy reign for Your Majesty.' Actually, some darkness hovered over his eighth house, but this was no time to mention it. 'All your subjects will bless your name when you leave us for Heaven.'

He leaned forward, his teeth tugging at his lips. 'And when will that be, Lady Solay?'

She swallowed. 'Oh, I am but a student and cannot determine such a thing.'

'You were skilful enough to deduce the correct time of my birth. I'm surprised you could not be so precise with my life's end.'

She lowered her eyes, hoping she showed proper deference. She had stumbled into a dangerous position. It would take all her talent to balance the King's belief in her with his fear. 'Forgive me for my ignorance, Your Majesty.'

He leaned back in his chair, peering at her over steepled fingers. 'And are some of these things also true of you, since we share a birthday?'

Trapped by her lie, she decided the truth might serve her well. 'It is interesting that you ask, Your Majesty. Since I have come to court, I found that I, too, was misinformed about the time of my birth. I was not born on the same day as Your Majesty.'

He smiled, pleased, and did not ask when she was born.

Hibernia pinched the bridge of his nose and shook his head. 'You can hardly take this seriously, Your Majesty.'

He would be wise to say so. The old astrologer was

right. Hibernia was bad for the King. She simply chose not to say so.

'Of course I don't,' the King said, chuckling, as if relieved to be given an excuse. He rose and nodded at Solay. 'You shall have a new, fur-trimmed cloak for your work.'

'Thank you, Your Majesty.' She sank to her knees in what she hoped was an appropriate level of deference for an extravagant gift.

'And Lady Solay. You shall not read the stars again.' The faintest sheen of sweat broke the skin between his nose and his lips. 'For me, or for anyone.'

She nodded, murmuring assent. Her work as a faux astrologer had accomplished its purpose. Her uncanny prediction had raised the least bit of fear in the King. Useful, if managed carefully.

Deadly, if not.

She must make it useful in finding a husband.

The King had turned back to Hibernia, whispering, leaving her again on her knees.

'Safe journey home,' the Queen said as she left the room.

This could not be the end. 'I had hoped—' she began.

The two of them turned to see her kneeling, as if surprised she was still there.

'I had hoped,' she continued, 'that Your Majesty might take an interest in my family.'

The King exchanged a glance with Hibernia. 'Ah, yes. "Generous to those of your blood," you said. What kind of interest?'

You'll get no money, Lamont had said. *Better to ask for a husband.*

She cleared her throat. 'In my marriage, Your Majesty.'

Hibernia smirked. 'Marriage? To whom?'

She let a cat's smile curve her lips. Would it be too bold to suggest the Earl? 'Any man would be honoured to be recognised by his Majesty.'

The King eyed her warily, indecision in his frown.

The Duke leaned towards the King, chuckling. 'She seemed to enjoy kissing Lamont. Marry the two of them.'

She felt as if a bird were trapped in her throat, desperately beating its wings. 'Oh, no, Your Majesty, that was just under the Lord of Misrule. Meaningless as the Duke's kiss of Agnes.' A kiss, she belatedly remembered, that was not meaningless at all.

But the King was not listening. 'Marriage to Lamont. A very interesting idea.'

Her damnable want warred with her family's need. She wanted no marriage to an enemy of the King, yet she dare not criticise the Duke's suggestion. 'How kind of the Duke of Hibernia to suggest it, but I'm sure Your Majesty was thinking of someone else.'

'You wanted a husband. If I choose to provide this one, are you ungrateful?'

Still kneeling, she looked down at the floor, hoping her deference would mitigate his anger at her small show of defiance. 'Of course not, Your Majesty. It would be just the expression of your generous ascendant planet to bring Lord Justin so close to the throne.'

She looked up through her lashes to see him frown at her subtle reminder that he was elevating an enemy.

A light flared in his blue eyes. 'And for my magnificent generosity, I ask only one thing of you.'

'Anything, of course, Your Majesty.'

'You will keep me informed of his actions for the Council.'

Suddenly, his purpose was clear. This marriage was to be for the King's benefit, not hers. She should never have thought otherwise. 'Do you not think they will be in constant contact with Your Majesty as well as Lord Justin?'

'That's what you are to discover.'

She bowed her head in defeat. 'Of course, Your Majesty.'

'Do your part and perhaps I will provide a grant for your family next year.'

Next year, when the Council's charter expired and she would still be married to a man who hated her. 'Your Majesty is ever generous.'

King Richard waved to a page standing outside the door. 'Summon Lord Justin.'

The King's summons bode ill, Justin thought, as he entered Richard's chamber with a brief bow to what looked like twin kings.

Solay stood before the King and Hibernia. She touched her lips when he entered and his blood surged as he remembered the taste of them.

The King's fury of two hours ago had been replaced with his dangerous, calculating look. 'It seems the Lady Solay would marry.'

Startled, he ignored the twist in his stomach. Was this not exactly what he had suggested? 'Most women do.' He should be grateful the King had backed down from a confrontation with the Council over the woman. Belatedly, the amount she needed seemed minor.

'You seemed to enjoy her kiss.'

No reason to deny the truth. 'What man would not?' He felt a flare of envy for the one who would be her husband and have the right.

'So, then, you will be pleased to have her as your wife.'

Lust surged through him from staff to fingertips, drowning logic. To be able to bed her, to take her, seemed the only *yes* in the world.

He saw a flash of fear in her eyes, but she blinked and it was wiped away. Lips slightly parted, she looked up through her lashes as if she were at once trying to seduce him and play the innocent.

He was sure, and the thought brought him pain, that she was not.

His mind regained control over his body. The woman had neither honour nor honesty in her. 'She is not what she seems,' he said, the words shaken up through a rusty throat. It was long past time for truth. 'She does not share a birth date with Your Majesty.'

She flinched and he fought the feeling that he had somehow betrayed her.

'So she told me,' the King said. 'She was misinformed about her birth.' He smiled. 'As was I. Lady Solay seems to have some talent as a reader of the stars.'

'Or so she has convinced you. Did she also confess that her flattering verse was borrowed?'

Her eyes widened in surprise. Justin smiled, grimly. Had she expected he would keep her secrets for ever?

The King frowned, shifting on his chair. 'So you already know what a clever woman she is.'

'I would prefer an honest wife to a clever one.' It was not only the King he must dissuade. It was himself.

'You have difficult requirements, Lamont,' the King continued. 'You've already turned down two honest heiresses most younger sons would have embraced with fervour.'

He met Solay's eyes again, full of fresh pain. Just as that first time when she entered the Great Hall, he could not break away from the force that flowed between them.

'Speak.' The King's voice seemed to come across a great distance. 'Will you have her?'

What would the King do if he said 'no'? Give her to Redmon? The man likely pushed his last wife down the stairs when she became quarrelsome over his dalliances.

Solay mouthed the word 'please'. Her pleading, desperate eyes held echoes of another woman, another time. He had not been able to save that one.

For a moment, nothing else mattered.

'Yes,' he said, his gaze never leaving Solay.

The word stood between them, a pillar of fire. She released a breath and a smile trembled on her lips.

Having broken the spell, he found a kernel of sense left in his brain. This time he would not sacrifice his happiness for a woman he could not trust. This time he would be sure there was an escape.

He faced the King. 'But I have a condition.'

The King frowned. 'Condition?'

'I must be convinced that she loves me.'

She gasped and he smiled at her. It was an unusual demand,

and, in this case, an impossible one. Yet he had seen the disaster of a marriage forced. He would not brook it again.

The King dismissed him with a wave. 'I never thought you a man who believed the love poems, Lamont. Love can come later as my dear wife and I discovered.'

Having planned his escape, he found he could breathe again. 'Nevertheless, the Church requires we both consent freely. If I have stated a condition that is not met, the marriage will not be valid.'

He and Richard glared at each other. Even the King could not deny the power of the Church.

Solay glanced at the King. 'Allow us a word, Your Majesty.'

They stepped out of earshot of the King. As she touched his arm, he struggled to keep his mind in control.

'I know you care nothing for my life, but have you no care for your own? You are angering the King beyond reason.'

'I told you not to let him force you. And I won't be forced either.'

'There is fire between us, Justin,' she whispered, but her fingers choked his arm. 'I am willing and I shall learn to love you.'

He steeled himself against the fear in her voice. 'If I believe a word of love you say, I'll be sadly deluded. I have bought you some time to find a man you really want to marry. Perhaps you can convince some other fool of your love.'

He stepped away from her to face the King again, relieved to be removed from her touch. 'I stand by my word.'

'Nevertheless,' the King said, smiling, 'I shall have the first banns read next Sunday.'

Sunday. The reality of what he had done pressed on his shoulders like a stone.

'So soon?' she asked. 'We cannot wed until Lent is over.'

Hibernia cut in. 'There's time enough for you to marry before Lent begins.'

'We won't be married at all unless I am convinced of her love,' Justin said.

The King shrugged. 'Very well. Lady Solay, you have until the end of Lent to convince him of your love.' His look turned menacing. 'And, Lamont, you have until the end of Lent to be convinced.'

CHAPTER SIX

SOLAY ran after Justin as he left the King's solar, determined to begin her campaign to convince him she would be a loving and pliable mate.

She touched his arm to stop him before he reached the end of the hallway.

'I shall ask the King's permission to visit my mother and inform her of the impending marriage,' she began. 'Would you accompany me?'

'No.'

'Later, then. I would not interfere with your work—'

'Solay, stop. This is folly.'

'You were the one who suggested I marry.'

'I did not mean to me.'

'Then why did you agree?' Surely her whispered 'please' could not have convinced him. 'You care nothing for the King's approval.'

He met her eyes with that cold honesty she had come to know, yet a hint of caring shadowed his gaze. 'I did not want him to force you.'

'I was not forced. I want this marriage.' If she said the words more loudly, would they sound more convincing?

'You want a marriage, not a marriage to me.'

I don't have a choice! The thought screamed in her head. Without this marriage, she would return home empty-handed.

She tried to calm her mind. Fighting him would get her no closer to learning the Council's secrets.

She leaned against his chest. All those courtiers who had fawned over her mother for the King's sake, what words did they use? 'I think the King suggested we marry because he could see how much I already love you.'

He undraped her like an unwanted blanket. 'For someone with so much practice, you're a poor liar.'

No one else had ever thought so. 'Why can you not believe me? You feel the attraction between us.'

His eyes burned into hers. 'Lust, yes. I would lie if I denied that.'

She could feel his breath on her cheek, feel the tingle starting again deep inside her. He moved nearer and she closed her eyes, lifting her chin. Now. Now he would kiss her.

Suddenly the air was empty of him. She opened her eyes to see him standing out of reach, arms crossed. 'But lust is not love.'

She forced her eyelashes to flutter. 'But it can be a start, can it not?'

He shook his head. 'I am not a senile King looking for someone to warm my bed. I demand more than your body.'

What else did a woman have? 'The King lusted after

many women who shared his bed. My mother shared much more.'

'Let me tell you why you said "yes".' He held a finger to her lips to stop her from interrupting. 'You agreed to please the King. And I assure you, whatever reasons he had for this marriage are for his benefit, not yours.'

She said a silent prayer that he never discovered the real reason. 'Perhaps they were for *your* benefit. Isn't it high time you took a wife?'

'I have no interest in a wife. And if I did, I would not want a viper in my bed. Do you think if we are married I will change my mind about the living you want from the Crown?'

Any ordinary man would. She held her tongue.

He did not wait for her to answer. 'If you think to share my life, then you will be wasting your time long past Lent. I agreed so you could have time to pursue one of those men who has stared at you moon-eyed. By the end of Lent, you could have a willing husband. One you want, or at least one who wants you.'

'If we are betrothed, I hardly think others will see me as a potential bride.'

'Marriage itself doesn't stop most men,' he muttered.

She shook his stubborn sleeve. The King had given her a husband. She would have no second chance. 'But I want this marriage!'

'Then you will be very disappointed come Eastertide. Nothing you say or do will convince me that you are capable of love for anyone, particularly me.'

As he walked away, she realised that instead of merely

pleasing the King, she now had to convince a man who hated her that he should be tied to her for the rest of his life.

Given the task, the forty days of Lent seemed no longer than a flicker.

Within days, Solay left Windsor, riding in solitary splendour in a cart driven by one of the King's men, to inform her family of the impending marriage.

She rubbed her nose in the fur trim of her new cloak, rehearsing the smile she would wear when she told her mother she was to be wed. She knew not how to explain that she had failed to secure the grant her mother was expecting. Alys of Weston had been away from court too long. She would never understand that a Council might gainsay a King.

Despite her worries, peace melted her bones as the two-storey dower house with the six chimneys came into view. Pretending to be a castle, it was surrounded by a small moat. The whitewash had yellowed and the thatch needed patching, but it was all the home she'd had for the last ten years and more dear now than Windsor's corridors.

Jane ran out to meet her while her mother looked down from her upstairs window, smiling. Her fair-haired sister, clad in tunic and chausses, seemed to have grown in the weeks Solay had been away. Her boy's garb could no longer disguise her womanhood.

As they gathered in her mother's chambers, her mother's blue-veined hands stroked Solay's heavy cloak with reverence. 'The King has given you a magnificent gift. You must have pleased him.'

Solay handed her mother a box. 'And here is his gift for

you along with a message of great importance.' The smile she had practised came easily.

Her mother opened the box and froze, not speaking, her hand still on the lid.

'What is it?' Jane asked.

Her mother lifted an amethyst-studded brooch, rubbing her thumb over the cabochon stones. 'It was yours, once, Solay,' she said, in a voice that held too much hope. 'A gift from your father.'

Solay reached for it, but her mother held the piece tightly in her fingers. 'Jane, please read the King's letter to us.'

As her sister read the clerk's prose announcing her betrothal, the lines in her mother's face deepened. When the simple statement was done, she rose and paced before the fireplace. 'What land does he bring?'

'He is a second son.'

'Even second sons can sometimes—'

Solay shook her head. 'He is a man of the law,' she answered, struggling to say the words without a sneer. Or perhaps the flutter in her throat was the memory of his lips on hers. 'He owns property in London.'

'How much? Where?'

How could she have been so ill prepared? 'I don't know.'

'What is his income?'

Solay flushed, ashamed she did not know. 'At least forty pounds a year.'

'A King's ransom, to be sure,' her mother said, archly. 'So he brings you no land and little money.'

'I bring little enough.'

Her mother drew herself straighter, trapping Solay with

her gaze. 'The King called you daughter. That is more than enough.' For her mother, it would always be thus. At Solay's age, her mother had been a King's mistress for three years. Her mother sat back, sad understanding dawning in her eyes. 'Tell me, Solay, what does he want from this marriage?'

He doesn't want it at all.

Perhaps she should confess. Perhaps she should prepare her mother for the possibility that in this, too, she might fail. But as the two expectant faces gazed at her, she answered with half the truth. 'He wants someone who will love him.'

'What does that matter?' Her mother shrugged.

Jane tilted her head. 'And do you love him?'

She swallowed. 'I will convince him that I do before we are wed.'

'God has blessed you with a face and body that heat men's blood,' her mother said. 'You can convince him of anything.'

She nodded, unable to disappoint her mother with her failure to do exactly that.

'Now,' her mother said, 'what about our grant?'

Now she could not dissemble. 'The Council has blocked it.'

'Council? No Council overrules a King!'

So Solay explained about Parliament's law and Gloucester and the Council's year to bring the King to heel.

When she had finished, her mother stared at the brooch in her hand. 'So, this is the King's recompense for what he cannot give.' She dropped it back into the box and shut the lid, disappointment creasing her lips.

Her mother had endured so much. Solay had to give her some hope. 'The King has promised a grant in a year if…'

Her mother settled back into her chair and raised her eyebrows. 'If what?'

'Lamont works with the Council. The King wishes to be kept informed.'

Jane gasped. 'He wants you to spy on your own husband? How can you love him and do that?'

No one answered her.

Solay's mother nodded, as if all had become clear. 'The King has a right to know what the Council is doing. And you will tell him. In a year, he will give us our grant. And if you persuade your husband well, we might not have to wait that long.' She turned, briskly, to the present. 'Now, we must begin the wedding plans, meet the man's family—' Her mother stopped in mid-sentence as she saw the truth on Solay's face.

'The King has his own plans.'

'I see.' A mask of resignation settled on her face. 'And will I be invited to this wedding, whenever it may be?'

'I do not know,' she said, though she suspected. 'This has all come about quickly.' She rose, unable to witness her mother's pain. 'I am to return to the court in few days. Lady Agnes would have me as a companion.' And as a cover for her affair, but she did not add that. 'And Justin's work is at Westminster.'

'Excellent.' Her mother smiled. She swallowed disappointment and moved on to necessity. 'I expect you to parlay this into bigger things for us all. Your sister needs a husband, too.'

Her sister threw down the message. 'Stop it. Stop it, both of you.' She ran from the room.

Solay shared a moment's sigh with her mother.

Her mother shook her head. 'Jane fancies herself a student, but she was never as wise as you.'

Nor as cynical, Solay thought, wishing that Jane could stay in blissful innocence. She had shared the situation too frankly for a girl of fifteen to hear. 'I'll go to her.'

Solay found Jane in her chamber, with the few books her mother had not yet sold. Her sister's eyes had seen much too much for her age.

Solay hugged her. 'Don't worry. After I'm wed, we'll find a husband for you.'

Jane was stiff in her arms. 'I don't want a husband.'

'Of course you do.'

She shook her head and sighed. 'Is there no escape from being a woman?'

'Escape? What do you mean?'

'I want to be free. Like a man.'

Solay shuddered at the thought. How did men live with only the blunt instrument of power? Unable to bend, they were forced to break. Better to be pliant, to accommodate the ever-shifting winds of power. But Jane loved books and horses and had never enjoyed womanhood.

'None of us choose the lives the stars give us,' Solay said, running her finger over the cut-velvet cover of her mother's Book of Hours with the charts of the planets in it. Now that it was forbidden, it called to her more than ever.

'No more than we can choose our parents,' Jane sighed.

'Nor our husbands.' Solay picked up the book. 'Perhaps Mother will let me take it with me. Would you mind?' She had taught Jane to read, but her sister had become more the scholar than she.

Jane shook her head. 'It should be yours. You are the student of the stars.'

'A poor one.' But perhaps better than she knew. She had discovered something about the King's birth even he did not know. And something about her own. 'Jane, I found out when I was born! It was St John's Eve.'

'What about me?' Jane asked, finally smiling. 'When was I born?'

The question broke her heart. The girl would rather have a birth date than a husband. 'I don't know, but I'll find out.' Perhaps Justin's mysterious laundress would have Jane's answer as well. 'I promise.'

Five days later, Solay held out the velvet-covered book as her mother laid the last of her few dresses into the trunk. 'May I take it with me, Mother?'

Her mother, never one to cherish books, nodded. 'If you like, but guard it well. The books and the jewels are easy to carry and easy to sell. This one could fetch nearly a pound, should we need it.'

But her mother's hand stopped hers as Solay lowered the trunk lid. 'The brooch was to be yours,' she said. 'I will keep it as long as I can.'

Solay nodded. The brooch would have to feed them, if Solay's husband could not.

'You must keep the favour of the King and your husband. We will need them both in the year to come.'

Dread knotting her stomach, Solay met her mother's eyes, hard with experience. A child no more, she must not expect to be taken care of like a child. 'This man, he is not like others.'

'All men are alike. Even a King. Discover what this man wants and give it to him.'

'How am I to do that?' *How did you?*

Her mother gazed out of the window, as if seeing the past in the clouds that scuttled over the winter brown grass that poked through the snow stretched across the flat Essex land. 'When the Queen was dying, the King needed nurturing, but he wanted people to see him as a warrior still. So it was necessary for me to…' she paused, searching for a word '…portray a desirable woman.'

Solay wondered, suddenly, whether she and her sister existed merely to prove that the King had been in her mother's bed. 'What did *you* want?'

Her mother brought her gaze back squarely to Solay. 'I got what I wanted. He made me the Lady of the Sun.'

And what do I want? Solay wondered, as she hugged her mother and sister goodbye.

No answer came as the cart pulled away, loaded with a trunk carrying her only possessions. It was just as well. What she wanted for herself was unimportant. She must provide for her family.

Yet for just a moment, she wondered what the stars might predict for her own life. She let the wind blow her wish away. The heavens gave answers for countries and Kings. Astrologers read their grand designs to find hints of

Christ and the Apocalypse, of comets and eclipses and wars, not to comfort puny individuals.

Right now, her fate was firmly entwined, at least until Easter, with Justin Lamont's. That was all she needed to know.

CHAPTER SEVEN

JUSTIN listened, grimfaced, as the first banns were read in Windsor Castle's chapel after the sermon on a sunny Sunday late in January.

Even though he had made his condition clear to the priest, a *frisson* of uncertainty rippled through him as the curate pronounced his name and parentage.

The last time his name had been called out with a woman's in a parish church, his family had stood beside him. This time, his family was not with him, even in spirit.

With the King's urging, familial negotiations that usually took months had been concluded in weeks. He would not assume her mother's debts. She would bring no dowry and make no claims on his family's land. It was almost as if the stars, that fate she so believed in, had brought him here.

Next to him, the shiny curl of her dark hair tempted his fingers. If he could push it away from her neck, he could kiss the pale skin—

He turned his eyes away from the dangerous vision. Being near her lured him into dreams of a home and a family—things he would never deserve.

Why didn't you refuse? she had asked.

I should have.

Solay stood serenely beside him, her back straight, never looking to Justin for comfort as the priest stumbled over the name 'Lady Alys of Weston' and that of her mother's ostensible husband. The congregation coughed.

As they left the church together, the tolling bell clanged like the door of a donjon cell. Solay was swaddled up to her neck in velvet and ermine, her cloak an extravagant gift from the King that Justin would no doubt find listed as an official government gift in the household expenses.

They were seated together at the *noonmeat* meal, sharing a trencher of chicken stew, while the rest of the Court tried to watch them without staring.

'When shall we travel to visit your family?' she asked, finally.

The hope in her voice made him wish he could dissemble. He had visited home last week, as she had. Like most of the Court, his brother and his wife had snickered behind his back, unsure whether to be insulted because she was a whore's daughter or honoured because her father was a king. 'There is no need for that.'

'But I was looking forward to meeting your parents.'

'My mother is gone,' he said.

'Oh, forgive me. I did not know. I'm so sorry.' She touched his arm, her eyes full of fake compassion.

He pulled away, wanting neither her touch nor her sham sympathy. 'It was years ago.' Half his life ago.

'That must have been hard. I cannot imagine losing my mother now, but to lose her as a child…'

Startled, he watched her blink back tears. Could she really love a woman the whole world reviled?

'What was she like?' she continued.

Nothing like you, he wanted to say, but he was no longer so certain that was true. 'Wise. Strong. Forgiving.' *And she loved my father very much.*

'And your father?'

Her examination made him uneasy. She already knew he had been dead two years and his older brother held the title. 'What about him?'

'What was he like?'

He had no ready answer. 'He was a judge.' It was more than his profession. 'He taught us to reach our own conclusions.'

'No matter what the King thinks?'

'No matter what anyone thinks.' Yet the words were hollow. He had let the King force him into this betrothal.

No, do not blame the King. It was not he who persuaded you. It was the lust-filled stones between your legs.

Looking at her profile, he fought the lure of her flesh. He had barely touched her since that kiss forced by the Lord of Misrule, but he could still taste her wine-tinged lips, feel her soft breasts against his chest. And if he relented for a moment too long, all the conditions in the world would not save him.

Consummation would mean consent.

'Would you visit mine, then?'

He stared at her, realising he had lost her meaning. 'What?'

'Would you come to meet my mother and sister?'

He blocked his curiosity about the Lady of the Sun and the sister with no name of her own. He refused to be dragged into her world or to insert her into his. It would only make the parting more difficult.

'Yuletide is over. I must return to my work.'

She put down her chicken without tasting it.

If he were a flatterer, he would say that a visit would be more convenient at another time or that the weather would make travel difficult.

But that would be a lie.

Around them, pages from the kitchen carried in dishes chilled from their journey through draughty stone corridors. He pushed a fried almond towards her side of the trencher, a poor apology for his rudeness.

She smiled and picked it up. 'Justin, which laundress was it? The one who knew of my birth?'

'Do you think to punish her for revealing your secrets?'

She lifted her chin and he saw the flash of pride defying his pity. 'I hoped the woman might remember my sister's birth as well. 'Twas no great thing for me to know my birth date, but my sister is still young and cares about such things.'

His anger at the King's whore flared anew. 'Your mother doesn't know?'

'A woman in the throes of childbirth cares little for dates and times. She remembers it was cold and the Queen was dead.'

'My mother could tell you how many roosters crowed the morning I was born.' He had always taken that for granted. 'She made me a tray of comfits each year to mark the day.'

'And what day was that?'

He squashed a vision of Solay bringing him sweet cakes on his birthday. 'You will not need to know.'

She made no more attempts at conversation, chewing her red-spiced chicken in silence.

His mother would have scolded him for his harsh words, he thought. Whatever Solay might be, nothing she had done today deserved his rude replies.

He cleared his throat. 'Your sister. Her name is Joan, too?'

'No,' she answered softly. 'My sister's name is Jane.'

'But…' Gloucester had said they were both Joan. Was every 'fact' about Lady Alys so wrong? 'The laundress is the heavy one. With her front teeth missing.'

The smile that blessed her face was the first honest joy he'd seen from her. It tempted him more than her kiss.

Bad enough her body called to his. He would allow no tender feelings to take root. In just a few weeks, Easter would come and he would be quit of her.

CHAPTER EIGHT

WITH the Yuletide log extinguished and Windsor emptied of guests, cold seeped through the very stones and crept into every corner.

There were not enough trees in all England to keep the castle warm, Solay thought, as she and Agnes huddled close to a fireplace in their chambers, burning a few sticks of hoarded wood and trading stories.

'I envy you,' Agnes said. 'Betrothed with the blessing of the King.'

She had not shared the King's reasons with Agnes. 'At least you have a lover who does not leave the room when you enter.' Envy bit her. What would it be like, to be loved so?

Agnes shook her head. 'He is not mine. He is only borrowed.'

'But you make him smile, you make him laugh. He can't wait to be with you.' Hibernia's wife had fled the court as soon as the Yuletide festivities ended and Agnes could smile again. 'Everything I say or do makes Justin angry.'

'So you envy me, too?' Agnes reached for her hand and squeezed it. 'Ah, we are a pair, aren't we? What are we to do?'

Agnes's sympathy touched her. She had never had a friend outside her family. No one had ever cared what she thought and felt. But with Agnes, she might at least confide her heart's foolishness, if not the King's plans.

'How am I to persuade him I love him?' She sighed.

Agnes chuckled. 'You are a woman. He is a man. It is not so hard.'

'He is not like other men.' Any other man would have been easier to fool.

Agnes put down her needlework. 'And your marriage will not be like other marriages. He must not suspect you report his every move to the King.'

The little heat left in her body drained away. She looked behind her, relieved to see the room's door closed. 'Hibernia told you.'

'Of course.'

She regretted her moment's candour. Agnes might act the friend, but the shared whispers of lovers respected no boundaries. What Solay said to Agnes might reach the King's ears through the same channel.

Yet knowing all, Agnes was the only one who could understand why she must succeed. 'Please. Help me. Tell me how you please Hibernia.'

Agnes's cheeks turned pink. 'Beneath the sheets, everything pleases him.'

No doubt. Between Justin and her there was no lack of fire. All the more reason, she suspected, that he avoided her. There must be some other way. 'But before that, how did you attract him?'

'It was over a game of Merrills. We were close over the

board, our hands touched, I looked into his eyes...' She smiled, remembering.

'You make it sound so simple.'

A dimple flashed in Agnes's cheek. 'I let him win every game.'

Solay laughed. Of course. She had been too forward, even asking to visit his family instead of waiting for him to suggest it. Justin struck sparks that made her want to spar with him, no attitude for a wife. 'I'll try it.'

If only she could concentrate enough to lose.

This was what came of misguided politeness, Justin thought, setting up the pieces on the Merrills board for the game with Solay. He should have refused to play, but the rest of the Court seemed party to a conspiracy to leave them alone together.

And as much as he tried to resist temptation, he craved her physical nearness. Her dark hair and her pale skin drew his eyes. His gaze traced the subtle curve of her lower lip as she tapped it with a finger, contemplating the board.

He made a move and took one of her pieces, realising too late that he had put his man directly in line for her to take on her next move.

Instead, she made a move that put her piece directly in harm's way, then looked up at him with a bland smile, hiding all the intelligence behind it.

He knew, clearly as if she had spoken, that she was trying to lose, pandering to her perception of what would give him pleasure.

He leaned back and crossed his arms, smiling to

himself as he looked at her pleasantly expectant face. Two could play that game.

Instead of taking one of her pieces, he moved his stick out of position.

She looked at him sharply and opened her mouth as if to question the move, then shut it.

He had left her in a quandary. Her only move would take one of his pieces. Struggling to keep his mind on the game, he watched her study the board, looking for a way out.

The thicket of her black eyelashes shadowed her fair skin and, although her sleeves nearly reached her hands, he could see the pale skin of her inner wrist and wondered how much paler it would be below her navel when he—

'Your move.'

He started. She had succumbed to the inevitable and taken a piece of his. 'You play well,' he said, goading her. 'You may be the victor in this game.'

'Oh, no. It was a lucky move. You are by far the better player. Perhaps your mind is not on the game.'

His mind *wasn't* on the game, but her voice was too innocent to suggest that she knew where his mind was. He nudged another piece into harm's way.

This time, she protested. 'Are you sure you want to make that move?'

He grinned. 'Can you suggest a better?'

'Oh, no,' she said, flustered. 'I would not know a better one.'

Boxed in by his play, all her available moves would take one of his pieces. All but the one she made.

'Are you sure you want to make that move?' he asked.

Reaching over the board, he touched her hand and moved it to one of the other pieces. 'Instead of this one?'

She froze, looking at his eyes, then laughed, a high-pitched trill. 'How foolish of me. You are so much the better player. I hadn't thought of it.'

He could swear she batted her eyelashes. 'You not only thought of it, you took time to think of every possible move trying to avoid it.'

'I need time to think because I'm not very good at the game.'

'On the contrary. You are deliberately trying to lose.' He grabbed her hand again, her fingers cold in his. 'Why?'

She met his eyes, taking his measure, then sighed. 'How did you know?'

He let go of her hand, savouring her moment of honesty. 'It can take as much intelligence to lose as to win. You must be a good player to make so many moves that lead directly to my strength.'

A genuine smile lit her face. 'My sister and I played often at home.'

'Then play as if I were your sister.'

Confusion dented her forehead. 'You won't be angry if I win?'

'I will be angry if I'm given a victory I have not earned.'

The smile that danced around her lips put him in mind of kissing. 'Then we shall start a new game.'

The game's pace quickened as both played to win. She let her cloak fall off her shoulders; more than once, his fingers brushed hers as both reached for the next move.

He liked the Solay who played her own game; when she bested him, he laughed with her.

When he rose and put the game away, the hall was empty and the fire burned low.

Solay pulled her cloak around her shoulders and stood, smiling, a sparkle in her impossibly purple eyes.

Her lips parted, ready for him.

He touched them with an unsteady finger, her breath brushing his skin. One kiss, just one. But a kiss would not be enough—

His pleasure ended with the thought and he pulled away.

'So you do punish me for winning.'

He could not tell whether her pout was genuine. 'You know better.'

'Then what harm is a kiss?'

'It would lead to more.'

'And if it does? It's what both of us want.'

She was a ruthless, unrelenting opponent and the real game was not over.

'No. It's what you want.' The stiffness between his legs belied his words. He rued the day he had agreed to this Devil's bargain, yet he could only blame himself. He had told her he would not marry her, but he had not told her he would not marry at all. If she knew why, she would surely refuse him as well.

Her gaze met his. 'You pride yourself on your truthful tongue, but I wonder whether you speak it about yourself.'

Silent, he watched her leave the hall and wondered whether he might regret unleashing an honest Solay.

Yet it was easier to know the true face of his enemy. Besides, if he could force her to reveal herself, this enforced betrothal might be worth it.

He would not give her marriage, but perhaps he could give her herself.

And spare the world another Lady Alys of Weston.

Ask Mother whether two days after Candlemas sounds right, Solay wrote the next afternoon, glad the knowledge would bring some light to Jane's winter. Solay had found the laundress in the damp warmth of Windsor's wash room. The woman had a gap-toothed smile, a prodigious memory and fond recollections of Alys of Weston.

'She made him happy,' the woman said. 'A King deserves to be happy.'

And what about the rest of us? Solay wondered wistfully. Do we deserve to be happy? Last night, Justin had laughed. It was the first time he had looked at her and not been stern, or judgemental or angry. His smile rekindled her hunger for someone who could look at her without seeing her mother.

Someone who might make a special treat for her birthday.

She shook off her daydream. It was Justin's happiness that must concern her, not her own. She must make him as happy as her mother had made the King.

Childish shrieks from the quadrangle pierced the wooden shutters. Pulling her cloak tighter, she walked to the window and peeked through a crack in the wood.

Winter's first snow blanketed the ground, but instead of a peaceful white pasture, the castle's inner courtyard had become a battlefield. Three pages and a kitchen boy flung snowballs at each other, running, ducking and yelling in turn. Hurtling snowballs with them, like a boy of ten summers, was Justin.

The sight brought a twinge of pain for the boy he must have been and the child she no longer was.

A 'thank you' for giving her the laundress's name would give her an excuse to seek him out. She left the fire's warmth, hurried down the hallway and stood in the shelter of the doorway, watching the mock battle, reluctant to step into the cold.

Justin looked up from his game, grinning. 'Lady Solay! Catch!'

A snowball came straight towards her, splattering the red velvet cloak with a dead aim.

She brushed the soft fabric frantically, wet snow numbing her fingers. If the King's gift were ruined, he'd think ill of her.

Across the lawn, Justin laughed, a sound so boyish that she forced a smile and a wave. He grinned back, delighted at his aim, of course, not because of her.

The young boys ran towards the Round Tower, still hurling snowballs, their shrieks echoing off the stone walls. Justin walked over to her, smiling up at the first snow as if it were a gift instead of a curse.

His smile deepened the cleft in his chin and softened the hard lines of his cheeks and jaw. Big, damp flakes dusted his hair and shoulders, his chest rose and fell with leftover exertion. Despite the snowball fight, he wore no gloves.

Never had he looked more tempting.

'Here...' he grabbed her hand, his fingers warm despite the wet snow, and pulled her into the courtyard '...look up.'

Obediently, she tilted her head back and let her hood fall off. Snowflakes skipped down from the sky, swirling, confusing, filling her vision. Dizzy, she could not tell up from down, ground from sky.

She stumbled.

He caught her arm, his heat blocking the cold. It was the first time he had truly touched her since that kiss. Even his gaze warmed her. For a moment, she let herself rest in his smile.

His needs. Remember his needs. 'You like the snow?'

He nodded, an unforced grin lighting his face. 'I like to watch it fall.'

Safe in his embrace, she did not feel the wind or miss the fire. She leaned into him as he swayed towards her, his breath a whisper on her cheek, coming closer.

Now, she thought, her lips parting.

Abruptly, he let her go. 'You want a kiss, Lady Solay? Then trade some truth for it. Tell me—do you like the snow?'

'Of course.' She lifted her hood to ward off the flakes prickling her head. The cold chilled her eyes. 'It's beautiful. I like to watch it fall.'

The light left his eyes and she faced her enemy again. 'How strange, Lady Solay. That's what I just told you.'

The icy wind swirled inside her cloak. She hunched her shoulders, missing the warmth in his eyes as much as the heat of his body. 'Does it not please you that we both like the same thing?'

'It would please me if you would tell the truth. About anything. I asked whether *you* like the snow.'

'Wouldn't you prefer I like what you like?'

'I would prefer you know what *you* like first. Now, once more. Do you like the snow?'

What did it matter what she thought? No one in power had ever questioned her for agreeing with him.

Except this man.

'I don't know.'

He crossed his arms, blocking the door to Windsor's blessed shelter, unmoving as a block of ice. 'Then we shall stand here and experience it until you do.'

Anger heated her cheeks. Why couldn't he be content with surface pleasantries? No one else forced her to consider her own opinion. She fought back a frown as the icy flakes weighed down her eyelashes.

Winter was a long, dark, hateful time of numb fingers and growling bellies, with the Lenten fast conveniently placed after the Yuletide feast, just as there was no more food to eat until the spring.

Shivering, she narrowed her eyes. 'I hate the snow.' She would give him the truth and more. 'I hate all of winter: snow, cold, ice, long, black, sleepless nights, short, sunless days.' He raised his eyebrows as she slapped him with the words. 'There. You have my confession. Now, where's the kiss you promised?'

Surely he would not kiss her after she had disagreed with him.

But a smile deepened the corner of his mouth.

Warmth…no, more than warmth, fire returned to his eyes. His palms cupped her cheeks and he bent his lips to hers.

His kiss made her dizzier than the snow. Head cradled in his hands, she felt at once vulnerable and protected. With the touch of his lips, strong and demanding, something below her belly caught fire.

Oh, for this, she would tell a thousand truths.

She slipped her arms around his waist, eager to steal his warmth. Her breasts pressed against his chest, her hips matched his, and everywhere she touched him she found heat.

His lips moved over hers and she kissed back, hungry for the taste of him and more. His chest rose and fell, as it had when he'd run with the boys.

Her lips clung to his as he pulled, gently, away.

He cleared his throat. 'You see, Lady Solay? Truth is not so difficult.'

Looking up at him, she smiled, full of the tender weakness the poets described. Now. Now, if she told him, surely he would believe her. 'I love you.'

He stepped back and his face became as ice. Snow fell between them again. 'You learn nothing. I weary of your lies.' He turned his back and walked towards the door.

She cursed herself for letting the words slip. She had badly miscalculated. No, she had not calculated at all. To be in his arms, to feel his kiss was so right that she had wanted to stay there always. It was just three words, three words she thought would keep her there for ever.

She ran after him, touching his back when she caught up. 'Wait, please. I wanted to thank you.'

He turned, eyes cold as dead ashes. 'What for?'

'For telling me about the laundress. She knew when Jane was born.'

A faint smile softened the harsh lines in his face. 'What was the day?'

'Two days after Candlemas.' She smiled. In little more than ten days, Jane could celebrate.

'And Jane loves the snow.'

'How did you know?'

His smile was not the one of boyish joy, but a thin line of triumph. 'You were born in summer and they call you Solay.' He turned back to the door.

'Wait!'

He did, blocking the door, as if happy to stay in the cold. She shivered, wishing she had followed him inside to talk. 'Would you like a game of Merrills tonight?'

He shook his head. 'I leave for Westminster tomorrow.'

She cringed at the very name of that dreaded palace. 'How long will you be gone?' Every day apart was a day of persuasion lost.

'Far past the end of Lent.'

She smiled to hide her fear. 'I would like to come with you if the King agrees.' Of course the King would agree. The King expected her to report on Justin's every move.

'You just flinched when I mentioned Westminster. You have no desire to come with me except to continue this futile effort to persuade me you can love. Stay here and find a husband you can keep.'

How could he read her so easily? 'I merely blinked to avoid a snowflake. I want to come, truly.'

'No, you don't. You think you *should* come.' Under the strong, dark brows, his eyes weighed her and found her wanting. 'I don't know who you are or what you want. And neither do you. Better discover who you are before you profess to love someone else.'

He closed the door behind him and left her shivering in the snow.

CHAPTER NINE

I DON'T know who you are or what you want.

Two days later, Solay woke with Justin's words still echoing in her head. *I have no right to want something for myself,* she argued back, full of truth as long as she did not speak aloud.

Did he think she should abandon her family for a selfish whim? For, for…for what? She could think of nothing selfish she might want this morning except to break fast.

Stomach growling, she rolled over in an empty bed, hoping Agnes would be back soon to help her decide what to do next. Justin was a hard day's ride away. How was she to woo him?

Want tangled with necessity. His judgement hurt in a way that the cruelty she had met from so many did not. He seemed to expect her to do something more, be something more.

The only man who is free is the man who answers only to himself.

A man such as Justin.

There could be no greater freedom than not to care for the opinion of others.

Yet he cared whether she loved him.

Fa! Head spinning with confusion, she forced herself out of the warm bed and into her dress. Love was only a word for poets to swoon over. If he looked at the evidence as the lawyer he was, he would know it did not exist. Marriages were made for money, power, position. As for other couplings—well, the connection of bodies was much more elemental than some invisible emotion.

The door opened and Agnes tiptoed in, carrying two smuggled sops from the kitchen to break their fast.

'Oh, thank you!' Solay savoured the wine-soaked bread, a secret little ritual they now shared each morning, despite the King's disapproval. The King believed that breaking fast before the midday meal was a weakness of the lower classes.

'The King has new plans,' Agnes said. No need to ask how Agnes knew the King's plans. 'We'll be travelling north within a fortnight.'

'And leave the Council in Westminster?'

Agnes smiled like a cat. 'Exactly.'

'Is that legal?' She surprised herself with a question that Justin would have asked.

Agnes tilted her head, as if she did not understand the problem. 'He's the King. He goes where he pleases. Won't it be wonderful?'

Wonderful for Agnes because the freedom of travel would leave her plenty of time with Hibernia. But what did it mean for Solay?

A knock interrupted them and Solay opened the door to the King's page. 'His Majesty summons you.'

Solay grabbed her cloak, brushing the mark left by the

snowball, and picked up the letter she had written to Jane. She had asked the King if he could spare a messenger to send it to Upminster in time for her birthday. He must have decided to say yes.

She entered his chambers, expecting him to smile at the cloak, or at least at her deep curtsy, but instead, she faced a frown.

'Why have you brought me no report of the Council's activities?'

She swallowed, her throat dry. 'I have not seen him since he left for Westminster, Your Majesty.'

'You saw much of him in the Upper Ward right before he left, Lady Solay.'

She shifted uneasily. Who had been looking out of a window and into their lives? 'We were speaking of other things, Your Majesty.'

'I've heard he's developing new charges against members of my household,' he said, glancing at Hibernia. 'Is it true?'

She assumed a serious expression, wondering who else was spying for the King. 'I believe so, but he did not say specifically who would be charged. I did not want to bring Your Majesty incomplete information.' She let the answer lie, hoping it would satisfy him.

'Did he say what the charges would be?'

She shook her head.

'Or how many would be named?'

'He was not precise.' How many might he charge at one time? 'No more than two or three, I think.'

'You know no more than I.' He looked down at her, standing before him, letter in hand. 'I can spare no messenger today.'

His threat was clear. He could remove more precious things if she did not fulfil her part of the bargain.

'Perhaps I should visit Westminster,' she said, subduing her hatred of the place. Justin would not welcome her, but she could learn nothing more here. 'I'm sure I could discover something else.'

'An excellent idea,' Hibernia chimed in.

Of course he would think so. If she were gone, he could share Agnes's bed at any time.

The King nodded. 'Go. They are plotting against me. I know it.' A small smile came to his lips. 'They think they have the upper hand, but all their legal tricks will come to naught.'

She stifled a shudder, not sure whether she feared the King or this trip more. But now that she had promised, she must not return empty-handed. What could she offer Justin to build his trust in her?

Something about the King. Something he doesn't know. Something that would convince him I am on his side.

Some small betrayal.

Justin moved closer to the west window, trying to catch the last of the faint winter light on the document before him. Through the cracks in the shutters, he saw snowflakes heavy as raindrops hurtling towards the frozen ground.

Safely back at Westminster and away from temptation,

his days had been feverish with activity. Messengers rode daily between the two palaces by the Thames, returning from Windsor with the King's reluctant signature over the Council's seal on the endless flow of documents needed to run the realm.

Yet even the hectic pace could not keep his mind off Solay. *Fool. You knew better than to touch her.*

Their kiss had released all the passion he had sensed from the first, along with something more. A hum in his veins of possession. Of knowing that she could be his.

Yet if he let his lust rule, they would share not only a bed, but a life and he'd find himself married to another woman of lies.

Still, none of that seemed to matter when he touched her. He had even hoped for a moment, that her kiss and her words were real.

I love you. Meaningless as *I like to watch the snow fall.*

Such desperation raised an ugly suspicion. What if her urgency came with a babe attached? He should have thought of that before. It was the way of women, he knew too well.

He looked back at his document, surprised that his quill had not moved and irritated that she would not leave his mind. It seemed as if he could smell roses, just by thinking of her.

A knock interrupted. 'Come,' he called, welcoming the distraction.

Solay paused at the threshold. The snow she so hated dampened the flowing red velvet cloak. She had thrown back the hood and her dark hair cascaded riotously over her shoulders. And, despite his distrust, when he met her eyes the very air in the room shimmered and his tongue seemed useless.

'Why are you here?' he said, finally.

Rude as he had been, she smiled. 'May I warm myself by the fire?'

'As you like.' He shrugged off his unease at her nearness and watched her cross the room. Her cloak covered everything.

It would even hide a change in her belly.

He looked down at the near-finished writ before him, the words now gibberish. The fire warmed his chest, but an inner heat smouldered as she walked closer. She dropped her hood and stood behind him, her hands caressing his aching shoulders. Her scent crept into his pores.

Refusing to face her, he shook off the comfort of her touch. 'You would have done better to stay at Windsor. I have no time for pleasantries.'

'The day is near over. Is it not time to rest?'

His shoulders sagged at the thought. He had not rested in years.

Always, his father had demanded one more task, one more achievement he could never quite attain. He had become a sergeant-at-law in thirteen years instead of sixteen, then joined the household of the Duke of Gloucester, finally rising to serve the Council itself. Yet after his mother's death, there was no one to soften the judgements or celebrate the triumphs.

Now, the year of the Council's charter stretched endless before him. 'Time enough for rest when the Council's work is done.'

Her hands soothed his knotted muscles. She leaned closer. 'What can be so important?'

Work seemed a safer topic than the scent of her skin. 'A subpoena.'

'A subpoena? What's that?'

Beneath her fingers, his shoulders sagged, relaxed. If he leaned back, his head would be cradled on her breasts…

He woke from his trance and sat up to escape her touch. Her interest in the law was feigned, no doubt. 'I am not at liberty to discuss the Council's business.'

She sat on the bench beside him. 'But I came to tell you something the Council should know.'

He shifted away from her, suspicious. 'What?'

'The week after Candlemas, the King will leave Windsor and he won't return until Eastertide.'

Absent from Windsor or Westminster, the King would be conveniently away from the Council's supervision, free to spend as he pleased. 'Where is he going?'

'He has not said, though some talk of Nottingham and Lincoln.'

If Hibernia escaped to the north, it would take an army to bring him back, not a piece of parchment. 'He's trying to sabotage our work,' Justin said, wondering whether the King already suspected their plan.

'What if you came along with the Court? You might serve as a link between the King and the Council.'

'The Council must work at Westminster.' Parliament had so stipulated in the law. 'The King knows that better than anyone.' No doubt that was the reason for this gyration into the countryside.

'Staying at Westminster seems a legal nicety.'

Nicety. As if the law were no more important than the King's protocol. 'We cannot follow only the laws we like.'

She pouted, which put him in mind of her kiss, a distraction he did not need. 'You are not a member of the Council. Surely Parliament would not object if you travelled with the King. Council business would be more smoothly conducted.'

Although he hesitated to take her at her word, her reasoning was sound. He reached for a clean parchment and dipped the pen into the ink. If he could not compel Hibernia into testimony, at least he could keep an eye on them both. 'I'll inform Gloucester in the morning. Take this demand to Windsor tomorrow.'

'No!' She gripped his hand.

Her cold fingers burned his skin. He stared at the moving shadows cast across their fingers by the fire.

'Why not?' The words struggled up from his throat. He forced himself to face her eyes again. 'You just said—'

'Don't you think it would be better if the King thought the idea his own? A demand from the Council might be ill received.'

An understatement. 'But now that I know he's leaving, I must act.'

'If you do, he'll know I told you.'

And Solay would bear the brunt of the King's displeasure. 'So you have a different plan.'

She nodded. 'If someone he trusted suggested it to him, he would surely agree.'

'Who?'

'Let me talk to a friend.'

This was what he hated about the Court. All was whispered behind closed doors. Arrangements were made in secret, for reasons that he could never quite understand. 'It is a simple matter, not a Court intrigue.'

'Not so simple as you make it sound.'

He wanted to protest, but she was right. If the King's objective was to avoid the Council, it would take delicate persuasion to allow a representative to travel with him. 'Why are you helping the Council? The King holds your loyalty.'

'You challenged me to prove I love you. The task will be impossible if we are separated for the rest of Lent. Do you intend for me to fail?'

Eyes wide, she waited for his answer.

He did, of course, feeling a guilty pang. At least she had asked an honest question. 'All right. Return to Windsor tomorrow. If I don't receive an invitation from the King within the sennight, he'll get a formal request from the Council.'

'Tomorrow?' The desperate edge returned to her voice. 'I had hoped to spend more time with you.'

First she wanted to talk to the King. Then she wanted to stay. Where was the lie here?

In the babe.

He struggled against black memories.

If she was with child, she would need to bed him quickly. That, he would not allow. Never again. 'We'll have time aplenty on the road.' He rose, a dismissal. 'The chamberlain will find you a room.'

And the farther from his, the safer he'd be.

* * *

Huge and oppressive, Westminster closed in on her as she wandered the halls, seeking the chamberlain to find her food and a bed. Solay had always hated this cavernous palace that the King shared with Parliament. Here, when they prayed, portraits of the King's wife and his nine legitimate children peered down at them from the walls of the chapel.

And here, her mother had faced the judgement of Parliament and lost.

Now her long, frozen trip to this gloomy place seemed for naught.

Agnes would persuade Hibernia to persuade the King to invite Justin on his gyration, but only if Solay could use him to gain information. The King already doubted her. She must discover some new titbit.

Something more about the document he was writing.

She tried to puzzle out a plan, yet the weak-kneed want she felt in his presence muddled her mind. Instead, she felt again the breadth of his shoulders and the power of his muscled back against her palm.

Stop brooding, she told herself as she ate the hearty cabbage soup the chamberlain found for her. If my want for him is a weakness, so is his for me.

It was in every breath he took in her presence. It was in his eyes that seemed to devour her. Justin might resist kisses, but if she bared her body, surely he would succumb. And afterwards, he might whisper secrets.

She put down her spoon and rose.

You must save your maidenhead for your husband, her mother had warned. *It may be your only currency.*

She ignored the voice. Banns had been read. Once she

unleashed his passion, he would be her husband in truth. There would be no more talk of conditions.

Now. Tonight. She must not return to the King empty-handed.

CHAPTER TEN

AFTER the castle was well abed, she crept through the echoing halls. Justin's room, the chamberlain told her, was well away from the smell of the river, in the shadow of the Abbey's towers. Faint firelight still showed underneath the door.

Heart pounding, she trailed her fingertips across the rough wood, afraid to knock.

Make his body want you and you can convince him of anything.

The door moaned as she pushed it open.

With his back to her, Justin stood before the window, staring out at the falling snow. She crept up behind him, slipping her arms, seductively, she hoped, around his waist and resting her cheek on his broad back. 'Husband.'

He slammed the shutters shut and pulled away from her. 'I am not your husband.'

Something hot, more than the fire's reflection, burned behind his eyes despite his harsh words. A muscle moved near his cheekbone.

So, he was fighting his desire.

She gentled her expression. 'Can you not spare me a word?'

'Talk.'

She turned away to compose her thoughts. Before her, his bed loomed, soft with a feather-stuffed mattress, deep blue curtains open to catch the fire's heat. Behind her, a log landed with a chunk. The fire licked it with a hiss, then it crackled into flame.

What must she do now?

Remember, her mother had said, *a man lusts with his eyes. He is helpless against what he sees.*

She did not understand how this could be so, but she knew when he touched her she was helpless. If seeing her would weaken him like that, surely he would bed her before dawn.

Back still to him, she reluctantly removed her cloak and draped it on top of the bed, grateful for the fire's heat.

Behind her, she heard nothing.

She shrugged out of the sleeveless surcoat, letting it slide to the floor to reveal her cote-hardie.

Nothing stirred except the snapping fire. Did she feel his eyes on her or was it only hope? She had expected him to touch her by now. Could she have been wrong? Perhaps he didn't desire her.

No. That was not true.

She tugged her front laces free.

Behind her, his breath turned ragged.

He was watching, then. The thought sparked an inner fire. Slowly, she threaded her fingers through her hair, then shook it down her back.

A sound, not quite a moan.

Her breath quickened as a plume of desire slithered up from her centre.

She squeezed her thighs against the weakness, waiting for his touch.

It didn't come.

What was she doing wrong? She thought she knew enough to fan his lust. It had never sounded hard. Men were all helpless that way, led by their staffs to drink at a woman's well, else how would a woman live?

She fumbled with the last of the laces and shrugged off her final gown. Now, covered only with the thin linen chemise, the fire still warmed her back, but chill air snaked across the floor and curled up her legs.

What was he doing? When was he going to touch her? She had only one more layer to shed.

She bent to reach for the hem of the chemise.

'Solay, stop.' Hard anger and rough desire clashed in his voice.

She dropped the hem and turned. Sitting by the fire, one leg flung over the arm of the chair, his legs spread wide enough that she could see his arousal.

Their eyes met and, for a moment, they breathed together.

He blinked, finally, breaking the spell.

'A pretty performance, Solay. No doubt you have used it successfully on many other men. Perhaps even on the father of the babe you carry.'

She crossed her arms over her shivering breasts. So that was what he feared. She should have realised.

'There is no child. Take me to your bed and you'll discover I'm a virgin.'

'If I take you to my bed, it will no longer matter whether you are a virgin.'

'If I had been so urgently in need of a husband, I would have asked the King for one. You were the one who suggested marriage, not I.'

Despite his frown, it could take little more, surely. She curved her lips in a slow, deliberate smile, knelt before him and reached for his staff. Perhaps he would like her to put her mouth on it. Men did, Agnes said.

He grabbed her wrists before her hands could reach him and held them apart. Now he was in control, his eyes taking in everything she had teased him with, forehead to toes, barely shielded by her linen shift.

She felt herself softening, aching for him to hold her.

No, no. There is no time for your wishes. You must satisfy his dreams.

She squeezed her thighs together as he stared at her belly. She knew her looks pleased him. If she leaned closer, surely—

He raised his eyes. 'You are so determined to display yourself. Let me watch you.'

As he stared at her, her mouth turned dry and her centre wet. 'What do you mean?'

'Don't pretend innocence. You know how to make a man covet you.' His glance fell again to the space between her legs. 'I'll be a willing audience.'

A hot, wild craving burned below her belly. She lifted her head with a seductive smile. Their eyes locked together and she felt the heat creep up from her centre, up through her breasts. Want muddled her thoughts. 'What would you have me do?'

He laced his fingers in hers and squeezed, his unyielding ring biting her flesh. 'You have needed no direction from me so far.'

'I don't know what you want,' she whispered, tilting her head, craving the kiss that must come. 'Show me.'

His ragged breath brushed her lips. A moment more and she'd have the kiss and whatever came next.

She pressed her lips against his.

He dropped her hands, threw her away from him, and stood. Without the balance of his touch, she fell, the cold floor raising bumps on the flesh of her thighs.

Towering over her, he wavered, swaying towards her, then pulling back.

The closeness she craved lay just out of reach. For ever out of reach.

She scrambled to her feet and clutched the soft wool of his tunic. She was so close, she must not let him slip away now. 'Don't you want me?'

He grabbed her hand, pulled her to her feet, and held her close, her breasts hot and full against his chest.

'Want you? I want to ravish you. I want to hear you cry out for me and I want to plunge into your body until the fire is ash and dawn lights the sky.' He let go and stepped back, shaking, as if his body were barely under his control. 'But I won't.'

'Why?' Panic edged the word.

'Because I will not trap us into this marriage.'

'It is not a trap. We agreed. Both of us.'

'I told you not to let anyone force you. I won't be forced either.'

'Loving is pleasure, not force.'

'Not when your body alone consents.'

'But you said I had to convince you of my love. That is what I am trying to do.'

'If you think a swift coupling will convince me of your love, you know nothing of lust or love. I told the King I would not marry you unless you were willing. I did not mean willing to lie with me. You've demonstrated that amply. To me and to how many others?'

'No others. There have been no others.'

'I don't believe you.'

'I am giving you the truth you asked for.' *And still you do not believe.*

'Regardless,' he said slowly, 'giving me your body will not convince me of your love.'

She gathered the remaining shards of her pride, stepped away and wrapped the King's cloak around her nakedness. What was left of the royal temper shot through her veins. 'You would not speak so to me if I were the King's legitimate daughter.'

He laughed, a hollow sound that fuelled her anger. 'You think not? I've insulted the King himself.' He waved towards the curtained bed. 'Take my bed. I'll find another.'

She bit her lip as her future walked towards the door. Stupid, stupid to let anger betray her. If he left now, what would she tell the King? She knelt and grabbed his leg, her body still pulsing to hold him, hoping the deference that pleased the King might work. 'Please. Stay. I will not try to tempt you again.'

He paused, eyes burning with want acknowledged. 'Do you believe that would make a difference?'

And then she realised she had not even needed to remove her cloak.

Wordless, she released him.

'Love demands more than your body, Solay. You must give your heart.'

After the oak door shut, she mourned alone before a fading fire, frightened at his words, for she had no heart to give.

He left the room, staggering, because he knew if he stayed he would take her. Take her and take her and take her again until every precious seed he had would be inside her and they would be married, never to be put asunder.

Clearly, she would say or do anything to hold him. Yet knowing why she had flaunted her body did nothing to bolster his resistance. His tongue craved her taste. Her soft skin tempted his fingers.

He was beginning to understand the old King's obsession.

He stepped outside, welcoming the blowing snow to chill the heat she had stirred in his veins.

He would not sleep tonight, knowing she lay in his bed. He only knew he must not touch her again.

But if he had any eyes at all, she had been honest about one thing. Virgin or not, her flat belly hid no babe.

He suddenly realised he had followed the path to the Thames, where the swirling waters rushed towards the sea. Cold. Dark. Final.

Please. Stay.

Desperation tinged her words. Beneath her scheming

lay a deeper pain, the one he had sensed the first time he saw her. Would his rebuff turn Solay to melancholia? Or something worse?

If so, it would be his fault. Again.

Please, the other woman had said. *Let me go.*

He turned away from the river's memories.

He must not let Solay return to Windsor until he could be sure she had not descended into despair. That would mean taking her to London with him tomorrow so he could watch her. The masters at the Middle Temple would raise their eyebrows to see a woman, but he dare not leave her alone. He must keep her close for at least a day and keep her mood jolly.

Unknowingly, he had become responsible for her. He should call it off now. Before it was too late.

But he was beginning to fear it already was.

CHAPTER ELEVEN

ALONE in Justin's bed the next morning, Solay lay half-asleep, imagining he lay beside her.

Wrapped against the cold, she would snuggle into arms strong and protective. When he opened his eyes, they would smile to see her. His lips would take hers in a sleepy kiss that would deepen until...

She opened her eyes to the dead fire, startled to realise she had been dreaming of love.

A gust of wind rattled the shutters and shook the thought from her head. She must have borrowed the foolish fancy from Agnes, mooning in hopeless passion for Hibernia, yet smiling from dawn to dusk.

She reached for her surcoat and dressed under the covers. Tugging her fingers through tangled hair, she assessed last night's disaster.

His want was plain enough. Strongly as he fought her, inexperienced as she was, she knew that.

But he was stronger than his want. What other man could have refused her protestations of love, refused her very body?

But then, as Solay climbed out of bed and opened the shutters to the soft pink echo of dawn behind the Abbey's towers, she remembered the worst.

Please. Stay.

The daughter of a king did not belong on her knees before a lawyer.

She left the window and stabbed the embers until a flame burst free. She must bury last night's humiliation and speak of it no more, but first, she must prevent Justin from sending her back to Windsor.

She opened the door and tripped over Justin, stretched out across the threshold.

He scrambled to stand, holding something behind his back, and stifled a yawn. Sleeplessness shaded his eyes, but when he looked at her the very air hummed between them.

She squashed the feeling. It was no good to her now.

'How are you? Did you sleep well?' He tripped over the courteous words, as if his tongue were unused to pleasantries.

'Oh, yes.' She covered her stomach to muffle the growl of hunger. She had barely slept at all.

'I thought you might be hungry.' He entered the room and held out a wine-darkened slice of bread, wrapped in a kitchen cloth.

Shocked, she took it, muttering her thanks. 'I did not think you would approve.'

'The law does not forbid it.' He smiled. Deliberately.

Surprise set off a giggle. 'Did you mean for me to laugh?'

'That was my intention.'

She did laugh then, a long, slow chuckle that warmed

her whole body. Was this the same man who had left the room last night?

'The weather has cleared,' he said, adding wood to the fire. 'I have to go to the City.'

Her smile faded. Next, he would say he had made arrangements for her to return to Windsor. Instead of bringing the King whispered secrets, she had only the strange word subpoena. She needed at least another day.

She leaned against the bed, clutching her belly with her free hand. 'I don't feel well.'

Instantly, he stood before her, pressing the back of his hand against her forehead, then her cheeks. 'Have you pain? Fever?'

She shook her head, surprised that her mild statement had sparked such strong concern. 'But I'm not sure I should travel.'

'Then we will stay here.'

'We?'

'I thought to take you to London with me.'

She swallowed her last bite in surprise. Last night, she could have sworn the man would never again seek her company. Had her words convinced him to give her another chance? 'What takes you to the City?'

'Council business. And there's a house for sale I must inspect. But if you feel unwell…'

'Thank you.' Surely she could learn something for the King by going. 'I would enjoy the trip.'

'But you just said—'

She wiped her fingers on the cloth and smoothed her

skirt. 'I must just have been hungry. I'm feeling quite well now.' She pulled her smile wide.

He looked at her keenly, gave a curt nod and put his hand at her elbow. 'Come.'

Shortly thereafter, Solay stood on the jetty at Westminster. A cold winter sun melted yesterday's wet snow at the river's edge as the boatman pushed off.

Justin gripped her hand firmly as she stepped into the boat. He had not let her out of his sight all morning, except when she visited the garderobe. The man who vowed not to touch her kept his hand on her back or at her elbow, even when he went to his workroom to roll and tie the document he had been working on yesterday. Once they were in the boat, his hand hovered near her arm, as if he wanted to be ready to snatch her at any moment.

Perhaps this change of heart meant he would speak more of the summons he carried. She dared not ask directly. Yesterday, that had raised his suspicions. Instead, she would babble nonsense while she pondered how to approach the subject.

'You wanted to know things I like,' she began. 'I like being on the water.' As a child, she had loved riding on the riverboats. How could she have forgotten?

Instead of coaxing a smile, her words made him frown. 'Why?'

'Why must there be a reason for what a person likes?' As the stars gave her hope and the sun courage, the water seemed to bring her peace. She smiled. 'Don't you like the river?'

'No.'

She did not ask why, not wanting him to dwell on a painful subject. Perhaps he did not have a boatman's stomach. 'The trip is so much easier than on land. And we enjoy this beautiful view.' As they rounded the river bend, London stretched before them, just as it had when she was a child ferried to her mother's house. 'I always loved the trip from Westminster to our house in London.'

'You told me you lived at Windsor.'

She gritted her teeth against his implication she had lied. 'We lived where the King lived, but Mother had a house in London.' When the court was in residence at Westminster or the Tower, she and Jane were shuffled off to the house by the river. She had not thought of it in years, but now she remembered the rush of the river, lulling her to sleep.

'Where was the house?'

'Near Cannon Street.' She rested her arms on the side of the boat, peering ahead. 'Look! We can almost see it.'

She leaned forward, hoping for a glimpse.

He grabbed her, nearly making her fall forward. The boat rocked, and the boatman yelled at them to keep low and to the centre.

His grip squeezed the air from her chest as he pulled her into his lap, his arms like iron chains.

'What are you doing?' he snapped. 'You nearly fell in.'

She gasped for a breath and smelled his scent, like fresh-cut wood, mixed with the crisp air and the tang of the river.

'I've never fallen overboard in my life,' she said, when she could breathe. 'I was just trying to see my old house.'

But he kept his arm locked around her until the boat

docked at the city gate and Justin relinquished his sword to the gatekeeper.

The river's edge usually harboured the rough side of society, yet beyond this gate they walked up a sheltered street surrounded by snowy gardens. Instead of sailors and strumpets, the street was filled with educated men arguing, many followed by servants.

'This isn't London as I remember it,' she asked. 'Where are we?'

His smile was genuine. 'The law may be made at Westminster, but the lawyers are made at the Middle Temple.'

She looked again, expecting to see horns and tails.

He didn't wait for a question. 'We eat, sleep, study, argue, work and live here. It is university, home and workplace.' Affection warmed his voice. 'Here, we speak of what matters.'

'What could matter more than the King's will?'

'Truth and justice. Right and wrong.'

What could she say that would please him? He understood nothing. Where was the justice in losing everything that should be yours by right? What was true except the need for food, clothing, shelter?

A young man, well dressed, walked by them, grinning. 'Your fine will be stiff for that one.'

'What does he mean?' she asked, glad to be spared from answering Justin.

His face reddened. 'The only women who come here are plying their trade. The fine for fornicating in chambers is six shillings eight pence.'

Her cheeks burned, thinking of last night. If he had been willing, the fine would have been worth a yard of russet wool.

He pointed out the hall, the chambers, the church, and she pretended interest in which ones were used to teach dancing, which for common meals, and which to learn the law, all the while wondering how she might get him talking about the Council's business instead.

They paused, finally, before a stone gate. London lay just beyond this private, orderly, serene world. And like a warning of what lay on the other side, black soot marred the stone, streaking upwards from dead flames.

'What caused that?' she asked.

'It happened during the rebellion.'

She had been safely away from London when the peasants rioted in the streets, yet she had hidden beneath her bed when angry voices echoed across the countryside, afraid they would come for her next. 'What happened here?'

'The peasants planned to hang the lawyers. When they couldn't find any, they burned the books instead.' His face was grim. 'We leave it as a reminder of what happens when there is no respect for the law.'

Solay nodded, for once in agreement. 'You dislike the King, yet it was Richard who calmed them.' It was a well-known tale, the fourteen-year-old blond King riding fearlessly out to the mob and telling them he was their king, too. 'He was the one who restored the rule of law.'

'And then ignored it.'

'What do you mean?'

'Do you not know? He promised justice and freedom for

the serfs, but afterwards, he hanged all the leaders and forced the peasants back to their lords.'

The King had given her his word, too. Would he ignore it so easily? 'But whatever the King wishes, that is the law.'

'It is power, not law. And certainly it is not always justice.'

Here was a hint of Justin's plan, but not yet enough to help the King. 'Have you come here today for justice, then?'

He ignored her question as they entered one of the buildings. At the door, Justin greeted a grey-haired man with a hearty handshake.

She peered beyond to a great hall, full of young men dining.

'Stay here,' Justin said to her, starting up the stairs. 'I'll not be long.'

Whatever reason he had come lay up those stairs. 'Can I not come with you?' She nodded towards the hall where several of the students had discovered her presence. 'Some of these young men look quite ready to pay the fine.'

'William will see you come to no harm.' Justin turned and mounted the stairs. 'And, William, see if you can find us some food.'

She watched him disappear, drumming her fingers in frustration. How was she to discover anything now?

'I am not accustomed to ladies in the house. Would you care for ale, milady?'

She started to shake her head, then realised William might have useful information. 'Yes, thank you.'

When he reappeared from the great hall, she put on her most dazzling smile. 'Justin neglected to introduce us. I am his betrothed. You must be an important man here.'

He preened, handing her a battered pewter goblet. 'The most senior masters of the law live and work here.'

'You mean the justices?'

'Oh, no. I mean the professors.'

'Ah, of course,' she said, nodding as if she knew what he meant. What could a law professor have to do with a writ? She should have paid more attention to her mother's longwinded stories about her legal affairs. Her mother had a keen mind for how the law might be used. And abused. 'You must know much of the law yourself.'

He smiled. 'I am no scholar, but I have learned many things. I have been here since King Edward's time.'

She could not resist the vision of Justin as a young man. 'Did you know Justin as a student?'

'Oh, yes. He had a special talent even then. He became a sergeant-at-law more quickly than anyone ever has.'

A surprising surge of pride brought on a genuine smile. 'Who does he visit today?'

'He still takes counsel with the master teachers when he has a particularly thorny issue.'

'He's mentioned working on a subpoena,' she said, then looked at the man with wide eyes and a smile. 'You probably know what that means. I feel so ignorant, but as his wife, I will need to understand such things.'

Would he take the hint and share his knowledge?

'It compels a man to appear before the jury and give evidence.'

'Ah, how interesting.' She nodded and took a sip of ale. She opened her eyes wider, tilted her head and smiled. Who would Justin force to testify? And about what? If a man was forced to tell all he knew to the jury, he might convict himself and many others before the questioning was through.

Justin came down the stairs, no longer carrying the document, took the bread and cheese William had found, and led her outside. They sat on a sun-warmed bench to eat.

'You forgot the document,' she said, as if she had just noticed.

'No. I left it with my old professor.'

'I thought you were through with training. Do you still need the approval of your professor?'

'Just because a man seeks counsel does not mean he needs approval.'

Now what could she tell the King? He took a document called a subpoena to an old man and left it? 'What sort of advice does he give you?'

'You have a new-found interest in the law.'

'Of course I do. It is your life.' If she were not careful, he would suspect the motive for her curiosity. She braved the feel of his bare skin to touch the gold ring on his left hand. 'It is even the ring you wear.'

He pulled back his hand, twisting the band without looking at it. 'My father gave it to me when I was called to the bar.'

His father. The judge. 'What does it say?'

'*Omnia vincit veritas.* Truth conquers all,' he translated.

She must not forget. All the untruths ordinary people needed to survive were nothing against this touchstone.

No wedding vows would bind him more tightly than this.

'Well, the law seems a tedious, slow-moving business,' she said. 'I had no idea it was so complicated.'

'Sometimes,' he said, 'the law is much more compli-cated than justice.' His stern expression softened. 'You've been patient this morning. You spoke of your old house. Would you like to see it again?'

A little flood of happiness surged through her and she squeezed his arm. 'The house by the river? Oh, yes.'

Even if he was being suspiciously solicitous, the law, and the King, could wait.

Finding the house again was not easy. Forgotten memories guided her as if she were groping through a dark room. Conscious of Justin's eyes on her, she turned down more than one dead end in the maze of streets.

Gradually, things seemed more familiar. A house with a dragon's head over the window. The smell of the river and then, at the corner, she saw it, the small white stone house, just as magical as she had remembered.

When had her mother lost this home? Of all the prop-erties, this one and the one at Upminster were the only ones she cared about.

Here, her mother even played with them, sometimes.

'We had a boat,' she said, drawn towards the house. 'The servant would take us for rides on the river.'

She gazed at the door knocker, the familiar head of a lion, a subtle reminder of the King's coat of arms. If she opened the door, could she walk back in time to the days when she had played barefoot on the jetty?

She raised her hand to knock.

'Solay,' he called, 'are you sure—?'

She knocked, for once not asking his permission.

A plump woman answered the door. A small boy hid behind her skirts and glanced from Solay to Justin. 'What do you want? If you are looking for the Lincoln family, they moved.'

'No, we're… I mean, I used to live here when I was a child. I was hoping to look inside again.'

'Are you one of the Lincoln girls?' The woman squinted with a suspicious eye, still blocking the door, shifting her gaze from Solay to Justin.

'I'm Lady Joan Weston.'

The woman frowned. 'One of the harlot's girls?'

'What did you say?' Justin moved towards the door.

Swallowing her anger at the insult, Solay held him back, nodding.

Wary, the woman looked at him. 'Are you here to force me?'

'No, but—'

The door slammed.

Solay choked back the burning in her throat. The wooden door blurred before her eyes. There was no room for happy memories in the real world. She blinked, refusing to turn until she could see the lion-headed knocker clearly again.

Justin put a hand on her shoulder and reached for the heavy iron ring. 'I'll see that she lets you in.'

'No, please.' She shrugged off his hands and looked past the house to the river one more time. She should not have confessed her affection for this house. Honesty only made your disappointments obvious.

She pushed the sadness deeper into her chest. 'It really

isn't much of a house compared to Windsor, is it?' She smiled, making sure her teeth showed. 'Shall we go?'

Justin's heart slipped when the door shut in her face. As her head drooped forward on her slender neck, he glimpsed the ten-year-old girl, thrown out of her home.

If this was what her life had been like, it was a wonder she had not fallen into melancholia years ago.

He had no words of comfort. Groping for some child-hood memories, she had been judged for her mother's sins. No wonder she tried so hard to please. Her very existence displeased.

Yet she squared her shoulders and put her brave smile back in place. As they walked to the dock, she talked easily, as if the last few moments had never been, asking him anew about the intricacies of the law. And he answered, hoping it would distract her.

Back in the boat, he kept his hand firmly on her arm, fearing this fresh humiliation had saddened her anew. As he peeled back her disguise, he faced a real person and he saw again the pain he had seen from the first.

It frightened him.

The last time he had cared for someone like that, he had killed her.

CHAPTER TWELVE

STEADIED by the oarsman's hand, Solay stepped into the rocking boat, burying her hurt next to her late-day hunger. She refused to mourn. Besides, her pain had an unexpected benefit. As they pushed off, Justin's arm circled her waist again, more gently than on the morning journey, and he answered all her questions about the law.

By the time Westminster came into view, she knew subpoena was Latin for 'under penalty', that it could compel a man's testimony and that the fine for failure to appear was one hundred pounds, a sum to make even a King think twice.

She still did not know whose name was on the writ.

Better to change the subject to frivolous things so he would not suspect her questions were more than idle curiosity.

'What colours do you like?' she said.

'Colours?' he asked as if he did not recognise the word.

'Yes.' She stroked the tightly woven wool of his tunic. 'This beautiful deep blue, for example. Is it your favourite?'

'It was the plainest the mercer had. The rest were gaudy enough for the King's fool.'

'And what foods do you like?'

'Good, plain food and drink.' He shrugged, as if he cared no more for food and drink than cloth. 'No need for it to be sugared and spiced.'

The oarsman's steady dip filled the silence. Plain dress, plain food. The man scorned comforts of any kind. No wonder the King's ways grated on him. 'Did you have a pet as a child?'

He pulled back and searched her eyes. 'Why all these questions?'

She fought a laugh. He had not wondered when she asked about the law. 'How am I to love you if I do not know you? As your wife, I will need to please you with meals and wardrobe according to your tastes.' She smiled, to forestall his objection. 'Yes, I know, you have not yet agreed to wed me.'

'Then talk of yourself. Did you ever have a pet?'

The sudden joyful memory did make her laugh. 'I had a popinjay.'

'A parrot?' He smiled. 'Did he talk?'

'I jabbered nonsense and he replied,' she remembered. They had kept each other company, the bright green bird half a world away from home and the lonely little girl who lived in borrowed houses. 'I think we taught each other to talk.'

She glanced at the boatman, then whispered, so he would not hear her naughty deeds. 'Once, I took him outside and it started to rain. He was so mad! He just kept squawking.'

She shook her head and raised her shoulders like a bird with ruffled feathers, then shrieked, 'Baad, baad', mimicking the parrot's cry just as well as she used to, when her imitation could fool Jane.

The boatman stared, round-eyed, and she started to giggle.

Justin's face, stiff with shock, dissolved into laughter, an easy rumble that came from deep in his chest. 'You sound exactly like a bird! What happened to him?'

Her laughter faded. 'We had to leave him behind.'

When the old King died, they had fled the palace in the middle of the night, jewels scooped up in darkness. There was no time to bring a useless bird to comfort a child. Only a King could waste money on such a trifle.

'I'm sorry,' he said.

She stared at him, unable to believe the word. No one had ever been sorry before. Many, like the woman at the door, had been hostile. Most had simply whispered and stared.

'Thank you,' she said, finally.

Hesitant to break the fragile peace, she sat in silence as Westminster came into view.

The boat touched the jetty and Justin stepped out, then gave her his hand. His touch coaxed some inner warmth, mixed with an ache for more.

Don't succumb. The King's velvet and ermine will warm you and your family long after this man turns cold.

Steadying herself on land, she slipped her hand away. She had enough to spin a story that would satisfy the King. 'I will leave for Windsor at first light.'

He looked at her sharply. 'You are feeling well enough?'

Puzzled, she finally remembered her feigned illness of the morning. 'Quite well now, thank you. You should receive your invitation to join the Court within the sennight.'

'If I do not hear from the King by Candlemas, he'll hear

from the Council.' He walked beside her. 'Who else goes on this gyration? Hibernia?'

And suddenly, Solay feared she knew whose name was on the legal document left at the Inns of Court.

She shrugged, avoiding his eyes. 'I do not know,' she lied. 'I thank you for taking me to London,' she said, huddling beneath her cloak. 'I learned so much about what you do and I'm so interested. That subpoena, for example. Whose name is on it?'

Suddenly, Justin knew why the visit, why the 'wifely' concern and the endless questions about his work. What a fool he'd been to be tricked by sad stories of lost parrots and houses by the river. 'Tell the King he'll find out soon enough, Lady Solay.'

She looked at him, eyes wide with imaginary innocence. 'What do you mean?'

He ignored the pain in his stomach. What had his truthful tongue let slip that the King need not yet know? All because he had thought, just for a moment, that her interest in the workings of the law was sincere.

'You did not drag yourself across the countryside in the snow for the pleasure of my company.' Anger burned in his chest that she let herself be so ill used. That he let himself be so ill used. 'You are here on the King's business, not your own.'

''Tis not true,' she said. 'I came to let you know about the King's gyration and to help you arrange to go with him. Why do you doubt me?'

'Because the King's desires rule your life, not your own. And certainly not mine.'

She faced him, then, eyes steady, though the wind whipped her dark hair behind her. 'The King's desires rule all our lives.'

'Not mine.'

She smiled a woman's smile, then. One of those that said *I know truths you never will.* 'Yes, at the end, even yours.' She pulled her cloak close and turned to go inside.

He wanted to argue, but as Gloucester came out to meet him, he realised that, every day he worked to restrict the King's power, his life, too, revolved around Richard.

Gloucester joined him, leering over his shoulder at Solay. 'A strange choice you've made for a wife, Lamont. Is she as good as her mother was?'

The vision of her skin, licked by firelight, warred with the haunted shadows in her eyes. She was the King's spy and, still, her smile seduced him. 'She is not yet my wife.'

Gloucester raised his brows, but let the statement lie. 'So where's the writ?'

'It's under review. We have only one chance. We can afford no errors.' No one had ever tried to compel a Duke into a court of law. A judge, even a brave one, would need an irrefutable case.

'Your endless details are costing precious time.'

'I'm aware of the urgency,' he snapped. 'The King is rumoured to be leaving Windsor soon.'

'What? How do you know?'

'The Lady Solay told me. Unless we serve Hibernia first, the writ will be useless.'

'Then let's take him. Now.'

'The other lords will never move against one of their own without cause.'

'He's not one of ours. He's an upstart whom the King has raised beyond his station.'

'He's a Duke. To take him without a reason would set a precedent. You could be next.'

Gloucester slapped his gloves against his sleeve as they entered the castle. 'Use what legal tricks you must, just get him out of the way. We must be in control and ready to rekindle the war against France by spring.'

Justin hoped it was only the man's temper speaking. 'Parliament charged us to investigate internal scandals. War remains the King's prerogative.'

'I will not sit idle while Richard loses land my family has held for centuries.'

'His behaviour is no excuse for us to violate our charter.'

Gloucester's look carried all the menace of his nephew's. 'Don't argue the letter of the law with me. Do what I need or I'll find someone who cares more for results than legal pleasantries.' Gloucester raised his eyebrows. 'An army makes the best law.'

As Justin made his way back to his workroom, Solay's deception mixed uneasily with the knowledge that, if the legal path failed, Gloucester would forsake it for something more direct.

And violent.

CHAPTER THIRTEEN

'He's done what?' The King's shout echoed off the stone walls of his solar. He raised a fist.

Solay cringed, expecting the blow to fall on her for bearing bad news. 'He wrote a document, Your Majesty, and took it to the Middle Temple Inn.' It was a titbit of truth, but she hoped it would satisfy.

The King slammed his fist into his palm and started pacing.

Hibernia took over the questioning. 'What did it say?' His patience with her had grown because she was Agnes's friend.

She raised her shoulders, palms open, to convey the confusion of a simple woman. 'I know little of the law.'

The King glared at her, narrowing his hard blue eyes. 'And where is this document now?'

'I don't know.' That was true. She didn't know which professor had it.

Hibernia shook his head. 'Best we start our journey now and leave Lamont behind.'

Solay gasped. Moments before, as she and Agnes had planned, Hibernia had suggested to the King that Justin accompany the court. 'But if he comes, I can watch what he does.'

'Lady Solay, if you cannot tell us something more useful than you already have, there will be no need for either of you to come with the Court.'

Useful. It would be useful to tell them Hibernia's name was on the writ, but, if she was wrong, she would suffer the consequences. If she was right, Justin would. 'I'm sorry I know so little. There were many words I could not read. I think he called it a "sup" or a "sub" something.'

'A subpoena?' Hibernia asked.

She rolled her eyes heavenward, as if trying to think. 'Perhaps.' How had he known so quickly?

The King exploded. 'He's coming after my household! This is treason!'

She swallowed and found her mouth dry. Justin Lamont would do nothing that was not by the law of the realm. Of that, she was certain. 'All the more reason for him to accompany the Court, as the Duke so wisely suggested. If he is left alone, he could cause mischief—'

The King interrupted. 'You expect me to allow him to travel beside me while he's trying to destroy me!'

'I'm sure Your Majesty can protect your household from a piece of paper,' Solay said. Justin himself could not take Hibernia physically with the King's soldiers all around. 'His legal demands can wait upon the King's pleasure.'

She held her breath, hoping flattering words would work.

'My pleasure!' the King snapped. 'My pleasure would be that he leave us alone until pigs fly backwards!'

Hibernia laughed, flapped his arms and walked backwards, snorting like a swine. That set the King laughing until they both doubled over and Richard was forced to use his little white cloth to wipe the laughter that had come through his nose.

And she suddenly saw why the King had raised him so high. A King had no peers. No one to trust. No one to laugh with. Yet with this man, for good or ill, Richard could be himself.

'No law clerk can best a King,' Richard said, in a better mood. 'The King *is* the law.' He put a hand on Hibernia's shoulder. 'Lamont may follow us to verify my seal on the endless documents that Council seems to generate.'

Solay released a breath of relief. The King, jollied, offered to send a messenger to her mother in Upminster with a letter explaining that Solay would be travelling with the Court, along with a gift of a cask of wine.

The Duke nodded at her, a sign of dismissal, and she curtsied, backing out of the room.

Everything was working out as she had planned, except that she seemed to have developed a foolish desire to protect the King's enemy.

As Solay had promised, Justin's summons arrived within the week. Now, as he entered Windsor through the towered gate where he and Solay had watched the stars, he wondered what she had said of the writ and his visit to the Middle Temple. Before greeting the King and Hibernia, he must know.

He found her huddled before a fireplace, studying the

pages of a red velvet book. She raised her violet gaze from the page and she looked glad to see him. Doubtless another whore's trick.

'Justin—'

'What did the King say when you told him about the subpoena?' he began, without preamble.

Whatever fleeting expression he had seen disappeared. She closed the book and rose, her bland smile unwavering as she dipped before him in submission. 'Welcome, husband,' she said, in the tone that lied.

'Cease your pretence.' If he could see her eyes, would he recognise a lie from the truth? He grabbed her arms and pulled her to face him, immediately regretting it. The soft rise and fall of her breath tangled with his own, threatening to make him forget his distrust

She lowered her lashes and ran her tongue over partially open lips. He gripped her harder, trying to hold on to his control instead of taking the kiss that tempted. 'What did you tell him?'

She shook off his hold and he let her, relieved when she stepped away. 'I simply told him you had a document.'

Did she lie still? 'What kind?'

She laughed then, a high-pitched tinkle that grated on his ears. 'Am I a lawyer to remember what the silly thing is called?'

'You remembered in London. In fact, for someone who despises the law, you seem to know a great deal and what you didn't already know, my flapping tongue told you.' He forced her chin up to face him. 'So he knows I am working on a subpoena. What else did you tell him?'

Her calm could have held truth or hidden lies. 'I told him you took it to the Middle Temple.'

He gritted his teeth against the disappointment, sorry to have been proven right. 'Nothing else?'

'What else was there to tell?'

He could not ask whether she told him Hibernia's name was on it. Hope remained that she did not know.

He let her go, wondering whether she told the truth. A creeping chill gripped his back. If the King knew about the writ, and suspected more, there was only one reason he would allow Justin to accompany the Court, a fact so obvious Justin was surprised he had resisted it so long. 'You are to spy on me as we travel.' The truth tasted surprisingly bitter.

She blinked, as if startled. 'Spy? What need is there to spy?' Her words held a practised lilt. 'You are here to keep the King informed, are you not?'

He consoled himself with congratulations that he had been clever enough to leave himself an escape from marriage to this woman. 'You are more than a simple flatterer. You would gladly see me in the Tower if it pleased the King.'

'How can you think so? You are my betrothed. I would do well to look after your head.'

'I am your betrothed for the nonce. Abandon hope of persuading me you are capable of any feeling for me.'

'Why do you still doubt me? I did as I promised and arranged for you to accompany the Court so you could mind the Council's business. These are all things of use to you, not the King.' She leaned against him. 'Do you not think you might enjoy the trip?'

At her touch, his blood again raced throughout his limbs. Her body had beckoned him from the first, but now that he had seen her, he seemed to be ever hard between the legs.

'Enjoy is not the word I would use.' Now that he'd vowed never to touch her, her nearness taunted him all the more. He could see few curves in a body bundled against the cold, yet the clothes that cloaked her mattered not. He saw her as she had been that night by firelight—her breasts peeking out from her dark hair, her skin, fair and smooth, the dark triangle hiding the sweetness between her legs.

'What word would you choose, then?'

He gritted his teeth. 'Torture.'

The damn vixen laughed. ''Tis torture easily ended.'

'Yes. I shall end it when Easter comes,' he said, leaving the room.

Tricked by a glimpse of false pain, he had let down his guard and stepped in like a chivalrous Galahad, thinking she needed rescue from the King.

It was obvious that she did not. In fact, he was the one in danger.

Her mother had shown no respect for marriage and neither did she. Perhaps she did not even realise what marriage should be.

Perhaps it was time he taught her.

As the Court prepared to leave, two grooms hoisted Solay into the sidesaddle Queen Anne preferred. Instead of riding firmly astride the horse, she perched precariously on a little chair with a footrest, balanced as uneasily as she was between Justin and the King.

Still, February's false spring lifted her spirits as they rode north towards Nottingham. She and Justin travelled with the Court. Jane had celebrated a birthday for the first time. Perhaps things could work out.

Without a clear place in the royal household, she and Justin also rode awkwardly between the riding household and the walking household staff. Behind them, moving slowly, followed servants, yeomen, household officials. Then lumbered the carts full of linens, clothing, beds, plates, musical instruments, vessels to celebrate the Mass, and hundreds of other items the royal household needed.

Before them rode the King and Queen, Hibernia, Agnes and the other gentlewomen, and a gaggle of footmen, grooms and armed men. Impatient, the King charged ahead at breakneck speed, catching the trumpeter heralding their approach. Soon, the monarch was a tiny figure in the distance, dwarfed under a clear blue sky.

The sky did not diminish Justin, she thought, as he pulled his horse up beside hers. The smile she had cherished had disappeared, replaced by a scowl of disapproval as he watched Agnes and Hibernia ride side by side.

'His wife would weep to see them thus,' Justin said. Tired of humiliation, Hibernia's wife stayed in their castle in Essex. 'It sours my stomach.'

'They do no more than the rest of the Court. Why do they disturb you so?' she asked, genuinely curious.

'He violates his vows,' he said, his tone a warning.

Her horse shifted from side to side with each step, and she clung to his mane, hoping she would not fall. 'What wife expects a faithful husband?'

'Mine.' The possession in his voice sent a rush of heat through her.

First he demanded love. Now he promised to be faithful. What kind of man expected such passion within a marriage? Marriage was about property and protection. Passion, if you found it, came outside the marriage bed.

'Then I shall have an unusual life,' she answered, trying to steady her voice. 'Even the poets write odes of love to the wives of other men.'

'Not only will I be faithful, I will demand a faithful wife.'

'Then of course I shall be,' she answered, by rote.

He grabbed the reins and her horse stopped, nearly throwing her out of her seat. 'Do not speak those words lightly.' A breeze whipped strands of his dark hair around his forehead. His eyes held her captive.

A frown creased her brow too quickly for her to stop it. All her efforts to please had failed and still he piled on new demands.

She grabbed back the reins and the horse walked again. Fresh air and an unfamiliar sense of freedom loosened her tongue. 'First, I must convince you of my love. Now, I must be ever faithful. Is there no end of conditions that I must meet?'

Justin raised his eyebrow and studied her. 'If you meet my first condition, the second will be no trial. How could I expect you to be faithful unless you come out of love?'

A flash of longing shook her, a leftover dream of love. 'A lawyer who demands proof of all things. What evidence have you seen of love in marriage?'

A smile softened his hard expression. 'My parents.'

Jealousy sharpened her tongue. 'Your parents were an exception to the rule. My mother's marriage served one purpose and it was not love.'

'How so?'

'You do not know the story? As a legal scholar, you would find it an interesting case, though a lengthy tale.'

'Tell me. The road is long.'

She looked around. The riding household had pulled away. The walking household was falling behind. No one would hear.

'After the King died,' she began, 'Parliament tried her as a *femme sole*, responsible for herself.'

'I know what it means,' he said.

She swallowed her resentment. 'They found her guilty, of course, of some imagined charge.' Telling the tale anew, anger sharpened her voice.

He opened his mouth as if to argue, then shrugged. 'The tale is yours. What then?'

'The sentence was banishment.' Remembered fear gripped her stomach. Her mother, four-year-old Jane and herself, nine, would be abandoned with nothing on a beach in France, at the mercy of predators with four legs. Or two. 'It was at that happy moment that Weston reappeared and claimed her as his wife.'

'Did he have proof?'

'What proof did he need? No one disputed his claim, least of all my mother. As his wife, her life and all she owned was his. Parliament promptly handed him her property and her person. He took the property, we took our lives, and he happily spent everything we had and more before he died.'

It was a fair trade, her mother had always said, without ever revealing whether Weston's appearance had been his idea or hers. Either way, no love had been exchanged.

He shook his head, frowning. 'With such an example, I'm surprised that you want to marry.'

'What else is a woman to do? The only women who do not serve men are those who serve God and even He requires a dowry.' Wife, nun, whore. Those were her choices. 'A woman must please either one man or many.'

He pulled her horse to a stop and leaned forward, his eyes demanding. 'Look at me and understand, Solay. Marriage is no game. Should I choose to wed you, you will please one man and one man only.'

Already she had bared her body, but his gaze demanded something more. It was as if he wanted to expose her secret self, the painful parts she would never share with anyone.

'Marriage is no game to me.' She met his eyes, trying to still her shaking hands. Somehow, she had never truly faced what it would mean, spending her life tied to this man. 'It is a matter of life and death.'

She pulled the reins away and rode on, hoping again that she would be able to escape being wed to this frightening man.

Agnes's laughter floated on the breeze and tickled her ears.

CHAPTER FOURTEEN

THE next night, in one of the guest rooms of an overfull abbey, Solay lay awake, listening to the snores around her, and puzzled over Justin's words.

One man and one man only.

As a woman, her only weapon was her body. The promise of it was all. Wisely used, concealed and revealed, she could tempt and tease until she got what she needed from any man.

But this one had resisted her as if he knew that the joining itself would cast a spell. As if there were something more to the act than the simple satisfying of need. Of course, she knew the wanting itself made you dizzy, but after that, when the wanting was satisfied, wouldn't that be all?

Next to her, Agnes shifted on the straw mattress.

'Are you awake?' Solay whispered.

'I am now,' she mumbled.

'What's it like with you and... I mean, when you...?' She did not know how to ask the question. 'He has not tired of you?'

'We want each other more each day,' Agnes said with a sigh that could not be healed.

'When you come together, what is it like?'

The straw crunched as Agnes turned on her back. 'When I lie with him, such loving as we have opens up the soul. There is no hiding.'

It was as she had feared. After such a joining, after he plundered her soul as well as her body, she would look in his eyes and see disapproval every morning for the rest of her life.

She pulled the King's cloak, spread over her like a blanket, up to her chin. 'Is there a way to be together without that kind of loving?'

'Oh, yes. That is the way with many marriages.'

Relieved, she turned on her side and pulled the cloak over her shoulder, muttering her goodnight. It was just as she had thought. Should she be forced to wed him, he would leave her bed soon enough to chase comfort elsewhere despite his threats of love and faithfulness. She would be left alone like Hibernia's wife, only meeting her husband on ceremonial occasions.

She ignored the little voice that kept reminding her this man was not like other men.

She had almost met sleep when Agnes's voice trembled beside her.

'Solay? Would you read the stars for me?'

The stars. Her days in the old astrologer's room seemed a lifetime ago. 'The King forbade it.'

Agnes turned over, whispering directly in her ear. 'Because he fears you may foresee his death,' Agnes said, in words she must have heard from Hibernia. 'But I am asking you to read my stars, not the King's.'

You would not ask me if you knew what a fraud I am.

Solay shook her head. 'I am not even a student.'

'Yet you told the King truths.'

'I had the old astrologer's notes.'

'But you found things he had not.'

Only because I was trying to please the King. She was lucky that her deception had stumbled on his real time of birth. 'Besides, the stars only tell of Kings and countries.'

'Please.' Agnes gripped Solay's arm. 'Help me. I love him so much. I must know whether there is any hope. If you look in your book, you might find something.'

In the urgent whisper of the woman who had been her only friend, Solay recognised the desperate need for something to cling to when there were answers nowhere. Hadn't she sought the same from the stars?

Well, what harm if she spun a little hope for Agnes?

'When we reach Nottingham, I'll try.'

Agnes bounced on the straw-stuffed mattress, stifling a squeal of glee. 'Thank you,' she said.

As Agnes's dainty snore began again, Solay lay awake, wondering whether the stars held any hints of hope for her friend.

Or for herself.

Halfway to Nottingham, the King's entourage descended on Beaumanoir Castle, commandeering the comparative luxury for a few days of rest.

Messengers on horseback travelled more swiftly than the King's household, so Justin spent the day reviewing the most recent documents from Westminster, then persuading the King, like a petulant child, to sign the most important.

Solay was never far from his thoughts. The more he knew of her, the less she was what he had imagined. Though he had glimpsed the long-buried, vulnerable child, he had discovered her pliancy hid strength of steel forged by pain and fuelled by anger. No matter how many blows were dealt her, this woman would not give up on life.

Unlike Blanche.

Yet her vision of life after the vows was more barren than he had ever imagined. All the more reason to avoid being trapped with her.

Despite it all, he looked for a glimpse of her graceful walk as he went about his work and he was relieved at the end of the day when she suggested a game of Merrills.

He was silent while they played, trying to ignore the tantalising whiff of roses every time she reached across the board to move a piece. Before the fire's heat, Solay cast off her cloak to reveal the body he'd been trying to block from his dreams. Firelight highlighted the curve of her breasts and cast shadows in her lap. Desire surged again, but try as he did to blame her, he had to admit that since that night he had rejected her, she'd done nothing to encourage it.

Nothing but exist.

Laughing, Solay scooped up the last of his undefended pieces, besting him again.

He sighed. 'You are the better player tonight.'

'My sister's game sharpened mine.' He was jealous of the warm smile that beamed when she spoke of her sister.

'Tell me about Jane,' he said.

'You would approve of her.' Her gaze was neither guarded nor full of guile. 'She's not afraid to speak her mind to anyone.'

'Is she near an age to wed?'

She rolled a small round Merrills stick between her palms. 'That will be difficult.'

'Why?'

Solay glanced towards the fire.

He regretted the question. It was self-evident that Solay was not considered highly marriageable. It would be no different for her sister.

'I think,' Solay began, 'that Jane would have been happier born a man.'

He frowned. 'It is not so easy to be a man.' Particularly now, when he watched her breasts rise and fall with each breath and struggled to keep his own under control. The fire between them threatened to consume his reason. It warmed him every time he looked in her eyes, scorched him when he touched her hand.

'Neither is being a woman.'

'What makes being a woman so difficult?'

She lifted her brows and stood, acting out the words better than the cleverest jester. 'Jane calls it "mince and curtsy, twitter and cling".' She looked at him over a lifted shoulder with a silly simper, batting her eyes fast enough to blur her lashes.

He laughed. Only one so thoroughly a woman could ridicule her sex so completely. 'And you think your lot is more difficult than a man's?'

She shook her head, serious again. 'It is my nature to be

a woman. I cannot imagine being anything else, just as you can only be what you are.'

He heard a trace of judgement in her voice. 'I am a man. What else do you mean?'

Instead of answering, she reached for his hand, running her thumb over the engraved letters of his gold ring. The whisper of her fingers on the back of his hand tempted him more than her fake kisses ever had.

'"Truth conquers all" you said. I think you have no choice but to believe that, even if it isn't true.'

He pulled his hand away.

Every minute with her was a lie. Not only was he hiding his past from her, he was withholding a truth of his present. Whether she ever loved him or not, he wanted her as he had never wanted another woman.

Their moment of closeness vanished along with the false spring. By the time they reached Nottingham, snow chased them across the drawbridge into the castle.

Solay saw little of Justin.

'Probably wandering through the snow, just to watch it fall,' she muttered, peering out of the window. Perched on top of a rock overlooking the city below, the castle caught the full force of the storm. Wind battered the shutters and screamed in the chimneys as it dropped fresh snow below and blotted out the daylight creeping longer into the sky.

Alone in the room she was sharing with Agnes, Solay moved closer to the fire, opened her mother's Book of Hours and stared at the pages.

The table of planets danced down the page, mocking her.

Oh, she knew the names of all five planets, the twelve signs, and the twelve houses, but how was she to create meaning from this incomprehensible list?

She spread her paper on a table and traced a square representing Libra, Agnes's birth sign, in the middle of the chart, then added empty triangles on each side, not knowing how to fill them.

One by one, she tried to decipher which planet would go in which house, never sure she was right. In the fading daylight, she squinted at the chart, staring as if she might force meaning to appear.

If she was reading the signs right, there was a change coming in the seventh house. Did that mean marriage, a lawsuit or a war?

Her experience with the King's chart had unsettled her. In the right hands, the stars *could* reveal truth. As she looked at the stubborn square in the middle of Agnes's chart, she fervently wished she had the wisdom to discover it and the courage to tell it.

She shook her head. She had been listening overmuch to Justin. She could spin whatever tale she wanted and Agnes would never dispute it.

'I thought you had abandoned the study of the stars.' Justin's voice leapt from her mind to her ears.

He stood in the doorway, his strong eyebrows shadowing his eyes. She closed the book, but the evidence lay spread before his hostile glance. 'Please tell no one.'

He shook his head. 'Always you give me your secrets to keep.' Yet there was no longer any question that he would keep them. He came closer, stroking the volume's velvet cover, then tracing the silver binding. 'Who do you flatter now?'

'I seek to help a friend.'

He sat on the bench beside her. At his nearness, her breath grew fast and shallow.

'You talk as if you believe you can read the stars. Do you?'

She put the book on her lap, frustrated with her traitorous body. He still believed her use of the stars a ruse. Well, it had been, once, and her fragile hope that she might actually decode the heavens was too new to share. 'The King has forbidden me to read.'

He frowned. 'I did not ask what the King thinks. I asked what *you* believe. Think for yourself instead of parroting what you think others want to hear.'

Not content with the surface smoothness most men craved, he urged her to declare her own beliefs, even—no, especially if they contradicted his, or even the King's. Perhaps he intended to trap her. If he told the King that she'd been reading the stars again, there would be no marriage and no grant. That would suit Justin's purpose.

She tapped her lips with her finger, trying to think.

He dragged her hand away and smothered both hands in his. 'Solay, I asked a question. What do you think about astrology?'

The warmth of his grip travelled from his hands to the centre of her being. He wanted to see the parts she did not dare examine herself. 'What do you want me to think?'

'Whatever misbelief you choose, so long as it is your own.' His hands gripped as tightly as his gaze. 'Just tell me something true.'

Trapped by his hands, dizzy with the scent of cedar, badgered by his questions, she had no escape. 'I don't know what I think!' The words exploded from her. For one moment, they were true.

He squeezed her hands more tightly. 'How can you not know? What you think is who you are!'

'No, it isn't.' She ripped her fingers away from the cradle of his hands and rose, clutching the book like a shield. 'I am what other people think of me. Even you. You asked for something true and I told you, but you will not believe it. You've already decided who I am. Nothing I say or do will change your judgement.'

'That's because you've done nothing but lie.'

She sighed. A lifetime with this man would surely be the Seventh Circle of Hell.

'What is it like to have no doubts that you alone possess the truth?' she whispered in wonder. She could not imagine being that certain, that uncaring for the opinion of the world.

An old ache seemed to fill his weary eyes.

'I am not always right,' he said, finally. The admission seemed dragged through his throat.

'I've never heard you express a doubt,' she said, surprised. 'What opinion do you question?'

'I no longer know whether I am right about you.'

Her heart thumped in her ears 'What do you mean?'

He moved closer and she forced herself not to back away. He did not touch her, but the very air trembled as he studied her face as if seeing it for the first time.

As the fire warmed her back, she studied him. Between his brow, two permanent frown lines carved the immovable stone of his face. Implacable features confronted her: the brooding brow, the sharp curve of high cheekbones, even the cleft slashed into his chin.

He was an inflexible enemy of the King and he hated her, yet when she stood this close, none of that mattered.

'You bow to power,' he said, finally, 'yet in defence of family and friends, you stand strong.'

'And you are stubbornly wed to the illusion that the law creates justice.'

'You are as stubborn as I.'

'You accused me of parroting what others say, hardly the act of a stubborn woman.'

'I begin to think your pliability is a feint. In pursuit of your goal, you stand resolute.'

She heard an echo of warmth and wonder in his voice. For once, instead of making her angry, his words gave her a quiet certainty. 'And you believe in speaking your truth no matter what others say.'

He searched her eyes. 'And I would have the woman who is to be my wife do the same.'

She hesitated. She wanted more. Before she spoke, she wanted to know that he wanted not only to hear the truth, but to accept it.

'Tell me...' he touched her cheek, forcing her eyes to his, yet his voice was gentle '...do you believe you can read the stars?'

His breath brushed her lips.

What would it feel like, to tell the truth? Would the words taste sweet, like honey?

'I believe the stars can illuminate our world,' she began,

surprised her throat did not close against the words. Instead, they triggered a rush that washed through her body, cleansing her of fear. 'I do not know whether I have the skill to discover their truths, but I have promised a friend I will try.'

He nodded and let go of her cheek. 'And what will you tell Agnes?'

She did not bother to deny the name of her friend. She had only one. 'Some things she wants to hear and some she does not.' Hibernia might be bad for the King, but Agnes's chart showed coming change.

'Is that a balanced answer meant to please?'

'No. It's the best I know.'

The hard lines around his mouth softened. 'Then I am proud of you.'

The warmth of his approval washed over her. Somehow she had pleased him without trying. She let his words rest in silence, not wanting to spoil this precarious moment of peace. Even the wind had quieted and outside the snow muffled the world like a warm blanket.

I love you quivered on her tongue.

'Thank you,' she said instead.

'If you can tell Agnes the truth,' he said, 'why can't you be honest with me?'

His words shattered her peace and her fear fluttered free again. He wanted more. More frightening, she wanted to give it to him. To tell him that his condition only encouraged lies. To tell him she wished he would love her, too, just as she was. To tell him—

Putting down the book, she donned her teasing mask. 'I'll

do for you what I'm doing for Agnes,' she said, lightly. 'Tell me your day of birth and I'll tell you what the stars say.'

'I have no wish to know.'

He had resisted the question before. She wondered at his reticence. 'It must be St Justin's Day, of course.'

'No.'

She rose to poke a fire already burning merrily. 'Then what day was it your mother remembered so clearly?'

He gritted his teeth and his lips moved, but he remained silent.

'You won't tell me?' She set down the poker and put a hand to her breast in exaggerated disbelief. 'Is there a truth Justin Lamont will not tell?'

She had expected him to smile and answer with the name of his saint's day. Instead, his face turned to stone. 'You have no need to know. We won't be together when my birthday comes.' Without a farewell, he left the room.

She stood unmoving before the fire, staring at the empty doorway. So Justin, too, was hiding something. While he was insisting she reveal herself, what did he fear for her to know?

Stomping around Nottingham's snow-filled inner ward, Justin filled his chest with icy air. He had acted like a petulant child, unable to tell a lie, unwilling to tell the truth. It did not matter whether his birthday was St Michael's, St Luke's or St Ann's. He should just tell her.

But he feared that, if she knew his chart, she could see into his past. Then she would know how unworthy he was.

His campaign to force her into truth was working. Gradually, so gradually, she was revealing more of herself.

God forbid she would ask the same.

No, he must keep her off guard. As long as she had to prove herself to him, he remained in control.

He must keep probing her, yet still make sure she got no closer to him. In just a few weeks, Lent would be over and he could end this betrothal.

What would the King do about her then? Well, that was not his problem. Despite the pain of her past, Solay would survive anything.

If only Blanche had been as strong.

CHAPTER FIFTEEN

AFTER being trapped in the castle for days by the storm, Solay smiled to see a clear sky on midweek Market Day. After the main meal, King and Court went to inspect the progress on the new St Mary's Church, leaving the castle strangely empty.

No one asked her to join them.

Restless, she put aside Agnes's chart and wandered the halls, puzzling over Justin's reticence to tell her his birthday. Was he plotting more against the King than she knew?

She was surprised to find him in the Great Hall, staring out of the window at the melting snow. Focused on her own lack of welcome at court, she had forgotten that he would not be embraced either. The King had taken this journey to be surrounded by his favourites and away from the Lords Appellant. In this company, Justin was the outcast.

That, they had that in common.

'I have been trapped inside these walls for days and would see something of the city,' she said. 'Would you accompany me?'

He flashed a lopsided smile. 'Since you have been so forthright as to ask for what you want, I can hardly refuse.'

As they left the castle, melting snow slipped off the walls, splattering like rain. He put a hand on her arm to guide her. Startled, she stiffened, but did not pull away. Then, his warm, ungloved hand moved down to curl around hers.

The market swarmed with activity. Sellers of wood, water, leather and pottery hoped to supply the needs of the castle's hundreds of visitors.

'We shall have to move on soon,' Justin said, as they saw the King's overworked cook bargaining for onions. The Court had nearly exhausted Nottingham's hospitality—and its stores of food.

'Stop that boy!' a voice cried. 'He's a thief!'

A small boy carrying a loaf of bread ran right towards them, the bread seller chasing after. Several in the crowd reached for him, but Justin grabbed the boy's shirt.

Squirming in snow-soaked rags, the boy looked up at him. 'He took my coin, sir, 'n wouldn't gimme my bread.'

Solay touched the lad's shoulder, pleading to Justin with her eyes. It was easy to cheat the powerless. She knew the desperation of an empty stomach. Did Justin?

His stern frown showed no sympathy.

The round-bellied baker, panting, came close and reached for the loaf, but the boy clutched it to his chest. Justin blocked the man's hand, shielding the boy with his cloak.

Seeing the ermine trim on Solay's cloak, the baker recognised he faced members of the King's party. He stepped back and bowed to Justin. 'Thank you, sir, for catching the thief. I will take him to justice.'

Crushed between the boy's skinny arm and his tiny body, the offending loaf was in plain sight.

'Thief? Are you sure?' Justin said. 'We were just talking about the depleted stores for the King's table when the boy grabbed this loaf of yours. Perhaps we should see more of your wares.'

It was all Solay could do to keep her mouth from falling agape. The words, all technically true, spun with a lawyer's ease into a story that was, indeed, a lie.

The bread maker licked his lips. His belligerent expression became obsequious. 'For the King, you say? Well, I make the best bread in Nottingham.'

The crowd that had followed the baker on his chase drifted back to their shopping.

Justin pulled the battered loaf from under the child's arm and held it in his palm, as if assessing its weight. The broken brown crust nearly cut the round loaf in two. 'This seems light. Are you sure it meets the specifications in the Assize of Bread and Beer?'

The bread maker's face sagged. 'Well, yes, I'm— Well, I mean…'

Solay smothered her smile with a cough as the man babbled on. Only Justin would think to threaten the merchant with violating the King's laws regarding weights and measures.

'Well, if you're certain, we can just weigh it to confirm.'

The man put his hands on Justin's shoulders, as if they were old friends. 'No need for that, sir. In case you have any doubt, I'll just give it to you.'

A smile only she recognised twitched at the corner of Justin's mouth. The boy leaned forward, ready to run, but Justin's hands kept him close.

'How generous,' Justin said, 'that would be fair, since you've already received your payment.'

The man paled and backed away, his eyes never leaving Justin. 'You'll find it good bread and a fair weight.' He pointed to a booth with a green banner fluttering. 'Come to my stall and you'll find many others, all fit for the King's table.'

As the baker escaped, Justin turned the boy around, keeping his shoulder firmly in his grip.

The child's round eyes held both fear and worship. 'Thank you, sir.' His voice trembled a little and he licked his lips, looking at the lost loaf. 'I hope the King enjoys his bread.'

Justin handed back the dented bread. 'I think you will enjoy it more.'

Blinking with astonishment, the child finally had the courage to smile. 'Blessings on you.'

'Next time I shall not be here to save you.'

The boy clenched his fist, ready to fight again. 'But he cheated me!'

Justin crouched down and looked the boy squarely in the eye. 'I know he was wrong, but that doesn't give you the right to steal, even to get what is rightfully yours.'

The boy hung his head. 'Yes, sir,' he mumbled.

'Do you have a mother?'

The boy nodded.

'Then give her this.' Justin stood and dug out a coin. 'And tell her to buy some good wool, ale and a goose.'

The child knelt in the snow and clutched Justin's hands in thanks, then ran, bread in one hand, coin in the other.

Solay watched wide-eyed, uncertain whether the Justin she knew still stood beside her. 'You let him go?'

Justin shrugged and they turned back towards the castle. 'The man cheated him. The boy made it even and no more. It was just.'

'But the law would have said both were wrong,' she said, puzzled. 'I thought you would take both to trial.'

He stopped walking to look at her, his eyes showing a sense of astonishment that she could not see the obvious answer. 'Who would believe the boy?'

It was on the tip of her tongue to taunt him with the proof that power was stronger than the law, when she realised what he had done. 'It isn't just about the law for you, is it? It truly is about justice.'

He tilted his head, as if not understanding her words. 'Did you think otherwise?'

She no longer knew what to think about Justin Lamont. Was he a man of the law who would do nothing not written in the law? Or was he simply using the law to mete out his own idea of justice?

'What will you tell the King?' His matter-of-fact question assumed she would tattle of all that had happened.

She lifted her chin and met his eyes. 'The King has no interest in a stolen loaf of bread.'

His lopsided smile was her reward.

Solay's words burrowed into Justin's brain as they walked back to the castle and the setting sun turned the horizon gold.

It truly is about justice.

The amazement in her voice stung him. 'Did you really think me such a monster as to punish an innocent boy?'

She tilted her head. 'You pride yourself as the caretaker of the law's letter. I thought you would do no less.'

His father would have. His father would have punished them both. 'I did what was fair.'

Her eyes, painfully violet as the early evening sky, searched his face. He met her gaze, surprised to discover he wanted his answer to please her. How had it come to this? She was supposed to earn his approval, not make him long for hers.

'How do you decide when to substitute your judgement for that of the law?'

He opened his mouth to say 'never', but then remembered one time, maybe two, like today, when the situation was so obviously wrong—

Startled, he snapped his jaw shut. Life had been easier when she merely flattered him. 'Those occasions are extremely rare.'

'You made a decision about the boy based on your concept of what was right. Would you apply the same to your work for the Council?'

Unease prickled the base of his spine. The King might not be interested in a loaf of bread, but he would be very interested in the Council. 'Parliament has given us full authority.' More than that, Parliament had passed a law prohibiting anyone to disagree with what the Council did.

'But if you can substitute your justice for the law's, what is the difference between you and the King who substitutes his justice for yours?'

'I care about what's right,' he said, in tones too close to a mumble. 'The King cares only about his own power.'

They entered the castle and he pulled her into a sheltered alcove, trying to read her eyes. Her body tempted him and this time, he did not fight it. He wanted to reassert his power. Perhaps if he kissed her, he would know whether his words had turned her towards or against him.

He took the kiss without asking, not caring who might see them, wanting to reach something in her core.

Remembering her bare skin caressed by firelight, he hardened with want. He teased her lips with his tongue, wanting to taste all of her, wanting—

She stiffened in his arms, her lips tight as the night of their Yuletide kiss. He tightened his grip, pressed closer, but this time, she did not surrender.

He released her, relieved. If she ever truly surrendered, she would conquer him totally.

He cleared his throat and pulled his tunic back into place. 'You're upset.'

'Not upset. I'm…' She pursed her lips and smoothed her skirt. 'Confused.'

'So you will not kiss me.'

'I do not know you.'

'What I did about the boy today—it was right.'

'I know,' she said. 'But it was not the law.'

That night, her words haunted him as much as the memory of her body melting, just for a moment, against his. Why, after weeks of temptation, had she resisted him? Puzzling over that question kept him from wondering why, after weeks of resistance, he had tried to take her.

Waiting for sleep that would not come, he remembered

lying in bed as a child, hearing his mother and father whisper in the bed next door. Her steady, loving voice had always soothed his father, when the judge's pronouncements began to sound like Moses's. Only his mother had been able to make him see another point of view.

After she died, there was no one to temper his judgements.

Now, he faced a woman who challenged everything he held dear, who would gleefully see him clapped in irons if it were the King's whim to do so. In probing his compassion for the boy, she had made him reveal a weakness that would undoubtedly reach his Majesty's ears.

He rolled over, pounding the feather pillow that gave disappointingly little resistance, cursing his candid tongue.

Her question had challenged him to be true to the words he had used to taunt her. Law. Truth. Justice.

He rolled out of bed and threw open the shutters, welcoming the cold air. He stared at the stars she so loved. Solay thought she might bring meaning to them. Could she do the same for him?

He pulled the shutters, closing out the sky. Lent was half over. The King's question would come soon.

There was only one answer he must give.

CHAPTER SIXTEEN

SOLAY loitered in the corridor outside Justin's room, listening to the voices, trying to understand the messenger's words.

The man had arrived, empty-handed. His message must have been too important to commit to writing.

She bent closer to the floor, hoping some words would slip under the door. The King's urgency to know Justin's business had become her own. Despite Justin's prideful honesty, he had been tightlipped about his work since London.

Perhaps his justice and the law had parted ways.

She had known from the first that he opposed the King, but she never thought he would go beyond the law. If true, she must resist the tug of feeling he sparked in her. When he kissed her, she had fought the desire that welled within her, strangely grateful that he had left them an escape, that she was not tied to him yet. If he could lie about the law, could his kiss lie as well?

She retreated down the hall as she heard the men's farewells. Strolling towards the room as if she had just arrived, Solay smiled at the messenger as he left, then stood in the doorway, waiting for Justin to invite her in.

He didn't.

'What news did he bring?' she said, finally, ready to try the honest questions Justin claimed to prefer.

'I will tell the King myself if he needs to hear it.'

'The news might interest the King. Particularly if it concerns treason.'

His eyes darkened. 'Treason is no jest.'

Her heart pounded in her ears. He had not denied it. 'And that is not an answer.'

He leaned back, looking at her. 'Do you even know what treason is?'

'Yes, I do.' She smiled with relish, not needing to pretend. 'My father's law was clear on this. There are seven offences.' Her mother had drilled them into her head. There was a time her mother had needed to know. 'I shall list them for you. First, killing the King, the Queen, or his heir. Second—'

'Actually, it is "if a man compasses or imagines the death of the king".'

She nodded at his correction. 'Yes, even the planning is treason. But if imagining the death of a King is treason, how are we to prove it?'

'And how many might be guilty?'

Are you? She bit back the question and continued. 'Second, killing the Chancellor, Treasurer or Justice while he is attending to his duties. This implies that killing the Chancellor while he is hunting boar would not be treason.'

'Legally correct, Lady Solay.' His eyebrows raised in surprise. 'For someone who protests she knows nothing about the law, you seem well versed in its vagaries.'

'Only of this one.' She fought back a satisfied smile.

'Next, violating the Queen, the eldest unmarried Princess, or the wife of the heir.' Her mother had noted, jealously, that there was no treason in bedding the King's mistress. 'But if the Princess marry, there is no treason in bedding her.'

He frowned. 'You have the mind of a lawyer. It is a shame you haven't the heart of one.'

'I never knew a lawyer who had a heart.' *Until you.*

She recited the rest until she came to the worst. 'And finally, making war against the King or giving aid and comfort to his enemies.'

'The last recourse of lawlessness,' he said, then tilted his head in a bow of respect. 'You *do* know the meaning of the word. I trust you do not accuse the Council.'

'The Lords Appellant on the Council are men like any others.' Gloucester's jealousy, coupled with his royal blood, might lead him to aspire to the throne and bring along the others who hoped for their reward. 'I do not know what they might think or do.'

'But you know me.' He rose, forcing her to look up at him.

'Do I?' She searched his eyes. In all she had learned of this stubborn, impossible man, she would have sworn he would do nothing outside the letter of the law.

Until the boy.

'You know the law and all its tricks,' she said. 'The King takes you for an enemy.'

His grim smile brought no light to his eyes. 'Then do not fear for your life, Lady Solay. You have given me neither aid nor comfort.'

Turning his back, he returned to his papers.

She stood, watching him for a long time. Perhaps if she

could look in his eyes again, perhaps if she could make him smile, then she might know his heart.

He did not turn.

What if the subpoena was just the beginning? What if he planned something worse? What would she do then?

The King summoned her to his chambers late in the day. She sank to her knees before him and acknowledged Hibernia with a nod.

'Well?' The King paced the room as rapidly as he galloped his horse. 'What happened today?'

'There was a messenger.'

'The gatekeeper could tell me so much.'

The red velvet cloak, the crackling fire, none of it warmed her icy fingers. She did not want to betray Justin, but if he planned treason, she could not stand by. 'I think he came from London.'

'What message did he bring?' the King snapped.

Anything I tell you will go straight to the King's ears. So, of course, she'd cajoled the answer directly from the messenger. 'He said the document was ready.'

'The subpoena?' The King was exasperated.

'The messenger did not say, Your Majesty. He brought nothing with him but the words in his head.'

'Whose name is on it?' Hibernia asked.

She looked at him and her heart squeezed for Agnes. 'I do not know.'

She would tell them later, in time for the Duke to escape. If she told too much too soon, it would be Justin at risk. Surrounded by the King's men, he could easily meet his death from an unfortunate accident and no one could prove otherwise.

'He's a traitor, I tell you,' the King muttered.

In his mouth, the words became a hangman's noose. Despite her suspicions, she did not want him dead. 'Surely not, Your Majesty.'

The King's scowl didn't fade. 'Find out what he plans. I'll decide whether it be treason.' He waved a hand to dismiss her.

She bowed her head and backed towards the door.

The King's voice followed her. 'The messenger from Rome will be waiting in Cheshire?'

'If the weather favours his journey,' Hibernia said.

'And the Pope our plea.' The King sighed. 'I am forced to deal with clerks to do what should be done on my word.'

Nodding at the guard, she lowered her eyes, pretending she had not heard.

What plea had the King made to the Holy Father?

When Agnes asked for the room to herself that night, Solay could not refuse. The King and Hibernia were leaving the castle tomorrow and Agnes longed for one night with her lover.

'You say you envy me,' Solay said, 'but I envy you. You have some happiness, even if just for the moment.'

'I may have even more than that,' Agnes answered, then hugged her. 'Thank you.'

A muffled knock announced Hibernia. He took Agnes in his arms, barely glancing at Solay as she left the room.

Agnes's moan followed Solay into the hall through the

closed door. Desperate to escape the sound, she staggered down the dark corridor, but still it resonated, triggering a buzz of desire. Desire, that was all. Not love, nay, surely not that fickle, weak emotion.

But desire, desire was not weak. Relentless, it gnawed at her resistance, conjured carnal dreams, and undermined her attempts to lead him on without losing herself.

She slumped against the wall, eyes closed, held captive by the growls and shrieks and gasps of love. What would it be like, that joining that seemed to wipe out everything else?

'What goes on there?'

She opened her eyes to see Justin, as if her wanting had created him.

He took her in his arms. 'Are you all right?'

Crushed against his chest, her breasts ached to feel his hands. His head dipped. Did his lips brush her hair?

The sounds of Agnes and Hibernia in heat echoed off the cold stone.

He lifted his head. She braced herself against his chest to stop him. 'Nay, you must not enter.'

An unmistakable squeal of feminine pleasure shook the walls. His arms tightened around her. 'You pander for them?'

'Why do you begrudge them their happiness?'

'Because he dishonours his wife. When we are wed, would I see you dally with every man who crossed your path?'

Amidst her dizziness, she heard *when we are wed*. 'No.'

'How can I believe you?' His breath, hot on her cheek, warred with his cold words.

He was hard with wanting. She was weak with it.

Once, she thought she would say anything to snare him.

Now, she would do anything to keep him. No logic, no clever words could triumph over her body's truth.

She tipped her head back to meet his eyes. She steadied her voice. 'You are the first.'

He crushed his lips to hers.

And if a voice in her head whispered 'traitor', she did not listen.

She had always believed that woman tempted man, yet her treacherous body, urged on by the rhythmic sounds beyond the door, curved into his. There was nothing left in the world but quenching the thirst he raised in her.

'Now.' A word. A gasp.

She was not certain who spoke it.

Unyielding stone met her back and the night air still held a hint of snow, yet she pulled up her skirts gladly, baring her flesh to his searching hands.

He seemed equally wild, pushing his breeches down past his knees, then straddling her. He was above her now and she missed the closeness of his hard, tender kiss, but the itch between her legs was more urgent. He teased her gently and she rocked, no longer in control of her mind or her body. Did all lovers feel this? No wonder it drove men mad.

And mad he seemed now, his lips close to her ears, his breath like another caress. And she could not tell whether the moan she heard was Agnes's or her own.

She started to spiral, empty, longing for him inside but consumed by what he was doing to that sweet, secret place. She was almost there, twisting, spinning to what? Her lips opened as if she could nearly—

Abruptly, he stopped.

She cried out at the sudden loss. Stripped of her clothes and his body, she dragged herself up against the wall and opened her eyes. He sat back on his heels, staring at the floor, clenched fist pounding his thigh.

Only one word fought its way to her tongue. 'Why?'

His chest heaved as if he had fought a great battle. 'You tease both of us too much, Joan of Weston.'

She sagged, unable to think, belly burning with a sort of hatred. It was not enough that she had begged him on her knees. He had used her desire to drag her to humiliation again.

She pulled her knees to her chest and covered her legs with her skirt, trying to catch a breath that was not a sob. 'You cannot blame me. You want me, too.'

He nodded, and when he met her eyes again, his looked sad, not cruel. 'I want more than a body.'

'More?' All the hot, wild feelings that had fluttered below her waist gathered in her throat. 'What more do you want?' He disdained her mother. Royal blood did not awe him. She brought no dowry. 'I am nothing. I have nothing except the body you've so forcefully refused.'

He shook his head and she closed her eyes against his pity. It had sounded so easy, to bare her body. Yet this frightening, immovable man had stripped her soul, then found it lacking. His bullying demands for honesty had ripped away the armour that shielded her from the world's scorn. Now, her heart lay naked, veiled by not so much as the thin linen that covered her nipples.

His fingers brushed her forehead, pushing aside the hair that had fallen across her face gently, as if the fury of the last few minutes had never been. 'Until you know who you are, you cannot love anyone else.'

She pulled her head away, angry at his insinuation. 'You know who I am. You have known from the first.' *Harlot's daughter.* Words too painful to speak. Would anyone ever look at her and see neither a harlot nor a princess, but simply a woman? 'That was what this tumble was about. For you to prove you were right.'

He shook his head, his eyes patient and sad. 'That's not true and you know it.'

'Do I?' She lifted her head, gritting her teeth to hold back the bile. She was the daughter of a King. She would not grovel. 'You are the one who claims to know all truth. Tell me what it is, then.'

Justin did not answer. At some point while they had grappled, Agnes and Hibernia had quieted and silence loomed, filling the hall.

She watched, shocked, as he seemed to be unable to speak, as if the truth were as hard for him as for other mortals. Unsteady, he rose to his feet and pulled up his breeches and hose, avoiding her eyes.

Finally, he faced her. 'The truth is this. If you knew me, you would want this marriage no more than I.'

He did not wait for her answer, but walked away, fists clenched. The flickering torchlight glinted off his gold ring.

Truth conquers all.

She hugged her knees and dropped her head. Truly, if she loved a traitor, the truth would defeat them all.

CHAPTER SEVENTEEN

A FEW days later, Solay looked at Agnes's hopeful, round face and then at the chart spread between them on the bed. The King and Hibernia had gone to Lincoln so she could give Agnes's reading without fear of discovery.

If only she could decide what to say.

Despite her lack of training, the outlines were clear. The house of relationship was full of passion and there were signs of great upheaval. Was this change to come, or the upheaval when Agnes came from Bohemia with the Queen?

Just tell the truth, Justin would say. Yet while he spoke of truth he had hidden it as well. Since that night, they had not spoken a word.

Agnes clasped her hands, squeezing her laced fingers until her knuckles turned white.

'Please, proceed,' she said, with the slight quiver around the 'r'. 'You've found something good, yes?'

'Well, perhaps—'

'I knew it!' She bounced on the bed, giddy with happiness.

Solay's good intentions evaporated. If she stretched the

truth to give her friend a little happiness, what harm could there be in that?

Agnes leaned forward, eager as a child for a Yuletide treat. 'What do the stars say?'

She gathered Agnes's hands in hers. 'I see a great change in your house of relationships.'

'So we are to be together?' Agnes held her breath as if her very life hung on the answer.

Solay nodded. It was not exactly a lie.

Agnes's eyes filled with tears and she stood up, tugging against Solay's hold. 'I can't wait to tell him.'

Solay tightened her grip, holding the girl back. 'No! You mustn't. The King forbade me to read. The Duke has no secrets from the King.'

'But he will be so happy. He will make the King forgive you.'

Solay jerked her to a standstill. 'Please. It would go ill for me. Just know in your heart that all will be for the best.' A vain hope, but all she could say.

'It will work, then,' Agnes whispered to herself. 'I had not believed it.'

She released Agnes and watched the girl twirl happily around the room, envying her joy. Perhaps for some, perhaps for Agnes, love was possible.

Until Justin's subpoena reached him and Agnes might find her lover on trial.

There it was, right before her, the disaster warned of in the stars. She had kept the information from the King, but Agnes was her friend.

Was she certain that Hibernia was named? Certain enough to tell Agnes? If she did, what would happen to Justin?

Agnes hummed and giggled, suffused with happiness beyond what Solay had ever imagined.

No, no need to tell Agnes anything yet.

'Oh, Solay, it will be so wonderful! The Pope will say yes and then we'll—' She bit her lip. 'I can tell you no more.'

If the Pope favours our plea. Could the messenger the King was expecting have something to do with Agnes?

Agnes knelt before her, eyes teary with joy. 'I will make certain you are rewarded when all this is over.'

Solay answered with a rueful smile. 'You could suggest to Hibernia that the King would be better served if I married someone other than Justin.'

Agnes nodded. 'Don't worry. The King will find you someone else. I'll make sure of that.'

Someone else. Someone who didn't hate her. Someone who didn't make her weak with desire.

She thanked Agnes and, as they hugged, waited in vain for a feeling of relief. Instead, she remembered a line she'd seen written in the old astrologer's notes.

The stars speak in riddles that we interpret as we wish, never seeing the true meaning until the time has passed.

Until it would be much too late.

The King and the Duke returned the following week. Hibernia approached her after the main meal and asked her to walk with him. Justin's frown and Agnes's smile followed them into the corridor.

Solay waited for him to speak. Dark and slender, the

Duke was a perfect foil for the King's fair splendour. A small and merry mouth perched under a straight and handsome nose. Perpetually raised brows topped light brown eyes, ever moving.

She saw in him neither the threat that Justin did, nor the passion that Agnes did. He was, simply, a man.

'Agnes tells me you have been a good friend,' he said.

'And she to me, your Grace.'

'She tells me you want a different husband.'

She hoped Agnes had not put it so bluntly. 'The King's wishes are mine. I simply hope my husband will feel the same loyalty to him that you and I do.'

'You speak of loyalty, yet you disobeyed his express orders not to study the stars.'

All heat left her body. Beneath the covers, lovers have no secrets. Well, too late to deny it. 'I read only hers, not the King's.'

'Ah, but in reading hers you read mine and in reading mine you read the King's more than you know.'

'I meant no harm.' The King might banish her from court, or worse, for such disobedience. 'Please—'

Hibernia held up a hand, smiling. 'Worry not. I can keep secrets that Agnes cannot. You gave her the courage to accept me.'

She murmured her thanks, certain again of one truth she had always known. Nothing was more powerful than a woman's words, whispered in darkness.

'When Lamont rejects you, who would you like the King to choose?'

Relief warred with a pang of loss. She struggled to

picture the Earl of Redmon, but Justin's image rose instead. Surely after the betrothal was broken she would want another man. 'The King's choice shall be mine.'

A smile played on his lips. 'Of course it will. We would not tie such a faithful friend to an enemy. And you need not worry about garnering any more information from Lord Justin. We've taken care of that.'

She took no comfort in the thought.

After supper, Solay approached Justin for the first time in days, carrying the Merrills board as a crutch.

Easter was little more than a fortnight away. Assured that the King would find her another husband, she no longer needed to curry Justin's favour. Besides, there was no doubt Justin would reject her.

Was there?

She must be sure of his mind. That was the reason she sought him out. The only reason.

'Easter comes soon,' she said, after losing the third game in a row. She would be glad to be free of Justin, yet huddled over the board, her body warmed with desire and something more she refused to name.

'And this long disguising will be over.'

She pursed her lips against unwelcome disappointment. Over the weeks, she had donned fewer disguises with him. He might not believe she loved him, but had he not noticed something different about her?

She lifted her chin. 'I am not the same person that I was at Twelfth Night. Don't you agree?'

'What I think is not important. It's what you think of yourself.'

'You play word games.' She slammed the leftover pieces down on the board, angry that he had noticed no difference in her and angrier that she cared. 'It is what *you* think and whether *you* can be convinced that I love you that is in question. It is evident that you cannot.'

His dark eyebrows rose and he blinked, for once speechless.

How appalling she had let her tongue run free. She wanted him to reject her, but she should not sound angry about it. 'Forgive me. I should not have spoken thus.'

'Do you think I will leave if you anger me?'

She drank in his obstinate gaze and the stubborn set of his narrow lips, memorising him for later. She might not love him as he wanted, but she felt something for him she hadn't weeks ago.

She wanted to believe in this man, to believe he would cleave to the law despite the temptation to turn traitor, to believe in choices beyond those made by the stars.

'I think,' she said, rising, 'that you will leave no matter what I do.' Truth, it seemed, tasted of rue as well as honey. 'Because the one thing that has not changed is the one thing I cannot change.'

'Solay.' The word echoed with agony so deep that it stopped her.

'Yes?' she whispered.

Pain etched lines around his mouth and eyes. 'I am sorry. The other night.' Each word seemed pulled from him like a stone. 'I should not have treated you thus.'

She blinked back tears. 'Thank you.'

'The faults are not all yours. They are mine.'

A pretty lie meant to soothe, she thought. Had she taught him something after all?

They walked towards her room together in silence.

'Justin…' she began, then held her breath. He must know that the King's sword was at his back. Glancing around, she saw no one near. She leaned to whisper in his ear, as if giving him a goodnight kiss. 'Be careful. The King watches you. He needs no help from me.'

'But he will get it anyway, won't he?' he whispered back.

Pride straightened her spine and she looked at him. 'No. And the pity is, you do not understand that.'

She closed the door on him, unable to say more. Listening to his fading footsteps, she sighed, relieved this would all be over soon.

Liar.

You didn't tell him you loved him because you were afraid you would have to marry him. Better to find some other man, one who will only require your body and, later, not even that.

Someone who won't care who stares back at you from the mirror each morning.

She skewered the fire with a poker, then picked up Agnes's ivory-backed mirror, peering at the image for reassurance.

Let's be honest, my dear. What do you see when you look at yourself?

And the reflection in the glass seemed blank.

Justin grimaced against the raw wind as the King led his boar-hunting party to Sherwood Forest. Even after Solay's warning, he was surprised when Richard had ordered him to join the party.

The wind stung no more than the memory of Solay's honest outburst. For once, there was no question of how she felt. Well, that's what he had wanted, wasn't it? He could release her, confident that at least he'd taught her something about honesty.

And, he must grudgingly admit, she had taught him something as well. He had wielded the truth as a weapon, trying to keep her away from the things he wanted no one to know.

But her forthright warning had confused him. Had she developed some loyalty to him after all?

His disagreeable mood soured at the sight of a phalanx of unfamiliar knights sporting the badge of the white hart. A King should ride with the trusted barons of his Kingdom, not a collection of random knights.

As the fewterers let the greyhounds loose, Richard galloped ahead to confront the boar alone. Lacking battle credentials, the King was ever eager to prove his courage.

One thrust of the tusk and a boar could split a man in two. Even a King.

Fighting the low-hanging branches, Justin and the rest of the party charged after him, following the barks and squeals. What would happen to the throne if the childless King were careless enough to get killed by a wild boar?

The thought slapped him like the leaves. If he wondered, Gloucester had, too. He would be all too willing to take his nephew's seat. This was not Parliament's plan for the Council, but was it Gloucester's?

As they broke into the clearing, Richard stood crowing

over the dying boar, impaled on the spear. As the horses stamped the soil and the pages' lips turned blue, the animal heaved his last breath on the damp ground, his entrails staining the fading snow.

Justin turned his horse away. A useless kill. They would eat Lent herring tomorrow. Once again the King had wasted coin, even life, for his own amusement. Because he wanted to. Because he could.

Because he was the King.

The party had left the pages to truss the boar. On the way back to the castle, the King, rosy and smiling, brought his horse beside Justin's.

'I understand you are an expert in the definition of treason,' Richard said, finally.

Did every word he said to her reach the King's ear? 'I have studied the law. I know the definitions in all the Statutes.'

'And have you advised the Council on treason?'

He looked sharply at the man. 'The Council needs no advice in this matter. Nothing we do is treasonable.'

'And what about treason not covered in the Statute? What do you advise the Council about that?'

Treason is no jest, he had warned her. But reckless, she had put him in the path of the King's wrath, as surely as the dead boar. 'There is no treason if the law does not name it.'

'Justices on the bench decide that, not words on parchment.'

'But the Justices are sworn to uphold the law.'

The sinister expression turned petulant. 'Why must you fight me on all things?' Richard whined like Justin's six-year-old nephew struggling against bedtime.

'I do not fight you, Your Majesty. There is no conflict between the law and the King.'

'Exactly!' The King's whoop caused his horse to break stride as the castle came into view. 'God anoints the King, so I am the law! Only when all men unite in allegiance to me can there be peace in the realm.'

Suddenly, Justin saw Richard as if for the first time. Here was a man who truly believed he carried the entire realm on his slender shoulders. But the mortar of allegiance must bind to more than a man, else the country would be no more than a collection of warring tribes.

And he knew the King did not understand this, nor did he have the wisdom to learn it. The centre of earthly power while still a boy, he saw a world that had always revolved around his wishes.

'Your Majesty, even a King cannot breach God's law.'

A thin, satisfied smile lingered on Richard's lips. 'You might be surprised what a King can do.'

Justin cleared his throat. 'I have learned not to let Your Majesty surprise me.'

'So what do you think of your bride now, Lamont?' the King said, after a pause. 'Do you not long to have her in your bed? Or have you had her already?'

The vision of her, half-naked on the stone floor, rose before him. He still did not know how he had found the strength to resist her, but Richard's insinuation angered him. 'She will not share my bed unless, and until, we are wed.'

A page helped the King down from his horse. 'Well then, reject her. I shall find her another husband.'

Justin gripped the reins so tightly his horse jerked his head. Wasn't that what he wanted? To be rid of her? 'Not yet, Your Majesty.' Was it jealousy moved his tongue? He resented the King's interference in what had become a more complicated relationship than he had ever planned. 'Until Easter, she is mine.'

And suddenly, the weeks that had stretched endlessly to Easter seemed short, and, instead of being relieved, he glimpsed all the days afterwards, stretching forwards empty without her.

CHAPTER EIGHTEEN

THE riotous morning chorus of birds woke Solay on Easter day before sunrise. Their frantic chirping settled in her blood, whether in anticipation or dread, she was not sure.

Lent was over. Today, after the Easter festivities, she would be released.

Yet until then, they must act betrothed. Justin walked her to the church and sat beside her at the Mass. All the words blurred except those he spoke. Afterwards, at the feast, the long-awaited bite of beef and bacon from their shared trencher tasted no different from yesterday's red herring. Her saffron-yellow decorated egg and Justin's pale green one looked no better than Hibernia's, covered with gold leaf.

Justin's eyes never left her, asking questions his tongue did not.

Just a few more hours and he would release her. Of course he would. She had given up trying to please him.

When the page summoned them, she was surprised to feel Justin's hand take hers, his ring a hard wedge between her fingers.

Truth conquers all.

She gripped his hand, stopping outside the King's chambers, suddenly unsure. 'Tell me. What will you say?'

Something, not quite a smile, tipped his lips. 'What will *you* say?'

Mute, she tried to read the face that had become dear to her, but she caught no hint of what he wanted her to say.

Except that her hand still lay in his.

With a twinge of disappointment, Justin realised she had stopped trying to change his mind. She had not said words of love in weeks, even when he had given her the chance. He didn't know whether she had lost the desire to convince him or simply the hope that she would, but he would play this to the end and force an honest answer.

Yet his palm itched to stroke the dark hair drifting over her breast, to push it over her shoulder and then cradle her head and draw her lips to his.

'Now,' interrupted the page. 'His Majesty awaits.'

She tugged against his hand, but he would not release her as they entered the King's solar.

The King barely glanced at them. 'Lamont, since the Lady Solay has not met your condition, I release you from this betrothal.'

Beside him, she sighed and closed her eyes. Relief or regret?

'Not yet, Your Majesty. The Lady Solay and I are betrothed until and unless I release my condition. You must at least ask her the question.'

Her head snapped up. He tightened his grip on her hand and she turned to him, amethyst eyes full of something he could not decipher. Pain? Hope? Was she thinking of him or of the Earl of Redmond?

Richard sighed, exasperated. 'So tell us, Lady Solay, do you love him as he demands?'

'I have already told Lord Justin of my feelings.'

What had she told him? That she lusted for him. That he angered her. That she had changed.

But when he asked her one final time, she had not lied and said she loved him.

'What kind of answer is that?' the King said.

A small smile twisted Justin's lips. 'An honest one.'

The King waved his hands to hurry them to the expected conclusion. 'Lent is over, Lamont. Your time is up. Do you believe she loves you? Will you have her to wife? Yes or no?'

She gripped his hand. Behind her eyes, he recognised pain, fear, and something else he couldn't quite capture.

With just a word, he could be free.

'Yes.'

Speechless and numb, Solay loosened her grip on his hand, strangely disappointed, because she had come to know the cadence of Justin's voice.

And she knew that he was lying.

CHAPTER NINETEEN

'LADY SOLAY, what say you?' The King's eyes shifted between Solay and Justin. 'You must both consent freely for the marriage to be valid.'

Solay stammered, not knowing what to say. For once, she could not decipher Justin's expression.

'Yes' lay between them like a gauntlet.

She looked frantically towards the door, hoping to see Hibernia. Why was he not with them? Had he truly arranged with the King for her to wed another? Perhaps this question was the King's way of letting her escape.

Justin released her hand and she nearly stumbled. Arms crossed, he looked down at her. 'Solay, the time has come to speak of what *you* want.'

What she wanted. As if her desires were important. She suppressed a disgusted shake of her head. What would it feel like to care, as Justin did, only for your own opinion? If she displeased the King, it would not matter that she pleased herself. Unless Solay found a protector, not only she, but her mother and sister, would have nothing.

The King drummed impatient fingers on the arm of

his chair. If she threw away this man, he might not give her another.

Keep both men happy, her mother had said. She couldn't satisfy even one of them.

'It shall be as the King wishes,' she said, bobbing a curtsy towards his bent head.

'No.' Justin grabbed her arms and turned her to face him, ignoring King and protocol. 'It shall be as *you* wish. What say you, Lady Solay? *You* must choose what you want.'

She leaned into his strength, surrounded by the familiar scent of wood and ink. Until now, another husband had been a vague idea, but, faced with the prospect of another man, it seemed impossible that Justin should disappear from her side. She knew the feel of his fingers guiding her elbow, knew the sound of his step on the stairs, understood his favourite opening gambit at Merrills and how to beat it.

Beside him, her traitorous body yearned for the heat they shared and for something more. Lifting her eyes to his dark, demanding gaze, she lost her grip on time and space. Dizzy as when she watched the snowflakes, she clung to him, knowing that if this warmth were ripped away, nothing would ever be the same.

And in that moment, she lost herself.

'Yes. I want to marry you.'

Justin released her and the spinning room righted itself. A smile cracked his face without reaching his eyes.

'You have made your choice, Lady Solay,' the King said. 'Live with the consequences.'

And she wondered whether any of them had chosen what they wanted.

She walked out beside Justin. He did not reach for her hand.

'Why?' she asked, when they were out of the King's hearing. 'Why did you lie? I never said I loved you. You trapped me.'

'Trapped? Oh, no, my Lady Solay. The choice was yours.' She could not read his face. 'Did you not speak your mind?'

Caught between the King and Justin, she had blurted something. And she was terribly afraid it had been the truth.

'How could this happen?' Agnes moaned, as she and Solay packed to leave Nottingham. 'It was settled. Now the King is angry with Hibernia and Hibernia is angry with me.'

The impatient King had decided they would be wed before they left Nottingham to return to Windsor. Richard was honouring them with his presence and gifting her with a new gown for the occasion. With the King as witness, their marriage would never be plagued with the doubts that followed her mother and Weston. They would be bound through eternity.

Agnes sighed. 'Why didn't you trust me?'

Solay gritted her teeth. There had never been anyone she could trust before. 'The Duke wasn't there. I wasn't sure.'

Agnes blushed. They both knew where the Duke had been. The room had reeked of lovemaking when Solay returned.

'It is all Justin's fault,' Agnes said, pouting.

Solay shook her head. 'No, the fault is mine. I made the choice.' She could blame neither Justin nor the King nor even the stars.

'So you do love him. If you do, then it will all work out somehow.' Agnes, addled by her own romance, seemed willing to believe that love was an excuse for anything.

Yet what was she to call simultaneous comfort and distress that gripped her in his presence? Her mother had been right. Unruly want had made her weak. Her body had answered the question. Now, her heart and her mind had to deal with the consequences. 'Not the way he wants.'

Agnes gripped Solay's hands. 'If it does not work out, you could still find a new husband.'

She shook her head. 'Even a King cannot break God's law.'

Agnes waved her hand in the King's gesture of dismissal. 'There are ways. On the wedding night, if he can't…well, then you wouldn't have to…'

Solay laughed at the absurd suggestion, her cheeks hot. Giddiness and terror warred at the thought of bedding him at last. 'I certainly believe he can.'

'Ah, but the witnesses will look for proof.'

It would not be hard to wave a bloodstained sheet. 'He will be my first, Agnes,' she whispered.

One man and one man only. What would that be like?

As Agnes hugged her, Solay smiled. Now that they were to be married, he would not refuse her bed. Even if he hated her, her body might find a way to rule his.

And she might expose his heart, without risking her own.

As the wedding banquet stretched endlessly past sunset, Justin sat next to his bride, wondering how he had got here. He had vowed never to marry, yet the stars seemed to have aligned against him.

Since he and Solay had left the King's chamber, Justin had tried to answer the question she had asked.

Why?

He didn't want to answer. Wasn't sure he could. Hadn't known he would say 'yes' until they stood before the King and he faced losing her to a man whose previous wife had conveniently fallen down the stairs to her death.

So out popped the word. Misplaced chivalry coupled with a final effort to force Solay to choose what *she* wanted.

Still, her choice surprised him. Had she spoken truly? Perhaps he was the one who should be asking 'why'? She must have been desperate to provide her family with the security of a marriage. Or perhaps she had heard the rumours about the Earl's wife.

And only one thing had surprised him more than her choice.

His reaction to it.

As he had waited for her to speak, his desire to be rid of her had warred with his fear that he would lose her and he realised he was once again at risk of caring for a woman who cared nothing for him.

One woman had ended up in the Thames because she was to be married to him. At least Solay would have no reason to throw herself into the Thames because she wasn't.

Well, if she were that desperate for a husband, she would have one.

That and nothing else.

As the door closed on the rowdy group that had led them up the stairs, Solay sighed with relief, the taste of red wine and anticipation on her tongue.

Finally, she was alone with her husband.

Solay glanced at him through her lashes. The curve of his jaw, immovable as carved stone, had not changed since they had stood before the church door that morning. Surely, when they were alone behind the bed curtains, he would bend. Surely, now that they were married, he would reach for her and the fire she had felt so often would flame free.

The way to a man's heart is through his stones, her mother always said. Make him feel as if he is the most desirable man on earth.

Solay set aside her fading nosegay of lavender periwinkle and yellow cowslip and wandered the unfamiliar room where Agnes had moved her things. Beneath the aching want and the fear of surrender, she recognised something else in her desire.

A flicker of hope.

They were husband and wife now. She had provided for her family. Could she and Justin truly come together?

Silent, he still stood at the door. Drawn to the window, she looked out at the familiar sky, searching for something to say. 'The stars look beautiful tonight.'

'Then let them keep you company.'

The faint hope she had cradled so carefully crumbled to ash. She turned towards him, the floor unsteady under her feet. 'Where are you going?'

'To find a bed.'

The familiar pain burned inside her. She felt again the cold stone against her bare legs and the hot rage at his rejection. Until you know who you are, he had said. Well, she might be a harlot's daughter, but she was his wife now. He could not refuse her.

'Justin, we are well and truly married and your bed is here, with me.' Did he still doubt her past? She gentled her tongue and widened her eyes, for sincerity. 'There has been no other man.' She stretched out her hand, palm up. 'It shall be you and no other.'

She held the pose, her elbow rigid, as anger consumed desire and sweat dampened her back.

His eyes darkened with desire, but he did not reach for her. 'I will not share your bed.'

She pulled back her arm, open palm now a fist. 'It is grounds for ending the marriage if you do not.' Too sharp a tone. She swallowed and tried on a teasing smile, hoping to rile his pride. 'Or cannot.'

No trace of male conceit crossed his face. He showed no fear that his manhood might be questioned. Instead, he mimicked her bantering lilt, twisting his lips into grotesque smile. 'Oh, milady, this is the marriage you so fervently wanted. Do you wish to end it so soon?'

Her palm itched to slap his smug face. She ignored the ache in her chest and tried to think over the angry heart-beats in her ears. What possible reason would he have to refuse her now?

If you knew me, you would want this marriage no more than I. Was he afraid she would discover him a traitor?

She forced her tongue to move. 'You said if I knew you I would not want this marriage. Now that we are married, what is it I must not know?'

'You got the marriage you wanted, Solay. Since you

could bring no love to it, you will find no love in it.' He pulled open the door.

'What are you doing?' she whispered, tugging on his sleeve. Drunken laughter still echoed from the floor below, but soon the crowd would want to witness the consummation.

'I will not lie with you, Solay. Not tonight. Not tomorrow. Not for the rest of our blighted lives.'

The drunkards were weaving up the stairway. She pulled Justin's unbending arm. 'All right, but come inside. Sleep on the floor if you must, but don't let them think you did not sleep with me.'

'You made this bed. Lie in it alone.' He pulled his arm away from her and stepped into the corridor.

She looked down the hall, biting her lip. 'What will people think?'

'Whatever they want. You needed money. Our agreement gives you a percentage of my income and rental monies. Give your mother and sister what you will. You need not whore with your husband for it.'

Stunned, she watched him walk off, in full view of the drunkards coming up the stairs.

Gather your wits, Solay. He might not care for the Court's opinion, but you do. If she accused him of neglecting his marital duty, she could end it now. She could be free.

But the King, angry with her, would never reward her with another husband. Without a protector—husband, father or king—she had nothing.

She turned to the crowd and waved. 'He needs to clear

his head,' she called out, forcing a laugh. 'If he is to perform his husbandly duties.'

They laughed with her and returned to the hall and their drink. She shut the door. With luck, they would drink to slumber and not mount the stairs again.

She crawled into bed alone, regretting that she had not listened to Agnes and made preparations. She had never imagined he would not take her, once they were wed. If the sheets showed no evidence, it would be her virginity, not his prowess, that would be questioned.

Sliding her hand beneath the pillow, she touched something damp and pulled it out into the light.

A bloody cloth.

She smiled at Agnes's thoughtfulness.

After the castle had quieted, she rubbed the cloth on the middle of the bed sheet. It left a reddish smear. Not much, but enough.

She tossed the cloth into the fire and watched it burn, blaming the smoke for the tears stinging her eyes.

She had got what she asked for, squandered her choice on this man and now she must live with the sorrow. She had never expected love in her marriage. Why did she now regret that her husband did not love her?

Her family would be provided for. Compared with that, her happiness, really, meant nothing. It would be better this way. Better not to hope. Better to live at arm's length.

At least the hate in his eyes would not be her first sight upon waking.

CHAPTER TWENTY

ON SOLAY'S first morning as a married woman, the maid removed the bloody sheets with a smile. Late in the morning, when Agnes knocked on the door, Solay assumed a blushing smile and invented a long night of lovemaking for her enraptured audience.

'So you did not need my little gift,' Agnes said.

Solay coughed. 'I...uh...burned it so it would not be found.' Even the truth could be a lie.

But her friend did not notice. 'He's so stern, he frightens me, but it is evident that he desires you. Even the King noticed.'

The King. The thought stopped her tongue.

'Agnes,' she began, trying to look bashful, 'we did not speak of his work. If the King asks—'

Agnes patted her hand. 'Don't worry. The Council's power will be over soon.'

Solay shook her head. 'It's near half a year until November.' And, she had discovered this much, Parliament could easily extend the charter longer if they wished.

Agnes pursed her lips. 'Sooner than that.'

Her stomach turned over. 'What do you mean?'

'I've said too much.'

'Has this marriage come between us, then?'

Agnes laughed. 'Never! The stars brought us together as surely as they brought me my Duke. I'll tell you later, I promise.'

Not comforted, Solay laughed with her. She was hiding things from Agnes, too. But, bedded or not, there were some things a wife deserved to know. How was she to protect Justin if she did not know the truth?

Sly smiles followed her through the halls until she found him at his desk, looking as if he had slept no better than she.

He frowned as she entered. 'So we start our marriage with a lie.'

Which one? she wanted to ask. 'What do you mean?'

'All of Windsor castle is smirking at me and congratulating me on how well I performed my duty last night.'

'Would you have preferred the truth?' Too late to wonder whether she'd made the right choice. 'I could have put it about that you despise my touch.'

A hint of regret shaded his eyes and his cheeks reddened. 'That's not what I said.'

She squashed her quiver of hope. She would beg no more. It was her turn to wound. 'Perhaps I should have told them you were too deeply in your cups to find your way home.'

The anger in his gaze satisfied her. 'That's a lie.'

'Did you wish me to tell them the truth?'

'You did not need to tell them anything.'

'Consummation seals the wedding vows, as you told me many times.'

He frowned. 'Yes, but it was no one's concern but our own.'

''Tis done,' she snapped, anger fuelling her tongue. 'You were not there to be consulted.' She was tired of grovelling for approval that would never come. 'And now that we are bound I must know. What will happen at the end of the year when the Council finishes its work?'

His shoulders relaxed, as if he were glad to be again on impersonal ground. 'If all is in order, the King will resume his rule.'

'And if all is not in order?'

'I will do as Parliament decides.'

'You will not…' She stumbled over the word. *You have given me neither aid nor comfort.*

'Commit treason? You know very little of the man you have married.'

That, she feared, was true. 'And when I asked you directly, you would not tell me.'

'It is time for you to answer a question, wife.' He paced as if questioning an accused criminal. 'Where lies your loyalty? With the King or with me?'

She drank him in with her eyes, this tall, harsh man who was now her husband. She wanted to believe in him, wanted to believe in integrity that bowed to no man, not even a King.

And yet, he feared something.

'Why should I have to choose?' she said, finally.

'The King gathers a private army. Who do you think he intends to fight? The French?'

'Of course.'

'His barons would do that gladly.'

'Who else would he fight?'

'You, of all people, are not that naïve.'

She wasn't, but she couldn't face the prospect. 'You misunderstand the King's intentions. Unless you plan treason, my loyalty needs no dividing.'

As Justin shook his head in disgust, she prayed, fervently, that it would not.

Justin became familiar with the stars over the next fortnight as the Court travelled back to Windsor. Night after night he lay next to her, staring at the sky, his body burning, and wondered why it had seemed so important to resist her.

In the daylight hours, he would remember.

So he kept her at a distance, even after they reached Windsor, not telling her when he visited London and the Middle Temple again.

For if he lay with her, the last of his resistance would crumble. He would be able to withhold none of himself.

And when she discovered it all, even if he kept his head, his heart would be lost.

Justin sought out Gloucester after the hours of pomp as the Order of the Garter installation ceremony dragged to their conclusion.

The Duke was in a foul mood. 'It sickens me. All this for a lad who's never seen a battlefield,' Gloucester grumbled, as they walked across the Upper Ward to the banquet hall. 'My father created this honour for fighting men. I was not allowed to join until I was four and twenty. Now, he gives the garter to a boy of twenty and two women.'

Justin was in no frame of mind to listen to Gloucester's complaining. 'I went to London yesterday.'

'Good,' Gloucester muttered, leading him away from prying ears. 'When do we take Hibernia?'

Yellow gillyflowers dotted the Upper Ward and bobbed happily in the spring breeze. It seemed impossible that something so simple and beautiful could still live in the world in which right and wrong no longer existed. 'No judge would issue the subpoena.'

'Why? What was wrong with it?'

'Nothing.' He had checked and rechecked that. There was no legal reason for their reluctance. Judges can be bought for a farthing, Solay had said. She was wrong. Apparently, fear was as strong as a farthing. 'No judge would risk offending the King.'

'Then we'll take him without it,' Gloucester fumed, 'before the King escapes to the countryside again.'

Justin frowned. 'If we violate the law, we are no better than he is.'

'I don't care. We should have clapped him in chains months ago.'

Gloucester's patience, never long, was nearing its end. Unless Justin could make the law work as it should, Gloucester would turn to force and everything he had strived for would be for nothing.

'There's another way. Based on what I discovered in Chester, I believe we can impeach him.'

The man's eyes lit up. Instead of forcing him to answer

questions, impeachment could remove him from the Court, or even the country, permanently. 'Are you sure?'

'What he's doing is worse than what de la Pole did and the Commons impeached him.' Impeached him because Justin had laid an inevitable path of legal logic for the Speaker to follow. 'He's gathering a private army for the King.'

Gloucester's sputtering anger drained, leaving his face pale and his lips pursed. The only reason the King would need fighting men beyond those his barons would supply was to turn against them.

He nodded. 'Do it.'

Justin fought a pang of regret. Solay would hate the very thought of putting someone else through what her mother had endured. Besides, if she found out too soon, so would the King.

So he would not tell her.

When had he learned to lie? Had she taught him that?

A few days later, Solay received a message from home.

She smiled, homesick at the sight of Jane's careful letters. Solay had written home as soon as she returned to Windsor. Would they be pleased at her marriage?

But the message was short and terrible.

Weston's nephew was suing them for the last thing they owned: the dear little house where she had spent the last ten years.

'That house had never even belonged to Weston!' she yelled to the empty room. 'He has no right.'

But time after time, the unfeeling courts had determined what was right, taking property her mother had paid for in never-ending revenge for the fact that a well-loved King could age.

If only the law actually worked, as Justin believed it did, the law might actually help them.

Would Justin?

He still avoided her bed, but he could not avoid his duties as her husband. She had married him to protect her family. Now, she would discover whether her sacrifice had been for naught.

She entered his work room without knocking and spoke without preamble. 'You say you believe in the law.'

His eyes met hers. 'You say it as if you don't think I do.'

'I don't want to exchange meaningless philosophy. I need you to answer squarely. Do you believe everyone has a right to fair treatment?'

'Of course.'

She drew a breath. 'I know someone who is being sued for the last thing she owns.' She did not modulate her tone. 'And the man who is suing her has no right to it. No right!'

He raised his brows and leaned back as her impassioned words bounced off the wall. 'That's for the court to decide.'

She coughed, wishing she had started better. Unruly emotions were leading her tongue astray. 'This person needs help to fight this lawsuit.'

He leaned back, raising his eyebrows and folding his arms. 'So why are you telling me about this case?'

'She needs a clever lawyer to represent her. Will you help?'

'You've told me nothing about the case. Who is it?'

'I am your wife and I am asking you to do this for me. Do you have to know who it is before you agree?'

'It's a simple question. Who do you want me to represent?'

Would her answer end the conversation? 'My mother.'

Shocked as if she had slapped him, Justin didn't move. 'How can you even ask me to defend that woman?'

'You are judging her without knowing anything.'

Chagrined, he held his tongue. He had never seen her so direct. 'Tell me.'

'Weston's nephew wants our house. It's the last thing she has—'

'Her husband's nephew?' If what Solay had told him about the man was true, none of his relatives deserved a ha'penny more from Lady Alys of Weston.

She nodded. 'He has filed suit in the civil courts of London that he is Weston's rightful heir, not my mother. That means he's entitled to the house.' Her voice quivered. 'It's all that's left.'

He fought the sympathy her vulnerability raised. Her mother had amassed chattels aplenty she never deserved. 'Is the property rightfully his?'

'You said that was for the law to decide.' At his challenge, her shaky voice turned to steel. 'Or have you judged our case already?'

Her words stung. 'I was asking for the facts.'

She looked at him, head tilted, eyebrows raised. 'You talked as if you already knew them.'

He waved for her to sit.

She did, her voice calmer now. 'The facts are these: he claims my mother never married Weston and that her children were the King's. That would make us…' she hesitated '…that would make her children not eligible to legally inherit Weston's property. In that case, the property should pass to him as the nearest male heir.'

'And were they married?'

He watched her think, wondering what she would say. Her answer could make her legitimate or a bastard. Would she tell the truth? Did she even know it?

'Parliament decreed they were,' she said, finally. 'And with that ruling, Weston was content to take a husband's spoils. Shouldn't that prove the case?'

No wonder she was suspicious of the law. Her family had navigated many of its more unsavoury nuances, just to survive. 'So that would make you the daughter of William of Weston.'

'Legally?' She smiled, sadly. 'I can be the daughter of whatever man the law decrees, but we all know whose womb bore me. That seems all the evidence most men need to decide the case.'

He looked from Solay's challenging gaze to Hibernia's useless subpoena and the questionable outline for the man's impeachment.

If he took on the harlot's case, could he restore Solay's faith in the law?

Could he restore his own?

'I will meet with your mother.' Surely the woman could answer whether or not she had been wed. 'Then I'll decide.'

A flood of happiness washed over her face. 'Alys. Her name is Alys.'

Justin pulled up his horse before the house at Upminster. Unimpressive by royal standards, devoid of defences except for a placid pond too small to call a moat, it hardly looked worth fighting over. But he had seen men do battle before the judges for even less important property.

He helped Solay from her horse as a young, fair-haired lad jumped down from his perch on an oak-tree limb. The boy ran towards them and threw his arms around Solay as soon as her feet touched the ground.

The boy's head came up to Solay's chin and she hugged back, kissing both cheeks before she faced Justin, her arm still draped around the boy's shoulder. 'Jane, this is Lord Justin.'

He looked again. This, then, was no boy, but the sister.

Now that he looked closely, he could see the girl was on the cusp between girlhood and womanhood, but old enough to be wed. She had the King's fair hair and blue eyes, but while Solay had learned to flaunt her sexuality, Jane avoided hers altogether.

She stepped back and looked him over with a solemn, frank gaze. 'You are her husband now?'

'Yes.' One word. All.

'Is it because the King said you must?'

If Solay hesitated to speak frankly, her sister had no such qualms.

Solay squeezed her sister's shoulder. 'Jane, don't badger him.'

'She deserves an answer.' It was time to face the truth of it squarely. Yet when he answered, he looked not at Jane, but into Solay's questioning eyes. 'I made my own choice.'

In their violet depths, he saw a flicker of hope. Was it possible she cared for him?

Jane turned back to her sister. 'Did you?'

Solay closed her eyes, shielding her thoughts. No, he had never been her choice. Not from the first. But he held his breath, waiting for her answer.

'Perhaps,' she said, 'the stars chose for us one for the other.'

Jane sniffed and collected the horses' reins. 'Well, the stars will not choose for me. I shall choose *not* to marry.'

Solay sighed, watching her take them to the stable, her love for her sister unmistakable in her eyes. 'You see how it is,' she said, simply.

He nodded. Hard as it had been for Solay to find a husband, it would be impossible for Jane.

At the double door, Solay ran her fingers over the pitted wood. 'It does not compare to Windsor, but it is home.'

He fought back the guilt. Certainly, he had given her no new home.

Warily, Justin crossed the threshold, wondering how many of the threadbare tapestries lining the wall had been paid for by the royal purse. No one greeted them. No servants hovered at their beck and call.

Instead of coming to meet them, Lady Alys waited at the end of the Great Hall, sitting as if in a throne room.

Solay led him forward slowly, and as they approached, he decided that whatever riches the woman might have purloined from the crown were long gone. The plate on display was pewter, not silver, and the edge of her skirt, salvaged from the days of glory, was now frayed like a battle banner whipped too long by the wind.

'Mother,' Solay began, 'this is my husband, Lord Justin Lamont.'

She did not rise and he fought the urge to bow, searching the woman's face for a relationship to Solay. Her brows, dark as her daughter's, were plucked into unnatural black slashes. Years of frowns drew lines down from her mouth.

Yet even at twice her daughter's age, he could see a hint of what might have captivated a king.

'I am pleased to meet my daughter's husband at last.' The simple words held an accusation.

'Mother,' Solay began, softly, 'Justin has come about the suit. He must decide whether he can help us.'

The narrow black eyebrows arched. 'Ah, so he has an interest in our land?'

Solay moved to speak and he put a hand on her arm. 'On the contrary, Lady Alys,' he answered. 'From what I understand, you have only this property left, and unless I can win this suit for you, you won't even have that.'

Solay's mother blinked and swallowed, as if she'd had a bite of sour fish.

He could have sworn Solay smothered a smile. 'Justin believes in honest speaking.'

'So I hear,' Lady Alys replied.

'You will never need to wonder at my meaning.'

'Well, we welcome your help, though if I may speak equally plainly, I think you are young for a sergeant-at-law,' she said.

'He is chief legal adviser to the Council, Mother.' Solay's quick defence made him smile. It was the first time she had ever boasted of him.

'It is because of my skill that I earned my degree so young. You need not doubt my ability.'

'I'll know the difference. I used to sit next to the judges

to make sure the King's will was done. Then they banned me. Parliament said no woman could ever practise law, but they didn't mean any woman.' Her smile was pure pride. 'They meant me.'

He could not but smile back, despite his remembrance of his father's fury when he heard the Weston woman was interfering with the judges. And he had the strangest sensation that perhaps the King had loved her for her mind.

'The Commons,' she continued, 'is a bunch of witless country dullards who had no right to interfere with the King's wishes.'

He wrapped his temper tightly at her dismissal. 'I see, Lady Alys, that you, too, can speak plainly.' Between her mother and her sister, Solay must have had to smooth over many ruffled feathers as she grew. No wonder she had become circumspect of speech.

'Mother, Justin has not yet decided whether to represent us.' Her eyes held fear that he would not.

'I've never met a lawyer who wouldn't argue whatever side paid him the most. And unless you wish to seize the very land we fight for, we cannot pay you at all.'

'Solay is my wife. I would not expect payment. I only want to see justice done.'

'Justice?' She snorted. 'If you win this case, it will be the first time I have seen it. I have made my way and that of my children with no help from the law.' She reached for Solay's hand and squeezed it and Solay hugged her, awkwardly. 'And still, the King called my daughter his.'

The pride he always assumed came from her royal father

seemed instead the gift, or curse, of a mother proud to have risen from humble beginnings to a seat beside the throne.

But he could not let sentiment rule him. 'That does not help us. The suit hinges on Weston being her father. Was he?'

The woman smiled. 'According to Parliament, he was. With that precedent, surely a lawyer with your skills can prove it.'

Her taunt lay like a gauntlet. This woman would have kept the judges examining their logic. The legal argument was clear, but she had not answered his question.

Solay and her mother stood side by side, heads held at the same proud angle, in a shabby hall in the countryside, awaiting his verdict.

Lady Alys, world weary and resigned, seemed prepared for him to refuse. It would prove that, once again, life had treated her unfairly, that she must battle always alone.

But in Solay's eyes, he saw the hope, the 'please' she could not say and he could not refuse. Whether they lived as man and wife or not, he did not want her to grow old like the bitter woman at her side.

'I will take the case.'

His wife let go a breath and closed her eyes as in prayer. 'Thank you.'

Her mother narrowed her eyes and looked from one to the other. 'All right. Let's begin.'

CHAPTER TWENTY-ONE

LADY ALYS wasted no time showing him the stacks of documents she had kept, itemising the ownership and finances of every holding. Long after sunset, Solay led him up the stairs to the sleeping chambers. Despite his yawns, her swaying hips roused him and, for a moment, he regretted that they would sleep apart.

'My room looks towards the sunrise,' Solay said, pushing open the door. 'I hope you like it.'

He stopped on the threshold, refusing to enter her world. 'I told you we will not—'

'Shh.' She put her finger to her lips and pulled him inside, looking both ways before she shut the door. 'This is not a castle where you can come and go without notice. Mother mustn't know we don't live as man and wife.'

Fixated on the impeachment, on his doubts about Lady Alys, on Solay, he had not grasped what would happen when he went home with her. Truly, she had muddled his head so much that he could no longer recognise the obvious. 'So,' he muttered, a feeble protest, 'again, we start with a lie.'

But the lie was to pretend he did not want her. Rooted to the spot, his body clamoured for hers. Did he mean to live his life like a monk? He was married to the woman. Why had he refused to take her? He was having trouble remembering.

Back against the door, blocking his exit, she lifted her chin, her lower lip trembling in a gentle pout. 'I agreed to your terms. Please honour mine. I do not wish to flaunt our situation before my family.'

He nodded, silent. When he looked at her eyes and saw her honest plea, he could not resist. Just like the first time, something spoke to him, wordless. Irresistible.

She smiled, her entire body relaxing as she let go her grip on the door. 'Thank you.'

While he was working, a manservant had moved his trunk to the left of the room's fireplace. A bowl of dried petals sat on top of it and Solay pinched some between her fingers, releasing the scent of roses. 'All your things are here. I'll sleep on the floor,' she said, 'and leave you the bed.'

He turned his back on the beckoning bed. 'Do you think me devoid of all chivalry? You take the bed.'

'But you are the guest.'

'I'm not a guest. I'm your husband!'

She looked towards the door, as if afraid his shout would carry, then back at him, anger wiping out the pleading in her eyes. 'I was trying to adhere to your wishes, husband. Sleep where you will.'

Since the wedding vows, her patience for pleasing him had evaporated, making her previous simpering over his wishes even more transparent. Worse, he liked this scrappy woman with fire in her eyes who wasn't afraid to tell him what she thought.

He cleared his throat. 'I'll sleep on the floor.'

She pursed her lips, anger gone. 'Forgive me. I must seem ungrateful. For you to help means...' Her voice cracked. She met his eyes, at once humble and proud. 'It means everything.'

'I did not do it for her.'

Cynicism mixed with sadness. 'I understand. My family will be less of a burden if you are not our sole support.'

Had she no faith in him at all? 'I will not let them starve, no matter what happens, but that wasn't why I agreed.'

'Then why?' Eyes wide, head tilted, she reminded him of the little girl who had lost her parrot. The little girl who wanted a birthday, but didn't believe she would ever have one.

He reached for her hair, stroking it, the strands silk against his palm, and then brushed her cheek with his fingers. 'I did it for you.'

She dropped her head against his hands, eyes closed. So quickly, just with a touch, he had made her breath quicken.

He felt the answering throb below his waist.

He stepped towards her, taking her lips as he had wanted to do for weeks. Already boneless, she melted against him, her softness making him harder.

'I wanted,' he whispered, his lips moving against her hair, 'to prove something to you.'

She leaned back to see his face and he loved the hope in her eyes. 'What?'

'That the law can give you justice.'

'I hope you are right,' she said softly, curling against his chest again.

'Perhaps,' he said, not wanting to let her go, 'we could share the bed.'

As close as he had been to taking her, he knew it was madness, but the journey had been long and neither deserved cold stone.

He felt her nod against his heart.

'Just the bed, of course.' He let her go and walked to the far side of the bed, sitting to remove his boots.

Behind him, he heard the rustle of her clothes.

He closed his eyes, but he could see her in his mind. She would unlace her dress, slip it off her shoulders, and her dark hair would cascade down the white skin of her back. The curve of her hip would press gently against her chemise and, if she turned to face him, he would be able to see the pink shadow of her breast through the veil of linen.

Biting off a groan, he decided to keep his clothes on and lay on top of the covers on his left side, facing away from her.

The straw mattress shifted beside him as she slipped under the blanket and he nearly rolled into her. Less than a finger's-breadth away, her scent, rising and falling with her breath, wafted over him.

Back to her, he hugged the edge of the bed. His arms dangled over the side, his legs overshot the end, and he lay, wide-eyed and stiff limbed, staring at the patch of sky and stars he could see through the window. The soft night air of spring stroked his brow.

Beside him, she turned, pounded the pillow, then lay quietly again. He could feel something soft and round nudging him.

He stifled a moan.

'Am I pushing you off?' she whispered.

'No.' He did not trust his voice to say more.

'The bed is small. I'm sorry.'

'Stop being sorry for what is not your fault.'

Her silence vibrated with hurt.

He cleared his throat, angry at himself. 'Perhaps, if we both turned the same way, we could fit more easily.'

Behind him, her breathing stopped. He waited.

'As you wish.'

He rolled over just as she did. Face to face, breath to breath, only the thin blanket between them, he wanted nothing more than to cover her sweet body with his. Her breasts rose and fell, her lips parted, and it took every ounce of his strength to roll away from her.

But he did.

With a small sigh, she nestled against his back and her right arm crept around him, tucking him close. Her hand dangled dangerously close to his stiff member and he grabbed her fingers away from danger and held them against his heart.

'Is this better than before?' Her whisper carried a husky edge.

It was better. It was worse. It was a fire at his back, igniting the desire he so vainly fought. He clenched his jaw against the growl of desire. 'Yes.'

'It's cold,' she said, when he did not speak. 'I'll get another blanket.'

Fresh air cooled his back when she left the bed, and then the blanket covered them both, her quick fingers tucking it too close.

Sweat trickled down his back. He flung off the blanket. 'Let's turn the other way.'

Obligingly, she flipped to her right side and he curved himself against her back.

It was worse.

Now, her full breasts were within reach of his hand, the sweet space between her legs was his to explore, and her neck was open to his lips.

He placed a kiss beneath her ear. He felt her swallow and wiggle back into him. Surely she could feel him, stiff against the sweet roundness of her bottom, still cool beneath the linen shift.

His hand hovered near her breast.

Boldened, she pulled his hand close, cupping hers over it, then snuggled up against his staff.

'Solay.' His voice cracked with a plea and he pulled away, then leaned on his elbow.

She turned on her back, open and tempting, looking up at him, her face hidden in shadows. 'Are you again going to cast me off as a temptress and a tease because I sought to share a bed with my husband?'

Shame clutched at desire's throat. She had done nothing but try to please him, even when she despised him and it was more than he deserved.

I'm sorry danced upon his tongue. 'No,' he said, instead.

'This isn't about the King, is it?'

He shook his head.

They lay side by side, careful not to touch, breathing in unmatched rhythm, staring up at the darkness together.

He swung out of bed and stuffed his feet into his boots,

desperate to escape. 'It's not your fault. If you knew…' His words drifted into the dark. He stood, making his feet walk away. 'I will seek shelter in the stable.'

'Whatever it is, Justin, if you decide to tell me, I will not judge you for it.'

Silent, he closed the door behind him. He had planned to close her out of his life. Instead, he craved not just her body, but something more.

Her love.

All his life, he had prided himself on his honesty. Yet he was hiding more from her than his Council work.

He was hiding the story of Blanche.

He had told himself it had not come up. Or that he was waiting for the proper time. But as he entered the stable, inhaling the scent of manure and straw, he faced the truth. He had not told her because he cared what this weak, strong, stubborn, crazy woman thought of him. And despite her babble of forgiveness in the dark, if she knew the truth about Blanche, he would never, never get it.

A bark of laughter escaped his throat and his horse whinnied. How the tables had turned. Over and over, he had judged her for her lies, when all the time, he had been lying to win her love.

Solay rolled her eyes heavenward, then pummelled her pillow with both fists, sending a puff of chaff dust through the seams. This man, this impossible man, this husband of hers. What was she to do?

I did it for you. An answer she had never hoped to hear. He must feel something for her, but she wanted so much more.

She hurled the pillow against the wall, where it bounced harmlessly to the floor. Sighing, she rose to retrieve it, pausing to look out of the window.

The stable blocked her view of him as surely as the wall around his heart held her back. Yet it seemed this man, afraid of nothing and honest about everything, feared something. She had been so busy trying to protect herself from pain she had been slow to notice his.

She had dreaded the judgement in his eyes, but it seemed clear now that he judged himself just as harshly as he judged others. How painful it would be, to find yourself lacking every day of your life.

Who had taught him that?

His father. A judger. She had suffered from an absent father. Perhaps his had been too ever present.

She raised her eyes to the stars, spilled like a thousand wildflowers across the sky, searching for patterns. She had a husband, but, it seemed, she would never become a wife. Despite her every effort, Heaven's plans for her had not changed. She had done her duty for her family, but she was still alone.

This, then, was to be her life. Unable to please her husband, perhaps she could at least please herself.

It was time to discover what that meant.

CHAPTER TWENTY-TWO

THE next morning, Justin splashed off the smell of the stable with cold water from the stream. He entered the kitchen, surprised to find Solay there, flour dusting her arms like snow. The room was basking in the heat of the oven.

He knew little of domestic duties, but he had never seen a lady up to her elbows in bread dough. Yet she kneaded the loaf as if she had done it many times. 'Is the kitchen maid ill?'

She smiled. 'We have only the two servants. Mother and I do most of the household tasks. Jane helps in the garden and the stables.'

He had barely noticed last night, but thinking back, he had seen only an older couple helping with supper and carrying his trunk up the stairs. Despite Solay's desperation to marry, he had never fully realised how far the King's mistress had fallen. 'No wonder you want to stay at Court.'

She shook her head. 'I'd rather be here. The whole Court seems like a disguising.' She dipped and twirled around the room, scrunching her face into that of a simpering courtier. 'What does the King think of this? Will the King approve of that? When does the King want to eat? What if I'm hungry when the King isn't?' She broke her pose and shook her head. 'We can't even go to bed or waken or break fast if the King does not wish it.'

Surprised, he laughed at her imitation of the flatterers at Court. 'I thought it was your sole ambition to make a life there.'

'That's what Mother wanted.'

Rooted in past glories, the harlot had foisted her dreams on to her daughter. 'She coerced you into going?'

Solay turned the full force of her violet eyes on him. The look said *the King called me his daughter.* 'I wanted to go.'

Her pride mixed in some alchemical way with her vulnerability. Together, they gave her strength he was just beginning to understand. 'And you got what you wanted.'

'I got what I needed.'

A husband. You. She might as well have said the words aloud. He winced at the honesty he had demanded. Neither had illusions about this marriage. Why did he crave something more?

'And what do you want now?' He held his breath, wanting it to be something he could give.

Silence stretched before she answered. 'What do *you* want, Justin?'

He opened his mouth to scold her for asking what he thought before she would speak. Then he realised he was evading her question. He had berated her for not speaking her mind while he had concealed his own.

He cleared his throat. 'I would like to be a Justice of the Peace.'

'Like your father?'

He nodded. 'I want to bring the fairness of the law to ordinary people.' It sounded foolish, said aloud. Why had he shared dreams she would disdain?

'So you do not want a life at Court either.'

'I never did.'

She reached into the oven and pulled out two finished loaves. 'I understand. You have never liked the King.' No criticism tinged her voice.

The scent of warm bread filled him with peace and Westminster seemed far away. 'It's not just the King.' Always he had asked for her honesty. It was time to share his own. 'Sometimes I fear the Council has become more concerned with their own power than with the common good.'

'So as a Justice, you could ignore all that?'

'The King cares little about what happens with most people in the countryside.' He smiled. 'And they return the favour. Many don't care who the King is, let alone worry about his household expenses, unless he asks for more taxes. Nor do they care about the war unless they have to serve.'

She paused in her kneading. 'Even now, King and Court dominate Mother's thoughts.'

'So that is what I want, Solay. And you?'

'I want my family to be taken care of, for Jane to be happy.'

No surprise. It was why she had wanted a husband. 'But what do you want for yourself?'

Her eyes met his without barriers. 'I misrepresented my knowledge of the stars. I want it to be real.' She broke off her gaze and pummelled the dough with her fists. 'I want to learn their secrets.'

He had hoped, foolishly, she might have said something about wanting a life with him. 'No one will teach you.'

She leaned on her arms and glared at him. 'You ask what I want and the first thing you do is disapprove. Why should I share anything with you?'

He recognised her princess voice, the one that said *I can.* Wasn't that what he had tried to teach her? No wonder she did not dream of a life with him. She had just accepted his crazy desire to follow in his father's footsteps. Then he sat here dewy-eyed over baking bread, unwilling to do the hard work of supporting her dreams. 'You're right. I'm proud of you for deciding what you want.'

He wanted to hold her, but not just for the physical fire. To cherish her, somehow.

She smiled, as if she had seen it in his eyes, and then looked away. 'And when I discover what the stars have in store for me, then I shall want that,' she said, in the teasing tone that hid her feelings, 'so as not to be disappointed.'

Relieved to be sparring with her once more, he breathed again. 'So you will seek justice in the Heavens and I on earth.'

She touched his arm, her fingers leaving white smudges on his sleeve. 'Justin, if there truly were justice in the world, I would trust you to find it.'

He grabbed her hand, feeling like laughing with joy, and kissed her palm, the flour clinging to his lips.

Perhaps here, away from the Court, they could find peace.

Solay's mother had hoarded her legal documents as tightly as her jewels. Over the next few weeks, Justin read every one.

He set up a table in the upstairs solar, alternating

between reading them and working on the impeachment document when his mind grew tired of the details of property ownership. He could have asked for a clerk's help, but he could trust no one else with either task. He let Jane sort the documents and keep them in order, a job she seemed to enjoy.

He was learning a few things from Lady Alys's business acumen. It was common knowledge that the King's mistress had accumulated wealth far beyond her right and her station. He had never known how cleverly she had done it.

Forced to leave her old life, Lady Alys had left many things behind, but not even one of her documents of ownership. There were papers supporting control of at least fifty properties in twenty five counties, an accumulation of land an Earl might have envied. Had she been a man, she would have sat in the House of Lords.

Some of the properties were gifts of the King, yes, but the income from many more came under her control in other ways, all perfectly legal. In fact, she might have given those judges good advice.

Yet in all this mass, there were no loving letters between husband and wife. No exchange on affairs of mutual holdings. Perhaps a jealous King wanted no reminders of his rival, but there should have been at least a scrap that would bolster his argument.

'How goes your work?' Lady Alys's voice at his back startled him.

He put down a document and rose. 'You have a wealth of information.'

'The documents for this property clearly show my right to it.'

'Until Parliament acknowledged Weston as your husband. Then it all went to him.'

'Which should make my daughters' inheritance clear.'

'You speak of normal circumstances. Your daughters are universally acknowledged to be the King's. If they are to inherit, I must find a way to prove they are legitimate offspring of William Weston.' Any children born during the marriage would legally be the husband's unless he disavowed them. 'Can you even prove you were married to him when they were born? You have all these documents. Is there nothing connected to the marriage?'

'Lost, I'm afraid.'

Or destroyed. The woman cared for her wealth more than her husband. 'There must have been witnesses to the ceremony.' The witness of the community was sufficient to prove marriage.

'None living.' She turned her back on him, pacing to the window, the frayed edge of her gown, dragging the floor. 'Why do I need witnesses? Parliament decreed we were married. That should be enough.'

'Perhaps it would be if Lady Alys of Weston were not involved.'

The mother looked over her shoulder at him with a sad smile. 'Ah, so justice is not blind?'

Reluctantly, he shook his head. 'Perhaps it never was.' His pompous arguments about the law sounded foolish now. He had scoffed at Solay's cynical views, but she was wiser than he. It seemed impossible for Lady Alys to be treated fairly by the law.

She swept past him to leave, pausing at the door. 'This property is all I have left to protect my daughters' future. I hope,' she said, a furrowed line between her brows, 'that Solay did not make a mistake in asking you to take the case.'

'So do I,' he answered.

Despite Justin's prediction, Solay found a local physician who agreed to teach her something of how the stars affected healing.

She would return from a day's study, flushed and happy from her walk, chatting of all she had learned, more irresistible than ever.

Now, as he ached for her day after day, the glimmer of a life together beckoned like the first star of the night. And his pallet, once a haven, had become a lonely cavern.

Still sleeping apart, they had fallen into a habit of taking a walk after supper, away from the prying eyes of her mother, often returning after the rest of the house was abed.

'Today, we spoke of the five aspects of the planets,' she explained, munching the last bite of a meat pie, watching the sky turn red and the stars emerge.

'What does that mean?'

'That's how they relate to each other in the sky.' She licked her fingers, then ticked off the list. 'Let me see if I can remember. Conjunction means they appear in the same space. In opposition means just what it says, as if at opposite ends of a string. Square is like this.' She held up thumb and first finger to form a corner. 'Then there are two others, trine and sextile.'

'How do you remember all that?' The terms made his head spin.

'It can be no more complicated than the machinations of the law,' she said, smiling. 'Here, let me draw it out.'

She grabbed a stick and traced a circle in the dirt. As he watched her elaborate, intersecting lines, he had to admit there seemed a certain logic to the system.

'But what good is it to know what the stars say if you cannot change their decree?'

She looked up from her drawing, her eyes steady. 'So you know what cannot be changed. For example, it is the planet Venus, cruel fate, who decrees whom we love. You cannot demand love of someone as if it were a pound of flour in the market.'

'Venus?' He raised his eyebrows and forced a smile. Demanding her love in order to consummate their marriage. Had he ever been so foolish? Yet Venus seemed as logical as anything about love, which seemed to strike at will and whimsy. Which seemed to be striking him.

She raised her chin. 'When I am skilled enough, I will read my chart, and yours, if you will let me. Then we will see what fate has planned for us.'

'You will not. The King forbade it.' He should never have let her pursue this. If she displeased the King, he could have her tried as a witch or worse. And Justin would not be able to save her. He would fail her just as he had failed Blanche.

A dimple he had never noticed flashed in her cheek

with a lopsided smile. 'I thought you cared naught for the King's opinion?'

'I care about you.'

She searched his eyes, as if for once unsure whether he spoke the truth. He leaned towards her, his lips brushing hers. Her touch sent a shiver down his spine and back to his arms, which of their own accord, circled her.

His lips would not leave hers. Hungrily, he kissed her, cursing Venus, or God, or Fate, or his own treacherous body for giving him the one woman he could not refuse.

She gave herself totally. No teasing, no luring, no trying to entrap him. Just soul-deep surrender. As if she had truly forgiven him everything, even those things she did not know.

He broke the kiss.

Unable to let go of her, he held her close, chin on top of her head. Both breathed as if they had run a long distance. Her heart battered his chest, trying to break through. Her body always called to his, much as he'd fought it, but now, a sense of peace lay alongside the wanting, luring him to the dream that he might some day deserve love, too.

His mind struggled to regain control. His breathing steadied. He did not let her go.

'Solay…' He looked up at the sky, unable to meet her eyes, but knowing what he must say. 'Solay, I'm going to London.'

She stiffened. 'When?'

'Next week.'

'Why?'

'I need to file a response to Weston's suit.' And meet with Gloucester on the impeachment, but he let that pass.

'Will you come back?' she whispered, though there was no one to hear.

It would be easier to stay away, to disappear into his work and avoid the temptation of her body day by day and the gnawing pain of hiding his secrets. But there was a peace in this life, in this odd existence, that he was reluctant to leave. 'I'll return within a fortnight. But I want you to know something.'

'What?' She stiffened her elbows, as if expecting a blow.

'I cannot guarantee the outcome of this suit,' he began, 'but you have my oath. I am going to do the best I can.'

Under his chin, nestled against his throat, she nodded.

He let her go, then, and met her eyes, wanting to see that she believed him, berating himself for raising hopes he did not know whether he could fulfil. His vaunted earthly justice seemed more uncertain than ever.

'I know you will.'

'Now I need your oath, Solay.'

She did not answer 'of course', as the old Solay would have. 'My oath on what?'

'You must promise me to hide your studies when we return to Court.'

She smiled. 'Now the Great Truth-Teller wants me to keep secrets.'

What had happened to the woman who sought only to please? 'To protect you from the King's anger, yes. Promise me.'

She shook her head. 'You wanted me to speak my truth, Justin. It's too late now to change your mind.'

And the pain that poured through him as he faced what it would mean to lose her was just as terrible as he had always feared.

Justin's absence left a gaping hole in her world.

She missed their games of Nine Man Merrills that stretched longer as the daylight lengthened. She missed watching the sun set and the stars come out. Afterwards, he would walk her to her room, his hand at her back, and leave her at her door with a kiss, nothing more. But everything.

Except for wanting to be his wife in every sense, she could have lived this way always.

Now, without him, though her skin welcomed the warm spring sunshine, the air that filled her lungs was not as sweet. This, then, was what it meant to miss a lover.

'Are you sure he won't deliberately lose the case?' Her mother's harsh question interrupted her thoughts.

Solay threaded her needle expertly, darning a rip in Jane's last whole tunic. 'Yes.'

Her mother shook her head. 'You trust him too much.'

'Perhaps, but if he lost, it would only make us a greater burden on him. Besides, he believes everyone deserves justice.'

Her mother gave a brusque laugh. 'How can you know what he believes? He does not share your bed, daughter.'

Solay's needle slipped, jabbing her thumb. She sucked the drop of blood away. She should dissemble, reassure, gloss over the problem, lest her mother think something was wrong with her marriage.

But something *was* wrong.

She put down the needle. 'No, Mother, he does not.'

'Not for want of desire,' her mother said. 'Any fool can see what lies between you.'

Solay blushed, staring down at the half-mended tear. She had thought the desire would fade, but it had not. Sometimes she could almost see the want wrap itself around them like some undulating serpent in the Garden of Eden. 'You warned me.' What kind of strength did her mother have, to resist such a force of nature?

'So have you bedded him?'

She shook her head.

'Why not?'

There was a moment of silence. She picked up her needle and shrugged her shoulders. 'He demands my love before he'll bed me.' She smiled, trying to make light of it.

'And what do you demand?'

'How can I demand anything? I am lucky to be married at all.'

Her mother sat straighter. 'The King called you his daughter. Justin is the lucky one.'

'He doesn't see it that way.'

The black eyebrows arched. 'Are you certain? He is not here for love of me.'

I care about you. It was more than she had thought she might ever have, but a long way from *I love you.* 'We are bound. He feels his obligation.'

But she did not want him bound by oath. She wanted him bound by love, just as he had wanted her. And she laughed at herself for the foolish way the fates had turned.

'I have seen the way you watch him,' her mother said,

looking up from her knitting. 'You have fallen in love with him.'

Solay's cheeks went cold. Deny, she should deny it. But she was tired of lies. 'Do you think he knows?'

Her mother laughed. 'Of course not. Men are hopeless that way.'

'It's strange, isn't it? That was his condition and I fulfilled it, but now I dare not tell him.'

'Why?'

For all the reasons her mother had warned her against loving in the first place. *Because he is too important. Because he holds my life in his hands. Because if he does not approve of me, I have no life.* 'He wouldn't believe me.'

Her mother cocked an eyebrow. 'I can understand your want of his body, but I cannot understand why you want more.'

'He's...' She shook her head, laughing at herself. 'He's stubborn and pigheaded and judgemental, but he has honour and integrity.' She went on her knees before her mother, gathering the blue-veined hands in hers. 'He really believes, Mother. He believes truth and justice are possible here on earth. He believes so much that he makes me believe in them, too. And if he ever says "I love you," I'll believe that, too.'

'Have I taught you nothing? You must trust no one.'

'But I'm married to him.' Sweet relief even to say it. No man could put them asunder. Justin had promised that.

'Married, yes, but unless you share his bed you cannot know him and have no way of influencing him. You must end this separation and lie with him or you will be totally at his mercy.'

She looked at her mother's frightened face, pity staining her love. In the worry she saw there, she recognised the life her mother had led, one in which not even the sharing of bodies was sacred. Always something was held back. The body was never traded without a price. A prostitute not paid in coin, but in loyalty and influence.

And she did not want that life. Not in the Court, not in the bed. Justin had taught her that much. She did not know how far she could follow his path, but she could no longer follow the old one.

'When I lie with him, it will be because I love him and for no other reason.'

Fear darkened her mother's eyes and she squeezed Solay's hands until her nails left marks. 'Listen to me. You were the King's subject before you were born. You will be the King's subject no matter who your husband is, no matter whether your husband lives or dies. Always, always, your first loyalty must be to the King. Before your husband, before your family, even before God.'

'No, Mother. My first loyalty must be to myself.'

Her mother drew back her hands and clasped them in her lap, as if she would never touch Solay again. 'Then it seems I have no daughter.'

Solay pushed herself up from her knees. 'You have a daughter, Mother, or else Justin and I would not be here. But you no longer have a pawn.'

And she thought her mother stifled the hint of a smile.

CHAPTER TWENTY-THREE

'SOLAY, can I talk to you?' Jane, a gangly fifteen, shifted awkwardly from foot to foot at the threshold.

Solay looked up from puzzling over her birth chart. Each planet, each house was an uncertain victory she must earn without asking the physician directly. He thought she was interested only in herbs and healing. 'Of course.'

Jane's pale hair was gathered behind her, out of the way, and as she entered the room, Solay recognised the curve of breast and hip beneath the tunic and tights. How could the girl have grown so much without her noticing?

Jane began without preamble. 'What will happen to us? Without the house?'

Her words stole Solay's tongue.

Jane had been only five when they fled to the country, too young to remember much about her father, the Court, and its trappings. Her mother had planned for Solay to return to Court. Jane was to stay at home, tending to her needs as she aged. Solay had been schooled in airs and graces while Jane grew as she liked, half-wild, playing outdoors and with animals and books her primary companions.

Now, their indulgence seemed thoughtless and cruel. Dear God, if they lost the suit, how could this naïve, half girl live without the protection of this house?

She took a breath. Jane had always embraced the truth, even when she did not like it. 'We shall be at Justin's mercy.'

'Will he find us another house?'

Jane's question shredded the final bit of the gauzy dream she had clung to. Her fragile truce with Justin had created a timeless bubble that closed out King and Court. Now, reality loomed. What would happen to her mother and sister if the suit were lost? Even the King could not find a husband for a woman who knew only horses and books.

'Yes. Yes, I'm sure he will.' She had just extolled his virtues to her mother. Justin was a man who would do his duty. She knew him that well.

'He likes me a little, doesn't he? He said I was helpful with the documents he needs.'

Solay's heart ached. Beneath her boyish bravado, Jane had grasped for the first time the lesson Solay and her mother had always known: her life depended on pleasing others. 'Of course he does.'

'When I asked about the law, he explained some of it to me and didn't seem to mind. Maybe I could be useful to him. Like a clerk.'

'Don't worry, Jane. Everything will be all right.' But as she hugged her sister, she decided she could avoid the issue no longer. She would ask Justin when he returned, and pray she liked his answer.

After Jane left, Solay pulled out a new sheet of paper.

Could she find a hint in the stars of what was in store for her sister?

She drew the square of the Water Carrier, Aquarius, for Jane's birth date, then sighed. She had had little luck in developing her own reading. In the centre of her chart, Cancer the Crab crouched unsteadily, waiting for the proper planets to surround him.

She was not at all certain that what she had filled in was correct. In the Fourth House of family, she had expected a grand planet, a sign of royalty and power, Mars, or even Jupiter. Instead, according to the tables, the House sat empty.

It must mean she had much yet to learn.

Justin's trunk arrived home two days before midsummer, so all the next day, Solay listened for his horse, not sure until the moment she heard it that he would really return. Jane, eager to please, flew out the door, ready to lead the beast to the stable.

Solay was right behind her. As he dismounted and handed the reins to Jane, Solay slipped her arms around his waist and held him close, loving the feel of his arms tightening around her.

'I missed you,' she whispered into his chest, and thought she felt a nod above her head.

She pulled away, afraid she had revealed too much, but his eyes held a softness and his lips a smile. The sun caressed her face, but, gazing at Justin, she felt the dizziness of the snowfall. He bent his head. Her lips opened to him.

'Justin! What is the news from London?' Her mother's voice commanded attention.

Their mouths, so near a kiss, dissolved into smiles.

Solay sighed. 'She will want every detail.'

'I know.' He waved to Lady Alys at the upstairs window, then turned back to Solay and took her lips, hard, fast and with promise. 'I missed you, too,' he whispered.

Both Lady Alys and Jane had endless questions about the state of the suit. Solay was not alone with him again until the late-day sky turned pink. She relished each warm hour of summer, so they sat outside to catch the last of the daylight.

He took a sip of mead and stretched his legs as the pink clouds caught fire, then turned golden orange.

'Justin, did you hear news of Agnes?'

He frowned. 'It is said she now shares a room with Hibernia, as well as a bed.'

We are to be together, Agnes said. This must have been her meaning. His wife in the castle; his mistress at Court. It was happiness enough. Unless...

'Justin, the subpoena—what happened to it?'

He took a sip of mead, not meeting her eyes. 'Nothing. It is no more.'

She could not help but smile. If Agnes could find happiness, perhaps she could, as well. She twirled the stem of golden flowers she had picked. 'Shall I tell you what I have learned while you've been away?'

'Please.'

She thrust the stem close to his nose. 'This is Saint John's Wort. It can be boiled in wine and drunk for inward wounds or made into an ointment for those on the skin.' He listened patiently while she listed all the plant's uses.

'It's a herb of Leo, which is ruled by the sun, the gold of the flowers.'

'Piss-a-beds are yellow,' he said, grinning. 'Are they flowers of Leo, too?'

She wagged her finger at him, certain of her knowledge. 'Don't mock me. 'Tis just as logical as the law.'

He laughed, cleansing all fear, and looked up at the darkening sky. 'It's good to be back. I could barely see the sky at day's end in London.'

'It did not look the same when you were gone.' She hugged the silent moment of peace, working up the courage to ask him. 'Justin, what happens next?'

'What do you mean?'

'If we lose the house.'

Lines furrowed his brow. 'Do you doubt my ability?'

'No, but I do not have your faith in justice. I cannot leave my family's fate in the hands of the law.' She strangled the flower's stem, gripping it until her knuckles turned white. 'We are not powerful. My mother has enemies still, even you—' She bit her tongue.

He covered her hands with his. 'Solay, I knew my obligations when we wed.'

She nodded, looking down at his hand covering hers. Her family had become his burden, just as she had planned.

Unable to meet his eyes, she looked up at the sky. The first, faint star pierced the darkness. *I wish for his love, not just his duty.*

He put his arm around her and followed her gaze. 'You love the summer, but there is less time to see the stars.'

She leaned into his comfort with a sigh. There would

be no more talk of the future. 'True, but I don't have to shiver as I watch them.' She lifted her arm. 'Look. There is Hercules.'

He squinted at the sky. 'Where?'

So she drew the constellation of Hercules with her finger until he finally saw the upside-down kneeling warrior with his lifted club.

'Come,' he said, finally. 'I have something for you.'

She followed him to the room where he opened the trunk, lifted out a large, flat volume, and laid it in her lap. It was as big as a small table and he had to help her hold it. 'I found this in London and thought of your birthday.'

She pulled back the leather covering it to reveal a bound volume. She opened it with reverent fingers, her eyes wide as she realised what she held. 'It's a Kalendarium.'

He leaned forward, turning pages, pointing out each treasure. 'Here are the tables of the position of the sun in the zodiac on every day of the entire year. And here is a list of all the eclipses.' He pronounced the unfamiliar words carefully. 'It tells the proper time for bloodletting, so the physician will be impressed with your knowledge.' He turned the pages carefully. 'And here are all the charts.'

She touched the pages with reverent fingers. 'It's magnificent.' The copyist had filled the pages with clear, neat script. Such a volume would surely cost as much as a small cottage.

'I thought,' he said, his voice rough, 'that if you were going to anger the King, your readings should at least be accurate.'

The symbols blurred before her eyes.

He reached over to catch a tear. 'Don't cry. You'll spot the pages.'

She blinked, trying not to weep. 'Thank you.'

He rose and moved around her room. There was nowhere, not even the bed, that he could make his. 'Solay…'

She held her breath, not wanting to interrupt. Never had Justin been a man to have trouble speaking his mind.

'I want to stay with you tonight.'

'Of course.' She reached for the laces on her gown, vaguely disappointed. She wanted to be his wife, yet this seemed so cold now.

He took her hands in his. 'No. Just—stay.'

Her chest lightened with relief. 'I would like that.'

Together, they put the precious volume aside. She rose, feeling a stranger in her own room. He removed his boots and lay on his back on top of the bed. She unlaced her shoes and lay beside him, staring at the ceiling, afraid to touch him.

He would see her rumpled hair when she woke, might kiss her before she had freshened her mouth. Would he still want her after that?

Wordless, he slipped his arm under her shoulders, pulling her head to pillow on his shoulder.

And she slept until sunrise.

Justin woke to find himself sprawled across a bed empty of her.

He threw an arm over his eyes to block the sun, wondering what she would say to him this morning. He had held her until she fell asleep. Nothing more had happened.

Nothing physical.

Something more than their bodies had bonded, but it

was fresh and fragile and he was not yet certain whether to trust it.

The smell of baking bread made his stomach growl and he swung his legs out of bed, glad to be back with her.

He had missed her more than he expected. Through the busy days at Westminster, the work on the impeachment document and conferences at the Inns of Court, he would yearn for the peace of sunset. But at day's end, the sky turned red, then blue and the very stars reminded him of her.

He had been right about one thing. Truth drew you closer. Lies built walls.

Parliament wouldn't meet until the autumn, but he and Gloucester had met surreptitiously with two key members of the Commons to outline their plan of impeachment.

And he had found himself using the very methods he despised. Deceit. Stretching the Statutes. He had become the very thing he'd vowed to fight, manipulating the law for what he thought was a good end.

What happens next? she had asked. He was beginning to ask the same. After Hibernia, would Gloucester seek to depose the King himself?

He could tell her none of this so he told her the subpoena had gone away. A truth, but a lie, for it had been replaced by something even more dangerous: a plan to impeach Hibernia.

So he added another crime to the list of those he could not confess. All his distrust had only come back in kind. Now, she did not even trust him to protect her family.

He splashed some water on his face and reached for a

towel. The time had come. Once he shared her bed, once he was fully her husband, his body would know what his mind could not: whether he could be certain of her.

CHAPTER TWENTY-FOUR

SOLAY spent the day poring over her precious present, admiring page after page of tables, neatly written in dark brown ink. There were even two letters illuminated in gold. She saw and heard little else all day, neither the sun's movement through the sky nor Justin's step at the door of their bedchamber.

'Take off your apron,' he whispered in her ear, hands on her shoulders. 'There'll be no more work today.'

Heat spread from her cheeks to her centre. Did he mean to take her in the middle of the day?

The memory of a stone corridor in Nottingham made her damp between the legs.

She turned, trying to look stern, but a little smile kept tugging at her lips. ''Tis full light.'

'Exactly. And I have plans to celebrate your day.'

'My day?'

'Tomorrow is your birthday, is it not?'

This was the first birthday she could ever claim. She had always loved Midsummer's Eve, when the sun ruled the sky for longer than any other day, and now, now she knew why. 'It is, but you have already given me a gift beyond measure.'

'Well, the whole village begins celebrating tonight. You must join them.'

The laugh that escaped was pure joy. 'It's St John's Day they celebrate, not mine.'

He arched a brow. 'Well, either way, we're going to join the festivities.'

It's my day, it's my day. She sang the words silently, as she pulled on her good indigo-dyed gown. It was really St John the Baptist's Day, but she would pretend the celebration was for her. Tonight, she and her husband might share a bed. And more.

They asked the others to join them, but Solay's mother insisted she was too old and Jane too young, so Justin and Solay escaped alone.

'I hear the young people stay up the whole night,' her mother said as they left.

Justin's smile suggested what they might be doing. He took her hand as they left for the village and the tingle she felt spoke of promises for later.

Their dower house was attached to a castle that had passed to yet another absentee lord since Lady Alys lost her rights to it. The steward, mindful of summer's endless days of cutting hay and shearing sheep, had ended the midsummer work day far short of sunset, set up wooden trestles with cakes and ale, and joined the serfs in a brew.

Justin tugged her hand and pulled her over to the table full of small loaves of St John's bread. He picked up one and broke off a piece for her. 'Here's a bite of birthday bread.'

She took it, her lips brushing his fingers. More than the sun warmed her cheeks. On the other side of the green, the physician and his wife smiled and waved. They must think him a foolish love-smitten husband.

As they wandered the green, her every move echoed his, as if the air were water, rippling between them.

At the edge of the green, a shallow stream, too wide to jump across, ran merrily towards the Thames. Courting couples sent little wooden barks with candle stubs and precious wishes out into the stream, cheering when the boat touched the other side safely, meaning a wish would be granted, and moaning if the little boat sank.

'There's a good candle wasted,' she muttered, looking at them with longing as one of the little craft sank and doused a candle and a wish.

'The night is short. Do you want to make a wish?' he asked.

She nodded. She would cherish the gift of this day for ever.

Two village boys had carved extra bits of wood and gathered candle stubs, glad to trade them for Justin's coin. Solay knelt in the grass, dabbling her fingers in the stream, as Justin melted candle wax on the wood and stuck the stub in it.

'Shall I write your wish on the boat?'

She shook her head and reached for it. 'I know what I wish for.'

Holding the rickety boat steady with both hands, she knelt on the grassy bank, reluctant to let it go. As long as she held it, wish and candle intact, she had hope.

Justin sat beside her, close, as he had been all day. 'What do you wish for?'

She met his eyes, knowing he must recognise the want in hers for the first night of their life together. She saw want and something more in his gaze. Could she believe it?

Shaking her head, she looked down at the little bark. 'It must be secret or 'twill not be granted.'

She closed her eyes and let the boat go.

He held his breath with her as it rocked from side to side, splashing water on to the candle wax before it righted itself. Then, in the middle of the stream, another woman's wish drifted towards it, riding the downstream current.

'Go around!' he cried, waving to the other bark as if he could change its course.

In vain. It rammed Solay's and both careened wildly. She gasped. He grabbed her hand and she thought he held a breath. Did he care so much then, if her wish came true?

Would he feel the same if he knew what it was?

They bobbed back and forth on the water, then the other bark capsized as the young woman who sent it groaned, then laughed as her beau stole a kiss.

The little prow of Solay's boat touched the opposite bank and she gave a little cry of joy.

Justin hugged her. 'So,' he whispered, tickling her ear, 'now will you tell me your wish?'

What would he say if he knew she wanted them to be husband and wife? Safe in his embrace, surrounded by his scent, she parted her lips to tell him.

Then she stopped.

Every time she had tried to lie with him, he had refused

her. Refused her so violently that everything that had come before was tainted. Instead of telling him, she wanted to cling to anticipation, still hoping, like the little bark, that it might touch the bank.

Later. Later she might tell him.

She sat back on her heels on the soft grass. 'I wished,' she said, smiling softly, 'to know *your* birthday.'

She thought disappointment touched his eyes. 'That's all?'

'And do not lecture me about being forbidden to study. The King is not here today.'

He laughed then. She was beginning to love the sound. In giving her a celebration, he had given himself one as well.

She held her breath as he studied her, trying to decide whether to trust her.

'All right. You shall have your wish. I don't know why I didn't tell you long ago.' He leaned close to her ear and whispered, 'I was born a fortnight before Christmas.'

The vibration of her laughter tickled her heart. 'I was right! You were born under the sign of the Archer,' she said, unable to resist a prideful smile.

'But you were not sure, or you would not have wanted to know so badly.'

For the first time, it was a comfort that he understood her so well.

They joined hands and turned back to the green, where the boys held impromptu races while the men brought fallen branches from the orchard to pile on the bonfire.

A tall lad set a torch to the pile, sending sparks crackling towards a cerulean sky. The younger boys grabbed brands from the fire, then raced up and down the green like shooting stars. A few, the brave ones, leaped over the fire's flames.

She glanced sideways at him. Ale in his right hand, he watched the jumping boys. 'I used to do that,' he said, nodding at them. 'There's an art to it, to guessing when the flame will dip and timing your jump.'

His smile reminded her of the boy who had thrown snowballs in Windsor's Upper Ward and she longed to give him boys of his own to play with. 'Did you ever get burned?'

He shook his head. 'No, but when I singed my good tunic I got a lecture from my mother.' His left hand toyed with her fingers, lifting each in turn. 'I bet I can still clear it,' he said. A wicked smile tugged at the corner of his mouth.

'No!' She clung to his hand, but she couldn't keep him from rising. 'What if you fall into the flames?'

He simply laughed and downed the dregs of his ale. 'Watch me.'

She covered her face with her hands, peeking through her fingers, trying to remember how much ale he had drunk. At least he didn't stagger as he crossed the green. A dark figure against a sky of stained-glass blue, he looked back and waved, as if to be sure she was watching.

She waved back, gritting her teeth.

'They're all boys at heart, milady.' The physician's ample-bosomed wife had come up beside her to watch.

'What if he's hurt?' Barley seeds and eggs would be useless against a severe burn.

'Don't worry,' the woman said. 'Now be sure you're watching him or he'll do it again to make sure you saw him.'

She took a deep breath. 'If he's doing it to impress me, I'd rather he do something else,' she grumbled.

Justin was the next in line to jump when she saw the night's first star. *I wish for him to be safe.*

He took a running start and leapt.

Just as he jumped, the blaze soared skyward and he passed directly through the flame. A tongue of fire licked his tunic and it ignited before he crashed to the ground.

Solay ran, her heart in her throat, knowing only that he must not die.

He rolled away from the fire, smothering the flames as he went. She reached him before any of the men, falling to her knees, pounding the flames with her bare hands, vowing in incoherent thoughts that if he lived, she would no longer wait to bed him.

Thumping his back, she pounded the last smouldering spark on a ruined tunic.

'Ouch! Stop it! I'm unhurt.' He sat up and waved away the men who had run over to help.

She cupped his soot-streaked cheek. 'Don't you ever, ever do that again. Now let me look at it.'

Miraculously, Justin's back was red, but not blistered. The physician joined them, applied a cold cloth, and reminded Solay to apply ivy and comfrey when they returned home.

Justin stood, arching his back, and stretched out his hand to help her up.

She wanted to throw herself into his arms and cry in relief, but his grin was too cocky to be rewarded, so she let him help her up with what she hoped was royal disdain. 'I am beginning to understand your mother.'

He hugged her shoulder. 'I told you I knew how to do it.'

She shook her head. 'Enough foolishness. We're going home so I can get you out of that tunic and keep the cold compress on.'

He smiled and put his arm around her shoulder, pulling her to him. 'No need. It'll itch for a few days, but I've had worse.'

She put her arm around his waist, careful to avoid his singed back, and snuggled against him, shaking her head.

The sun's final blush left the horizon. The older folks drifted off to bed. What was left of the night belonged to the young. The village lads, the ones more interested in kissing than bonfires, slipped into the shadowed orchard to be alone with the girls.

As they walked up the path to the house, a moan drifted behind them on the clear night air.

'Midsummer's Eve is a night for lovers,' he said, the whisper raw in his throat.

His breath rose and fell, whether from the exertion of the jump or from want of her, she didn't know, but if she was to have her Midsummer's Night wish, she would have it now.

Here, there was no castle, no Court, no King. Only the two of them and the stars.

She wrapped her arms around him, raised her face and kissed him.

The wind caressed her throat like another hand of loving. All her fears lifted. She lay back in the grass and he undressed her, not gently, for his fingers shook with urgency. She writhed with anticipation, with some spark that moved her relentlessly towards him.

And the touch of the warm night air on the tip of her breast felt like his breath.

His fingers stilled.

Her muscles held their breath. Surely he would not reject her now?

She opened her eyes. 'Do you find me...pleasing?'

'You know I do. No more games, Solay.'

'But even so, you didn't, you wouldn't...' She stumbled, afraid to say the words. 'I thought...'

'That I didn't want you?' He stroked the hair away from her forehead. 'How could you not know?'

And if she didn't, he showed her with a kiss. He drank her lips and searched her mouth with his tongue, loving her inside and out. Then his kisses trailed down her neck with little nibbles that made her laugh with joy.

'You are mine, Solay,' he whispered. 'By this act, we shall be truly wed.'

He pushed her skirt away, and she unlaced his shirt and tangled her fingers in his hair, seeking the hidden heat of his chest.

She wanted to see him, to relish the sight, but now was not a time to look and savour. That would come later, after they were sated and the moon had risen.

With awkward fingers, lips and tongue, she explored his chest, his neck, the crook of his arm. His skin salt was on her tongue. He twisted now, hungry as she, shucking off his chausses until only the fragile barrier of skin came between them.

She reached for him, the heat of his staff branding her palm before he pulled away. Leaning on his arms, he loomed over her, dark against the cobalt sky.

Surely he would not resist her now.

'I want you,' she said. 'Please. I'm crazed by it.'

He shook his head, his breathing ragged. 'I want you to be ready.'

'I am ready.' She rolled her eyes to the heavens and grabbed his arms. 'I'm telling you the truth.'

He shook his head, slowly. 'Not the way you will be. Lie back.'

She did.

He leaned over her, holding her arms down with each of his. Her body swelled, aware of his eyes on her, just as they had been that night so many months ago.

This, this was so much more.

She opened her mouth, hungry for him to fill it, but instead of kissing her again, he took her breast. The soft scrape of his teeth sent lightning between her legs. They opened of their own accord, melting with anticipation.

Without lifting his head, he slipped his fingers inside her, teasing, preparing, until it seemed the entire world had collected at that one point. She thrust towards him, wanting to take him in everywhere, through her skin.

He was right. She had not been ready before. When he slipped inside, the opening that had seemed too small to hold him matched him perfectly.

Her breath and her body were one. There was inside and no outside, no difference between his skin and hers. No up or down. No earth or sky. Just this swirling oneness, dizzying as the fall of snowflakes.

'Look at me,' he commanded.

Her eyes fluttered open. Moonlight showed her a glimpse of his eyes and when she saw the fierce possession, she gripped him even more tightly. His eyes, relentless, wouldn't release hers. As he stroked her, she spiralled upwards, holding him so tightly that it seemed they would be joined for ever.

Eyes locked with his, just before his loving stole her speech, the words burst free.

'I…love…you.'

Then she cried out, and so did he, and then they lay together, needing no words.

And over his shoulder, she could see the stars, scattered across the heavens in a constellation she had never seen before.

CHAPTER TWENTY-FIVE

THE next morning, Solay opened her eyes as sunlight kissed the sky, creating the world anew.

Behind her, Justin held her tightly against him, his hand cupping her breast. His even breathing against her neck told her he slept. Relieved, she lay still, needing time to think about what she would say.

He rolled over on his back, wincing as the grass touched the burn, but he didn't wake.

She followed the rise and fall of his chest, wanting to thread her fingers through his hair again. Now that she had known him, he suddenly looked fragile as well as strong. If the heart that had pulsed against hers stopped, surely hers would follow it into death.

I love you.

She had meant every one of those three words. Now, they lay like rubies scattered on the path for him to gather.

Would he?

What if she asked *Justin, do you believe me?*

What would she do if he said 'no'?

Yet she wanted to ask another, even more frightening question.

Do you love me?

Such a foolish wish. But when he looked at her, the way he had loved her last night, oh, now she knew what Agnes had meant. Such loving opens the soul.

Now, her soul lay naked.

Waiting for him to wake, she sat up to watch the sun slip over the edge of the horizon. Bright and yellow and hot enough to sear her eyes, it burned a hole in the orange sky.

And it illuminated dark corners, shining light where she had never thought to look.

That was another, larger question.

Why was it so important to him that she love him?

I love you.

Justin lay on his back, arm flung over his eyes, savouring the words drifting through his memory, heady as the scent of roses.

If she had said it at any other time, he would have explained, excused, resisted. He could have told himself she didn't mean it.

He would have been safe.

But even Solay could not dissemble at that most elemental moment. Could she?

He pushed aside the doubt, wanting a moment of peace. He yawned and stretched out his arm, uneasy that she was no longer within reach. Sitting up, he rubbed the burn on his lower back and looked for her.

Wrapped loosely in the unlaced dress, she sat hugging her knees to her chest and gazing out at a golden-orange sky.

He moved behind her, pushed aside her dark curls and kissed the curve of her neck. She arched in answer, and he reached for her breasts, ready to love her again.

She stiffened and pulled away. 'Tell me about the other woman,' she said. 'The one you were betrothed to.'

The peace lay shattered.

'Why do you want to know?' When she knew the answer, her *I love you* would vanish. He had known loving her would lead to this, yet he took her still.

She put her hand over his, gently, but would not let him turn away. 'You are the one who has preached the power of truth.' Her violet eyes met his, full of acceptance, but demanding honesty. 'I told you I would not judge.'

He sighed, resigned. He should have told her months ago. 'You must know something already.'

'I know you were to be wed and the girl died.'

She did not know the worst. 'What more must you know?'

'I want to know what happened.'

He looked down at an ant crawling on the grass, trying to steady his thoughts before he was forced to speak. Why must a woman carve a man open, pick out his innards and expose all things private? 'There's not much to tell.'

'So about this, then, you cannot be fully honest.'

Shamed into speech, he spat the words as quickly as he could. 'Her name was Blanche. She came to me wide-eyed and tempting and I...' He shrugged.

'You and she...?'

'Yes.' He closed his eyes against the vision of their

mating, a tepid thing in the end, over as soon as he finished what she came for.

No. A woman could not lie in the moment of joining.

'How old were you?'

He opened his eyes and filled them with Solay. She had promised forgiveness, but that was before she knew. 'Youth does not excuse me. I was already at the Inns of Court.'

Did he see a wisp of disappointment in her eyes?

'So you agreed to marry.'

He nodded, trying to remember whether honour or hope had driven him the hardest. For those few weeks, he pretended he was loved without reserve, without judgement. A lie. All of it.

He had not been loved at all.

'The banns were read. Our families rejoiced.'

Each hard-won confession fell into silence. Each time, he hoped he had revealed enough to satisfy her.

But she probed again. 'Then what?'

'It became evident that she was with child.'

Solay looked down, as if thinking of the seed he'd planted last night. She was silent a long time. 'You would not be the first couple to anticipate the final vows,' she said, finally. 'But I did not know you had a child.'

'I don't. A week before the wedding, she confessed the babe was not mine and she told me she loved the father.'

Blanche's words, long buried, burst to life. *I could never love you. You love the law more than you will ever love a woman.*

'Then why didn't she marry him?'

'Because he was already married.'

He thought he heard her gasp, but he fixed his eyes on the ground and stabbed at the dirt with a short stick, knowing she would ask for the rest.

'And what did you say?' she said, finally. 'After she told you the truth?'

'I told her she had made this marriage and now we both must lie in it.'

'A marriage neither of you wanted.'

The stick between his fingers snapped. 'I knew you wouldn't understand. By the law, we were already wed.'

'So you chose to live a lie to abide by the letter of the law?'

He frowned, wishing for the old, accommodating Solay. 'There was no other way.' *It's what must be done, son.*

'Did you look for one?'

He flinched and hurled the broken stick at a tree. 'She was wrong! She trapped us. The banns are binding. There was no escape.'

Silence stretched up to the calm blue of the summer sky. He breathed again. Perhaps this would satisfy her.

Perhaps she wouldn't ask what happened next.

But Solay would not be fooled. 'She found one, didn't she?'

Her question seized his throat like murderous hands. This, this was what it was like for other people, those terrified by the truth.

She let him sit without answering for a long time, but she never looked away. And she never said *you don't have to tell me.*

'Yes,' he said, when neither the grass nor the wind nor Solay's eyes offered an escape. 'She went down to the river, loaded her pockets with stones, and took herself and her unborn babe to the bottom of the Thames.'

And because Blanche had not told her parents the truth, neither could he. Blanche's mother had shrieked and torn her hair. *She's condemned to the Seventh Circle of Hell for ever.*

Solay tugged his fingers from their fist and laced their hands together. 'I'm sorry. I'm so sorry.'

He pulled his hands away, grabbed another twig and snapped it. 'She shouldn't have lied.' He no longer knew whether he argued with Solay or with his past. 'If she'd just been honest from the beginning—'

'Yet when she was honest and wanted to leave the marriage, you refused her.'

'It was not me! It was the law.'

'So this time, you made sure you had a way out.'

He searched her eyes and knew she had seen through him, through everything. *I have a condition.* He heard the echo of his voice, desperate to control the feelings for her that had swamped him, even then. 'I would not risk that again. And I could not force someone else into a marriage with someone they didn't love.'

'Do you love her still?'

He rummaged amid the painful images, searching for the answer. 'I'm not sure I loved her at all.'

'Yet you had not taken another bride.'

He shook his head. 'You may blame Blanche for that.'

'*You* do not blame Blanche. You blame yourself.'

Pain ripped through his chest, sharp as an arrow. He could see her still. He always would. Her blue eyes, first seductive and then, on that last day, so full of pain. He could have set her free with one word. She and the babe would have lived.

He must admit the truth to Solay, then lose her. 'I killed her. That's the truth I haven't told you.'

'No,' she whispered. 'That's the lie you've told yourself.'

Shocked, he searched her face. No judgement touched her eyes. No blame. Only compassion and tenderness and understanding.

He resisted her comfort. 'You can't know. You weren't there.' He had worked so hard, hoping that some day, he could bring enough justice into the world to atone for his sin. 'My judgement was her death sentence. I can never forgive myself for that.'

'Until you do, she holds you at the bottom of the river with her.'

And the love in Solay's eyes as she held out her arms looked like absolution.

CHAPTER TWENTY-SIX

SOLAY and her mother sat quietly in the solar later that week when she decided to brave the subject of William Weston.

Justin had faced his past. Perhaps she could do the same.

Her mother was reading documents in preparation for the case. Odd, that the mysterious William Weston consumed their lives as fully as the King once had.

She hardly remembered the man her mother had married. He had swirled into their lives when she was eleven and was gone within two years, most of that spent persuading Parliament that he was Lady Alys's legal husband. Three years ago, when he died, they did not even see him laid to rest.

Yet he had married her mother. And the few times she had seen him, though he had barely spoken to her, he had watched her like a dog stalking a deer.

She took another stitch, then put down Justin's tunic. 'What was William Weston like?'

Her mother looked up from the parchment. 'Why do you ask?'

Solay smoothed the singed threads' edges and shrugged,

as if the answer were of little consequence. 'How can I not be curious? Our lives and our lawsuit revolve around him. Did you know him well before your marriage?'

Her mother's gaze did not falter. 'He was at Court. One knows people at Court.'

'Did I ever see him there?'

'You were very young. He was much in Ireland. The King sent him to subdue the rebellion.'

'What was he like?'

'A man. Just a man. Certainly not a king.'

'What did he look like?'

'What does it matter?'

'I want to know.'

'It was a long time ago.'

'He was your husband. Don't you remember?'

Her mother sighed. 'He was much older than I.'

'So was the King.'

'As I remember, he was tall, strong and had very dark hair.'

'What colour were his eyes, Mother?'

'Blue, like the King's, but deeper.'

'When did you marry him?'

'I don't remember.'

Solay put down her mending and stared. 'You don't remember? How can you not remember your marriage?'

Yet there was much her mother had not remembered. Her birthday. Jane's.

'What difference does it make?'

'It makes a great deal of difference in this lawsuit.' All her life, she had known some things were not to be spoken of. She had never questioned. But not now. No longer.

'Justin trusted me and I trusted you, yet you have no proof that you ever wed the man and now you say you can't even remember?'

Red spots flared in her lined cheeks. 'You are cruel and you know nothing.'

'I know you are not telling the whole truth.' She crushed Justin's tunic in her fists and stood. 'If Justin loses the case, the fault will not be his alone.'

Lips pursed, her mother let her leave the room without a word.

She dropped the mending in their chamber and went to his workroom. He should know, at least, what her mother had said.

At the door she paused, relishing the sight of the straight, strong back her fingers had stroked this morning before they rose. For a moment, nothing else mattered. If only the two of them could close the door on the world for ever.

She sighed and he turned and smiled to see her. The pile at his left elbow had dwindled. 'I'm almost done.' His fist tapped the stack in frustration. 'There's nothing here.'

'Mother has done her best to hide the truth. She claims not even to remember the day they were wed.'

'There's no record of it.' He waved the stack, the last few documents. 'Another deed, another bill of sale—'

A folded document with a broken red wax seal slipped out.

She sank on to the bench beside him and stared at the cracked imprint of a lion rampant. The Weston seal.

She picked it up, her hand shaking. Undated, it carried only a few lines, written in an informal hand with no signature.

News of the birth of your daughter has reached me. I

hope all went as you wanted. This amethyst brooch is hers.
When she is grown, tell her the truth.

And an icy certainty chilled her spine.

'What is it?'

'A note from Weston. Accompanying a birth present to me of an amethyst brooch.'

An amethyst brooch like the one the King had sent back to her mother. *It was yours, once, Solay. A gift from your father.*

And all this time, she thought her mother had meant the King.

'It seems,' she said, forcing her lips to move, 'that I am no more royal than you are.'

He grabbed the letter, skimming the lines, vague enough that if the King had read them, he might have been fooled. 'There could be another explanation. Perhaps Weston was currying favour with the King.'

She gripped her elbows, trying to cover the emptiness. She had pranced proudly at Court, but her very presence was the biggest lie of all.

'"The King called you his daughter." That's what Mother always said. Not that I *was* his daughter.'

His jaw settled into grim determination. 'Come. It is time for your mother to tell the truth.'

He rose, but she stopped him. 'No. Stay here. I must do this alone.'

Bits of her life floated across her memory as she walked to her mother's solar. No wonder Weston had spent all they had. He must have counted it small payment for having his child stolen.

She stood in the doorway, the note trembling in her hands. 'Why didn't you tell me, Mother?'

Her mother looked up. Her eyes flickered to the letter, but she did not reach for it. 'Tell you what?'

'That I am not the daughter of a King.'

Colour drained from her mother's face and she seemed to shrink inward, ageing before Solay's eyes. 'You were not to know,' she whispered, looking towards the door for someone listening. 'No one was to know.'

It was true, then. Alys had smuggled another man's child into the bed of the King. Discovery would surely have meant death.

All her life, Solay had clung to her royal blood, the only thing that made her special. Now, even that was a lie. Her entire existence was an elaborate disguising.

A hollow ache opened in her chest, but she didn't know whether the pain was for herself or her mother. 'Why?' She refused to whisper. She was done with secrets. 'Why did you call me the King's?'

'He could have no children.'

'How could that be? The man fathered ten children.'

Her mother shook her head, staring at the floor. 'That was in the days before. Later, he could no longer...' She couldn't say the words.

All of a sudden, too much made sense. A precise birthday would allow too many calculations. 'Jane, too?'

Her mother nodded. 'Her fair hair was a lucky accident.'

'And were you married to Weston when we were born?'

'It was part of the bargain. I helped his career with the King.'

Solay sighed. 'Tell me one true thing, Mother. One thing that was done out of honest feelings. Something you did for something other than personal gain.'

'I loved him.'

Love. Her mother had never used the word before. 'Who?'

'The King.'

'Loved him so much you made love with another man?' The idea was absurd. 'You never even called him by his name.'

She straightened her back and lifted her chin, once again the most powerful woman in the realm. 'He was the King, not some ordinary man.' She looked up at the ceiling, seeing things far away. 'He still needed to be as powerful in bed as in battle. It was the one thing I could give him.'

It was necessary for me to portray a desirable woman. 'The King would not call that love.'

Her gaze returned from the past. 'No, *you* would not call it love.'

And as she looked at her mother's face, she realised how much love that took.

But in the end, the deception was all for naught. 'It is over, then. Now, everyone will know who fathered me.'

Her mother grabbed her arm, her nails sharp on Solay's skin. 'No!'

She lifted her mother's fingers away and rubbed the four crescents on her forearm. 'How can it matter now? The King is long dead.'

'I did not do it only for him. It was the only thing I could give you. I will not let you destroy it.'

'Even if it means losing the house?'

Her mother lifted her head, the moment of desperation shed. 'What is one house to the daughter of a King?'

Nothing, it seemed. A house could be bought anew.

Solay left the room, moving in a body she no longer recognised. In her left hand, she clutched Weston's words with fingers that no longer seemed to belong to her. She touched her cheek, wondering whether she wore the same skin as when the sun rose, then stared at her right hand, veins blue with the blood of a man she'd considered a stranger.

Standing in Justin's doorway, she let the air fill her chest, each breath an effort.

'It's true, then,' he said.

She nodded, searching his eyes, praying she would find forgiveness. 'They were married. I am his daughter. So is Jane.'

'And you never suspected?'

She laughed, sadly, remembering her puzzlement at the emptiness of her Fourth House. 'No, but the stars knew.'

He squared the stack of documents as if the matter were closed. 'So you and Jane are Weston's only legitimate offspring. When we prove you are Weston's daughter, the property will be yours.'

'We are not going to tell them.' The certainty came across her, strong as her mother's lifetime of pride.

'Do you think ignoring the truth will change it? Why can't you just be who you are?'

Crushed in her damp palm, Weston's note stuck to her skin. 'Be who I am?' She heard a scream. Was it hers? 'Who am I? Suddenly proven I'm not the King's daughter. That leaves me only what I've been called all along: the daughter of a whore.'

He who so loved to speak the truth was struck dumb when she uttered it. And the small sense of triumph she felt at his pain died. If he loved her, he would understand.

But he'd never said he loved her.

'You've been like all the others.' She spoke with an unearthly sense of detachment as her marriage lay smashed before her. She was a different woman now. Not the King's daughter he thought he'd married. 'You look at me, but you see her.'

'That's not true.' His jaw clamped around the words, releasing no others.

'You've demanded I prove my love again and again. What if I ask you to prove you love me?'

She waited. For interminable minutes she waited while he stood there, unable to move from the cage he'd built.

'Even a whore's daughter deserves love, Justin.' The whisper almost choked her. 'And she needs it so much more than the daughter of a King.'

His silence was her answer. She locked her hope away with her illusions. The reality of her life was before her. And knowing all her mother had sacrificed, she knew what she must do.

She walked to the table and picked up the candle he had lit, touched it to the note from Weston, and flung it into the hearth. No one else would ever know. Even Jane. 'There's your blessed legal proof. Fleeting as a flame.'

He knelt to reach for it, but grabbed only ash. Black

smoke drifted up the chimney and the note disintegrated into powder, like passion, not something that could last.

He looked up at her. 'I wanted to save this house for you. Is perpetuating a lie more important?'

'Not for me. For her.'

With a sigh, he rose and engulfed her in his arms. 'If it's that important to you, I will do as you want.'

Burrowed against his tunic, she consoled herself with the solid feel of his arms and the reassuring thump of his heart. If she could not have his love, then this, this must be enough.

She lifted her head, drinking in the softness of his brown eyes gazing at her. 'An Act of Parliament says they were wed. If Parliament can control a King, it should allow us to keep a house.'

'What will you say,' he said, 'when they ask you?'

'I will tell the truth.' She smiled, sadly. 'The King called me his daughter.'

CHAPTER TWENTY-SEVEN

JUSTIN watched Solay leave to prepare the evening meal, wishing he had a right to speak his truth.

What if I ask you to prove you love me?

Her question stuck in his belly like a sword thrust. Buffeted by his demands, the King's threats and her family's needs, sustained by pride or anger or by knowing who she was, she had demanded his love.

And it was too late. Much, much too late. While he had required her to convince him of her love, he'd fallen for her.

He stared at the empty doorway and laughed with a sad abandon, for she had neatly turned the tables. Now, if he told her he loved her, she would never, never believe him.

All his posturing, all his accusations, all his arguments were vain attempts at denial. He had implied she was not worthy of love, but all the time he was the unworthy one. She had forgiven him, but he could not forgive himself.

Words alone would not be enough to claim her. He would have to earn the right, to show her, with deeds, not words. He must give her what she wanted most in the world.

This house.

He stacked the documents and blew out the candle. He had dallied here because he loved to be with her, but tomorrow, he would return to London to better prepare for the case. What he had must be enough to convince a judge.

And then, what he did must be enough to convince Solay.

Solay shivered as October's raw wind swept the few remaining leaves from the trees in the courtyard of the Middle Temple, relieved that her statement to the judge was over.

Justin walked up to her. As she stood next to him, for the first time in months her skin felt warm and whole.

'What do you think? How were my answers?' she asked. The opposition's lawyer had been a mean-spirited man, accusing her of lying at every turn. 'Have we a chance?'

'I'll do everything in my power.'

'But…?'

'But it will depend on the whims and the prejudices of the court.'

She shook her head. 'At one time I wanted to hear you admit that the law was flawed. Now, I wish you'd tell me that justice will be done, no matter what.'

He put his arm around her, pulling her close. 'Justice will be done. No matter what.'

And just to hear him say it made her smile.

'Now,' he said, 'here's something happier to think on. Agnes is back at Windsor. I thought you would like to see her.'

She nearly skipped. 'Oh! That would be wonderful.'

'If we start early tomorrow, we can be there before day's end.'

'Thank you.' She squeezed his arm in gratitude. She

had barely seen him in the weeks since he left the house. He was, if anything, more gaunt than ever. 'You have not been eating enough.'

'I live in chambers and eat in the common hall. The cook cannot compare with you.'

'Have I finally taught you the art of flattery? My cooking is not so good.'

'I said nothing about the food.' He grinned. 'Only that the cook could not compare with you.'

Her laughter pealed and his smile broadened. 'So tell me,' she said, moulding her body against his side as they walked, 'what has kept you too busy to eat?'

'Parliament meets next month. There is much to prepare.'

'More subpoenas?'

'No. An impeachment.'

Her every muscle went rigid.

She forced herself to softness again, afraid he would notice her reaction. 'Oh?'

'I'm sorry. I knew it would bring unpleasant memories.'

She shrugged. The Court seemed years away. What did the intricacies of power matter now? She had her husband and he had promised to take care of her family. 'Who has earned the wrath of the Lords and Commoners?'

He stopped and looked at her, his eyes searching her face. A restless wind fluttered through his hair like fingers, but the narrow set of his lips did not part.

He's wondering whether he can trust me. After all this, he still wonders.

She reached up to lace her fingers with the wind in his

unruly hair. 'It's all right. I only asked because I knew it was important to you.'

A shadow of the old suspicions lingered in his eyes. 'I must be sure you will not tell the King.'

Her hand slipped on to his cheek and he pressed against her palm. The King, still on gyration, had forgotten all about her. She knew where her loyalties lay. Everything she needed now, Justin held. 'I am your wife, not the King's.'

He took a breath, and released a sigh. 'Hibernia. It is Hibernia.'

She swallowed a gasp, then forced her lips to smile. 'Hibernia,' she whispered, wanting to know nothing more. 'No, I will not tell the King.'

But how could she keep this secret from Agnes?

The question still haunted her as she hugged Agnes the next day. Her friend's round face had narrowed somewhat, but she glowed with an inner light.

'You look happy,' Solay said, settling into a chair before the fire.

'I am. The King has made Hibernia justice of the Northern Counties.' She put a solicitous arm around Solay's shoulder. 'And you? How goes marriage to Lord Justin?'

Solay tried to smile. 'I am content.' The happiness of a mistress was beginning to look more appealing than the state of her marriage.

'You do not love him, I know.'

Solay shrugged, not correcting her. If she opened her mouth to confide, the truth would escape.

'Oh, Solay, I'm so sorry. All the happiness you saw for

me is coming to pass. There is something wonderful I must tell you.' Firelight reflected in Agnes's soft blue eyes, as if it burned inside her. She closed the door. 'But you must keep the secret.'

Solay's heart was heavy with secrets. Surely it would crack with one more. 'Agnes, I'm not sure—'

Agnes sat and gripped Solay's fingers. 'We are to be married.' Each word was a smile.

Solay shook her head, sure she misheard. Justin's set jaw flashed into her mind. *One man and one man only.* 'But he is already married.'

'He has put his wife aside.'

Solay touched Agnes's forehead with the back of her hand. Surely a fever had taken her senses. 'Agnes, that is not possible.'

'Ah, but it is! The King's own lawyers wrote the papers and sent them to the Pope months ago, along with a special appeal from the King.'

'By all the saints,' she whispered. The King now placed himself above even God's law. 'And his Holiness agreed?'

'He did not object. Their marriage is dissolved.'

'On what grounds?' Solay whispered weakly, surprised to hear Justin's words in her mouth.

'Grounds? I know not, neither do I care. But it is all thanks to you.'

'Me?'

'The Duke told me last winter that he had petitioned the Pope and he asked me to marry him, but I hesitated. Then, when you told me what was in the stars, I knew God had destined us to be together!'

Solay's stomach turned over. She clutched Agnes's shoulders, forcing her to meet her eyes. 'You mustn't do this.' How naïve she had been to think that her reading would cause no harm. 'There was more I didn't tell you. The stars predicted disaster!'

Agnes's smile never faltered. 'You are my friend. You would have warned me of danger.'

You would have warned me. Her fingers turned to ice and she could not look away from those trusting blue eyes. Before she left this room, she would betray someone.

Agnes, seeing her shocked face, patted her knee. 'Don't worry, Solay. The worst is nearly over for all of us, including the King.'

Grateful for a change of subject, she let her hands fall to her lap. Let Agnes talk. It would give her time to think. 'You mean Parliament will not renew the Council's charter?' She prayed so. Perhaps then there would be no impeachment.

Agnes shook her head. 'It's more than that. The Council will be destroyed. The King has arranged it with the judges.'

An uneasy feeling rippled through her. As little faith as she had had in the law, it sounded strange to hear such a thing spoken aloud. 'What do you mean?'

'The King called a secret meeting of senior judges and they rendered their legal opinion. They said Parliament cannot impeach anyone without the King's approval.'

She tasted remembered bitterness. 'They did not believe so when my mother was brought before them.'

She should have found it amusing. She should have been able to share it with Justin and laugh. *See, even the King seeks the counsel of the judges.*

But Agnes was not smiling. 'The judges said the Council members are all traitors.'

'Traitors?' Her blood ran cold. 'How can that be? The Council was created by Parliament. They've violated none of the tenets of the Statute of Treason.'

'They said it is the word of the King that is the law, not the Statutes.'

Suddenly, everything Justin had said became clear. If the King put himself above the law, then neither the laws of Heaven nor of Earth were sacred.

'So you see,' Agnes said, smiling, 'it means the King doesn't have to do anything they say.'

For all her years at Court, Agnes remained naïve about the ways of power, unless it affected her personally. It meant much more than that. Once condemned as traitors, they would all be hanged. Drawn. Quartered. Dead.

All perfectly legal.

Not Justin. Oh, please, not Justin. 'When? When will this happen?

'By the time the Council's charter expires all will be ready.'

'But Parliament!' Amazing what straws she clutched, expecting Parliament to save instead of condemn her world this time. 'When Parliament meets, they will confirm the law.'

'The King has thought of that. He told the sheriffs that anyone elected to Parliament this fall must be "neutral in the present disputes".'

Solay did not doubt that the sheriffs would manipulate the elections.

What will you do, she had asked Justin, if the King has

not reformed? Always his answer had been what was right and legal. Now, his respect for the law left him vulnerable to those who cared only for power.

Solay rose. Justin must flee. She must keep him safe.

Agnes put a hand on her arm. 'You must not tell your husband.'

Husband. She had used the word so lightly once. 'I cannot let him die.'

'Then you do love him, yes?'

'I will not let him sit in ignorance and be destroyed. Agnes, if I mean anything to you, please, please help me.'

Agnes pouted. 'He's a stubborn, ill-dressed dullard. How can you love such a man?'

Solay's smile warred with her tears. 'And Hibernia is a peacock who laughs too loud. How can you love such a man?'

Agnes dabbed at her eyes with her sleeve. 'Big oafs.'

'Would that they let us rule the world instead,' Solay said.

Agnes laughed. 'What a world that would be! Full of nothing but music and needlework and love.' She sighed. 'All right. How can I help?'

Solay stood, knowing what she must do. 'I need to see the King. Now. And no one but you and Hibernia must know.'

She must be careful and swift. She knew only one thing she could trade for Justin's life.

Agnes guided Solay, bundled in her cloak, via the private corridors and directly to the King's personal solar, where he and Hibernia were relaxing before the fire.

Startled and angry, he rose and growled at Agnes, 'What is this intrusion?'

'The Lady Solay begs a word.' Agnes backed away to stand with Hibernia.

'What is it, Lady Solay?' the King asked.

'Forgive me, Your Majesty.' She dipped in a deeper curtsy than usual. 'But I have information that is vital you know.'

'So? What is it?'

'First I would ask a favour.'

'No bargains, milady. I have already given you more than you deserve. Tell me the information. Then I will decide if I will grant any favours.'

She took a breath, trying to steady the panic in her belly. 'I believe Lord Lamont is planning to impeach the Duke.'

The King laughed and sipped his leftover wine. 'Ah, Lady Solay, marriage has finally made you a better informant. But you only confirm what I already knew.'

'What? How?' Shocked, she forgot to watch her tongue. Had she betrayed Justin for naught?

'I had spies in the Middle Temple who keep me informed. But at least you have belatedly proven your loyalty. I had reason to wonder, since you married a traitor.'

There was the confirmation. If she did not succeed, Justin would die. 'It is for his sake that I have come.' She took a deep breath. 'He plans to move against Hibernia on the morrow. If the Duke is to escape, he must go tonight.'

'I should never have let him back into Windsor.' He slammed the goblet on the table and turned to his friend. 'Call the guards. Take Lord Justin to the dungeon.'

Agnes gasped.

Before he could move, Solay knelt, her knees no longer

strong enough to hold her. 'Please, Your Majesty. I will keep him occupied tonight. By tomorrow, the Duke and Agnes will be far away. Then if you will let Justin escape Windsor unharmed tomorrow, I will keep him with me where he will trouble you no more.'

'Why should I?'

'Parliament meets next month. You have many challenges ahead. Wouldn't you like to know what the stars have to say? Give me some time to prepare, then I will come to you whenever you choose.'

His eyes shifted and she recognised the fear that drove the power. 'Go to Chester,' he said to Hibernia. 'Both of you.'

Hibernia took a final swig of wine. 'I'll gather your badged men and return within a month. We will crush the Council before Parliament even sits.'

Solay gasped. 'An army? Will you not put them on trial?' Surely that was why he had gone to the trouble of speaking to the judges. She had expected Justin to have his day in court. She had expected justice.

'They've broken the law,' the King said. 'They do not deserve its protection. Traitors deserve to be hunted down like wild boar. By the time their charter expires, we will wipe them off the face of the earth.'

She rose, fearless because, if Justin were dead, she would not want to live. 'If you do not spare him, I shall not read.'

He eyed her in silence. 'Even a King cannot control the battlefield.'

'Leave that to me.' Justin had always disdained illegal force. Surely he wouldn't join the Appellants army? 'Just let him escape tomorrow.'

The King's eyes turned gentle and he nodded. 'So, Lady Solay, it seems you do love him after all.'

'Should he ever discover our bargain, Your Majesty, I do not believe he will see it that way.'

'Your Majesty?' A shaky whisper. Agnes.

'What?'

She had stood in the shadows behind the Duke, but now she stepped forward. She sank to her knees, her head down as if ducking her head at the King's temper. 'Forgive me, Your Majesty, but if the Duke and I are to leave tomorrow, might we be wed tonight with your blessing?'

Solay's heart squeezed. The King and the Duke exchanged glances.

The King's said *what you ask is impossible*.

The Duke's said *please*.

The King sighed and reached out to lift Agnes to her feet. 'I will call the priest.' He looked over his shoulder. 'Would you stay as a witness, Lady Solay?'

She wanted to protest that the banns had not been read. That she was not even sure that a divorced man could remarry. She wanted to say that if she stayed away too long, Justin would wonder where she was.

And she looked at all the hope and happiness in Agnes's eyes and could not refuse.

For now she understood what a woman would do for love.

CHAPTER TWENTY-EIGHT

JUSTIN put another log on the fire, knowing the autumn chill would make her cold.

He waited for her, his body only slightly less patient than his mind. She had been with Agnes since after the evening meal. What did women find to talk about for so long?

He had planned this evening for weeks. He had even reread the romances, to see what the heroes did.

But his body and hers—well, she had been right about that all the time. Their bodies did not lie.

He had planned the fire, the wine and cheese, the gown, and most of all, the loving, to get to the quiet time. After she had exploded at his touch, in the peace after the love-making, he could hold her and whisper *I love you*. Then they would laugh and whisper of the future. Of where they would live. How many children she would give him.

The door opened and she was there.

'Husband.'

His wife. After all. His wife.

'You were gone a long time.'

Fear flickered in the depths of her purple eyes, but it must have been a trick of the firelight.

'Agnes and I had much to say.'

Relieved she did not talk of it, he took the cloak from her shoulders and flung it across the bed, then poured Burgundian wine into the goblet, resenting the need to look away from her. 'I wanted to spend the evening with you.'

'Oh, yes,' she answered in a fierce whisper. She sipped the wine, and looked at him over the rim of the cup until he was lost in her eyes.

He took the goblet from her hands, then ran his fingers through her hair, delighting in her shudder. Her eyelids drooped with pleasure. Then, she caught his hand and kissed his palm, tickling it with her tongue.

He crushed her against him and took her lips. Already he was hard, his careful seduction wiped from his head. She answered his tongue with hers, sharing the same urgency that had nearly driven them to mate in the corridor at Nottingham.

Reluctantly, he pulled away. Tonight must be more than that. Tonight, he would worship her with his body. Then, surely then, she would know.

She reached for him and he captured her hands and brought them to his lips, tickling the little valleys between her knuckles with his tongue. 'Tonight, I will pleasure you.'

She laughed, huskily, and pulled him towards the bed. 'Can we not both be pleasured?'

'In time. You shall be first.'

He turned her around, like a limp doll, and slid the surcoat off her shoulders.

'Wait. Here.' He reached for what he had hidden in his trunk. 'Open this.'

'What is it?' she asked, but he let her discover for herself, delighting in her gasp as she pulled the robe of purple silk from the box. 'It's beautiful,' she said.

And he knew his search of London for one that would match her eyes was worth it.

'Put it on,' he said, hungry to see her wear it.

Shy now, she pulled the bed curtains, giving herself privacy to change. He ripped off his clothes, burning with heat that came not just from the fire.

When she stepped into view again, his body rose to meet her.

The robe fitted her like a lavender shadow, caressing the curve of her hip, sculpting the shape of her breast, and veiling the darkness between her legs.

'I feel like a princess,' she said, running her palms over her hips and thighs. 'Thank you.'

He managed to choke out two words. 'Sit down.'

She settled in the middle of the bed, her back to him, the blue-black strands of her hair tumbling over her shoulders, fine spun as the silk. He pulled her against his chest, loving the feel of her hair on his skin.

He reached for her breasts, each a perfect fit in his palm, and teased the tips with a squeeze.

A low moan rumbled in her throat. 'Take me now.'

He laughed. 'Always so impatient. Not until you are ready.'

She twisted to face him and put her arms around his neck, whispering against his lips. 'I am ready.'

'I'm a better judge of that.' He parted the silk and slipped a finger into her. Sheathed inside, he felt her grip his finger. She was wet, but not as wet as he would make her.

'Lay back.'

She obeyed, but only by kissing him and pulling him down with her. He had a mad moment of wanting to make love on the cursed cloak, as if that would mark her as his instead of the King's.

Instead, he rolled over, pulling her with him, and kicked the red velvet on to the floor.

She did not turn her head to look.

He pushed her boneless legs apart and knelt between them. The robe, open in front, exposed the untouched pale skin of her inner thighs. In the shadows, the dark nest was even blacker than he remembered.

She pulled his hand to her lips and put the finger inside her mouth that had been inside her, her tongue a sweet echo of the pressure inside.

Heat washed over him, from the fire, from her, from within him, and he nearly exploded right then, but he gritted his teeth. Tonight was to be hers. He must show how much he loved her.

He pulled his hand back and let his fingertips roam from her shoulder to inner elbow. She arched against him, writhing, reaching, nearly ready, as she claimed, then his fingers caressed her inner thighs and brushed between her legs.

She stretched wider, an involuntary invitation.

'How do you know what to do? How do you know how to make me so wild?'

He smiled. 'I just listen to your body. Now lie back.'

And he bent his head to kiss her.

* * *

When she felt his tongue, she nearly leapt off the bed.

Tongue, breath, a thousand fingers roamed around and inside her. With each touch, each kiss, she spiralled higher, until she felt as if she really were dissolving, as if all barriers would be gone and they would merge into one being.

She stiffened at the thought. If they did, if they were finally and for ever that close, surely he would know everything she had done before she said a word.

All night long, he caressed her, yet each time she reached the brink, all she had done rose like a wall in her mind.

So throughout that long, luscious night of lovemaking, not once did she reach her release.

He woke, dull with failure, the mid-morning sun bright in his eyes.

Their bodies had always been their one sure connection. Now, even that had failed him.

It all began as he had planned. She had screamed, she had moaned, she had gasped for breath. But not once did she cross into the Elysian abandon where he wanted to take her.

Now, she clung to him, her head on his chest, the dark silk of her hair spilling over his loins, her breathing too erratic for sleep.

'I did not please you.'

She lifted her head, meeting his eyes. 'Yes, you did.'

'Not enough.'

'The fault was mine, not yours.'

He shrugged her away and swung his legs off the bed. 'I thought we were done with lying.'

She lifted her chin. 'I could have pretended, but I did not want to…lie.'

He walked over to the basin, splashing water on his face, cold as the realisation of what she had said. He wiped his face with a drying cloth, wishing he could wipe away the vision of her face in ecstasy in the half-light of Midsummer's Eve. 'So your body has lied all along.'

Eyes wide, she scrambled from the bed and wrapped her arms around him. 'No. You must believe me.'

He pressed her cheek against his chest and held her close, not wanting to face her eyes, no longer sure he could tell her truth from her lies. But even betrayed, he wanted her again. But he wanted not only her body. He wanted whatever it was she could not give.

He let her go and turned away, pulling on clothes, desperate to leave the room and his failure. 'I'll get you a sop.'

Tears choked her throat and spilled over as soon as the door closed.

So this, then, was the price of lies. To destroy the one true thing they had shared.

Now, out there, he would discover the truth and suspect her part in it. And when he came through that door again, he would bring with him the lonely future she did not want to face.

CHAPTER TWENTY-NINE

When she heard the door creak, she closed her eyes. So soon their peace was ended. Now, she must persuade him to leave Windsor quickly, or everything she had done would be for naught. And how could she sway him now that the bond of flesh had broken?

When she opened her eyes, he loomed larger with each silent step he took towards the bed. Strength and power, hard as carved stone, nothing remained of her lover except a lock of uncombed hair, still rumpled from sleep.

'You knew.' Instead of the hot anger she had expected, his voice shimmered icy certainty. 'You knew and you said nothing.'

'Knew what?' She must find out what he had discovered before she could release the rest.

'Stop it, Solay. Hibernia and Agnes have disappeared. There's even wild talk that they are married, though that's impossible. You saw her last night. She must have told you.'

'Yes.' She forced her voice to stay soft, low. 'It's true. They married in the King's private chapel and left before dawn.'

He gripped the bedpost and glared at her. 'And you

pleased them and the King with the blessing of the stars, no doubt.'

'I told her there was hope she might be happy.' So many, many months ago.

'The man is already married!' He clung to the post as if the world was careening beneath him. 'He cannot take another wife!'

She must stay calm, speak softly, explain things step by step so he would understand what he must do, else he would be in the dungeon by sunset. 'Hibernia is no longer married to the Duchess.'

'That's not possible.'

'But it is. The Pope allowed Hibernia to put his wife aside.'

'On what grounds? They are related by neither blood nor marriage.'

She wanted to share the story with him. *See, Justin? When Agnes told me, I asked the same thing.* But the time for shared smiles had past. 'He did it because the King asked him.'

Momentarily stunned, Justin stared at her. 'But the King is on earth to enforce God's laws through man's. He cannot violate them.'

Blind. Still he was blind. 'If Pope and King agree, your precious, immutable law, God's or man's, has no more power than their desires.'

He paced the room, pounding his fist into his palm, as if looking for someone to hit. 'Mismanagement of the Privy Purse, exalting Hibernia to the rank of a King's son, refusing to fight France—these were all reprehensible. But to allow the man to put aside his wife, the King's own cousin, for his Bohemian mistress is an outrage.'

She let him argue with the walls, knowing she must tell him much, much worse.

'The Council will not tolerate this,' he concluded, flatly.

'The Council will have no say.' She slid off the bed and circled her arms about his waist, wanting to hold him when he heard the worst. 'The King has declared the Council traitors.'

He staggered as if the word was a sword blow. She could not hold him. 'What?'

A question, from a man who never questioned. It bent her heart. 'The King asked a panel of judges for their legal opinion on the Council's actions. They told him that to obstruct the wishes of the King was traitorous.'

'No.' His stunned face was that of a child whose favourite toy lay broken before him. 'That's not right. That's not the law. No judge would say that.'

Always, always, he saw only the world he believed in, a world in which good and bad, white and black, battled uncompromising enemies, never sullied with messy grey.

'Just because you defy power for right you expect everyone to do the same. There are many, even judges, who do not want to spit in the King's eye.' She touched his arm. 'Most just want to be left alone to live the life we dreamed of. A life in the country, where we speak of the King only if he rides through on his way somewhere else.'

He shook his head. 'The Council has done nothing to violate the Statute of Treason. We can prove that at the trial.'

She took his face between her hands, forcing him to look at her eyes. 'You think justice is blind, but it is you who cannot see. There will be no trial. Hibernia has gone north to gather an army that will hunt you down and kill you, all of you.'

He blinked, then realisation touched his eyes. 'If the King will not honour the law, there is nothing left but brute force.'

She sighed, his pain tight in her chest. Finally he understood. She had been right all along. And she had not wanted to be right. 'Now, gather your things. We must leave quickly. We'll be safe in Upminster.'

'If the King does not respect the law, no one is safe. Gloucester was right. We will have to take up arms against him.'

'No!' Now she was the one in shock. 'You hate war.'

'I would rather die in battle than in a traitor's noose.'

She had hoped she would not need to tell him all. 'You won't be hanged. If we leave now, he will let you live.'

'What do you mean? How do you know?'

'He promised.'

'Who promised?'

She lifted her chin. 'The King.'

His eyes met hers and she knew everything was about to change in some final, terrible way.

At his silence, she broke the gaze, lifting her cloak and shaking it, as if all were settled. 'But we must escape this morning while everyone is distracted by Hibernia's disappearance. If we go home and stay out of the fight, the King will let us alone.'

'I don't know whether to be disgusted by your treachery or stunned that you think I would believe the promise of a King who's never kept one.'

Anger burned her cheeks. 'Would you have preferred I let him take you?'

'I can see why you are a survivor. Nothing else, no one else matters but what you want.'

'You matter!' She drank in the stubborn set of his jaw, the pain in his brown eyes, the cleft in his chin, all the little things she loved. 'Why else would I bargain for your life?'

'And what is worth so much to the King that he would give up the joy of my death?'

She swallowed and touched her fingertips to her lips. How could she not have seen that he would ask? 'I told him I would read his stars for the coming year.'

'Valuable, to be sure, but that's not all, is it?' Light dawned in his eyes. 'You told him about the impeachment. Everything I told you, my wife, my helpmeet, went straight to the King's ears.'

'It wasn't like that—'

'I loved you and you betrayed me!'

His shout bounced off the walls and she tried to clutch the echo of the word before it slipped away. Loved. Once, but no longer.

'I did what I had to do to save you,' she whispered.

'I even thought it might be true, what you said.'

'It *is* true.' *What you said.* He could not even say the words *I love you.* Could not even understand that she loved him so much that she would save his life, even if it meant losing his love.

'Don't expect me to believe you.' There was grim determination in his eyes, in the set of his jaw. 'If you really loved me, you would have honoured my principles.'

'Instead of keeping you alive?' She turned on him with the vengeance of a warrior. 'You don't want love. Love isn't enough. You want love on your own terms. It isn't enough that I save your life. I must save it by your rules, rules you just admitted don't apply to the world we live in.'

She shook with the effort to push it into his stubborn brain. 'Don't you understand? I don't want you to die.'

He snorted. 'Yes, it would be useful for you to keep me alive. That way, if the King loses and the Lords win, you can come crawling back to me. Don't expect me to welcome you. Or maybe I will. Maybe I'll welcome you by saying "let's have a roll in the hay". That shouldn't be too hard for a harlot's daughter.'

Of its own accord, her hand flung itself at his face, the slap stinging her fingers, leaving a red imprint on his cheek.

'You don't deserve the love I've wasted on you.' She gasped for breath, but he had stolen the air. 'I sold my soul for your life. You owe me the courtesy of saving it, at least today. We are leaving for Westminster. When we get there, you can warn your beloved Council and raise an army and start a war or do whatever you please. I'm going home.'

He shook his head, sadly. 'If Hibernia can dump an inconvenient wife, you can certainly be freed of an inconvenient husband. You've finally convinced me, my dear. If I return alive, I will find a judge who's not too particular to set us both free.'

The thought of losing him ripped her heart away, but he had never, truly, been hers. If he hated her now, it was not because of the past or because of her mother. It was because of what she had done.

She wanted to put her arms around his waist and hear his heart beat for the last time, but the few feet that separated them were as wide as the Channel. 'All this time, you've demanded love, but you know nothing about it. Love has its own laws, Justin, and they care nothing for your legalities.'

He turned away without a word, as harsh and cold as he had been the day she first saw him.

She closed her eyes, unable to watch him go, and waited for the sound of the door closing. It was long in coming.

'Goodbye, Solay.'

She didn't answer. There was nothing to say.

CHAPTER THIRTY

FOR the next two months, as the Lords Appellant gathered their men to stop Hibernia's army, Justin had no thoughts, only feelings.

Rage, at her, at the world, at the King, even at Gloucester, burned through his veins and drove his preparations for battle.

Her betrayal cut more deeply than any sword's blow. Convinced of her love, he had succumbed to the temptation to believe her. Now, because of her deceit, they were marching to fight Hibernia on the field instead of in court.

And if he sometimes remembered that he owed his own life to her devil's bargain, he ignored it.

But in the dark hours of the night, when the winter stars watched over the sleeping soldiers and even the exhaustion of his body would not let him rest, he could not turn away the memory of the forgiveness he had found in her flesh.

Then, the vision would dissolve into their last, angry words.

Over and over, he saw the scene until the clash of swords

and the bump of shields could not blot out the truth. *You don't want love. You want love on your own terms. Love has its own laws, Justin, and they care nothing for your legalities.*

The answer screamed at him from the darkness. The failure was not hers alone. When she made her own decision, uncowed by his opinions, he had cut her down without mercy. He should have cut out his tongue instead.

All the time he had insisted she prove her love when he had done nothing to earn it.

So he marched towards a final confrontation, hoping a blade would find him because he didn't want to live, now, without her.

And all that kept him alive was knowing there was one more thing he must do for her.

At the sound of an approaching horse, muffled by the December snow, Solay put down her bite of mincemeat pie.

Huddled in the upstairs solar around the only fire in the house, she and her mother exchanged a wordless glance over Jane's head. Who would come to their door on Christmas Day? The country was at war and marauding armies threatened civilians as well as soldiers.

Yet when she opened the shutter, she hoped, as she always did, that she would see Justin.

Under a shadowless afternoon sun, a peaceful white blanket hugged the cold ground. Justin would have liked the snow, she thought, wondering where he marched, whether he was cold. Praying he was safe.

She shook off the feeling. She should be planning to cajole another man into marriage. Or less. After Justin cast her off, even to find a man who would take her as a mistress would be no easy task now.

'Is it him?' her mother asked, her voice soft with compassion. They had become close over the months, bound by the foolish things they had done for love.

She shook her head. 'It's a squire, alone.' She peered more closely, catching her breath when she saw the badge of the white hart. 'He's come from the King.'

Her mother stood as he pounded on the front door. 'Jane, light a fire downstairs. Solay, bring him to the Great Hall. We must greet the King's messenger with honour. What will he think that we have no wild boar to serve him on Christmas Day?'

Downstairs, Solay opened the door to a shivering boy, with chapped lips and a runny nose, who looked barely older than Jane. Had the King no seasoned men left?

Her mother waited in the Great Hall, seated before a hearth that yawned empty where a Yule Log should be burning. Jane touched a brand to some of their precious kindling. The boy eyed the flames with longing.

'The King commands the Lady Solay to come to him,' he said, when his teeth stopped chattering.

'Where is the King?' she asked, dreading Windsor at Yuletide.

'London.'

His answer told her little. Had Hibernia's men beaten the Council's army? Then where was Justin?

'I trust his Majesty is in good health,' her mother said, in her most regal tone.

The boy's reddened cheeks paled. 'His army was defeated a fortnight ago.'

Her mother swallowed a gasp.

Solay sagged, relief pouring through her veins. Justin was on the winning side.

Agnes was not. 'Where is the Duke of Hibernia?'

The boy inched closer to the fire. 'No one knows.'

She gripped her hands and bowed in silent prayer for Agnes and for forgiveness. Without Solay's cheery assurances, her friend would never have married Hibernia. Now, no doubt she was cursing Solay for false predictions of a happy future.

Never again would she shade her words. Her study of the stars had become a sacred calling. She would not dishonour it with a lie.

Her mother, ashen-faced, sat unmoving, her hands gripping the arms of the chair. 'Does the King still reign?'

The boy leaned forward, whispering as if spies lurked in the chimney. 'The King and his councillors have locked themselves in the Tower. The Lords Appellant approach the city. No one knows what will happen when they arrive.'

So the Lords had triumphed and Richard wanted to know whether this was his hour of death. She had spent the autumn and early winter with Justin's gift and the King's chart. She knew what she would tell him.

'Jane, I will need the horse at dawn.'

'Must you go?' A note of fear rang in Jane's voice. 'You'll miss Saint Stephen's Day. We had planned—'

Her mother put a hand on Jane's shoulder. 'Hush, child. It is an honour that the King summons her.'

And more. It had been the price of Justin's life. She prayed he still had it.

* * *

Tiny snowflakes skipped around the Tower's courtyard as the squire took Solay's horse.

It was Yuletide and she had come to the King again.

She clutched a folded chart beneath her cloak, and followed a guard upstairs and through corridors until he paused before a closed door.

'Wait in here,' the guard said, knocking. 'I'll tell them you've arrived.'

A voice answered beyond the door, 'Come.'

Heat from a brisk fire washed over her as she opened the door. A broad-shouldered man looked out of the window at the snow falling into the Thames.

She caught her breath. 'Justin?'

When he turned, she searched this stranger's features for the husband she had known. Cheekbones carved sharp lines in his gaunt face and new muscles curved his shoulders and arms. He had wielded a sword, then, despite his hate of force.

He took a step towards her.

She matched it.

He did not take another. 'Solay.'

A question echoed in her name and she longed to answer it. She wanted to run into his arms, to pretend they were still on a midsummer hill, watching the sun rise over a beautiful new world.

She straightened her shoulders. Their summer closeness had been swept bare as the trees, the halcyon days of love a midsummer fancy. That hill was miles and months away and she had traded his love for his life. There would be no forgiveness.

'The King sent for me,' she said.

'I know. I wanted to see you first.'

His last words had cracked the stone of her heart in the engraving. *If the Lords win, I'll just say 'let's have a roll in the hay'*. She could not bear it if he said that. 'You won a great victory over the Duke.'

'Solay, I found Agnes.'

She took that step and then another. 'Is she all right? Where is she?'

'She's safe. I took her to the convent at Readingdon.'

She pursed her lips against sudden tears. How fleeting Agnes's joy had been. 'Thank you.'

He held out a handkerchief and she took it, unsure whether she cried for Agnes or at Justin's unexpected kindness.

'Sit,' he said. 'Please.'

He motioned her to a bench by the fire and pulled up its companion. She untied her cloak and placed the King's chart on the table.

He leaned forward, elbows on his knees, his fingers near enough to touch. 'We haven't much time and I have much to say.'

She closed her eyes against the memory of his hand caressing her hip, but she could not shut out the familiar hum that linked them. It sang in her blood and turned her centre to molten metal.

She leaned away, struggling to remember her mother's lesson. *Don't trust the wanting.* But in the last year, all the certainties she had clung to—the power of the King, her birthright, her ability to please, her attempts to influence the future—all had melted like snow. Only the wanting remained, binding them as strongly as it had that first moment, as if nothing had come between.

'What is it you would tell me?'

'I have drawn up papers that give you the income from three of my London houses in perpetuity.'

She thought she had accepted her fate, but hearing his cold calculation turned her tongue to lead. *I will find a judge who's not too particular and set you free.* They would be no different from all the other former lovers at court, averting their eyes with a nervous cough when forced to pass in the carolling ring.

He had not waited for an answer. 'It's the only way I could—'

She held up her hand to ward off his words. 'Thank you. You are generous.' There would be enough for food and firewood and feed for the horse and a new gown for Jane come spring time. Now, she only wanted to return to home, where the sight and the scent of him would torture her heart no more. 'We will be quite comfortable.'

'No.' Despite being on the winning side, his eyes were hollow with irreparable loss.

Dread crept up her spine. 'There is something more?'

'The courts grind like millstones, no matter who sits on the throne. I lost the suit. You have lost the house.'

She reeled, breathless, at this final blow. 'I should have told the truth, despite what Mother wanted, I should have—'

He gripped her knee and shook it. 'The fault is not yours. You were right. I can't guarantee justice on earth. I'm sorry.'

His eyes spoke as strongly as his lips. And as she looked at the dear face she would not see again, the last little wall that had kept her heart safe crumbled.

'Then it was not to be,' she whispered. 'I know you did everything you could.'

How foolish she had been, chiding him for his conditions. All the while, she had held back one little portion of her love until he had earned it. And now that he no longer belonged to her and she had nothing to gain from him, she had never loved him more.

The guard knocked and opened the door without waiting. 'They are ready for her.'

'Tell them we are coming,' Justin said, and the guard withdrew.

She tried to rise, but he grabbled both her hands in his. 'You must know before you go. You are walking into a den of lions. The Lords no longer argue over law or even justice. They talk of a new King.'

She shivered. A new King would not be crowned while the old King breathed. 'What has that to do with me?'

'They think the stars will tell them Richard's reign is over.'

She swallowed the fear fluttering in her throat. She had been too long away from Court. Focused on the heavens, she had forgotten to think of earthly snares. 'Who would they see on the throne?'

Gloucester was the son of the old King, but he was not the only one who could make a claim. And the others would relish the title of Kingmaker.

'Richard only lives because Gloucester cannot get them to agree to make him King. Slant your words with care.' He squeezed her hands between his. 'Gloucester will be there. He wants you to predict Richard's death.'

'And if I do not?'

'He will accuse you of practising black arts.'

She did not need to ask the penalty for that. 'So he sent you to warn me that Richard's life is not the only one hanging in the balance.'

His finger touched her cheek, bringing her gaze back to his. The urgency in his eyes had nothing to do with lust. 'I will protect you. I swear.'

She rose and his hand dropped away. 'I know you will try.' But they both knew it was an empty promise.

When she turned, he dropped her cloak over her shoulders and whispered in her ear, 'What will you tell him?'

She had no husband, no home, no surety left in her life except the learning that had given her a glimpse into Heaven. Strange, what stayed, what didn't. 'The truth.'

There was nothing else left.

Stunned, Justin watched her walk out of the door without waiting for him. Belatedly, he remembered she knew the Tower as well as he and caught up with her halfway down the corridor, grabbing her arm to stop her.

'That will save you if the truth is what they want to hear. Is it?' he whispered fiercely, uncertain who might overhear.

'You will find out when the King does.'

Her tongue had become tart over the last year. 'You are good at games. Spout some nonsense they can interpret as they please. They won't know the difference.'

She never broke her stride. 'I will not seek to please Gloucester because he now holds the power.'

'When did you become a warrior for truth? You've bent it much further for much less reason.'

'You don't even care what the truth *is*.'

'Tell me later. After this is over.'

'So the great defender of truth wants me to lie?'

'If it will save your life, yes.' He would break any oath, defy any rigid soulless code that wouldn't let her live.

'Then how can you be angry at what I did to save yours?'

The ground shifted beneath his feet. 'You never craved the King's power, did you?'

'Only his power to give me what my mother and sister needed.'

Loyal to flesh and blood and friends, she had sacrificed everything else for those she loved. For him.

He cupped her face in his hand. 'You are stubborn, foolish and incredibly brave,' he said.

A flush touched her cheek, but she turned away without a nod or a smile.

And as the guard opened the door, Justin had no idea what she was going to say.

Shaking, Solay swept into the room. Finally, too late, Justin had understood. But she would not violate her vow. Not to please him, or Gloucester, or even the King. She had worked too hard to find the truth.

When she paused, face to face with Richard, she stumbled to a curtsy. But no command came, neither to rise nor to kneel. She looked up through her lashes, keeping her head low.

The proud King she had known was gone.

Richard was slumped in a rough chair, his wife within touching distance. Faithful Hibernia no longer stood beside him. Instead, Gloucester and the other four Council members circled the room, ready to pick his bones.

She glanced up at Justin, who raised his eyebrows and shrugged. She had been prepared for Gloucester alone. It seemed the other Council members would not trust his report.

A cask of wine had been tapped, and red drops of Burgundy spotted the floor. The smell of fear hung in the air beside that of the leftover wine.

She rose, and Richard did not prevent her. Sunken above thin cheeks, his blue eyes had become those of a trapped and angry animal. 'It seems a crowd has gathered to hear my fate, Lady Solay.'

'I shall tell it the same, Your Majesty, whether to a crowd or to you alone.'

He did not move, but the Queen waved a hand for her to proceed.

She spared a glance for her scowling audience. Besides Gloucester and the grizzled Earls of Arundel and Warwick, she was surprised to see Henry Bolingbroke and the young Earl of Nottingham, both Richard's age. How things had changed since those snowy days in his castle.

She cleared a place at the table, moving aside two half-empty wine goblets.

'Wait,' Gloucester said, before she could sit. 'I must have your oath that you will interpret the stars truthfully.'

Justin spoke before she could. 'Gloucester—'

'I asked Lady Solay.'

She smiled at Justin and shook her head. This, she must do alone. 'To come among you, I have risked death.' She would speak the truth for herself, not for him. 'I would not risk it on a lie.'

And she did not really care whether anyone except Justin believed her.

'Then swear on the grave of your father, the King.'

Justin's hand tightened on her shoulder. She reached up, covered his fingers with hers, then touched the amethyst brooch pinned near her heart.

'I swear on the grave of our late and beloved King Edward.' She looked at Gloucester. 'Your father.' Then at Richard. 'Your grandfather.' And finally at Justin. 'And the man who called me daughter.'

Gloucester's mouth twitched, as if he were not satisfied, but could not think why. 'Proceed.'

She settled at the table. Justin poured a goblet of wine and set it at her right hand, then stood behind her, his hands on her shoulders.

She started to shrug him off. Their marriage was over. She must go on alone. But the feeling of him, warm at her back, comforted her.

She let him stay.

As she unfolded her chart, Gloucester and the others moved closer, peering over her shoulders as if they could decipher the neatly labelled squares and triangles.

She cleared her throat and concentrated on the chart, letting everything else fall away. 'In the twelfth year of his Majesty's reign, there continue to be powerful planets in the Twelfth House, the house of enemies.'

Richard slumped in his chair with a tired laugh and

looked around the room. 'You need not look to the stars to know that. Just look around the room.'

'We are not enemies of the King,' Gloucester said, glowering at his nephew.

The Queen snapped at them, protecting Richard like a cub. 'Do you claim you are his friends?'

'We are friends of the realm,' Gloucester answered.

'Then perhaps,' Solay continued, 'you belong in the Eleventh House, the house of courtiers, councillors, and friends both false and true.' She raised the goblet with a shaking hand and touched it to her lips. Still, her mouth tasted of dust. 'Here, the planets show disruption, change and even endings.'

'Endings?' Richard asked. 'Of the Council or of my councillors?'

It was so quiet, she could hear Gloucester swallow his wine.

'The stars do not have men's names attached,' she said, relieved for once that she did not know the truth.

She continued through the houses calmly, speaking of wealth and possessions, of brothers and fathers, of sickness and health, of love and marriage.

No one spoke again until Gloucester sputtered an interruption. 'What you say is meaningless. It tells us nothing.'

'Not so,' she answered, evenly. 'Look at the Tenth House. It is the house of Kingship. There have been shadows in this house during the last year, but now, Saturn leaves this house and Jupiter enters.'

'What does that mean?' Gloucester said.

Richard sat straight and smiled at Gloucester in the old

way. 'Beneficence to the King and punishment to my enemies.' His kingly voice had returned.

'You were born of royalty and born to rule, Your Majesty,' she said. 'I know the signs.'

The signs so lacking in my own chart.

Anne's quiet voice floated softly into the hush. 'You have not spoken of the Eighth House.'

Bolingbroke, eager. 'What is that one?'

Richard answered for her. 'The House of Death.'

Silence blanketed the room.

'Well, Lady Solay, answer him. What is in the Eighth House?' Gloucester asked.

'Nothing.'

'Nothing?' Richard's voice cracked.

'The heavens have given us no guidance.'

His glance skittered to his foes, then he leaned forward. 'I did what you asked,' he whispered, though they all could hear. 'Can you tell me no more?'

She heard the plea in his voice. He wanted to know whether he was to live or die. Yet no matter what the stars said, what she said now would determine his destiny.

'The stars do not guarantee the future, Your Majesty,' she said, loud enough for all the lords to hear. 'They only tell us what circumstances will test us. We create our own lives by meeting our fate bravely. You were born a King, Your Majesty. As long as you honour the laws of the realm and the advice of your barons, I'm sure the stars will shine favourably on you so that when you die, whenever that may be, you will still be our rightful King.'

She held her breath.

Richard pursed his lips, as if reluctant to capitulate, then sighed. 'The King embodies the law and so must fully express it. I always welcome the instruction of my dear uncle and the other lords in these matters.'

Gloucester glared over her shoulder at Justin. 'It seems your wife parrots your opinion, Lamont. You must have told her what to say.'

Justin's hand tightened on her shoulder.

She felt the war within him and covered his hand with hers. 'He told me what I would face in this room. Only I could decide how to meet it.'

'It is I who agree with my wife, Gloucester,' Justin said. 'Richard is the King Heaven has given us. The law of earth can do no less.'

Behind Gloucester, the others murmured assent. His shoulders slumped. There would be no more talk of a new King.

She stood, letting Justin's hand fall away, and met each man's eyes. Gloucester's angry ones, so like the old King's. The minor Lords Appellant, by turns wary, relieved and irate. Then she looked into the Queen's grateful brown eyes with a woman's understanding. Richard's gaze now showed kingly pride instead of craven fear.

She turned to Justin.

His eyes were full of warning and fear and affection and a strange sort of pride.

Gathering her chart, she walked out beside him, their bodies joined by that invisible cord that had bound them from the first.

My wife. I agree with my wife.

Hope rose in her heart.

She glanced over at him, looking for the little quirk of his eyebrow, for the twitch at the edge of his mouth that came just before a smile. She watched brown hair curve around his ear and the blunt fingers that had brought her to ecstasy. She watched all these things for what might be the last time, and heard him say nothing.

'I spoiled Gloucester's plans,' she said, finally. 'What does that mean for you?'

'I shall leave his service. We will both be glad of it.'

'Will you be safe?'

He smiled. 'Are any of us safe?'

'What will you do?'

'What I was trained to do. Practise the law.'

They returned to the little room, where the fire had burned to embers and her cloak was welcome in the early winter darkness.

He had called her brave, but to be brave before the King had risked only her life. To be brave now, with him, would risk her heart.

But she would do it anyway.

She reached for his hand, wanting that touch one more time. Unable to look into his eyes, she played with his fingers, watching them as if they were magic, unable to tell him goodbye.

But he spoke instead.

'Stay with me, Solay,' he said, stroking the back of each of her fingers, one by one. 'Perhaps justice can only come from the Heavens, but I think we can find love on earth, now.'

She held her breath. If he took back his words, she would have this one memory: the crackle of the fire, the taste of leftover wine, the scent of cedar and ink, his clenched jaw and that whisper of hope in his dark eyes.

'Have I convinced you that I love you?' she asked.

'I have become convinced that I love you.'

'If I say I love you, will you believe me?' She wanted him to say yes. More than she'd ever wanted anything in her life.

'Should I?'

She lifted her head and caught the twitch at the corner of his mouth. 'Yes, you should. And be honoured to have earned the love of the daughter of Lord William Weston and Lady Alys Piers.'

He wrapped her in his arms. 'We are already bound by the laws of heaven and earth.'

'And more than that,' she said, needing the silly white cloth again as she looked up at him. 'We are bound by the laws of the heart.'

He swept her into his arms then, and it was hours before the kiss was complete.

EPILOGUE

SOLAY opened her eyes to the midsummer sunrise and a kiss from her husband. She laughed against his lips as the baby inside her kicked with satisfaction.

'Good morning, my love,' he said. 'Your day has come again.'

Despite all convention, Justin persisted in celebrating St John's Day as if it belonged to her instead of the saint, and he was planning to spoil their child the same way.

'Isn't it nice that my day happens to be the longest one of the year?' Later, they would all join Justin's brother and his family for their first midsummer celebration. 'All the more for me to enjoy.'

He bounded out of bed. 'Wait. Stay right there. I'll be right back.'

She rolled over, content, as he slipped out of the room.

They had come back to the country from London for the midsummer celebration, leaving the bustle of the city and Justin's law practice for the dower house on his brother's property. It was small, no grander than the house in Upminster, but her mother had been happy here.

And Jane? She wished she knew how to make her sister happy. Justin had a marriage offer in hand from a wealthy London merchant, but when they broke the news, Jane ran from the room crying and had barely spoken since.

Solay curved her arms around her growing stomach, hugging her soon-to-be-born babe, wondering what the stars in the sign of the Virgin had in mind for this one. They had been right about the King. The next session of Parliament had been stormy. Safely away from Court, she and Justin had watched, horrified, as Richard's chief advisers had been tried, convicted and killed.

But the King kept his life. And the throne.

Hibernia and Agnes had escaped across the Channel to the Low Countries. She missed her friend, but she was glad they had finally found a place to love in peace.

Justin opened the door. 'I've a birthday gift for you.'

She sat up in bed as he pulled something from behind his back.

Inside a small cage, a bright-eyed, shocking green popinjay blinked and cocked his head. Open-mouthed, she stared at the alert eyes.

'Awk!' the bird squawked.

'Teach this one to talk and you'll always have a companion who mimics you.'

Her eyes lit up and her laughter pealed out like bells.

There would be more, later. An appointment for Justin as Justice of the Peace in a village near the Thames, where their house would have windows facing east so she could always see the sunrise.

But for now, this, this would be enough.

AUTHOR'S AFTERWORD

This story was inspired by real people and events, though I have taken many fictional liberties.

The notorious mistress of Edward III, Alice Perrers, who I called Alys Piers, was reviled by the chroniclers as greedy, avaricious and power-hungry. She sat on the bench with the judges, was impeached by Parliament, and was accused of stripping the rings from the dead King's hand. Alice's trial, the convenient appearance of her husband, Lord William Windsor, and the later lawsuit with his nephew over Great Gaynes in Upminster happened much as I described.

Alys had two daughters: Joan and Jane. (I ignored her son for the sake of the story.) Little is known of the girls, not even their exact years of birth. Their parentage is also the subject of speculation. And some reports call them both Joan.

We do know that Joan the Elder married a lawyer, Robert Skerne, and they lived in Kingston-on-Thames. A monumental brass with their images is still there, marking their tombs after a seemingly long and prosperous life.

Everything else about Joan in this book comes from my imagination—her return to Court, interest in astrology—and any role in Richard's reign is strictly conjecture.

For the historical figures in the book, I have tried to adhere to actual events during 1386-7. King Richard was ordered by Parliament to submit to a Council of Lords Appellant, headed by his uncle, the Duke of Gloucester. To escape their control, he did go on a 'gyration' across the country. And he did submit ten questions to a panel of judges, who then declared the Council traitors. History also suggests he had some interest in astrology.

The character I called the Duke of Hibernia is actually the Duke of Ireland. He divorced his wife with the Pope's blessing and ran away with one of the Queen's ladies, Agnes Lancerone. As I've tried to show, the King's favouritism for Ireland, and his flouting of the laws of marriage, triggered the Lords' decision to go to war with the King's men, who were soundly defeated. Ireland fled the country and died abroad. I chose to believe that Agnes went with him.

No one knows exactly what happened between the Lords and the King during his imprisonment in the Tower, but there is speculation that he was removed from the throne for a time.

History has not looked kindly on Alice Perrers or the Duke of Ireland. I have tried to show them as human beings, with both flaws and strengths.

Richard survived this 'constitutional crisis' and emerged stronger than ever. Eventually, he took revenge on those who had thwarted him. In the end, he was deposed and killed and the new king was Henry Bolingbroke, who had been one of the Lords Appellant in the Tower.

The Regency

LORDS & LADIES
COLLECTION

More Glittering Regency Love Affairs

Volume 17 – 4th January 2008
One Night with a Rake by Louise Allen
The Dutiful Rake by Elizabeth Rolls

Volume 18 – 1st February 2008
A Matter of Honour by Anne Herries
The Chivalrous Rake by Elizabeth Rolls

Volume 19 – 7th March 2008
Tavern Wench by Anne Ashley
The Incomparable Countess by Mary Nichols

Volume 20 – 4th April 2008
Prudence by Elizabeth Bailey
Lady Lavinia's Match by Mary Nichols

Volume 21 – 2nd May 2008
The Rebellious Bride by Francesca Shaw
The Duke's Mistress by Ann Elizabeth Cree

Volume 22 – 6th June 2008
Carnival of Love by Helen Dickson
The Viscount's Bride by Ann Elizabeth Cree

Volume 23 – 4th July 2008
One Night of Scandal & The Rake's Mistress
by Nicola Cornick

The Regency

LORDS & LADIES
COLLECTION

More Glittering Regency Love Affairs

Volume 24 – 1st August 2008
The Reluctant Marchioness by Anne Ashley
Nell by Elizabeth Bailey

Volume 25 – 5th September 2008
Kitty by Elizabeth Bailey
Major Chancellor's Mission by Paula Marshall

Volume 26 – 3rd October 2008
Lord Hadleigh's Rebellion by Paula Marshall
The Sweet Cheat by Meg Alexander

Volume 27 – 7th November 2008
Lady Sarah's Son by Gayle Wilson
Wedding Night Revenge by Mary Brendan

Volume 28 – 5th December 2008
Rake's Reward by Joanna Maitland
The Unknown Wife by Mary Brendan

Volume 29 – 2nd January 2009
Miss Verey's Proposal by Nicola Cornick
The Rebellious Débutante by Meg Alexander

Volume 30 – 6th February 2009
Dear Deceiver by Mary Nichols
The Matchmaker's Marriage by Meg Alexander

Wanted: Wife

Must be of good family, attractive but not too beautiful, but calm, reasonable and mature... for marriage of convenience

Spirited Charity Emerson is certain she can meet Simon "Devil" Dure's wifely expectations. With her crazy schemes, warm laughter and loving heart, Charity tempts Simon. However, the treacherous trap that lies ahead, and the vicious act of murder, will put their courage – and their love – to the ultimate test.

Available 19th December 2008

"There is a dead man stinking in the game larder. I hardly think a few missing pearls will be the ruin of this house party."

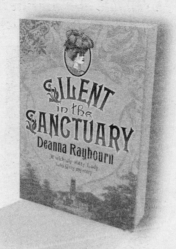

England, 1887

Christmas festivities at Bellmont Abbey are brought to an abrupt halt by a murder in the chapel. Blood dripping from her hands, Lady Julia Grey's cousin claims the ancient right of sanctuary.

Forced to resume her deliciously intriguing partnership with the enigmatic detective Nicholas Brisbane, Lady Julia is intent on proving her cousin's innocence. Still, the truth is rarely pure and never simple…

Available 19th December 2008

www.mirabooks.co.uk

Immerse yourself in the glitter of Regency times through the lives and romantic escapades of the Lester family

Miss Lenore Lester was perfectly content with her quiet country life, caring for her father, and having no desire for marriage. Though she hid behind glasses and pulled-back hair, she couldn't disguise her beauty. And the notoriously charming Jason Montgomery – Duke of Eversleigh – could easily see through her disguise and clearly signalled his interests.

Lenore remained determined not to be thrown off-balance by this charming rake.
The Duke of Eversleigh, though, was equally determined to loosen the hold Lenore had on her heart.

Immerse yourself in the glitter of Regency times through the lives and romantic escapades of the Lester family

Jack Lester had every reason to hide the news of his recently acquired fortune: he wanted an attractive, capable bride who would accept him for himself, not for his new-found riches.

But he had to make his choice before the society matrons discovered the Lester family were no longer as poor as church mice. He must convince Sophie, the woman of his dreams, to marry him as poor Jack Lester.

MIRA